THE STRUGGLE FOR INNOCENCE
A *Bridge of Magic* Novel

Robert E. Balsley, Jr.

Illustrations in Collaboration with Jim and Shelley Charles

THE STRUGGLE FOR INNOCENCE

Robert E. Balsley, Jr

COPYRIGHT

Copyright © 2020 by Trient Press

Except for the original story material written by the author, all songs, song titles, and lyrics mentioned in the novel THE STRUGGLE FOR INNOCENCE are the exclusive property of the respective artists, songwriters, and copyright holders

THE STRUGGLE FOR INNOCENCE

Trient Press
3375 S Rainbow Blvd
#81710, SMB 13135
Las Vegas,NV 89180

Ordering Information:
Quantity sales. Special discounts are available
on quantity purchases by corporations,
associations, and others. For details, contact
the publisher at the address above.
Orders by U.S. trade bookstores and wholesalers.
Please contact Trient Press: Tel: (775) 996-3844;
or visit www.trientpress.com.

Printed in the United States of America

Publisher's Cataloging-in-Publication data
Balsley, Jr., Robert E.
A title of a book : THE STRUGGLE FOR INNOCENCE
ISBN Hard Cover 978-1-953975-62-1
Paperback 978-1-953975-60-7
E-Book 978-1-953975-61-4

Robert E. Balsley, Jr

The Bridge of Magic

The Salvation of Innocence
The Struggle for Innocence
The Loss of Innocence *(Forthcoming)*

THE STRUGGLE FOR INNOCENCE

<u>Dedication</u>

Freedom! A word that means many different things to people all over the world. For many, it's the quest of a lifetime. A quest to break the shackles of an impoverished or state regimented existence. The quest to find and preserve the dignity of self-determination.

Freedom! To others, it's a dream wherein one can think and say what they mean without fear of punishment or repudiation. Political correctness is in direct conflict with freedom. But freedom comes with responsibility. It's a responsibility to abstain from words that cause destruction or pain. It's a responsibility to understand that others have the same right as you to think and say what they mean. Limiting speech is the antithesis of freedom.

Freedom! To all freedom means equal opportunity to succeed... and equal opportunity to fail... without regard for race, sex, religion, or all the other things that combine to make us who we are. "Freedom for all" makes us one united people.

Freedom! The foundation block upon which all civilized societies are built.

Freedom varies and can have different meanings to different people. For some it could be freedom from physical captivity. For others, freedom from addiction... or from financial hardship. Each person views their manacles of slavery differently... whether it be slavery of the body or slavery of the mind. But the one thing regarding freedom that remains forever constant is the sacrifice necessary to attain, and subsequently defend, its spirit. Each of us owe a great debt to those who make it their life's work to provide us with the freedoms we enjoy today... and routinely take for granted. I dedicate this novel to all military and law enforcement, past, present, and future... and to the families of those freedom warriors who have suffered the gravest of consequences. No sacrifice is more honorable than that which ensures another's freedom... and life.

Robert E. Balsley, Jr

Table of Contents

PREFACE

From the Book of the Unveiled:

Empath: An extraordinary group of healers unique to the elven city of Elanesse and believed to have the power to control the thoughts of another mortal being. As the empaths grew in prominence, fear of their rumored mind control abilities gave rise to suspicion and civil unrest. The elven lords of the city declared empaths outlaw and issued orders for their systematic capture and execution. Because the accepted truth was no magical spell could guard against the empath ability to control thoughts, the clerics of Elanesse devised powerful magic to ward against this talent. This magic also gave those who sought the empath the means by which the empath could be tracked. This magic, known as the Purge, was designed to be wielded by all willing rangers in Elanesse and the surrounding Forest of the Fey... for it was the rangers who were the enforcers of the law and the legal executioners. All empaths discovered within city limits were put to the sword. No quarter was given. Any empaths who escaped this slaughter were methodically hunted down by elven rangers and destroyed.

The goddess Aurora, to whom many rangers owed allegiance, did not favor her followers being used as executioners. Aurora, however, couldn't force her rangers to ignore the law of their mortal masters, nor could she stop the magic that allowed her rangers to be the instruments of this horrific slaughter. Other than making the participating rangers outcast, there was little she could do to prevent the carnage. Mortals had a right to govern their own affairs. Althaya, the goddess of healing and the immortal champion of all things magical, was just as helpless. She could only provide succor when possible and ensure the souls of the doomed empaths found eternal rest.

Unknown to the elven overlords of Elanesse, the empath ability often skipped multiple generations. Thus, while all known active empaths were murdered, the bloodline of the empath may not have been completely exterminated. This has never been proven, however, since there have been no reports of the existence of empaths for over three thousand years. The level of involvement, if any, played by the higher powers in this mystery is unknown.

The true power of an empath: Contrary to the belief at the time, the empath does not control thoughts. The empath is attuned to what people feel emotionally, love and hate being the two strongest. Hate can kill an empath. It was reported that many of the empaths killed in the Purge were so overwhelmed by the feeling of hatred emanating from their ranger executioners they died before suffering physical harm. While hate can kill, love can serve to protect the empath. For this reason, empaths were never alone during their childhood. To be so in the world would mean death. Their protection came from a bond that was forged with another who has a strong emotional attachment to the empath. This was usually the mother. It was only after the empath matured into an adult were they be able to thrive on their own, having by then developed sufficient internal coping mechanisms against pure emotions.

Empaths can also sense the state of the soul. They can feel good as well as evil. No evil deed or intent can escape the detection of the empath. But this ability made them a target of unnatural evil such as the undead and demonic forces.

The empaths greatest ability, however, is their natural aptitude for healing. They do this by accepting the injury or disease from their patient to their own body. Their empath power within would then heal the transferred injury. Empaths freely sacrifice themselves for others if the need is great. This healing ability has one significant benefit for the empath. It gives them an unusually long life span. It has been rumored that the empath and the long-lived elf age at the same pace.

Author Unknown

THE STRUGGLE FOR INNOCENCE

FORWARD

From the Book of the Unveiled:

The Elves of Aster: The Elves of Aster don't call the world of Aster their homeland, for they are not native to that world. Known as the Elves of Light, they were settlers from the world of the Alfheim who arrived on Aster many thousands of years ago. Why the original elven colonists left their home world remains a mystery to this day... though the most logical explanation is that they saw an opportunity to explore new lands. The Elves of Light traveled from the Alfheim to Aster through a portal created by the power of the Ak-Samarië Shard. This elven relic of unlimited power linked the two dimensions. Little is known about the passageway except that it's a permanent connection between the two worlds and can only be activated for travel if the appropriate magic is used and the link between the shard and the magical Ak-Séregon stone, a piece of the Ak-Samarië Shard, is maintained.

Many present day elves feel a strong desire to return to the Alfheim. Numerous scholars suggest this need to return to the Alfheim is intrinsic to the elven race. There are others, however, who speculate the real reason is that Aster is no longer the natural forested world of its past... that the other races, particularly humans, have expanded to the point that a bastion for the elven race on Aster is no longer possible. Even the elven migration from the mainland to InnisRos had failed to stop incursions into elven sovereignty and, perhaps even more importantly, elven privacy.

Elanesse: The Elves of Light arrived on Aster in a richly wooded area which they claimed as their own. This became known as the Forest of the Fey, and the city they built within the forest was named Elanesse. In the elven way, a large portion of Elanesse was grown from magically induced crystal and the surrounding trees. Though the world of Aster did not have the same capacity for magic as the Alfheim, the world was in its infancy and the magic held within untapped and strong, particularly in this forest.

Unplanned and unknown to the elven sorcerers who wielded the magic, however, the manipulation of the magic of Aster to grow the city of Elanesse ignited sentience. The city of Elanesse was born both physically and spiritually. As the city grew, so too did its soul. Like all children, however, Elanesse needed guidance. She needed to be taught the difference between right and wrong, good and evil, and all the gray areas in between. Elanesse also suffered from the loneliness caused by being the only one of her kind... for no mortal being could mentor her or provide companionship. The inhabitants of the city didn't even know she existed.

Observing the unintended consequences of the elven actions to build their city was Sehanine StarEagle, Goddess of the Five Elements... earth, wind, fire, water, and aether, or quintessence, as it is sometimes called. Though the elves had long ago replaced Sehanine StarEagle with the discipline of science, she remained an active force in the Pantheon of the Gods, championing good, kindness, and compassion. Upon seeing Elanesse's distress and isolation, the goddess filled the void in Elanesse's heart… a heart that beat as sure as any other corporeal being.

   Over the thousands of years that has passed since the "birth" of Elanesse, Sehanine StarEagle was her mother, father, sibling, best friend, and teacher. This relationship between the goddess and Elanesse will remain until the end of time.

Author Unknown

THE STRUGGLE FOR INNOCENCE

PROLOGUE

The Alfheim

(193 Years Ago)

Having the blood of royalty coursing through one's veins offers many advantages not available to the common person... wealth, power, and access to all the things that makes existence more than just a constant struggle to carve a comfortable life out of reality. The royal who sees his duty as service to the people he rules, however, pays a steep price for those advantages. The good royal will bleed for the devoted.

-Book of the Unveiled

Martin Arntuile was seething. He didn't understand how the king could demand such a high price. "You ask too much, Argonne," he said hotly. "I can't leave my daughter behind. Nefertari is our oldest!"

King Argonne Quarion, leader of all the Alfheim, leaned forward in his throne and pointed a finger at Martin. "It was you who decided to take your family and all your people to this world called Aster." Leaning back and slumping down slightly, Argonne sighed. "I'm sick and dying, Martin. I can't be cured. You know that."

Martin softened. "I know, Argonne, and I'd change that if I could. But you have two brothers to succeed you. And the Alfheim's been secured from the Elves of the Dark."

"Thanks to your generalship, Martin," Argonne said.

"It was my duty, my King. The Army is in superb hands, I've seen to that. My family and people aren't needed here, but we are needed at InnisRos on Aster."

"You wish to be a king. Trust me when I say it isn't an easy tasking," Argonne countered. He had hoped to put doubt in Martin's mind.

"I don't wish it, Argonne, but I have a duty," Martin replied. "Someone over there traced my lineage back to their dead king. It's a stretch, I know, but if someone they consider having royal blood doesn't sit on the throne, chaos and anarchy will rule on InnisRos. Innocents will die when I could have prevented it. I don't want that on my conscience. But leaving behind Nefertari... my King? Why? It makes no sense. She's just a child. Think what it'll do to my wife Denairis, Lessien, and Nefertari to be forced apart like that."

"Families are torn apart all the time, Martin," Argonne said. "I've observed Nefertari at my court and see a spark of intelligence I rarely see in someone so young. I believe she'll make a difference here someday and I want to give her the opportunity to make that difference. She can only get the training she'll need under the tutelage of my First Councilor. Martin, think about Nefertari's future. It's for the best... and there's precedent for such an apprenticeship." He paused and tapped the arms of his throne with his fingers, thinking. "I should've had that damn portal closed decades ago." Argonne understood Martin's motivation, however... to keep together his family. It was much the same motivation that was driving Argonne, the survival of his monarchy. He looked at Martin and could tell he wasn't accepting his reasoning for keeping Nefertari in the Alfheim. After a few seconds, he looked at his guards. "Leave us," he said. Hidden doors throughout the throne room silently closed as the guards did the king's bidding.

"Stay, Martin, and I will make you king," Argonne said as he looked pointedly at his Chief General. He would make this one last plea.

"Argonne, please," Martin replied shaking his head. "Your brothers…"

"My brothers are both power-hungry fools who anxiously await my death!" the king shouted. "They'll fight each other over their right to rule. There'll be bloodshed as they tear this kingdom apart. Neither are capable of assuming the crown I wear or the Mantle of the Sovereign, Martin! You know that!"

Martin held his tongue and didn't dare argue...not when Argonne was so worked up. Besides, the king was correct, there'd be bloodshed. However, Martin suspected the only blood to be shed would be that of the two brothers and their sycophants… no real loss. There probably wasn't anyone else in the kingdom who liked either of the two enough to help elevate them to the throne.

"Well, Martin? Care to respond?" Argonne asked impatiently, drawing Martin from his thoughts. "You're going off to be a minor king on some damn island on Aster and I'm offering you the entire Alfheim. Surely this is more preferable."

Argonne's tone rekindled the anger Martin had relieved himself of just a few moments before. "Are you mad?! You know as well as I that would mean civil war," Martin replied crossly. "Your brothers would finally find the one thing they could agree upon, and the council would think you're implementing a dictatorship. My armies follow me, but they're loyal to the crown and the monarchy first. Someone without a royal connection will never succeed." Martin paced, attempting to ease some of his rage. Calmer, he turned back to face his king. "If I were to be named heir upon your death, everyone I hold dear would be killed as traitors. Even still, you hold my daughter hostage in the hope I'll acquiesce?"

"Even still," the king said. "Martin…" the king paused as he looked down at his gem-studded, multicolored ring of office, immersed in the same thoughts that had been swirling around his head for the last month… his mortality.

Martin looked at Argonne and noted his vacillation. "Speak your mind, Argonne. Let us have no secrets between us. I've been commander of all your armies for decades. We've battled the Elves of the Dark together as well as elements of those within your own kingdom who would tear you down."

Argonne looked up at Martin. His eyes had become hard, his tone of voice authoritative. Now he was a king talking to a subordinate, not a friend. "Trust me, General Arntuile, when I say I'll spare no one to guarantee my kingdom is safe after I'm gone. The monarchy must survive for everyone's well being. Without it, we're lost."

Martin recognized the king's change in attitude and shook his head. "That has nothing to do with me, Highness. I can't rule for reasons I've already made clear. Your brothers…"

"My brothers will soon be dead!" Argonne shouted as he stood. Martin was tall for an elf, but Argonne was taller, and the height of the dais upon which the throne sat made him even more imposing. "I've had them arrested! They're to be executed as traitors to the realm within the hour."

"But the rule of law..." Martin began, surprised to hear of this news.

"The rule of law be damned!" Argonne interrupted as he stepped off the dais to stand in front of Martin. "I'm the king! Do you understand, General? The king! My word IS the law!"   Argonne studied his general for a moment. He knew he had been taking a calculated risk. "If I so choose, you can join my brothers, buried in a shallow grave without fanfare and soon forgotten... like you never existed," he said quietly.

Martin drew back, stunned, at a loss for words.

Argonne rubbed his temples as pain flared in his eyes... eyes that had receded and had become unnaturally dark. "Damn headache," the king said as he went back to his throne and collapsed into it. He looked weak and frail.

"Your Highness, perhaps you should rest. We can continue this discussion later," Martin said, willing to use any pretense as an excuse to escape what he was witnessing... fearful the pain from the disease that was killing Argonne would cause the king to make rash decisions about his own future.

The king looked at Martin shrewdly. "You'll not be dismissed so easily, General Arntuile," Argonne said. "As for the pain, it'll be gone soon enough."

Martin bowed. "Yes, my King."

"Is your refusal final, then?" Argonne queried.

"To be king of the Alfheim, Your Highness?" Martin asked. "Yes, I'm afraid it is. I've given those on InnisRos my word. My word…"

Argonne waved his hand around as he interrupted. "Your word is your bond. Yes, yes, I know all about that," he said. "Sometimes it strikes me as being rather high-browed. I also find it somewhat tedious." Argonne leaned forward in his throne. "Here's a piece of advice about your 'word'. Never let them see you break it… but don't always keep it. Call it… oh, let's say 'king's privilege', if you will. When dealing with your enemies and your subjects alike, you must allow yourself that leeway. Politics is not honorable battle, Martin. It's dirty. Believe me when I tell you the strength of your conviction will not deflect the danger you put you and your family in as soon as you put on that crown."

Martin looked down at the crystal floor. The conversation had taken an uncomfortable turn. He heard Argonne whisper, "Very well," before he yelled for the guards. When Martin looked up, he saw Argonne's personal contingent of warriors return from behind numerous door that had been invisible until now. Though they had made no hostile movement toward him, he recognized their vigilance, defensive posturing, and subtle movements to ready their weapons. Two of the larger guards stood shoulder-to-shoulder with Martin, while two others flanked the king.

Martin sighed. He was no longer a friend of the court. "So it has come to this, my King?" he said.

"I have only begun, General Arntuile." Argonne said. Turning to one of the guards at his side, "I want the full council here immediately," he ordered. "Accept no excuses."

The guard saluted. "Yes, Your Highness," she said before running out of the audience chamber. Two other guards followed closely behind.

Shifting his attention to Martin, the king said, "I believe you have something that belongs to me."

Martin was momentarily confused. "I...?" Then he understood. It had been so long he had forgotten."Yes, Highness, I believe I do," Martin said as he started to unsheathe his sword.

Eighteen blades appeared in the hands of the nine remaining guards, two for each guard. Martin found himself surrounded by a wall of razor sharp steel. He looked at the elves behind the swords. He knew most of them since he had handpicked each one himself for service to the king. The eyes, however, were unrecognizable as they stared back at him. Martin let the sword fall back into his scabbard and looked at the king.

"These men are mine, General. You no longer hold standing in their eyes." Argonne answered Martin's silent query. Waving the guards to step back, he said, "Leave the sword in its scabbard and present it to me. You've lost the right to use it on my behalf."

Martin did so without feeling. He'd seen the king's wrath before, but never towards one of his own. As Martin stepped back, he heard the sound of many footsteps enter the chamber from behind. The council members had wasted little time arriving.

Argonne rose from his throne to address the newly arrived council members. In his hand was Martin's sheathed sword. All signs of the headache had disappeared. "I'll make this simple for you," he said, addressing the council. "I have several announcements to make. All are being made by royal proclamation, so no discussion will be tolerated. I only bring you here to follow protocol... and to warn you that any attempt to counter these proclamations by either direct or indirect action will result in your execution as traitors. Am I understood?"

There were general nods of agreement amongst the council members, though some were reluctant... not so reluctant as to challenge the king, however. Argonne nodded. "Good," he said. "You've all made a wise decision. As is customary, I'll have all the necessary paperwork drawn up and distributed in a day or two for your perusal. Just so everything is legal and transparent, you understand." Argonne looked at the council, daring even one to argue. No one did.

Withdrawing Martin's magically gleaming sword from its sheath, Argonne used it to slice his hand. Several of the council members gasped at the sight. As each drop of blood hit the floor, the magical link contained within the sword between king and guardian became weaker and weaker until it was completely drained of its magical power. "This sword was spelled to be in the hands of my most able general who, for all intents and purposes, is my closest protector," Argonne said. "For who can protect a king better than the general wielding the king's armies? But if it should ever draw the blood of the king it was meant to protect, the magic and power of the sword will exist no longer." Taking the now magic-less sword, Argonne pointed it at Martin. "Martin Arntuile is no longer that general," he said. Holding the sword by the hilt and grabbing the tip with his other hand, he brought the flat of the blade down hard on his knee. The metal broke in several pieces. One shard flew forward and pierced Martin's cheek and imbedded itself in his jaw bone. Taking what was left of the sword in his hand, Argonne threw it to land at Martin's feet.

Argonne then pulled his own sword, *Ah-RahnVakha*, from its gem-encrusted sheath. It blazed with strong magic as soon as it cleared the scabbard. The Mantle of the Sovereign covering Argonne's shoulders glowed as well. Argonne pointed the fearsome sword at Martin and said, "You are hereby exiled, along with your wife, Denairis, and youngest daughter, Lessien, to the world of Aster. There you will live out your days. Any return to the Alfheim will cause an arrest warrant to be issued for your capture and immediate execution. The same arrest warrant also applies to Denairis, should she ever return. The child, Lessien, may petition for return, but no sooner than one hundred years from the day of this judgment."

Martin kept his mouth shut and let this scene play itself out. Argonne was giving Martin what he wanted while avoiding the shamed of being abandoned by his Chief General.

Argonne voice drew Martin away from his thoughts. "Martin Arntuile, you have six hours to settle your responsibilities and obligations, collect your family and possessions, and say your goodbye's. At the end of that time, you'll report to the gateway and leave the Alfheim forever. Do you have any questions?"

"Your Highness, I'm sorry it had to come to this," Martin answered. "Perhaps…"

"Enough!" Argonne roared. Argonne took a few deep breaths. "The time for talking is over, Martin," Argonne said quietly as he regained control over his emotions. Even still, he couldn't keep the sting of losing Martin's leadership, and camaraderie, from his voice. "My decision has been rendered. You no longer hold standing at this court. You'll be escorted back to your home by members of my guard, so I suggest you do not stray nor tarry overly long. In six hours' time you'll go through that portal." Waving a hand at two of his guards, Argonne said, "See to it."

As Martin was marched from the audience chamber, the sound of his boots and that of his guards echoed throughout the otherwise silent and still room. Martin knew he would never see his home world again. Martin's attention suddenly diverted to the shard embedded in his jaw. It tingled. Surprised, Martin realized it still radiated magic... enough to create a new sword. Martin smiled. His old friend Argonne hadn't completely abandoned him after all.

Argonne watched with sadness and regret as his former Army commander left the chamber... sadness that Martin did not accept his offer and regret for the charade he had to play to banish him. There's so much Argonne wished to say to his general. He wanted to tell Martin of the time Denairis came to him, lonely and despondent because Martin had been on campaign for so long. She only wanted to be reassured by the king that her husband was still safe, but both soon found themselves caught up in simple lust… a lust fueled by a need to feel comfort from another person. There was an unintended consequence of that weakness… Nefertari. That's why Nefertari had to stay. After Argonne's two brothers, Nefertari was the only person left with royal blood. For the survival of his imperial lineage, she must become queen. But those secrets would have destroyed Martin, a thing Argonne didn't wish to see happen.

If Martin had accepted the offered kingship, Nefertari would've had time to grow into a great queen with her father's tutelage. But now he wasn't sure. Argonne could only hand her over to his most trusted advisor and pray to the gods that all would be right after his passing.

A door to the right of the throne opened and a female elf dressed in a resplendent floor-length white dress and purple robe entered the audience chamber. All the guards noticed her entrance, but none made any move to stop her approach to the king.

Argonne looked over at her as she stepped onto the dais and moved over to his side. Bending over, she whispered, "Nefertari's with us."

"Denairis was allowed to say her goodbyes?" Argonne asked.

"Yes, Highness, all went well. Lessien is much too young to understand and Denairis, though despondent, understands the necessity. I regret we didn't allow Martin to say goodbye, however."

Argonne nodded. "As do I, Kyleigh. But Martin's very intelligent, and he's going to figure out Nefertari's importance to me sooner or later. Right now he'll be too busy getting the rest of his family ready for the transition to give it serious thought… at least I hope that's the case. When he does make the connection, he's going to be hard to restrain. I don't wish to hurt him further, so would prefer he didn't come to the truth until after he's crossed over to Aster. Where do you have Nefertari?"

"She's at my home, Highness," Kyleigh replied. "I'm the one who'll instruct her on what she must learn to be queen, so she'll stay with me. She's had a meal and is now sleeping. I have several people watching over her."

"Excellent! What about Martin's elite guard, his Sword Masters?"

"As expected, they are loyal to a man, Majesty," Kyleigh said in answer to Argonne's query. "Their captain regrets he has to stay behind to command your next Chief General's security detail, but Lieutenant Van-Gourian resigned his commission and the rest accepted discharge."

Argonne smiled. "I can always count on you, Kyleigh," he said. Kyleigh nodded and turned to leave. "No, stay," Argonne said as he caught her arm.

"Very well, Highness," Kyleigh replied as she turned to face the council and remaining guards. She stood at Argonne's right side and slightly behind. Everyone in the room knew she was extremely devoted to her king as well as to the Alfheim. She would not bend on her principles and was impossible to bribe. Kyleigh Angelus-Custos, First Councilor to the King, was an honorable person who truly cared about the people. She also had the king's complete trust.

As Martin was escorted out of the king's audience chamber, the council members parted to make way for the small procession. Martin, using his soldier's instinct, briefly studied each person. Instead of the derision, contempt, and even hate he expected to see in their eyes, he saw fear… fear and confusion. These emotions he understood all too well as a general and a veteran of many campaigns against the Alfheim's foes. Once he saw either in his enemy's eyes, he knew he had won. Many times Martin overwhelmed an opponent on the battlefield because they either feared him or his tactics confused and kept them off balance. Undoubtedly the council members feared for their own futures, which put them squarely in the palm of the king's hand. Whatever Argonne had planned for the realm after his death, none of the council dare gainsay him. Martin sighed inwardly, "How sad," he thought. "Other than the King and Kyleigh, none of them cared about the kingdom short of what it could do for them. When I'm king of InnisRos, I'll have people advising me who are willing to sacrifice their lives for the people."

Martin and his guards walked through the audience chamber entrance. As they left the room, the massive wooden doors closed behind them. Martin stopped and turned to the sergeant at his side. "You don't need to escort me further, soldier," he said. "I'm sure you have other, more important business to attend.

I'll do as the king has instructed. Upon that you have my word."

The sergeant looked at Martin as if he were delusional. "No disrespect, General, but what could possibly be more important than following the king's instructions exactly as he gave them," he replied.

Martin nodded. "Perhaps it was wrong of me to ask, but I don't like being herded," he said. "I'd also like to know that my word still means something here. The King would understand."

The sergeant shook his head. "Your word means everything to every man in the Army, General," he said. "But the King's our Commander-In-Chief. His orders trump our respect for you."

Martin didn't reply as he started to walk forward again. "They're good men," he thought. "That's exactly the answer I would've expected if I were still their general."

They left the palace and crossed a courtyard to the stables. Martin's warhorse was saddled and ready to ride. An orderly stood at attention while holding the reins and saluted as Martin mounted and settled into the saddle. After Martin took the reins from the orderly, he returned the salute. By this time, his escort had also mounted their horses. It would be a thirty-minute easy gallop to Martin's quarters outside the palace.

As the countryside passed by, Martin's thoughts returned to his conversation with Argonne. He suspected why the king wanted to keep Nefertari early in the discussion... and that suspicion was confirmed when Argonne said he was going to execute his brothers. Not that they didn't have it coming. Their constant manipulations turned treacherous long ago.

But with Argonne's deadly illness, the king would be left without an heir… with one exception. Martin knew from that moment forward he had no hope of keeping Nefertari with him and his family when they moved to Aster. Though Argonne would never admit it, Martin had known for years she was the king's illegitimate daughter. Denairis had confessed to him as soon as he returned from campaign. Martin understood how people sometimes responded to loneliness and, though he wished Denairis and the king had shown more restraint, didn't get angry... believing Denairis when she said she was sorry and that it'd never happen again. He decided to raise Nefertari as his own, even though he knew the risk this would entail emotionally should the king ever claim her. While he had prayed daily to the gods that Nefertari would be spared the responsibility, he knew someday the unavoidable consequence of his wife's indiscretion would eventually come home to roost. Though Nefertari was now lost to him, he consoled himself with the knowledge she was going to be the Alfheim's queen, which not only was her rightful place as Argonne's last living heir, but also her duty. Martin understood duty.

As the doors closed behind Martin and his escort, everybody turned and looked at the king nervously. The guards, a small force of brutally effective soldiers dedicated to the protection of the king, had stationed themselves at strategic areas throughout the room. Not all the council members were intimidated by Argonne's behavior in the sudden dismissal of his chief general. The king's impending death was no secret, and most, though fearful about the short-term, were calculating how they were going to keep power once one of the brothers took charge.

Argonne, as he sat on his throne, studied his councilors. Only about half of them cared about the kingdom and gave advice with that consideration always on the forefront. The other half, however, were appointed by his brothers and served those interests at the expense of all other things. This selfish contempt for the wellbeing of a nation and its people disgusted Argonne. He hoped that what he was about to say... and the decisions he had made over the course of the last few days... would solidify, secure, and most importantly, protect the leadership of the kingdom from self-serving appointees after his death.

Argonne rose from his throne and looked out into the audience chamber. He reached inside his purple and gold-trimmed cloak and produced a scroll. Holding the scroll up for all to see, he paused for a few seconds before speaking. His weary and blood-shot eyes gazed into the eyes of each council member. As he did so, those who followed his brothers broke away from their king's scrutiny and looked down at the floor.

"As you all know, I'm dying. But now, I stand before you to explain that my impending death is not the result of a foreign disease for which there's no cure." Argonne shook his head. "No... no... were that it was so simple. I've obtained conclusive evidence I've been poisoned by my brothers... and parties as yet to be determined. At some point I was given the venom of the Harvester centipede, which, as you know, has no antidote and is always fatal. But death does not come quickly with this poison. The victim will languish for several weeks, getting weaker and weaker. Then the brain starts to liquefy, slowly robbing a person of his or hers identity. It's a most cruel way to die... particularly for a monarch."

Everyone started to talk at once. Argonne waited until the clamoring had quieted down before continuing. "Oh spare me the theatrics!" he said. His voice was granite hard. "Your righteous indignation astounds even me." Argonne looked around the room. "This document I hold in my hands is the signed execution order for Bastione and Jurial Quarion... my brothers." Argonne paused to study his audience once again as everyone started to talk. As king, he excelled in speechmaking, drawing out emotions and reading reactions as he spoke. He learned to recognize subtle body movements which indicated betrayal. But it was the eyes that told the real story. Any wise leader knew that the eyes were the window to the soul. In many of those eyes he saw fear. Leaning over to Kyleigh at his side, he whispered, "Did you see the panicked look in some of their eyes?"

"Yes, Highness," Kyleigh whispered back.

"Start your search with those," Argonne replied softly. "Watch them, but wait a few weeks until after my funeral before building your case. Let them think they've gotten away with it."

Kyleigh studied the council members and nodded. "It'll be in accordance with our laws, Highness. But be assured... those who helped your brothers will meet the executioner."

Argonne nodded. "I trust in you to make that come to pass. It's part of the reason I choose you," Argonne responded while he watched the general pandemonium. "There's one other thing, Kyleigh. Seek out Robert Gareathe. He's junior of all the council members, but perhaps the one most trustworthy. And he's smart. Vet him as you would anyone else, but I don't think he had a part in this."

Kyleigh took Argonne's sword-callused hand and bowed her head. "You have my word on it, Highness," she said with tears in her eyes.

Argonne squeezed her hand as he gently wiped away her tears before turning his attention back to the room. "Silence!" he roared. The deep bass of his voice, though emasculated by the poison, was still powerful enough to resonate throughout the chamber.

The impact of the king's order was immediate. The sudden stillness soon became once again a crescendo of nervous anticipation. One person, however, came forward to challenge the quiet.

"Excuse me, My King, but all execution orders shall be approved by the full council. That is the law. There are no exceptions," the councilor said. His bearing, his continuance, even the tone of his voice screamed defiance.

Kyleigh started her rebuttal, but Argonne held up his hand, stopping her response to the challenge.

"Councilor Merlotia, your king assures you we've done everything to make sure the letter of the law has been strictly followed," Argonne replied calmly. He was now in his element... politics.

"Then why haven't we seen your proof, or been given a chance to investigate for ourselves, Highness?"

Merlotia asked. "According to Article Fifty Seven of the King's Agreement with the people, trial of royalty or high-ranking individuals for a capital offense must be preceded by an independent investigation of the full council."

Argonne nodded. "You're correct, Councilor Merlotia. You ARE aware, however, of the codicil to the second subsection of that article?" the king asked.

Merlotia snickered. "Of course I'm aware…" he said before he stopped. "You mean you suspect one on the council of treason?"

"Your august body shouldn't be held above suspicion, Councilor Merlotia. My brothers couldn't have acted alone, and it would take someone with inside connections to help. Who better than one of you," Argonne said, "or perhaps more than one." Several council members shouted out denials. The king held up his hand for silence. "My brothers haven't been forthcoming, and I have no doubt they'll go to their death holding on to that secret. But First Councilor Angelus-Custos will get to the bottom of it, have no fear. If no blame falls upon any of you, there's nothing to worry about. Are you satisfied, Councilor Merlotia?" Argonne purred as he re-directed his focus back to the councilor. "Have I met all the criteria for the execution order?"

Merlotia bowed. "It would appear so, My King."

Argonne acknowledged Merlotia's bow with a short, curt one of his own. "Excellent!" he exclaimed. "I knew you'd see it my way! Now, let me explain to all of you how the succession will proceed. Upon my death, First Councilor Angelus-Custos will become the provisional sovereign over the kingdom. She'll use her own advisors and she'll have the latitude to appoint her own council. The First Councilor is keenly aware that most of you hold your positions due to family connections and political expediency. In other words, I suffer some of you because I owe favors to your families. But be warned, upon my death, the slate is wiped clean. Each of you, at least those of you who had no part in my assassination, will be vetted again for loyalty and, most importantly, your desire to serve the people of this kingdom."

Argonne gazed upon the now depressed-looking throng. "Oh come now, it can't be all that bad. Stand on your merits! If you've been honest, forthcoming, and competent, you'll have nothing to worry about. I caution you, however. The First Councilor has the complete backing of my military forces. Any threat to her, real or perceived, will be prosecuted rigorously."

As one, the entire guard unsheathed one of their swords and beat them to their armored chests. "Hail First Councilor Angelus-Custos!" they shouted in unison, surprising the councilors.

Argonne leaned over, smiling, and whispered to Kyleigh, "Don't you love a little theatrics?"

Kyleigh didn't smile back. "My King, you shouldn't be mocking them," she said.

Argonne whispered back, "Probably not, but I want to make sure they understand. I'll do my best to protect both you and Nefertari after I'm gone."

Kyleigh's voice became hard. "Don't fear on that score, My Lord. If they don't understand now, they will shortly," she said.

"I wish I could see that. I wish I could see so many things." Argonne replied wistfully as he gazed around the audience chamber like a parent who must say goodbye to a well-loved child.

"Your Highness?" Kyleigh asked with deep concern in her voice. "Are you feeling well enough to continue?"

Argonne shook his head. Everyone in the room was closely studying him. "Damn," he thought, "I've just shown weakness."

"Yes, of course, First Councilor," he replied, putting as much strength as he could in his voice for all to hear.

"Then allow me to ask a question, Your Highness," Councilor Merlotia said.

Argonne nodded.

"You mentioned that First Councilor Angelus-Custos is only the provisional sovereign. That implies ruler ship of the kingdom will eventually be handed over to someone else, yet you have no heirs other than your condemned brothers."

"But I have an heir… an heir that has been kept out of the public eye until now," Argonne replied. "I have a daughter."

Martin and his escort arrived at his small country villa to a bustle of activity. Soldiers, his Sword Masters, were scampering about helping to load several wagons with the contents of Martin's home - furniture, clothes, household items, expensive art - which, in some respects, defined who he was. Slowing his horse, Martin watched quietly for a few seconds. "The trappings of a successful and comfortable life," he thought. "Is that my legacy?"

Denairis, holding Lessien's hand while carrying a sack slung over one shoulder, came out of the main building. Her eyes were wet and red though she was not crying. Looking at her, Martin saw that a spark, no, a part of her soul, had been torn out. At that moment Martin knew that the king had already claimed what he felt was his, Nefertari, and that he would not have a chance to say goodbye. "Damn!" he swore silently. "Argonne, you could at least have given me a chance to hug her and tell her I love her one last time!"

Denairis, spying Martin, stopped suddenly and looked down. She couldn't meet Martin's eyes. Even after all this time, even after the wonderful gift of Nefertari, she was still ashamed by her betrayal of him with Argonne. All Denairis could see was the pain she thought she was still causing to those she loved. Martin groaned in frustration. He didn't know how to convince her she had been forgiven long ago. Perhaps the new start on Aster would provide the cure.

Martin got off his horse and walked over to Denairis and Lessien. Picking up his five year old daughter and giving Denairis a kiss, he turned to the military detail that was packing and loading his family's possessions. "Lieutenant Van-Gourian!" he called.

A lieutenant put down a crate and stepped forward, saluted, and answered, "General!"

Martin shook his head. "I'm no longer a general, son," he said.

"Begging your pardon, sir, but you'll always be our general," the lieutenant replied. "Do you recognize any of these soldiers?"

Martin took a few moments to study the work party. "I do, Lieutenant," Martin answered. "I see that everyone from my security contingent is accounted for. But I don't see how any of that is relevant."

"We're going with you to Aster," Van-Gourian stated firmly. His tone told Martin they were going regardless of his wishes.

Martin handed Lessien back over to Denairis. "You're deserting?" Martin asked.

The lieutenant frowned. He was surprised that Martin would suggest such a thing. "Of course not, sir," he said. "I resigned my commission. The noncom's and enlisted have been discharged. We're free to take up our posts for you once again in Aster."

Martin considered what the lieutenant said. "No one gets discharged from the king's Army unless they've reached the end of their enlistment, Lieutenant. I don't think all these soldiers just happened to reach their enlistment termination at the same time. So explain to me how they were discharged."

Van-Gourian shuffled his feet in the soft dirt. He was clearly uncomfortable. "Well, Lieutenant?" Martin asked for a second time.

"It was suggested by the First Councilor," Van-Gourian said, then shaking his head, "Don't get me wrong, General. All of us decided that as soon as we had fulfilled our obligations to the king, we would follow you over to Aster anyway. Somehow the First Councilor caught wind of our discussion and thought it was a fine idea. She was the one who proposed an early discharge for my, or should I say, your men. She even gave us traveling money."

"Why would she do that, Lieutenant?" Martin asked. "Did she give you a reason?"

Van-Gourian shook his head. "Not specifically, but she did say the king would look the other way. If you'll permit me, General, I have some sense for what's going on. Scuttlebutt, sir. Your daughter will be in good hands with the First Councilor."

Martin sighed. "Thank you, Lieutenant. There won't be any easy way to come back to the Alfheim if you so choose. Are you and the men ready for that?"

Lieutenant Van-Gourian smiled. "Yes sir, we are!" he replied enthusiastically.

"Then stop what you're doing and mount up. We leave within the hour," Martin replied.

"But your…" the lieutenant started to say.

"We leave it," Martin interrupted. "I think a fresh start will do us all some good."

"By your command," the lieutenant said as he saluted. Turning to his First Sergeant, he said, "See to it." The sergeant came to attention and saluted Martin first and then the lieutenant. "Sirs," he said. Several of the elves nearest the three also saluted and, along with the First Sergeant, ran to pass the orders along to their comrades.

Before turning back to his waiting wife and daughter, Martin touched the lieutenant on the sleeve. "Thank you," he said.

The lieutenant nodded. "We've always been yours," he replied with a confused look on his face. To him and those he led, that explained everything. Why would they do anything different?

42

Argonne, Kyleigh, the council, and the king's guards stood against the walls of a cold, damp, circular room. In the center of the room was a wooden block scored with numerous sword and axe marks. Though the block had been meticulously scrubbed, dried blood remained, absorbed by the wood. On this day the simple chunk of carved wood seemed to come alive, anticipating the meal about to satiate its hunger. Sitting next to the headsman's block was a bucket of pristine holy water, blessed by several clerics hours before. Several torches were lit and placed in sconces around the room, revealing the stormy dark look on each face. There was not a soul in the room who looked forward to what was about to happen. Many of the council members were shuffling their feet nervously on the straw covered floor.

Argonne leaned over to Kyleigh. "We should have brought Nefertari to watch this," he whispered. "One day she must order and witness executions."

"You're correct as always, Highness," Kyleigh replied. "But she's still too young and the pain of being taken away from her family still too new. I don't think we should traumatize her further."

Argonne nodded. He always deferred to Kyleigh's judgment in such matters. Turning to the dungeon guard, he said, "Bring in Jurial first."

The dungeon guard saluted and left through the only door in the room. Argonne nodded to two of his guards who followed. During the interim, everyone waited in complete silence. The only sound that could be heard was the quiet crackling of the fire at the end of each torch. That silence was broken by the sound of scuffling outside the door.

Two muscular guards, one on each side, had their hands firmly clamped on Jurial's arms as he struggled. Except for an occasional foray into nearby forests hunting one of his falcons, Jurial had taken no effort to keep his body toned and strong. His thrashing about proved futile against the combined strength of the two guards. When Jurial saw the headsman's block, his struggling stopped as the true implications of his actions, and subsequent penalty, finally sank in. As Jurial was brought to stand before Argonne, he struggled again with renewed vigor.

"Get your hands off me!" Jurial screamed.

"For once in your life act like an adult," Argonne scolded.

Jurial stopped resisting and spit in Argonne's face. "You whoreson!" he yelled.

One guard cuffed Jurial in the back of the head, but Argonne held up his hand to stop it as he cleaned the spit off his face with the other. "Let him speak his mind without repercussion. Say what you will, Jurial, before I carry out your sentence."

"I have no regrets except that I could not live long enough to watch you die," Jurial replied with a smirk. "The venom from the Harvester centipede is particularly cruel, which is why we used it."

"Jurial, I'm your brother… your own flesh and blood," Argonne said. "Who helped the two of you to assassinate me?"

"And why would I tell you that, Argonne?" Jurial replied angrily. "Will you commute my death sentence?"

Argonne shook his head. "No, I will not, Jurial. But it'll allow you to die with some measure of recompense for the evil deed you took part in."

Jurial closed his eyes for a moment while everyone waited to see what he would say. When he opened them again, the hate for his brother was stronger than ever. "You stopped being my brother long ago. I saw an opportunity for power and you were in the way. Now let's get this over with. I can no longer tolerate your stink," he said.

Argonne nodded to the guards holding Jurial. He then took his place alongside the headsman's block as the guards chained the prisoner's arms to the sides of the block. When they were finished, Jurial's head lay across the block, his neck exposed.

Argonne unsheathed his sword *Ah-RahnVakha.* The glowing blade felt uncharacteristically heavy. Whether this was because of the weight of regret or venom-induced weakness, Argonne couldn't tell.

Lifting the sword into a horizontal position, tip leveled at Jurial's neck, Argonne said, "You've been found guilty of high treason and regicide. The sentence for this is death. Do you have any last words before I carry out judgment?"

"Just get on with it!" Jurial shouted.

When Argonne lifted the sword straight up, the radiance of its magic became brighter than the sun. All the witnesses in the room had to glance away as the brilliant light burned into their eyes. A lightning bolt exploded from the end of the sword and danced along the ceiling of the room. For a moment the power of the sword transcended the king wielding it, but then quickly returned to its master. As the blade descended on its righteous path, Jurial knew true terror the moment before the sword struck.

Thunder reverberated throughout the room, momentarily stunning all except Argonne. As quickly as it came, the sword relented and smothered its awesome power, becoming once again the gleaming, glowing blade everyone was accustomed to.

Argonne looked down at the headless body of Jurial. There was no blood. The heat of his sword cauterized the blood vessels as it sliced through. The block of wood had also been slashed, leaving two charred and smoking halves. Looking at one of the dungeon guards, he said, "Please remove the body and the head."

"Right away, my Lord," the guard replied. "Do you wish another block of wood be brought in?"

"Yes. And bring me a chair," Argonne said.

Within a few moments a chair was brought in and Argonne collapsed into it. Kyleigh immediately stepped to his side. "I didn't know *Ah-RahnVakha* could do that," she said as she wiped Argonne's sweaty brow with a silk handkerchief.

"It only happened on one other occasion. On campaign, years ago, my command post had been overrun by dark elves. Martin and I found ourselves back-to-back and fighting for our lives. Its power saved us. Since then I've done extensive research about the sword. It only comes alive like that in defense of the monarch wielding it, and to serve justice. When I'm gone, only Nefertari, as queen, will be able to use its full power. Make sure she gets the proper training."

"Of course, My King," Kyleigh replied, "For now rest a few moments. You look weary." She had noticed a little blood coming from Argonne's ears and knew, from all the information she had gathered about the Harvester centipede's venom, that once he started to bleed from body orifices, he only had a few days to live.

The execution of Bastione went much the same as Jurial's, except Bastione was less combative and more resigned to his fate. Afterwards, Argonne went to his quarters to lie down while Kyleigh administered the details that typically followed an execution. She wanted to make sure she abided by the strict letter of the law. Afterwards, she held a late meeting with the council, listening to tiring denials of treason and promises of cooperation and bipartisanship. Robert Gareathe, the council member Argonne pointed out to Kyleigh earlier, leaned in a corner and was talking privately to Councilor Merlotia. Both seemed unaffected by the ongoing pandemonium being caused by the other councilors. Finally Kyleigh could stand the bickering no longer. She called for a dinner break so she could escape the room full of popinjays. She also wanted to check on the king.

As she passed through the seated and standing throng, she was almost out the door when she was hailed.

"First Councilor Angelus-Custos, a word if you please." It was Councilor Gareathe who had called. Councilor Merlotia stood by his side. Kyleigh stopped and studied the two. She saw that Councilor Merlotia had allowed himself to take a subordinate position in favor of the junior council member.

"Of course," she said. "But please make it quick. I've much to do, including reining in this rabble." The last was intended for the two councilors standing in front of her as well as the others.

Robert nodded. "We haven't made things too easy for you, have we?" he replied calmly, taking no offense at her subtle slight.

"No, not really," Kyleigh admonished, "but I understand everyone's apprehension, considering some, if not all, of you are going to be replaced or arrested as accessories to the king's murder."

"As is your right, First Councilor," Robert agreed. "We should all be well scrutinized and our usefulness challenged. It's your duty to the Alfheim."

Merlotia nodded enthusiastically. "Yes, please, replace me. I know the law, but I don't want to be on the council. My family never bothered to ask when they drafted me to replace my dead father."

Kyleigh frowned. "You certainly seemed in your element when you challenged the king," she said reproachfully.

Merlotia looked away before answering. "As I said, I know the law… its purity, its detachment from emotion, its beauty. I had to at least ask about the legitimacy of the execution warrant. It was my duty. But please believe me when I tell you I would much rather be teaching the law at the university then spending time on the council."

"I see," Kyleigh said. "Yet the king managed to school YOU on the law."

"You mean the codicil?" Merlotia said. "Yes, madam, he did. It's a mistake I'll never make again."

"If I still require your services after this, see that you don't," Kyleigh responded. "Now, I'm very busy. Is there anything else?"

Robert held out his hand. In his palm was a signet ring, the face of which shaped like a flame, the base of the flame made from red crystal while the top clear crystal. "This is my family's insignia," he said. "The flame represents the pain of sacrifice we all must undergo. The clear crystals symbolize our transcendence to the higher calling each in my family gives oath to at a young age. Not all endure…"

"… the flame," Kyleigh finished for him. "That's your family motto. I know it well."

"Then you know what it means to have one of our signet rings presented," Robert said.

Kyleigh studied the young elf. "Argonne is a good judge of character," she thought. "It would seem he read this one's heart correctly." Kyleigh closed her hand around the ring. "We shall see," she said. "All in this room will be investigated most vigorously with no exceptions. I'll not allow the new queen to be jeopardized until she has come of age… and not even then."

"I strive for the same goal," Robert responded. He sighed. "In this, we both failed King Quarion."

Kyleigh couldn't prevent the flash of pain that escaped her eyes.

"The ring represents my solemn oath given to you and our new queen, whoever she may be. Both of you have my complete loyalty, devotion, and life, should you require it," Robert said.

Kyleigh nodded, her stance softening somewhat, but her voice was still firm. "I would expect nothing less," she said before walking away.

Robert understood Kyleigh's apprehension. As she walked away, he called after her, "Check the king's belongings, First Councilor. You'll discover that I gave him a ring as well."

Martin was riding his horse while holding Lessien in front of him, one arm encircling her tightly. She had fallen asleep and her head was resting on his chest. He looked over at his wife, Denairis, who was riding next to him, and couldn't help but cringe at the dead look in her eyes. Her movements were automatic and made without strength of will. Even Lessien seemed lost to her.

"Sir," Lieutenant Van-Gourian said as he approached Martin from the front of the column. "The portal's just over the next rise. Besides the normal sentries and sorcerers, the king has also seen that an honor guard will see us off."

Martin considered the lieutenant's remark. "I wonder why he did that?"

"It's fitting for your station, General… or should I say Highness," Van-Gourian said as he smiled.

"Let's not get ahead of ourselves, Lieutenant," Martin replied.

"Yes, sir," Van-Gourian replied. "What're your orders?"

"None right now… no wait," Martin called as the lieutenant started to ride back to the front of the column. "On the other side of the portal are sentries much like what we have here. I haven't received a communiqué from InnisRos for several days and assume they know to expect us. But I'm not completely sure about my status, so warn the men I want no trouble. That's going to be our new home. Treat it and those living there with respect."

Van-Gourian saluted and rode off.

Martin kicked his horse gently and started forward again. He looked over at Denairis and asked, "How are you?"

Denairis shook her head, clearing her mind of a self-induced trance, and focused on Martin. "I don't know, my husband," she answered. "It's been a long day."

"It has," Martin agreed. "In a few minutes we'll be through the portal. Once on InnisRos, you'll be able to rest."

"How can there ever be any rest… any escape… from the loss of Nefertari?" she asked, though she didn't expect an answer. "Martin, it hurts so badly. A piece of my heart's been ripped out today."

Martin reached over and grabber her hand. "We both know why Argonne had to insist she be left behind. I suppose I should've known this would happen once I accepted the kingship of InnisRos. Argonne would never let a potential heir slip through his fingers considering the relationship he had with his brothers." Martin sighed. "By agreeing to go to InnisRos, I took a calculated risk in the hope I could get Nefertari safely away. I knew if his brothers had ever caught wind of her existence and claim to the throne of the Alfheim, they would have her killed. But that's no longer a concern and she'll be safe enough now."

Denairis shook her head. "Martin, you have no reason to blame yourself," she said while squeezing his hand. "It's simply… life."

Martin looked down at the sleeping Lessien ensconced in his arm and squeezed a little harder, wishing she would never leave his embrace… his protection. "Life is a cruel master," he said.

About that time they reached the apex of the small hill they were climbing. The open portal was visible below, swirling vapors of black and gray seemingly built out of nothing. Four sorcerers surrounded another who was holding a brightly glowing staff. All five of the sorcerers were casting spells of enchantment. Two rows of twelve mounted knights formed a steel corridor leading to the mouth of the portal. Lieutenant Van-Gourian had stopped the column.

"Are you ready?" Martin asked Denairis.

She nodded. Still holding hands, Martin, with Lessien sleeping in front of him, and Denairis, moved their horses to the front of the column and slowly approached the portal. Martin acknowledged the salutes from the honor guard and entered the portal without hesitation. Travel through the portal was simply a matter of stepping into the mist and appearing on Aster. Everyone who accompanied Martin disappeared from the plane of the Elves of Light. It was as if they had never existed.

Eight days after Martin Arntuile left for Aster, His Royal Highness, Argonne Quarion, King of the Alfheim, and Keeper of the Light, lay dying from the poison of the Harvester centipede in his bedroom. At his side were First Councilor Kyleigh Angelus-Custos and the commander of Argonne's personal guard, Captain Tori Emanidore. The king's sword, *Ah-RahnVakha*, was by his side, pulsating with each beat of Argonne's heart. The power radiating from the sword was noticeably weaker as the link between wielder and magic slowly dissipated.

Kyleigh, exhausted from the vigil she held the last two days, was sitting in a padded chair next to the king's bed, dozing. Captain Emanidore shook her gently.

"Kyleigh, look," the captain said as she pointed to the sword. Its magic was no longer visible.

Kyleigh looked from the sword to the side of Argonne's head. Brain matter was leaking out in a grayish, thick, gruel-like liquid. "It is finally over," Kyleigh whispered.

"His heart still beats," Captain Emanidore said after placing her hand on Argonne's chest.

Kyleigh nodded. "It does not yet know the brain is gone, Tori," she replied as she gripped the hilt of *Ah-RahnVakha*. "I will not tolerate the king's humiliation by this poison a moment longer!" Standing up and positioning the tip of the sword over Argonne's heart, she thrust with all her might. With the heart destroyed,

Argonne's body finally succumbed. The sword suddenly disappeared in a flash of purple light.

A gasp escaped the captain. Kyleigh glanced over at her and touched her on the arm. "The king told me this would happen. Do not fear... the sword will present itself once again when Nefertari becomes queen. Now go let the waiting clerics and servants in. Prayers must be said and the king's body must be prepared for the funeral and burial."

Captain Emanidore replied, "Yes, First Councilor!" as she came to attention and saluted before exiting the room.

Kyleigh shook her head. "I hope Nefertari's a fast study," she said to the empty chamber. "I don't relish being the provisional sovereign for any longer than absolutely necessary."

It was, however, not to be.

After three days of lying in state, the king was cremated in a lavish ceremony, his ashes scattered to the four winds. A crystal plaque with his likeness was mounted on the Wall of Remembrance, located outside the palace, maintained and patrolled by a round-the-clock honor guard. During nighttime hours, each plaque on the wall glimmered with magic and released beams of light into the heavens where, as legend told it, the dead rulers of the Alfheim lived. By following the magical beams, these legends of lore could return during times of trouble to once again offer their wisdom, protection, and blessings. One more beam had joined the nightly climb into a starry sky.

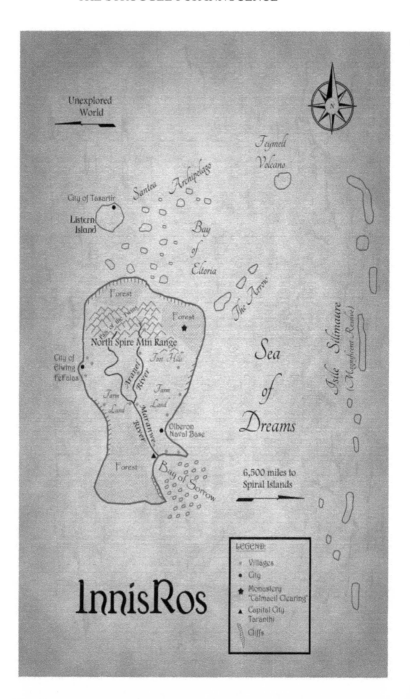

CHAPTER ONE

InnisRos

(193 Years Ago)

The plight of the honest person is sometimes preordained, for the nature of the honest person is to unequivocally trust those to whom friendship is given. The friendship of an honest person is priceless beyond imagining. That friendship, however, can pave the way for deception.

-Book of the Unveiled

It was late afternoon on Aster. Martin Arntuile and his entourage dismounted their horses and handed the reins over to waiting hands. Martin, holding tightly onto Lessien, stood on InnisRos soil for the first time. He was facing a gathering of the island's most highly ranked individuals. All the members of the ruling body were present as were the wealthy families, each wanting a glimpse of their new king and perhaps find an opportunity to draw him aside for an informal audience. However, First Councilor and InnisRos' acting president, Amras Sáralondë, successfully intercepted Martin and his followers to steer them away before the lords and ladies of the island descended upon him. Standing at First Councilor Sáralondë's side and directing the military honor guard was his associate, a sinister-looking elf with a fake smile. Martin didn't like him.

"You're First Councilor Sáralondë?" Martin asked.

"Yes, Your Highness. I'm the one you've been communicating with," Amras replied. "We've been waiting for this day ever since we first learned you represented the continuation of our dead king's bloodline. This is Mordecai Lannian, Second Councilor and InnisRos' Chief Executor of the Ministry of Finance."

Martin shook hands with both.

"All of you look exhausted, Your Highness," Amras said. "We need to get you to the palace so you can rest."

"It was just a single step, First Councilor, but it's still a trip between worlds of existence," Martin replied. "I've heard this would happen, but I had no firsthand experience… that is until now. And please, don't call me 'Highness' just yet."

Amras shook his head. "You don't understand, Your Highness. The actual coronation is just for show. You became our king as soon as you crossed from the Alfheim."

Martin paused a moment while he wrapped his mind around his new position. "Very well, then. When is the coronation?" he asked.

"In a week, my Lord," replied Mordecai.

Martin nodded. "Thank you, Second Councilor." Redirecting his attention to Amras, Martin said, "First things first. We need to rest. My men and I are trained to function while fatigued, but not my wife and daughter."

"The palace is just over there," Amras responded as he pointed to a large, ornate crystal structure. "If you wish, I could have a coach brought over."

Martin looked at his wife, Denairis, who shook her head. "No, First Councilor, we can walk. I have a question, however. Why so long before the coronation?"

"There's still much to do to make everything ready," Amras replied.

Martin shook his head. "It's not necessary, you know. The coronation, I mean. It seems like a lot of trouble just to…" Martin said before being interrupted by Mordecai.

"Tradition, my Lord. The people expect it."

Martin smiled. He understood tradition… the Alfheim reeked of it. "You understand that I was the general of all the Alfheim's armies?" he asked.

"By the gods yes, Your Highness," Amras exclaimed. "When we first found out that there was a distant relative to our dead king alive in the Alfheim, though relieved, we feared you might be a candlestick maker or some such simpleton. We couldn't have been happier to learn of your status."

"Candlestick makers are skilled practitioners of their craft," Martin replied. "But I take your point. The reason I mentioned my past occupation is so you'd understand my first orders as your sovereign. Between now and my coronation, I want a complete briefing as to the state of affairs on InnisRos… our strengths, our weaknesses, our assets and debts, our allies, our enemies… that sort of thing. Nothing sugarcoated. I also want a complete report as to the potency of our military forces and their ability to defend this island. After the coronation, I intend to visit and inspect every nook and cranny, especially our military bases and bivouacs, so I'm completely familiar with the 'terrain', so to speak. Are there any questions?"

"No, Your Highness," Amras said. "After you've rested, we'll bring in all of your advisors for that discussion. Mordecai, please see to it."

"As you wish, First Councilor," Mordecai replied. To Martin, he said, "My Lord, I'll have your security detail ready for your inspection as soon as it is convenient."

"That won't be necessary, Second Councilor Lannian," Martin said as he shook his head. "I already have my security detail in place. The warriors I brought over with me... my Sword Masters... are sufficient to handle most contingencies. I trust each with my life."

"But, my Lord..." Mordecai was halted by Martin's stare.

"They were the finest warriors on the Alfheim," Martin said. "I expect those abilities have not changed simply because we're now on Aster."

"As you wish," Mordecai said. He kept the disappointment out of his voice. "Damn!" he thought.

As the group drew closer to the palace, Martin noticed a curious thing. Three large dire wolves were sitting around a young priest. The wolves watched everything with uncommonly intelligent eyes. The priest watched only Martin and his assembly. Everyone else on the streets had given the cleric and his wolf companions a wide berth.

"Oh great, beastie boy is here," Mordecai whispered.

"Hold your tongue!" Amras scolded. "Your Highness, that's Father Horatio Goram from Althaya's monastery at Calmacil Clearing. No doubt you'll meet him later. His family and the deceased king were quite close."

"And the wolves?" Martin asked.

"They never leave his side," Amras replied. "Father Goram has them under his complete control. It's amazing to watch him with them… almost as if he can speak to them directly. They pose no threat. Well, except for our friend Councilor Lannian here. He and the good father don't like each other. As a consequence, the wolves aren't very polite whenever the two are together. Isn't that right, Mordecai?"

Mordecai nodded. "One of these days I'm going to kill that old bastard," he thought.

The wolves watched with interest as the group passed. Father Goram bowed slightly to Martin, who acknowledged the priest with a slight nod of his head. Lessien, half asleep, suddenly reached out to Father Goram as if she knew him. He smiled and waved at her. Lessien whispered, "Wolf," and nestled back into Martin's arms and fell back to sleep. "That's bizarre," Martin thought as he continued towards the palace. "How could she know about the dire wolf. She's never seen one before."

The royal palace in Taranthi, the capital city of InnisRos, was a thing to behold. Martin, as well as

61

those who came with him, were not overly impressed. As beautiful as the palace might be, nothing on Aster could match the magnificence of the architecture on the Alfheim.

Entering the courtyard, servants were lined up and ready to do Amras and Mordecai's bidding. Before either could give orders, though, Martin put Lessien in a surprised Lieutenant Van-Gourian's arms and shook the hands of each of the servants, taking the time to learn their names and what they did in his service. Both Amras and Mordecai frowned, but said nothing.

After thirty minutes, Martin dismissed the servants to their duties. A handmaiden led Denairis and Lessien, who was now awake and walking on her own, to the king's quarters.

Martin turned to Lieutenant Van-Gourian. "You're now a major. Bump each man up two pay grades except for First Sergeant Inglorian. He's now second-in-command holding the rank of lieutenant… unless you have someone else in mind."

"No sir. Inglorian will do just fine," Van-Gourian replied.

Martin nodded. "See to our horses and then get your folks food and rest. Make sure to set a perimeter watch."

Amras shook his head. "Really, Your Highness, there's no need for that. The palace guard…"

"First Councilor, I'll make those decisions," Martin responded in a no-nonsense tone. Turning back to Van-Gourian, Martin said, "Finally, Major, make sure we have no one fraternizing with the female servants, at least not yet."

"Righteous hearts and righteous minds, My King," Van-Gourian replied with a smile as he saluted.

"Yes, well, be off with you then," Martin said as he returned the salute.

"Shall I show you to the royal bedchamber?" Mordecai asked.

"I think I'd prefer a drink," Martin replied. "Where's the sitting room?"

Amras pointed towards a door to everyone's left. "Through there, Your Highness. Shall I call for wine?"

Martin shook his head. "Think I need something stronger," he said.

"Right away, my Lord!" a servant said from behind them, startling Martin. "I must be more tired than I realized," he thought to himself as Amras and Mordecai led him into the large and ornate sitting room.

Sitting in a comfortable chair, Martin allowed himself to close his eyes for a few moments until the whiskey arrived in a crystal decanter. Each of the three poured for themselves, sat back in chairs, and sipped their drinks, letting the burning liquid warm their bodies. "At least their whiskey is as good as what I had in the Alfheim," Martin reflected.

Amras cleared his throat and said, "Highness, may I ask a question?" Martin nodded. "We were led to believe you had two daughters," Amras said.

Martin grimaced. "I do," he said. "First Councilor, it's a complicated matter. She'll not be joining us. In fact, she's probably lost to us forever."

"I'm so very sorry!" Amras said with genuine compassion in his voice. "That must be why your wife seemed so sad."

"That's certainly part of it," Martin replied quietly as he stared into his drink.

Both of the councilors waited expectantly for Martin to continue. Martin looked up and rubbed his eyes. "I don't really care to elaborate," he said. "I have a question for you. That priest… the one with the wolves…"

"Father Goram," Mordecai replied sourly.

Amras put his drink on a table. "He's a most interesting fellow, Your Highness. He's the heir apparent to a large fortified monastery northeast of here at Calmacil Clearing. Though not really on the council, he did have the king's ear in matters of magical healing, which seems to be his specialty."

Mordecai swallowed the rest of his drink. "He follows a pagan goddess called Althaya. Personally, I never had any use for him. But the king felt otherwise. His family and the king's family have been acquaintances for a long time. If I were you, I wouldn't trust him."

Martin looked at the Second Councilor. "If Mordecai doesn't like the priest, I probably will," he thought. Aloud, Martin asked, "And the wolves?"

As soon as Martin mentioned the wolves, he saw two opposite facial reactions. Amras smiled while Mordecai frowned in disgust. "Wonderful creatures," Amras exclaimed. "People are always so afraid of them, yet they are at all times perfectly behaved. I've never known Father Goram to travel without them… or the rangers who keep close yet discrete watch over him."

Martin nodded and considered Amras' information. "That's why Mordecai has a problem with the wolves," he thought. "They're the perfect bodyguards. There's bad blood between those two, that's for sure." Martin redirected his attention back to Amras, who hadn't stopped talking.

"… seems the wolf pack and the monastery have an almost symbiotic relationship," Amras was saying. "The wolves offer protection while the monastery provides healing and, during severe winters, shelter and food. But I believe it goes beyond that. The pack leader of the wolves, Hector, loves Father Goram. Of that I'm certain."

"Thank you, Amras. I wish to meet Father Goram," Martin said. As he looked at the distressed look on Mordecai's face, he added, "And the wolves. Especially Hector."

"I'll see to everything, Your Highness," Amras replied. Mordecai looked relieved he wasn't going to be ordered to make the arrangements.

During the subsequent pause, a knock came from the opened door of the sitting room. It was Major Van-Gourian. Martin, pleased to see a familiar face, hid his smile from the two councilors. "Yes, Major, what is it?" Martin asked.

"My King, the watch has been set and the rest of us are settled in our quarters," the major said. "Is there anything else you need?"

"No, I think…" Martin paused, and instead waved Major Van-Gourian into the room. "Have a seat, Carl, and pour yourself a drink. There are few things I want to discuss with you before checking on Denairis and Lessien."

Major Van-Gourian rubbed his hands together as he crossed the room and seated himself on one of the over-stuffed leather chairs. Mordecai watched in horror and contempt as the major poured a glass of Taranthi's most premium and costly whiskey. "At least the idiot didn't gulp it down like a common drunk," Mordecai said to himself as he watched the major sip his drink.

Martin decided it was time to dismiss the councilors. "Gentlemen, I think that'll be all for now. I appreciate your time and consideration."

"It was our pleasure, Your Highness," Amras responded with a smile as he got up and bowed. "Please don't hesitate to call upon us at any time."

"Thank you," Martin said as he stood up and shook the hand of both councilors. "By the way, Councilor Lannian, I want to talk to each advisor individually... with you and Councilor Sáralondë present, of course. Let's start the interviews on the noon hour, say, day after tomorrow? I'll need a directory of the advisors before then. Be sure this information contains personal backgrounds, duties and responsibilities, idiosyncrasies, their weaknesses and strengths as you perceive them, plus any other pertinent notes you might want to add. Any questions?"

"No, my Lord," Mordecai replied. To Martin, he seemed eager to leave.

Martin nodded. "Very well. Meet me for lunch tomorrow so we can go over your findings." Martin looked at the two. "Anything else for me tonight?" he asked. When neither responded, he nodded. "Good evening to the both of you, then."

"Until tomorrow, Your Highness," Amras said as he ushered Mordecai out of the room.

Martin waited until both councilors had left the building. The butler came into the room. "Begging your pardon, Majesty, but shall I have dinner brought in?

The cook has made a most excellent pheasant and vegetable pie… still steaming hot from the ovens. And if I may say so, Your Majesty, his biscuits are the best on InnisRos."

Martin looked over at Carl who nodded his head enthusiastically in silent agreement. "That'll be excellent, Fëanáro! Please bring two plates, biscuits, and wine."

"Superb, Your Majesty," Fëanáro said with a broad smile on his face as he slipped out of the room and quietly closed the door.

Martin sat back down. "Well, what do you think?" he asked Carl.

"I don't trust that Mordecai fellow… he oozes condescension. Trust me, General, that chap means no good. I'd watch him very closely."

Martin nodded. "Agreed," he said. "That's why I gave him the responsibility of developing the list of InnisRos' current advisors. Maybe he'll give something away."

"You mean if he writes something bad, it's someone he wants to see 'kicked to the curb', so to speak?" Carl replied as he nodded his head. "Good plan. It's plain he doesn't like you, so maybe it will give some insight into those he considers allies."

"He may recognize it for what it is, but it's worth a try," Martin said as he reflected on the day's events. "I think I want to talk to Father Goram tomorrow, but I want to do it secretly and in private. I suspect he'll give me valuable... and truthful... information concerning the comings and goings on InnisRos." Martin thought about Lessien's reaction to the wolves. Little ones can sometimes read the soul of people better than adults. Perhaps he had an ally in Father Goram.

After dinner arrived, the two ate with vigor, realizing just how hungry they were. Fëanáro was right. The biscuits were the best either had ever tasted.

The meeting Martin had with Father Goram the next day had gone well. A plan had been germinating in Martin's mind and Father Goram and his wolves would be essential if it was going to succeed. After meeting, talking with, and observing the priest and his dire wolf escort, Martin was satisfied they wouldn't pose a danger to Lessien. Martin discovered that, as he had been informed by Amras, the wolves, particularly Hector, loved Father Goram. At first Lessien was shy with Father Goram and wary of the wolves. But by meeting's end, Father Goram was bouncing her on his knee while she clutched Hector's thick, rich fur, giggling and laughing as only a five year old can.

As Father Goram left, he had turned and nodded to Martin before smiling and waving at Lessien. Buoyed by the meeting, Martin felt at peace. He had found Denairis and Lessien a haven at Calmacil Clearing should the need ever arise. With the safety of his family assured, he could now concentrate on other things.

Martin began his inspection tour of the island the day after the coronation. He took Lessien with him so she'd be exposed to the realm she would one day rule.

Denairis had decided not to accompany him. This worried Martin, but he reasoned she still needed time to sort things out.

In his absence he was confident Amras would manage InnisRos' affairs adequately. He had done so after the death of Martin's predecessor... and had done it well. Also, though Martin was reluctant to admit it, Mordecai was a superb administrator. Martin didn't trust Mordecai, but he didn't think there would be a power struggle this early in his reign. Martin also knew, considering Amras' advanced age, he'd have to make a decision about the first councilor position after Amras retired. Perhaps Father Goram might be a good candidate? In retrospect, probably not, though, since the leadership of Althaya's monastery at Calmacil Clearing would soon fall to the priest. Martin made a mental note to himself to place finding Amras' replacement first on his agenda once he returned from the tour of the island.

Amras Sáralondë was dozing in his sitting room before a cozy fire. The previous week had been a hectic one... but the arrival and subsequent coronation of King Martin Arntuile happened without incident and everything had gone exactly as Amras had planned. It was a grand affair. An affair fit for a king. Amras smiled. Now it was time to relax for a few days. The king was off on his inspection of InnisRos and there was little to do while he was gone except oversee a very competent government.

Amras lived alone in a large mansion just outside of the city limits of Taranthi. He never had the time for a family, but he had become infatuated with a small, furry creature called a cat. This animal had been brought over from the mainland by humans hundreds of years ago... and they provided companionship for many. They were also great rodent hunters. As he petted Mr. Twinkles who was sitting in his lap, he found himself thinking about retirement. He'd served InnisRos for a long time and was tired. Amras picked up his glass of mulled wine and drained it. Relaxed by the wine and the purring of Mr. Twinkles, he decided it was time to retire to his bedroom for welcomed sleep. Holding Mr. Twinkles in his arms, he stood.

Amras never saw the black mist that seeped underneath the main doors of his mansion, breaching ill-prepared magical wards and rolling along the floor and into the sitting room. As a fifteen foot high, eight clawed monstrosity rose up behind Amras, Mr. Twinkles hissed, the back of his fur rose, and he jumped out of Amras' arms to find a safe place behind a piece of furniture. He watched as Amras was reduced to a dried husk. In the empty mansion, only Mr. Twinkles heard Amras' terror filled scream. When the demon left, it took what was left of Amras' body with it. Mr. Twinkles, indifferent to his master's fate, jumped out of hiding and raided the pantry.

The death of Queen Denairis Arntuile was sudden and unexpected. Shortly after Martin and Lessien left, Denairis emerged from the rooms that served as the king's private residence and informed her ladies-in-waiting she wanted to go on a day-long trip. It was to be a short visit to the cliffs on the southeastern tip of the island which overlooked the Bay of Sorrow. Denairis told them she wanted to look out across the Sea of Dreams as the sun rose the following morning. "It will soothe my soul from the heartbreak of losing my home on the Alfheim," she said.

The commander of her security detail, a well-trained bodyguard who had served the previous king in the same capacity, advised against such a quick-notice trip. The first councilor, who normally advised him on such matters, was nowhere to be found. But since the commander's intelligence arm discounted any knowledge of a threat, he reluctantly allowed himself to be persuaded by his new queen. He believed little could go wrong... and the king hadn't restricted such an outing. There was no way the commander could know the fragile mental state of his queen. The following morning her body was discovered lying in the rocks at the bottom of the cliff, broken, mangled, and partially eaten by sea-crabs. They never found out how Denairis breached camp security that evening without being noticed.

Martin was notified of the queen's apparent suicide the following day as he was inspecting the facilities on Olberon Naval Base. The news felt like an arrow had pierced his heart. In less than two weeks he had lost his daughter, Nefertari, to duty, and now Denairis to unresolved guilt. But Martin, if nothing else, was a warrior above all else… and as such was equipped to handle grief without letting it affect his judgment or actions. After a few hours in isolated contemplation, Martin, with Lessien, his Sword Masters, and the few advisors who had accompanied him, returned to Taranthi. Three days later the King of InnisRos buried his dead queen. The whole island mourned for seven days and seven nights. Speculation as to what drove a new queen with a young child to such a terrible fate ran rampant during this time and for years thereafter. Martin took the real reason Denairis committed suicide to his grave.

Martin's rule ushered in a golden era for InnisRos. He expanded trade between InnisRos and the mainland, particularly with the Dular family at Palisades Crest. Though InnisRos was self-sufficient, trade for elven goods allowed the population of InnisRos to expand their proclivity for luxury items… an elven weakness. Martin doubled the size of the island's self-defense force and put in place the means by which the islands' rangers could be mobilized to supplement the Army in cases of national emergencies. He had convinced Father Goram, who by now led Althaya's fortified monastery at Calmacil Clearing, to give up long-standing neutrality accords and place his followers in the service of the king. Twenty-five years after Martin ascended to the throne, the economy was strong, and the island had the most powerful military in the known world of Aster.

During this time Lessien grew into a beautiful, elegant young lady. Her abilities seemed endless… to the extent some of her instructors believed she was endowed by the gods. Though she proved to be very deft with swords and excelled with the longbow, it was her aptitude for diplomacy that exceeded all expectations. She mastered everything she attempted, was charismatic, and had a natural predilection towards leadership. Lessien, in every way, had grown into a queen-in-waiting, well ready to rule after her father. Unfortunately, this responsibility would fall upon her sooner than anyone expected.

It was the twenty-fifth year of King Martin Arntuile's reign. Martin, Lessien, Major Carl Van-Gourian, and Father Goram, with his usual bodyguard of three huge dire wolves at his side, were in the king's personal meeting chamber. Seated on a chair in front of this imposing audience was a young female elf. She was the housekeeper for General Camthalion Tîwele, the chief-of-staff of Martin's armed forces. At the present moment the girl was trembling uncontrollably, her face as white as a freshly laundered bed sheet.

"What is your name, child," Martin asked.

"Idril, Your Highness, Idril Tinehtelë," she replied shakily.

"Carl, pour her a glass of wine," Martin said. "Horatio, can you use your magic to calm her?"

"I could, Martin, but it'd muddle her mind," Father Goram said. "We need her memories to be clear. I'll ease her fears after we've heard what she has to say."

Martin nodded.

Lessien bent down on one knee in front to the terrified Idril and took her hands. They were cold as ice. "Father, get a blanket. She's freezing."

As Martin did Lessien's bidding, Carl handed over the glass of wine. Idril took a deep drink, smiled, and bowed her head. "I'm sorry to be such a bother, Princess," she said.

"Please, don't concern yourself. You're among friends," Lessien said as she tightened the blanket that Martin draped over the shoulders of the girl. "Now, tell us what you saw. And don't worry, we'll protect you."

Idril nodded. "It was late. I was upstairs turning down the General's bed before retiring myself. He was downstairs enjoying a small snack and a glass of mulled wine. It's kind of nightly ritual for him." Idril took a sip of wine and closed her eyes.

"It's okay, Idril. Take your time," Lessien said as she put her hand on the side of the girl's head, reassuring Idril with a gentle stroke of her damp, sweat-soaked hair.

"I'm fine, Princess. I just get shivers whenever I think about what I saw." Idril composed herself and resumed her narrative. "As I was going downstairs to say good night to the General, I heard a slight commotion coming from the sitting room. As quiet as I could, I investigated, not really knowing what to think.

When I got closer to the door of the sitting room, I felt a wave of… darkness, I guess you could say… coming from the room. My King, it took every bit of courage I could muster to keep moving forward. I wanted to run… no, I felt a compulsion to run... for my life. I've never felt anything like that before."

Martin clasped Idril on the shoulder. "You were very brave."

Idril bowed her head. "Thank you, Your Highness." When she raised it back up, there was a look of uneasy determination in her eyes. "I peeped around the corner of the door. I saw this huge, red-black, fur-covered monster. It had to be a demon. It had four arms on each side that were buried into the General. He was struggling, but he couldn't break the monster's embrace." Idril paused and took another sip of wine. "It raised its head and I saw two sword-like fangs. It… it… it saw me. Its eyes were twin swirling iridescent globes. I couldn't move. I think that thing forced me to watch. Then it buried its fangs into the General's chest and…"

Idril whimpered softly. Lessien cupped Idril's face between her hands. "Listen to me, Idril. None of us are immune to life's cruelty. But we must learn to cope with it or we'll lose our sanity. You're safe here in the palace…"

"NO, my Lady," Idril cried out as she shook her head. "No one can be safe from that… that… demon!" It was becoming clear to all within the room she was just moments away from a complete breakdown.

Father Goram walked behind the frightened girl and placed his hands on her shoulders. A soft blue glow radiated from them and the girl's trembling calmed. Martin raised an eyebrow. Father Goram shook his head. "Don't be concerned, Martin. It's just magical courage and won't interfere with her memory. It's very delicate and precise." Bending over to talk softly in Idril's ear, Father Goram said, "I'll take you back to my monastery when we're done here. It's a holy place which no demon can violate and survive. You have my word. But now, and for the sake of many others, you must face this and complete your story. That's all we ask of you."

Idril nodded. With Father Goram's help she regained control of her fear. "The fangs sucked away the General. Within the space of a few seconds, his struggling and screaming stopped, and he became nothing but a dried shell of bones and skin. That thing removed its fangs and looked directly at me, gore dripping to the floor, and then it… it seemed to smile. I thought I would be consumed next. But it turned into a mist along the floor and left the room, caressing my feet and ankles as it moved past." Idril shivered. "It was awful. I couldn't move. After it was gone, I finally found the courage to look back into the sitting room. The General was gone. I came here as fast as I could. I know how important the General is."

Martin considered for a few moments before addressing the General's young housemaid. "You've been very helpful, Idril. The people of InnisRos are in your debt."

"Please, Your Highness… duty," she replied.

Father Goram had gone over to the door and opened it, whispering to one of the two guards standing on the other side. Before long one of the palace maids appeared. "Please show Idril here to my quarters,"

Father Goram said. Turning to Idril, he asked, "You're not afraid of wolves, are you?"

Idril smiled for the first time. "Not these wolves."

"Argos, Ishmael, guard!" the priest commanded. As one, two of the three dire wolves followed Idril and the palace maid out the door which was closed by one of the guards. Agamemnon, the pack leader and son of Hector, stayed at Father Goram's side.

Martin started thinking out loud. "Something about this is vaguely familiar." Martin then looked at Father Goram. "Horatio, your thoughts about this demon? What are we dealing with?"

"The description matches one of my tomes," Father Goram replied as he paced the floor. "It's an Assassin Fiend or Huor Súrion, as the tome calls it in the old language. They can only be called from the Abyss by powerful sorcerer magic and only stay long enough to perform the 'contract' they make with the sorcerer. A lot of that, of course, depends on the nature of the contract. Any sorcerer making such a demon contract must be extremely precise with the wording, or they could very well end up like the General did. That is also probably why the Assassin Fiend didn't harm Idril. She wasn't in the contract... and apparently whoever made the deal didn't allow for collateral damage... a mistake that generally isn't made."

"Can a contract be amended?" Carl asked.

Father Goram stopped his pacing. "Yes... yes it can. Martin, I've got to get Idril out of here and back to the monastery where I can best protect her as soon as possible. When that thing reports back..."

Martin held up his hand to stop him. "Yes, I know. When that beast reports back about Idril, whoever had it murder General Tîwele is going to assume Idril will make a beeline here to report what she saw."

"Fair assumption, Your Highness," Carl said. "We'll be ready for it."

Father Goram shook his head. "It's not that easy, Major. Being able to transform into a mist at will makes it extremely dangerous and difficult to kill. You need to use magic to stop that transformation. Even then, only the gods can help any warriors who get in its way. The best hope is to lure it into a blessed place such as a chapel."

"But if all that's true, why would the demon allow itself to be manipulated into that situation in the first place?" Martin asked.

"Because they have to abide by the contract... it's their one great weakness," Father Goram answered. "I can kill it, but only in a place of my choosing, such as the monastery. That's why we need to get Idril there as quickly as possible."

Martin turned to Major Van-Gourian. "Get an escort detail put together. They need to ride fast... Rangers... yes, I think rangers would be best."

"Right away, Your Majesty," Carl replied as he saluted. He turned to walk out the door when Martin called him to halt. "Carl... I want you and the Sword Masters to go as well."

"Please, Your Majesty!" Carl pleaded. "Martin, don't order that."

Martin smiled. "My friend, I love you as a brother and trust you with my life. I also know of no other I'd trust more with the life of my daughter."

Lessien shook her head. "No father, I'm not leaving. Whatever we face, we face together."

"Lessien…" Martin started, but closed his mouth. He knew nothing he could say would change her mind or make his decision easier on her. "Lessien, you'll go with Father Goram, Major Van-Gourian, and the rest of my Sword Masters to the monastery at Calmacil Clearing. There you will wait until I have sent for your return. This is not a request."

"Father…"

"I'll not argue with you, Lessien. There's too much at stake. Now do your duty!" Martin interrupted.

Lessien bowed her head. "Yes, My King," she whispered, and then looked up. "I love you, father."

Martin embraced her for a few moments and kissed her on the forehead before releasing her. "I love you to, my daughter. Now go."

Martin was alone in his meeting chamber. It was much later and Lessien, Carl, the servant girl Idril, and Father Goram were well on their way to Calmacil Clearing. As he sat thinking about the evening's events, he suddenly realized what had been nagging him…what seemed familiar about the death of General Tîwele. He remembered, right after he had been crowned king and while he was on his initial inspection tour, Amras

Sáralondë, his original First Councilor, had disappeared under mysterious circumstances. Martin wondered if the General's death and the First Councilor's disappearance were connected. But who benefitted the most? Obviously Mordecai had the most to gain all those years ago. He was next in line to replace Councilor Sáralondë. But what about this time?

Martin abruptly stood. "Of course!" he said aloud. General Tîwele's second-in-command and most likely his replacement, General Maglor Narmolanya, must be on Mordecai's payroll. He'd seen the two together many times. That was the connection. Martin knew it as sure as he knew the sun would rise the next morning.

He rushed over to the door that lead to the waiting room and opened it... but the guards weren't there. He found their dried husks stuffed in a closet a few minutes later. Pulling his sword from its sheath, he turned, looking for any hint of the assassin. Martin then felt an evil presence... and from out of the corner of his eye saw a huge shadow spring up behind him. His sword flashed brilliant white light to challenge the evil, but Martin knew his sword was not only too little, but also too late. He whispered, "Lead InnisRos well, my little girl," before turning to meet his fate.

The assassin materialized into blackness. He sniffed the air and extended his senses outward, but couldn't detect anything. Was the mortal even in the summoning chamber? Was HE in the summoning chamber? Strange! How had the mortal managed to steal his senses? Then the demon heard a slight chuckling and turned towards the sound. "What have you done?!" he roared.

"Come, come, Aikanáro. Surely you can appreciate the modifications I made to the summoning circle," the voice said.

Aikanáro roared again, but this time in frustration. His greatest desire was to destroy his mortal master… the one who summoned him. Unless the mortal breached the contract, however, he was powerless to do so. If Aikanáro defied the code of the contract, his punishment in the Abyss would be excruciatingly painful and last for an eternity. Better to admit to his failure and be dismissed than allow that torture to occur.

"Were you successful?" Mordecai asked.

Silence.

"Answer me! WERE YOU SUCCESSFUL?!" Mordecai shouted.

"The General and the King are dead," Aikanáro replied. "But there was a complication. There was a witness to the General's death."

"And," Mordecai asked.

"She was not in the contract," Aikanáro said, smiling because he had found a way to defy his mortal master within the code of their agreement. The letter of the law worked both ways.

"Damn it! Don't you know the necessity of collateral damage?" Mordecai asked, not really expecting an answer.

"She wasn't…"

"Yes, I know. She wasn't in the contract," Mordecai snapped. "So this is your way of telling me the Princess escaped?"

Aikanáro laughed. "Precisely," he said. "The mortal female must have warned your king. Princess Lessien was well out of the city by the time I visited the King. The contract…"

"… doesn't allow for you to leave Taranthi's boundaries. I get it," Mordecai said in annoyance. "Next time I'll damn well use Nightshade. At least she can be trusted."

"Can she?" Aikanáro asked.

There was a pause before Mordecai replied angrily, "That's enough, Aikanáro. You're dismissed."

Alone in his summoning chamber once again, Mordecai sat at his desk thinking. "No doubt Goram has the Princess… now Queen, I guess. I have plenty of time. Yes, plenty of time. This really isn't that much of a disaster when thought about rationally. Who knows what the future holds? After all, I am the First Councilor." Mordecai smiled. "Think I'll visit Amberley," he said out loud as he got up from his desk.

CHAPTER TWO

The Alfheim

(168 Years Ago)

Curiosity is a two-edged sword. While great good can come from a curious mind, it doesn't come without risk. There is a saying on some worlds that goes, "Curiosity killed the cat." In the Alfheim, however, the saying is, "Curiosity took a queen."

-Book of the Unveiled

Seven year old Nefertari's training started the day after the funeral and was still ongoing twenty-five years later. As Kyleigh had hoped, Nefertari was a quick study. She was extremely intelligent, wise beyond her years, and very mature for her age. Kyleigh also noticed that Nefertari's adopted father, Martin, had instilled a strong sense of duty in the child. Nefertari never questioned why her family was taken away from her. She never let the loneliness she undoubtedly felt break her spirit... was the perfect student who reacted well under stress... and had a particular aptitude for tactical and strategic thinking. Nefertari also had a voracious appetite for knowledge and an unparalleled curiosity for all things mystical.

But Nefertari's training to be queen did not come without difficulty. Though Nefertari never gave Kyleigh reason to doubt the strength of her convictions, Kyleigh nevertheless felt that perhaps being a queen was not Nefertari's true calling. She was constantly veering from the path provided by Kyleigh... instead always moving towards disciplines that involved the supernatural, the unexplained, the possibility of things thought impossible. More than once Kyleigh became so frustrated with Nefertari that she ended lessons early, usually angry at herself because she couldn't convince Nefertari to stay on point.

As for the realm, Kyleigh found the act of ruling was, though stressful, somewhat exhilarating. After a thorough investigation into the poisoning and subsequent death of Argonne, several council members were found to have staked their futures on one or both of the king's brothers. That gamble didn't pay off. Kyleigh presided over several more executions. But theirs was not the honorable death by the blade of a sword that the King's brothers had received. Instead, Kyleigh had them hanged as common criminals.

Argonne had been right regarding Robert Gareathe. Kyleigh followed up the investigation of him by her special prosecutor with an interview of her own. She found he was intelligent, trustworthy, and as devoted to the Alfheim as the deceased king had said he was. She also came to understand the significance of the ring he had presented to her and decided to keep it. She then promoted him to First Councilor, jumping him in rank ahead of the others. These actions served two purposes, both personal and political. By accepting the ring, she strengthened the bond of his allegiance, as well as that of his family, to her. By promoting him, she served notice to the remaining council members that things would be done her way.

After Kyleigh formally gave Robert the Sash and Dagger of office in a small ceremony, she handed over the ring she'd found in Argonne's belongings. It was the ring Robert had given to Argonne. She instructed Robert to give it to the new queen upon her coronation. Kyleigh also discharged Councilor Merlotia from service so he could teach full-time at the university. She insisted, however, that he be kept on retainer. She had no doubt he'd earn the monthly stipend he was paid for his services.

Kyleigh worked hard to strengthen the military. She knew from the Alfheim's long history that changes in the power structure of the monarchy meant brief times of chaos until a new king or queen had been crowned. It was during these times that the dark elves from the Svartalfheim were most dangerous. She deeply regretted the loss of Martin Arntuile's leadership, but his second-in-command, General Eärendur Fyriss, turned out to be an amazingly quick study… one whom Martin had trained well. Within a decade after Argonne's death and Kyleigh's rule as the provisional sovereign, the armies of the Alfheim were as strong as they had ever been. Though there were a few minor incursions by the dark elves near the portal between the Alfheim and the Svartalfheim, no serious attempt to invade ever materialized. Kyleigh looked into closing the portal link between the two planes of existence, but that idea did not come to fruition. It was created by the gods and mortal magic would never tear it down.

As the time to crown Nefertari as queen drew near, Kyleigh felt she had taken all the necessary steps to turn over an Alfheim that was as strong as ever both economically and militarily. She had also ensured the realm was guided by loyal, experienced, and intelligent advisors. There would never be a repeat of what happened to Argonne… at least not as long as Kyleigh lived. Satisfied all was well, and she had given Nefertari the best chance at a long and successful reign, Kyleigh, more than ready to relieve herself of the responsibility of provisional sovereign, counted the days to the coronation.

Kyleigh, Robert, and the commander of Nefertari's Royal Guard, Colonel Megyn Tasardur, were standing over a table and making last minute preparations for the coronation of Nefertari when there was a knock on the door. Without waiting for a response, one of the Royal Guard opened it.

"Provisional Sovereign Angelus-Custos, please forgive the interruption, but the king's butler is waiting outside and says he has urgent news," the guard said.

Kyleigh nodded and a middle-aged elf was shown into the room. No one spoke until the door had been closed. "Daniel?" Kyleigh asked.

"Madam, please pardon the intrusion."

Kyleigh shook her head. "You wouldn't have come if it wasn't important."

Daniel nodded. "I'm afraid the king's inner sanctum has been breached."

Kyleigh sat down. She said nothing at first as she digested the news. Looking up at Daniel, she asked, "The book?"

Daniel shook his head as he broke protocol and poured himself a glass of wine from the decanter sitting on the table without asking permission. He sat down and took a drink. "Madam, it's open."

"Damn!" Kyleigh said. Everyone in the room other than Daniel stared at her. It was unlike Kyleigh to even whisper a vulgarity. Each held their tongue, however. They knew Kyleigh would explain eventually... but from her reaction and the look on her face, they knew they weren't going to like that explanation.

Kyleigh got up suddenly. "Let's go," she said. "I'll clarify on the way. Megyn, lock down the palace. Daniel, go find Nefertari." She walked around the table and out of the room. Colonel Tasardur repeated Kyleigh's orders to the guards outside the room who ran to do their commander's bidding.

As they were making their way to the king's suite, Kyleigh began her narrative. "The inner sanctum was Argonne's little 'get away' when he couldn't really get away. It's a large, comfortably furnished room he used to relax, think, and sometimes escape the responsibilities of being a monarch... even if for just a little while. Only Argonne, Martin Arntuile, Daniel, Nefertari, and I knew of its existence. Argonne also used it to store some very valuable items, reasoning it would probably be the safest place in the palace. Most of the items are just unusual magical tomes and trinkets of little consequence. Anything powerful enough to be used for the good of the kingdom was never hidden. Argonne was very good about that."

"There's an 'except' in this tale, isn't there," Robert said.

Kyleigh weaved in and around people in the hallway. The palace was on full alert now. "A book," Kyleigh replied. "A very dangerous book. It was taken from a dark elf war general decades ago."

"What's the title of this book?" Robert asked.

"The *Book of Scattered Souls*," Kyleigh replied. She had gone several steps in the now quiet and empty hallway before realizing Robert wasn't behind her. Turning, she saw he had stopped and was staring at her. "What is it?" she asked.

"That book was supposed to be destroyed… at least that what the legends say. How the hell did the Elves of Dark come by it?"

"I don't know, Robert," Kyleigh replied as she turned to continue towards the king's quarters. "And I don't care. I only know that whoever opens the book disappears, forever lost. If it was Nefertari…" she didn't finish her thought.

Once in Argonne's former quarters, Kyleigh knelt next to a luxurious rug, flipped it back, and touched magical runes hidden within a large mosaic on the floor in a specific sequence. A doorway into the inner sanctum opened in one wall.

Robert, following, entered and saw a book sitting on a pedestal in one corner, opened. Kyleigh was looking at the book. "The magical wards protecting it are broken. That wasn't an easy thing to do," she said.

"Could Nefertari have done it?"

Kyleigh thought about that for a moment. "Yes, she probably could, now that I think upon it. Why did I not see this coming?" Kyleigh said before she suddenly gasped.

"What's wrong?" Robert asked.

Kyleigh bent down and picked something up from the floor. Reaching out her hand towards Robert, she opened it to reveal a broken necklace in her palm. "This was given to her by her mother. She'd never leave it behind willingly."

About that time Colonel Tasardur and Daniel rushed into the room. "Nefertari's not in the palace," Colonel Tasardur said, worry plainly written upon her face. "And there's no sign that she was kidnapped and forcibly taken away. It's almost as if she disappeared."

"There are magical ways to capture people," Robert stated as a matter of fact.

"Yes, Robert," Kyleigh replied, "but not without setting off magical wards and alarms." Kyleigh looked at the opened book, walked over and slammed it shut. "We've lost our queen."

Five days later Kyleigh Angelus-Custos, by popular acclamation, was crowned Queen of the Alfheim and the Mantle of the Sovereign placed on her shoulders. During the coronation, *Ah-RahnVakha,* the sword of elven royalty that had disappeared upon the death of King Argonne Quarion, appeared over her head, raining bolts of lightning and using thunder to voice its consent. As its hilt settled into her extended hand, the sword turned purple. A new royal bloodline had been established for all to see.

Nefertari remembered a book. It was a book that was only rumored to exist in the physical world... a point of contention between many scholars and theologians. As she stared at the book, she could feel its great antiquity and enormous power. It was the *Book of Scattered Souls.* She had learned of its existence in one of the tomes of mystery she often read during her spare time. That she should find it in the secret sanctuary of the dead king was incredible.

She knew, even as she opened the book, she was making a mistake… a foolish, childish mistake. But she couldn't stop herself. She couldn't overcome the curiosity of youth. The pages were mesmerizing… paralyzing. The words twisted and turned, then jumped off the pages and became hideous spirits, caressing Nefertari, exploring every inch of her body as if they were measuring her for a new dress. Satisfied, the ethereal beings flew back into the book. It was then she was taken. The last thing she thought to do before she disappeared was to tear off the locket given to her by her mother and drop it on the floor.

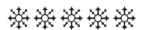

Nefertari felt nothing as she fell into the book, becoming incorporeal herself. The room around her faded and was replaced by blackness. Her connection to the material world snapped. She mourned the memory... which was all she now had. Then she remembered a voice from long ago... her father's voice... tell her that a true warrior wasn't afraid to face the consequences of their actions. Nefertari pushed back her fear and accepted her fate.

The blackness soon began to recede as if whatever journey she made between realities was coming to an end. The blackness soon gave way to a smoky gray. She couldn't see much in the grayness... a few feet at most. The ground she was standing upon was rocky and barren. No sound came out of the grayness... or if it did, it was inaudible, muffled by the strange fog. Feeling the loneliness, Nefertari shed a tear for her loss, but quickly re-composed herself. She was determined to acknowledge whatever penalty she must pay for her moment of weakness. She'd make her father proud. At this point, it was all she had.

Taking stock, Nefertari saw she no longer looked like a queen-in-waiting with a silk dress, jewels, and soft slippers. But rather her semblance was closer to that of a servant. She now wore a simple home-spun dress and cloak. A corded belt surrounded her slim waist, and hard-soled boots snugly fit her feet. Instead of finding this disconcerting, however, Nefertari appreciated the change.

Looking around, swirling misty clouds of gray, black, and white surrounded her. No one direction differed from another. Though Nefertari had no idea what she'd find, she decided movement was better than standing still. She heard the crumble of rocks beneath her feet as she took a few tentative steps. Stopping, she stared into the grayness to see what the sound of her footfalls might bring. Shadows upon shadows made it hard to determine what was reality or what was imagination.

Something other than gray clouds moved. Though it was barely perceptible, it had the feel of substance... and Nefertari didn't doubt it was threatening and lethal, if death was even possible in this reality. Instead of choosing to stare toward the menace, she closed her eyes to let her other senses come to the fore... to let her warrior's blind fighting training take over. But she could sense nothing. Helpless to prevent the assault she instinctively knew was about to come, she opened her eyes and prepared herself as best she could.

With unimaginable speed, a figure jumped out of the gray. Nefertari had no opportunity to avoid the strike. The figure, dog-like in appearance, bit her in the arm. With equal speed, the attacker retreated back into the anonymity of the gray. The bite at first looked like it barely broke the skin, but there was yellow ichor around the puncture wound... venom. Then Nefertari felt the pain as the injected venom radiated up her arm. It felt like caustic acid was running through her veins... burning and freezing simultaneously. As the poison crept up toward her torso, Nefertari saw the coloration of her skin change. First it turned blue and then white. Huge rends appeared... valleys in her skin that exposed tissue, muscle, and bone.

She stared in horror as the venom traveled up her arm. The pain she felt exceeded anything she'd ever experienced. Nefertari dropped to her knees as a scream of agony escaped her lips. Soon her whole body convulsed. As she writhed on the rocky ground, small, sharp-edged stones ripped her home- spun dress and cut into her skin.

After a few minutes, the convulsions ceased and the pain mercifully receded. Nefertari's mind only barely registered this before she heard movement in the gray once again. Paralyzed and exhausted, she could only wait for what was to come. The dog-form returned and ate her body organs – intestines, lungs, liver – and everything else exposed by the venom-induced cracks in her skin.

Nefertari's screams of agony began anew.

The torture of Nefertari was occurring on so many different levels she could almost admire the inspiration. The chase, bite, and suffering occurred over and over again for what seemed like an eternity. Each time after Ghost, as Nefertari had come to call it, made a meal of her internal organs, Nefertari fell into a dreamless asleep and awoke whole. There was never any pattern to when Ghost would attack. Sometimes it felt like days, and other times only a few hours. As hard as Nefertari tried, she could never track Ghost. She could never defend herself against its devastating molestation. What made Nefertari suffer the most, however, was the anticipation of the next assault. The attacks were always the same, as was the outcome. Even the pain was something Nefertari had learned to cope with. It was the waiting for the inevitable that soon became unendurable. Perhaps that was the whole purpose of this macabre game.

As Nefertari woke from the last attack, she was determined to end the cycle. Although the timing always varied, the method never did… movement, attack, pain and paralysis, approach and feasting, more pain. This progression of events somehow had to be broken. Nefertari needed to find the key that made the routine pleasurable for Ghost. She knew that she no longer had a physical body… at least not as she knew it… so Ghost was not actually feeding on something to fill an empty belly. After all, she herself never felt hunger. Ghost was feeding either from her terror and pain, from the hunt itself, or some other unknown imperative.

Steeling herself, Nefertari awaited the next attack. When she spied the barest hint of movement in the gray, instead of preparing to defend against its aggression, she simply sat down to await its coming. It was not long before Ghost made a move toward her. Although she could hear it, she could not see it. Closing her eyes, she took several deep breaths. The hint of movement, which is what she only ever sensed, stopped. Cautiously, Nefertari opened her eyes, not sure what to expect. She was shocked by what she saw.

The surrounding gray had dissipated, and it was as if she were in a glass bubble. Directly across from her sat Ghost. It looked like a great dog, but with wisps of itself drifting around its body, as if it were not completely substantial. There was a look of great age to it. A look of something extremely complex that made Nefertari feel "Ghost" was a misnomer… too simple by far. Then it spoke.

"So you think you have it worked out," Ghost said. "You think that our little game will stop because you alter the routine? My dear Nefertari, only the gods can change our destiny."

"May I ask your name since you already know mine?" Nefertari said. "I've come to call you Ghost, but I know that can't possibly be correct. If it so pleases, I would know the name of the one who tortures me so," Nefertari wondered if she would get an answer. True names are powerful weapons and can be used against the owner.

Ghost stared at Nefertari and considered. "You have no power over me in this dimension, so it doesn't matter," he answered. "I'm Rictus Tor. As you, I've been trapped in this alternate reality. But unlike you, I am here to act as predator while you are my prey. In this reality we can neither control nor change this aspect of our existence."

Nefertari shook her head. "But we already have, Rictus Tor. We're now sitting and communicating of our own free will," Nefertari responded. "It seems to me we have, independent of any mandate or destiny, freely decided to have a conversation. On my world we have a saying:

'Destiny. Fate sealed?

Or purposely directed
by free-willed action?'

"It's an interesting concept, Nefertari, but irrelevant nevertheless. This doesn't mean that our intertwined destinies have changed... only delayed for a short time."

"You mentioned only the gods can change our destiny?" Nefertari asked, hoping to get as much information as she could.

Rictus Tor paused as he mulled over her request. "Very well," he said. "I don't see the harm. We have, after all, eternity. You were captured by the *Book of Scattered Souls*. This is an Elder God relic and very powerful. Once a soul enters its dominion, the book attunes itself to that soul... and the soul to it. There can be no escape, no mortal 'magic or spell' that can break the will of the book."

"Does that mean you have to turn to evil?" Nefertari challenged.

Rictus Tor grimaced. "I was not always this way," he said sadly. "However, I freely chose the role I play in this ghastly reality. In this way I make sure I'll never become prey."

"Evil is absolute, but that doesn't mean you personally can't change. I've seen others practice a lifetime of evil yet beg forgiveness before they die," Nefertari said. She was beginning to get desperate because it started to look like her gambit may have failed. It didn't appear she would be able to break the pattern.

"No doubt just before the hangman released the trap door," Rictus Tor replied angrily. "It's easy to repent when it may spare your life."

Nefertari had no answer for that simple observation. It was the truth. A condemned man will usually say anything to gain favor in either this life or the life beyond. Knowing it was futile to delay longer, she held her arm out so Rictus Tor could bite it. "I won't give you the satisfaction of tasting my fear," she said. "And eventually I'll learn not to let you consume my pain. As you said, we have an eternity. I WILL learn to make you go hungry."

"A bold statement for one so weak," Rictus Tor replied. Getting up, he walked over to Nefertari's extended arm, but paused, as if distracted by something. He sniffed the arm but didn't bite. "It is not your fear or pain that sustains me, Nefertari, but rather it is the act itself," Rictus Tor said as he drew away from the proffered arm. "The evilness of it keeps me well fed. It would seem, however, that you now have a benefactor. I'm no longer permitted to bite."

Rictus Tor faded away as the gray once again surrounded Nefertari, leaving her confused and unsure. Then she remembered Rictus Tor saying only a god could break the pattern of the book. But she followed no god or goddess while she grew into adulthood.

Nefertari suddenly heard a voice, loud and clear, sweet and gentle, speak to her in her mind. "That's true, my child. But it doesn't mean I've not been following YOU."

"Who are you? Show yourself!" Nefertari exclaimed as she rose to her feet to meet this new challenge, trying to withhold her surprise lest she show weakness.

A beautiful female elf appeared in front of Nefertari. She was dressed in a flowing purple gown with long white hair billowing around her head. On her brow a precious gem, woven within flowery tattoos that move across her forehead. A larger match to the gem was inset in a silver necklace around her neck. She had a kindly smile… a smile that at once set Nefertari at ease.

"I am Sehanine StarEagle, one of the Elder Gods so long ago forgotten by your race," she said. "I've come to lead you out of this place."

"Why," Nefertari asked, astounded and eager for an answer.

"That is a discussion for later. I'll tell you this, however. You must sacrifice much," the goddess replied. "What are you willing to sacrifice for your freedom?"

"Everything," Nefertari said as she lost consciousness.

Rictus Tor searched for new prey and sensed movement within the gray clouds of billowing mist. As he had done for thousands and thousands of years, he stalked its every movement. He studied how it walked, how it breathed, the number of heartbeats per minute, and every other thing he could garner from close observation.

When Rictus Tor felt he was ready, he began his attack, but soon stopped his approach. Something was very wrong. This creature was not playing its part. As he stopped to consider this unusual and perplexing state of affairs, the creature laughed… LAUGHED… before suddenly disappearing. In an instant Rictus Tor heard an inhalation of breath from behind, followed by intense pain as he was swathed in searing dragon fire. Rictus Tor realized his mistake. It was now he who would be the prey. It was now he who would be tortured for the rest of eternity, for no god or goddess would save him. Rictus Tor, shortly before mercifully losing consciousness as he was being bathed in dragon breath, was delighted by the irony.

The goddess Sehanine StarEagle had teleported Nefertari out of the *Book of Scattered Souls* and into a series of underground chambers. Everything Nefertari needed to survive was there. The living quarters were comfortable yet simple, as was her clothing and the food that nourished her. A hasty inspection of the chambers revealed there was no way out to the world above.

"With all due respect, Lady StarEagle, am I to trade one prison for another?" Nefertari asked her hostess.

Sehanine StarEagle smiled. "Nefertari, you wouldn't survive on the surface of this world," she said. "It's very inhospitable. There also can be no distractions while you learn what you must do to advance my cause."

"Which is?" Nefertari asked.

"To become my priestess," the goddess answered.

Nefertari frowned.

"Don't be concerned," the goddess replied to Nefertari's scowl. "You still have the freedom to leave even if you deny my request. I did what was in my power to help right the wrong that is the *Book of Scattered Souls*. That abomination should never have been created by my brethren. So you owe me no debt. I can this very instant send you back to your world. But as my priestess, there's much good you can do. And..."

"And what," Nefertari asked.

"There will come a time in the future when your sister, Lessien, will have great need of you and the powers I will teach and grant you."

Nefertari hesitated, steeling herself to ask the question she didn't want answered. "What about my mother and father?"

"I'm sorry, Nefertari. They're gone."

"How?"

"Oh child," Sehanine StarEagle said. "I'll not keep this from you, but it's hard to hear."

"Please go on," Nefertari replied. "I'm no longer the child I used to be."

"Indeed you are not," the goddess said. "Your mother committed suicide shortly after she moved to Aster with your father and Lessien. Your father was betrayed and assassinated for the power he held. Your sister faces that same obstacle to her rule."

Nefertari sighed. Though inwardly she knew what the answer to her question would be, Sehanine StarEagle's confirmation still momentarily took her breath away. She started to get angry, but realized no good could come of it. She wouldn't seek revenge... but justice. After a few moments she looked at the goddess and nodded. "I understand. Is there anything else I should know?"

Sehanine StarEagle bowed her head. "I also need my priestesses to help one other. She is like a daughter to me." Looking up, Sehanine StarEagle had tears in her eyes. "Her name is Elanesse and she's been suffering for a very long time. Nefertari, there's a storm coming. It's a storm I fear will destroy her."

"Can't you just, oh, I don't know, wave your hand to save her?" Nefertari responded.

The goddess shook her head. "It's a bit more complicated than that. There are restrictions to our interaction with the physical world. That's one reason why we rely so heavily on our priests and priestesses. You'll understand more once you're fully indoctrinated. Besides, the same evil that threatens my daughter will also endanger your sister."

Nefertari nodded. "You're not finished, are you? Go on," she said as she crossed her arms.

Sehanine StarEagle studied the young elf. "Even after all I've told you, still there is defiance."

Nefertari studied the goddess herself, unafraid. "I've already decided to accept and help you, but I must know everything."

"You're very intuitive," Sehanine StarEagle replied. "Intuitive and strong-willed... an excellent combination. Very well. I'd like to have someone who believes in me again. How else can a god or goddess have relevance?"

"I believe in you… you're standing right in front of me," Nefertari replied.

"Yes child, but are you willing to follow me? Of your own free will?" the goddess asked.

"I don't know what you stand for, Lady StarEagle," Nefertari responded with caution. "Are you good or evil? Have you perhaps tricked me? How can I be a believer and follow you if I don't know these things?" Nefertari shook her head. "No, my Lady, I will not satisfy your need to exist in my reality once again if you're evil, regardless of the consequences. And if my sister has grown up to be like my father, she won't either."

Sehanine StarEagle smiled. "I've chosen wisely," she said. "As a goddess I've many powers of persuasion as well as the ability to easily deceive a mortal. I've not done this. I'm not evil, but there's no way I can show you this beyond doubt. You must rely upon your own instincts and decide for yourself whether or not I speak truthfully."

Nefertari was at a loss. How does a mortal verify a god or goddess is speaking the truth? Then she remembered something her father once told her as she sat on his knee. *The people need to have confidence you have their best interests in your heart. You can only prove that through your actions. SHOW them they can have faith in you.* Certainly Sehanine StarEagle's actions have given Nefertari reason to think she has her best interest in mind. But how could she be sure?

"We are perhaps at a cross-road," the goddess said. "You don't know for a fact you can believe I am of good intention. And there's nothing I can do to satisfy your reservation. You must have faith. You couldn't follow me if you didn't. Know this, however. To follow me it must be of your own free will. This cannot be changed. If I disappoint, you may choose to stop being a follower. Even I have no control over that. In this respect you have as much power over me as I do you." Sehanine StarEagle then opened her arms and her mind, giving Nefertari the ability to truth-read her. "Perhaps this will ease your fears."

When Sehanine StarEagle did this, Nefertari, stunned that the goddess would be willing to reveal so much, took a step back and looked down at the marble floor of the chamber. "I can't do that," she thought, "no matter how willing she is. Perhaps that gesture is enough." Looking at Sehanine StarEagle, Nefertari made the decision to have faith in the benevolence of the goddess. "I accept you with all my heart. What must I do, my lady, to become your priestess? What must I sacrifice?"

Sehanine StarEagle nodded at Nefertari's acquiescence. "We start at once, my child."

"No child, that's not how it's done," Sehanine StarEagle said. The goddess' patience was never-ending. "I want my priestess to be more defensive minded. You're still thinking with a warrior's mentality. While that will serve you well, it should never be your first instinct."

Nefertari was breathing heavily. "My Lady, that thing was trying to kill me! I doubt if it could be persuaded to go away. So I used air to hold it and earth and stone to kill it," Nefertari, somewhat vexed, replied. She knew what the Lady wanted, but she was having a hard time bringing her fighter instincts under control when she had to act without thinking. "Shouldn't evil be eradicated from the world... from the universe?" she asked.

"My priestess, there's a delicate balance between good and evil in the heavens. So too is that true in the mortal realm." Sehanine StarEagle explained. "Rarely is absolute evil, or absolute good, a mortal trait. Think of the worst a mortal can do to another. Then multiply that act by an immeasurable number. Now you understand absolute evil. Nor can the nature of evil always be viewed as finite. There are degrees of evil. Some evil can be used for good... or even changed. You must ask the question, is it only the act that's evil, or is it the soul? It's an important distinction... and one you must learn to make. But this isn't the lesson I wish to teach you now. I want you to learn constraint. I want you to rationally decide to hold back your killing instinct and decide if that's the best course of action for the circumstances at the moment. I want you to make these decisions within one beat of your heart."

"What you ask is a hard thing for a mortal," Nefertari said. "We're born with an overpowering impulse to fight or flee when confronted with danger. I was trained to stand and fight... to protect. You're asking me to throw that away."

"My child, you're no longer being trained to be a queen," the goddess replied, allowing the statement to take root in Nefertari's mind before she continued. "I understand your argument, Nefertari. That's why we do this so often. You've learned much... more than I could've hoped. But you must learn this one lesson before the test. We've talked about what lies ahead. You won't be free to help your sister... to take my ministry out into the world once again... until after the test has been successfully completed. To do that, you'll have to act with instinct AND forethought." The goddess wiped Nefertari's sweat-soaked brow. "There are people who need my help. Help I can only give through a priestess. Rest for now and regain your strength, for tomorrow we shall do this once again."

Nefertari nodded tiredly. "As you command, Lady StarEagle." She turned and made her way back to her quarters and drew a hot bath. Many muscles were in need of relief. Nefertari was in top physical condition, perhaps more so than any time in her life... but these sessions were extremely demanding.

The sessions went on... over and over... for what seemed like decades before the elder goddess Sehanine StarEagle felt Nefertari was ready for the test.

Nefertari awoke after another hard day of exertion. Her thoughts wandered to the dream that was already beginning to slip away. She was sitting on her father's lap in front of a fireplace. The night was cold, but the fire and her father's arms around her were warm and comforting. A few feet away Lessien was being rocked to sleep by Denairis as Martin regaled Nefertari with a fairy-tale about giants, dark elves, the gods, and other exciting things that make for a good bedtime story.

The dream forgotten and now fully awake, Nefertari sensed something was amiss. She rolled with astonishing speed just as a gigantic reptilian head was coming down to snap her up in its powerful jaws. Without conscience effort she drew forth the elements of both Air and Earth, creating a thick barrier of the former which caused the head to slow as it moved towards her. Immediately after she used the element of Air to give her much-needed time, she built a barrier of earth between her and the head that was still trying to grab her.

Nefertari found herself kneeling next to a stream... sharp pebbles dug painfully into her knees. Glancing up, she saw her attacker was an enormous red dragon. Looking back down to the ground, she noted her StarStaff, a magical staff that amplified her potent magical abilities, was lying several feet away. Even from this distance, and in full daylight, Nefertari could see the familiar power aura radiating from it. But it would be no help to her if she couldn't reach it, and the dragon was already breaking through her first line of defense. Then the dragon saw the staff and recognized it for what it was. A dragon would disregard prey altogether if it could add to its horde… and the staff would be a highly treasured prize.

Using air once again, Nefertari snatched pebbles up from the stream bank and, as she released the air that was slowing the descent of the dragon's head, flew them into its face to distract it. At the same instant, the force of her will flew the staff into her waiting hands.

However, by now the pebbles had dropped back to the ground, and the dragon had re-directed its full fury back at her. Clearly it intended to turn her into a cinder with dragon breath. Nefertari heard the rumble coming from the belly of the dragon just as it opened its mouth.

With a wave of her arm, Nefertari drenched the dragon's mouth with a water elemental she called forth from the stream. Nefertari knew, however, that simple water wouldn't deter dragon's breath for more than a few moments. She called forth a huge fire elemental. Sometimes fire can be fought with fire. As she dodged to the side, she let her elemental absorb the dragon breath while she stood. She pointed her staff at the dragon. A lightning bolt flashed from the staff. It struck the dragon on one of its wings and moved down its length. The dragon roared in agony and looked over at her, keeping its dragon breath streaming forth. The fire elemental moved with the dragon, ensuring it kept itself between the dragon and its master, thwarting the dragon's deadly breath.

Nefertari decided it was time to prove a point. She once again called upon the element of Air, and used it to direct the last of the dragon's flaming breath up into the sky where she formed it into a ball before snuffing it out. The dragon paused and looked at Nefertari, then at the scorched path along it wing caused by the lightning bolt.

"Very impressive, mortal," it said. "You're not the easy prey I thought to have for my breakfast. I suppose I should've known better when I saw the staff, but I'm hungry. When we continue, I'll not be again taken by surprise."

"Why do we need to continue?" Nefertari asked. "I've proven to you I'll not be an easy kill. As for my staff, it's attuned to me alone. Its power fed by my life force. If I die, it will become nothing but a stick. Is that worth risking your life over?"

The dragon snapped its head back as if it had been slapped. "IF you die!" the dragon roared. "Risking MY life? What impertinence! You don't really think you can survive this encounter, do you?!"

Nefertari waved her arm in practiced movements as she whispered words of command. An earth elemental appeared and glided across the ground to hover next to the fire elemental. The earth elemental had several sharp appendages sticking out which spun at an incredible rate as it moved. Each one of the knife-like arms could do considerable harm in a very short period of time. "I'm not alone," Nefertari remarked.

"That does appear to be the case, mortal, for I can sense the power in you as well as the allegiance to you held by your allies," the dragon replied. "But I've never run from a fight or from a meal... and especially never from treasure. You can't win, but it does seem you can hurt me. We're at an impasse. Give me the staff and I'll seek my breakfast elsewhere."

"I've told you..."

"Of course I don't believe you," the dragon interrupted.

"Then take the staff, if it so pleases you!" Nefertari replied as she threw it to land at the dragon's feet. As she did so, she snapped the link between her and the staff. This made the staff powerless and therefore useless to the dragon. Though Nefertari knew she could always make another, it was a dangerous ploy, for it left her with fewer defenses against the dragon in the here and now.

The dragon, as surprise and irritation crossed its countenance simultaneously, backed up a step so it could study the staff more closely. It was no longer radiating magic. "Damn mortals to the hell they deserve!!! What trickery is this?" the dragon roared.

"I told you it'd be useless without my life force connected to it. I spoke the truth," Nefertari replied. "What I didn't say was that I could break that connection any time I wished. So now you're left with a wooden stick … and me. Even without the staff, as I've already said, I'll not be easy prey."

The dragon lowered its head closer to Nefertari and studied her. The elementals moved to re-position themselves. "You cannot defeat me," the dragon said, though with much less conviction than before.

"Possibly not, but for the trouble I'll cause, there'll be little reward," Nefertari replied. "Go find yourself a cow to break your morning fast!"

The dragon continued to stare at Nefertari as it considered its options. With the StarStaff rendered useless as treasure, and the female standing before him a mere mouthful, the thought of two juicy, less troublesome cows was suddenly much more appealing. "Perhaps there's wisdom in your words, mortal," the dragon conceded.

"Wisdom can come from surprising sources, can it not?" Nefertari replied with relief, knowing the battle with the dragon was over.

"Harrumph!" the dragon snorted as it launched itself upward.

Nefertari immediately retrieved the staff and re-attuned it to her life force. By the time she was done, the dragon was but a speck in the sky and no longer posed a threat. Dismissing the elementals, she knelt down by the stream and delicately took a sip of water from a shaking cupped hand. "That was close!" she said aloud.

"Tests aren't supposed to be easy, StarSinger," the goddess Sehanine StarEagle said as she appeared standing beside Nefertari.

"StarSinger?" Nefertari questioned as she quickly moved to get up. She was used to her goddess appearing without warning, so she wasn't particularly surprised. It was the first lesson she was taught.

Sehanine StarEagle smiled. "You've earned the right to be called that. You've passed the test and are ready to be my priestess, if it so pleases you."

Nefertari dropped to her knees. "Of course it pleases me, my Lady. I'm yours to command."

Sehanine StarEagle placed her hands on Nefertari's shoulders and bid her to rise. "You need not kneel before me, StarSinger," she said as she placed two fingers on Nefertari's chin and looked deeply into her eyes. "You've made me very proud. Now, let's talk about what you must do to help your sister and my daughter on the world of Aster."

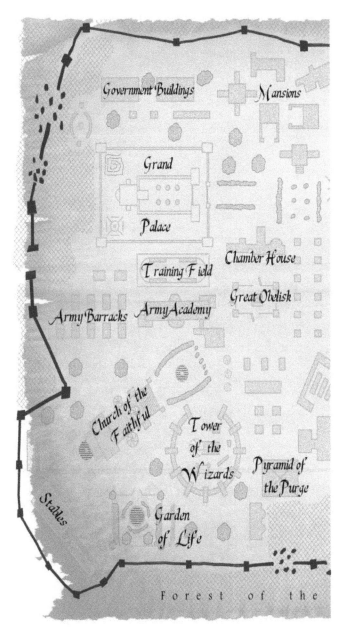

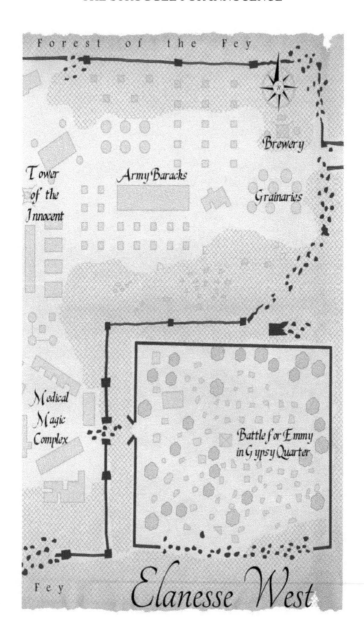

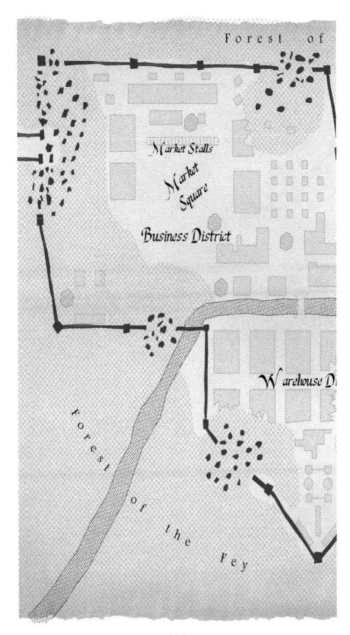

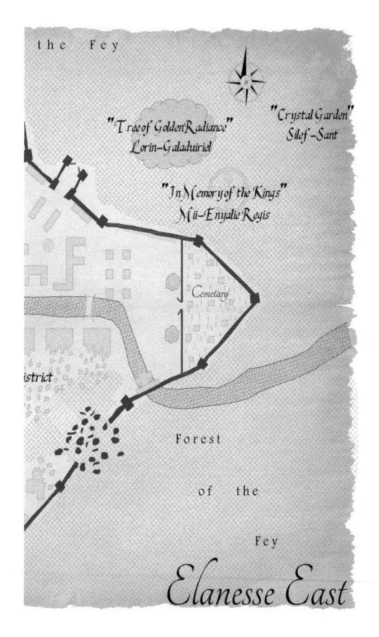

CHAPTER THREE

Elanesse

(Present Day)

"Death was here."

-Esmeralda, the Last Empath

<u>Death's Lament</u>
Eternal, insidious, black as night.
Regal ruler of landscape blight.
Friend or Foe, mortal's waiver.
Sometimes a devil, sometimes a savior.
Death does not care, duty bound.
To end each life that fate has found.
Though stoic and unrelenting, Death does shed
a tear.
For those it takes with life so near.

-Author Unknown

Kristen, holding Emmy's hand, started to follow Tangus and Jennifer out of the room, but was stopped short by Emmy. "What's wrong, dear heart?" Kristen asked, thinking maybe the shock of the battle with the vampires had finally taken its toll on the child.

"We're too late, mother. Both Euranna and Christian are gone," Emmy replied with tears in her eyes.

Kristen knelt in front of the empath. "Dear, how can you…"

"I'm sure. There's nothing either you or I can do. Death never gives back what it has claimed. You know that." Emmy then put her arms around Kristen and hugged her tight. "I'm so sorry. I know they were special to you."

Kristen nodded, accepting Emmy's pronouncement. She knew it was true for she could feel the certainty through the bond. Kristen returned Emmy's embrace and buried her face in Emmy's silky, long blond hair. She did her best to keep the great sadness she felt far away, but Emmy already understood, and was using the bond to support Kristen.

Tangus appeared in the doorway of the room with an impatient scowl. "Ladies, we need…" He didn't finish when he saw the two comforting each other. As he walked toward them, he asked, "What's wrong?"

Kristen stood and wiped away wet, stinging tears from her face with the back of her sleeve. "Tangus, my love, there's nothing we can do for Euranna and Christian. They're dead."

"What do you mean?" Then Tangus looked at Emmy and understood. He nodded and took both of them into his arms. After a few seconds, he said, "Let's go. The others will be waiting."

"Father," Emmy said. "I… I… your friends died because of me."

"Oh no, dear heart," Kristen exclaimed as she shook her head. "Don't think such a thing!"

116

Tangus knelt down so he could be at eye-level with Emmy and grasped her shoulders. "Sweetie, they died acting in defense of something they strongly believed in. Their death helped to bring a great treasure back into the world."

"Me," Emmy said. "I'm that treasure. Tangus, I save people. I don't want the responsibility of causing their deaths."

Tangus frowned. Before he had a chance to respond to Emmy, Jennifer appeared in the doorway to the room. "Father..." Jennifer said before Tangus held up one hand to stop the interruption. He knew this was important to Emmy's development. He couldn't let her conscience destroy her.

"Are you a goddess then?" Tangus said, gently chiding the child. "Or perhaps fate itself?"

Emmy stared down at the floor and shook her head. She looked back up and locked eyes with Tangus. "But... "

"But I was their commander, Emmy. Where does the blame for their death really lie?" Tangus asked pointedly.

"Not with you, Tangus!" Emmy exclaimed.

"Perhaps you're right, perhaps you're not. Regardless of how we feel about it, however, they're still dead. That can never be changed." Tangus glanced up at Kristen uncertainly. Who knew what Emmy was capable of? Kristen shook her head. "You can't self-recriminate for choices THEY freely made," Tangus continued. "To deny them that choice would have been the same as forcing slavery upon them. To deny them that choice would have been the same as refusing them an honorable and heroic death." Tangus cupped

Emmy's face in his callused hands and kissed her on the forehead. Emmy closed her eyes as she let the warmth of his love spread through her. "We have to go, sweetheart," Tangus said as he picked Emmy up. Even though she was a powerful empath, she was still a little girl.

The scene upstairs was surreal. The shadows from the pre-dawn light went from shades of gray to absolute dark, refusing to yield anything sinister hidden within. Lying in the middle of the floor was a headless corpse, the blood from its neck was already congealing in a wide swath of red and black. The head was nowhere to be seen... presumably lying somewhere in a dark corner. The body had two arrows sticking out if its back and one in its chest. Tangus, even in the dark of the room, recognized the fletching of both Safire and Euranna.

Outside in the small courtyard, the smell of charred flesh from the burned horses permeated the air. Tangus, still carrying Emmy, saw one of the more bizarre sights of his lifetime... Euranna and Christian as they had died. Christian, missing a leg, was sitting with Euranna's head in his lap. He had been stroking her face. Now both were just still forms. Lester, helmet discarded, was kneeling and had the point of his bloody sword resting on the cobblestone floor. He touched his forehead to the sword hilt while he said silent prayers. Kristen at once walked over, knelt, and joined him.

Safire joined Tangus, Jennifer, Emmy, and their animal companions, shaking her head. "I thought at least Christian would survive," she said to Tangus.

"I've seen this happen before," Azriel said as he walked over to the small group. He bowed slightly to Emmy who was now standing and holding Tangus' hand. "You think you've done enough to save a life and suddenly their heart just stops. It's as if they've lost the will to live. The surgeons call it... let's see... a..."

"Blood clot," Emmy finished for him. Everyone looked at her. "With severe wounds such as, well, leg amputations, sometimes it's not enough just to heal the open wound. It becomes necessary to remove the clots that had formed as the body tried to stem the flow of blood."

"Where did you learn that?" Jennifer asked.

Emmy frowned, thinking. "I didn't learn it, Jennifer. I feel it," Emmy replied haltingly, as if she had to find the words to match the meaning. "It's part of my power as an empath."

"The lassie has the right of it," Azriel stated. "When someone's been grievously wounded, one of the healing protocols is to thin the blood after the injured blood veins and arteries have been closed. This is done either magically or with a combination of the right type of herbs."

"That's impressive, Azriel," Safire said.

Azriel shrugged his shoulders. "I spent time assisting a healer when I was younger. Tangus, it'll be daylight soon, and you can bet those explosions from the vampyre's first attack will bring someone calling. We need to seek shelter... and soon."

"I know," Tangus replied.

"The Purge knows where we are," Emmy said. "It can track me."

Tangus frowned as he looked down at Emmy... though at this point he wasn't surprised she'd be able to sense such a thing. "We need to run," he said. "As far and as quickly as we can until we're out of the Purge's influence."

"It won't do any good," Kristen said as she and the others joined the conversation. "Each day the Purge grows stronger... holds tighter the agents it's already recruited... and brings more under its spell. Tangus, it must be destroyed. Only then will Emmy be free of its threat."

There was complete silence. Finally, Max asked the question everyone else had been avoiding. "How are we going to destroy the Purge once we find it?"

"I don't know, but we'll think of something," Tangus said. "First, though, we have to find it."

"Seems to be an impossible task," Lester replied as he shook his head.

Emmy squeezed Tangus' hand and looked up at him. "Get me to the Purge, father. I'll destroy it."

Kristen grabbed Emmy by the shoulders and turned her around to face her. "You'll do nothing of the kind, Emmy!" she exclaimed. "I won't let you." Kristen looked at Tangus pleadingly. "She must be protected at all costs, dear. You know the stakes. It's the reason we're here."

"Mother," Emmy said. There was something in her voice that demanded everyone, not just Kristen, hear what she was about to say. "The Purge was born with a perverted connection to all empaths. That's the only way it could track down empaths to butcher them.

And that's why it knows where I am. The stasis protected me while I slept... but it can do so no more. It's through that same connection, however, that I'm able to understand its greatest weakness. Mother, I'm the only one who can destroy it."

"There has to be another way," Kristen begged. She was frightened for Emmy. "Tangus, find another way!"

"He cannot, mother," Emmy said with finality.

"Then I'll take your place! I have empath blood. Show me the weakness, Emmy. Please..." Kristen stopped and put a hand to her brow. She looked over at Euranna and Christian, who had been laid out by Lester and arranged side by side. She knew the sacrifice they had already made... that they died doing what they felt was their duty. How could she do differently? She nodded. "Yes, of course. I'm sorry, Emmy. I should've known getting to you was only part of what's required of us."

Emmy put her arms around Kristen. "I'm still scared," she whispered.

Kristen wrapped Emmy in an embrace and kissed the top of her head. "I know you are, sweetie. But you'll never be alone again," she whispered back.

The woman lay on the bed... naked, beautiful, tantalizing, and beckoning with a finger. The man stared, not truly believing his luck, and then decided he'd ask no questions as he took off his combat boots.

This stroke of luck turned out to be a soldier's dream come true.

As he was removing his pants, nearly falling over because of all the beer he had consumed, she called his name, "Warfel." His pants off, he struggled with his shirt and vest. "Damn these buttons!" he thought.

"Sergeant Warfel!" screamed Lieutenant Arnish as he shook Warfel's shoulder roughly.

Warfel came awake instantly. "Yes sir," he said, as he tried to muster enthusiasm for his commanding officer while hiding his annoyance at being roused.

"I want the men up and ready to move within the hour. I now know where we must go to find our quarry. Full combat gear and rations for a week."

"What about the civilians?" Warfel asked.

"Nearly all have already left. We may have to fight them for possession of the prize."

"That's fine," Warfel replied as he stood. "I don't much like most of them anyway."

Ishiro, one of the two assassins employed by Nightshade, wasn't happy with their tactical situation. "How do we establish a perimeter, even a small one, with just the two of us," he asked. "We're assassins. We don't defend!"

Mariko shrugged her shoulders. "Our training covered this. You just don't like sitting around," she said staring out into the early morning light. "We have our orders."

"Yes, impossible orders," Ishiro replied with distaste.

Mariko looked over at her companion. He was a well trained fighter, but had little discipline. He also had no scruples. While she hated working for Nightshade, she was bound by the contract her guild agreed to with the demon. But the killing she did now wasn't always justifiable and she found much of it morally repugnant. Not so Ishiro. He relished it. He laughed as he killed and butchered, gleefully playing with his over-matched opponents just to see the fear in their eyes before he made the killing thrust. Mariko long ago decided she wouldn't work with this assassin again.

"Well?" Ishiro asked, impatient for an answer. "What's our next move?"

Mariko sighed in disgust, but looked out towards the northwest part of the city. "Most of the activity's in the heart of the city," she said as she pointed in that direction. "I think that's where the main threat will originate... not behind us. For whatever reason, even Nightshade didn't want to go east of the gypsy quarter. Now that the empath child's hidden sanctuary has been found, other seekers will undoubtedly follow. Let's spread out and wait."

Ishiro grunted and silently moved off. Mariko went to the roof of a nearby three story building to begin her watch. As she looked out across the part of the city visible to her, she studied routes that would allow her to quickly position herself to defend the empath and her companions. She knew their protection meant she couldn't hide in the shadows for long... that she'd eventually have to make her presence known, even if that went against Nightshade's orders. But it was a risk Mariko felt she had to take. She reasoned Nightshade would be even angrier if harm came to either the empath or the female who was bonded to her.

Mariko spotted movement between buildings in the direction Ishiro went. As she looked closer, she saw Ishiro move to intercept. But from her vantage point she also saw Ishiro was about to unknowingly assault a force large enough to give even him pause. Fool! He was so eager to attack he didn't study his adversary beforehand. Mariko drew her hand crossbow, attached lightweight nylon rope to a bolt, and fired into the side of a wooden building at street-level. She tested the strength and tautness of the line. Satisfied it would support her, she slid down the rope, hit the ground running, and made a mad dash to reinforce Ishiro. As she ran, she unsheathed the two katanas that made her such a dangerous opponent… and such a successful weapon.

Victor was the fifth son of a minor lord in Madeira. With few prospects, he had hoped to make his fortune by discovering unclaimed treasure and riches in the abandoned elven city of Elanesse. Accompanied by several friends suffering from the same financial malaise, they spent the better part of a year fruitlessly searching. As the unsuccessful days added up, Victor became angrier and angrier. He couldn't understand why the city wouldn't give up its secrets. As supplies dwindled, he wondered why he ever left Madeira in the first place, where at least his father would feed him.

Then he heard the voice... the voice whispering in his head, promising wealth and power if he'd only follow it. Mesmerized, Victor persuaded his friends to do the same. "Just stick it out awhile longer," he argued. "We'll soon have our reward."

Then the call came from the voice in his head. It was the call he had been awaiting for several weeks. It was a call strong enough that even his friends heard it. "The treasure is in the gypsy quarter in the southeast part of the city," the voice said. With rusty daggers, swords, staves, and any other weapon they could get their hands on, they, along with many others, charged to where the voice told them to go. Rushing towards them from between two buildings was a figure dressed in black, swirling two katanas.

Victor wondered what one person could possibly do to stop the tide of treasure hunters. As the figure rush past him, he thought, "Good, let the others handle it. It means I'll get to the treasure first." In his fanatical, delirious state, he didn't notice two of his friends running next to him had dropped to the ground, their headless bodies jerking and spitting blood. After a few more steps, his legs suddenly stopped working, and he dropped to his knees. He felt pain for the first time. He looked down and saw his intestines spilled out on the ground. He reached to gather them up, but blackness engulfed his consciousness as other internal body organs also slipped out of the slit across his torso.

He was dead before his head hit the ground… dead before he realized he'd been eviscerated.

Ishiro had killed or maimed the first group of humans he attacked with little effort, suffering only a few minor scratches. None of these men were trained fighters and Ishiro wondered why they fought so ferociously… just like the group he and Mariko faced earlier. What made them so determined? Surely it wasn't the child, was it? But why else would a demon be sent to retrieve it if it wasn't very important. Why would he and Mariko be ordered now to protect it? It was a dilemma Ishiro put aside to think about later.

After the last man went down, Ishiro stopped and looked over the killing field he'd just created. It was impressive. "The guild should pay me double!" he boasted to himself aloud as he laughed. The laugh died out almost immediately. From several directions, through alleyways and streets, dozens of men poured into the small intersection. He was surrounded. Even then, though, his arrogance wouldn't allow him to be concerned. That changed when an arrow took him in the leg.

Mariko saw the arrow hit Ishiro. He didn't stand a chance if the archers weren't neutralized. As she worked her way to them, moving silently and blending into the background, she felt the earth move beneath her feet and heard a slight rumble coming from the direction where she knew the empath to be. She didn't let that act as a distraction, however, as she positioned herself behind the archers. There were only two and both were relatively close to each other. Just before she made her attack, she saw one archer release an arrow, and then, over the din of the battle, she heard Ishiro grunt and several humans let out a victory yell.

Mariko quickly dispatched the two archers and stormed the remaining humans. They were entertaining themselves by sticking their swords into the body of Ishiro and laughing. One took an ice pick and drove it into both of Ishiro's eyes. Distracted as they were, the humans could never mount any semblance of defense against the angry battle maiden… not that it would've mattered. Mariko's dance with her swords was delicate, efficient, and brutal. Each human suffered sudden, bloody deaths… the only outcome possible.

After the last human had fallen, clutching at bleeding stumps where legs used to be, Mariko paused, closed her eyes, and breathed deeply. She opened them and looked around. No one was alive except for her. She then carefully picked her way through the sprawled bodies and knelt next to Ishiro. The last arrow had hit him in the neck, one of the few places on his body not covered in light armor. Reaching down, she closed what was left of his eyes and bid him farewell. As Mariko stood, debating within herself what to do next, she heard movement. It was still several blocks away, but she recognized it instantly… a military column. The mercenary unit that had been bivouacked in the western part of the city was on the move and heading in the direction of the empath.

"We can't just leave them, Tangus," Kristen said. "I know we need to leave quickly, but they were our friends… our honored friends."

Tangus looked at the bodies of Euranna and Christian. Though he appreciated the sacrifice Christian had made, he was a soldier through and through who understood the risks. Christian died a warrior's death. Euranna, however, was so young and innocent. In many ways she was the most delicate flower of them all. Tangus shook his head. "I'm sorry, child," he whispered. "I let you down." Tangus looked up at his wife. "Of course we're not going to leave them to the vultures, human or otherwise, who inhabit this city," he said. "Elrond, I'll need you and that staff of yours. Everybody else…"

"Wait," Elrond said as he held up a hand. His attention appeared directed inward. He was clearly having a discussion with Elanesse. "Yes, that will work," he said.

"Elrond, are you alright? Max asked.

Elrond nodded. "Tangus, Elanesse can arrange a proper burial. We need to get their bodies back down into the chamber where we found Emmy."

Tangus stared at Elrond. Kristen grabbed his hand. "Let's do it," she whispered.

Emmy tilted her head and then nodded. "Elanesse says we must hurry."

"You can hear Elanesse's music?" Elrond asked.

Emmy smiled. "I've always been able to hear her, Mr. Elrond. I just didn't know who it was until now."

Lester, Azriel, and Max picked up the bodies of their fallen comrades. "She hardly weighs anything at all," Max remarked to no-one in particular as he cradled Euranna in his arms.

Within a few minutes they had both bodies downstairs in the small chamber that was Emmy's prison for over three thousand years. Euranna and Christian carefully laid side by side with their arms interlocked. Tangus, as the de facto leader of the group, spoke a short eulogy. Everyone then took a few moments to be alone with their own thoughts.

"We need to go," Elrond said. "Elanesse's going to collapse this chamber."

As they made their way up the stairs and out into the courtyard, the ground beneath their feet suddenly trembled and the sound of collapsing stone rumbled from inside the building. Dust, left undisturbed for millennia, flew out the doorway unhindered. After the earth had settled back down, Tangus and Kristen, leaving Emmy holding Jennifer's hand, went back inside to check the collapsed basement of the building.

As they were waiting for Tangus and Kristen to return, Elrond exclaimed, "I don't hear her anymore!"

Emmy released Jennifer's hand and went over to Elrond. "That's okay, Mr. Elrond. She's exhausted after making the tomb for Euranna and Christian. She needs to sleep for a while. Then she'll be well."

Elrond looked at Emmy and frowned. "You know much for such a young person," he commented.

"I'm seven, Mr. Elrond, but my soul's much, much older," she said. As she spoke, her complexion took on a faint bluish glow.

Everyone was staring at Emmy when Tangus and Kristen came back out of the building. Emmy's appearance, however, had returned to normal before Tangus or Kristen noticed anything amiss.

"Elanesse did a good job," Tangus remarked. "Their resting place will never be found or disturbed under so much stone. They'll be together for eternity."

But no one was listening. They all were still staring at Emmy and didn't even notice Tangus and Kristen's return. Kristen snapped her fingers to get everyone's attention. "What's wrong?" she asked.

Elrond shook his head, still looking at Emmy. "Oh, nothing," he replied. "We should be going."

At that moment Romulus and Bitts both growled a warning. Kristen grabbed Romulus by the scruff of his neck. "What's wrong, boy?" That question was answered when a figure clad in black stepped out from between two buildings with her empty hands held up. Everyone drew their weapons as they established a defensive perimeter around both Kristen and Emmy. An arrow from Jennifer's bow was already streaking towards its target as Max whispered. "Damn, I didn't even notice she was there!"

CHAPTER FOUR

InnisRos

(Present Day)

Power, like the hammer and chisel, is a tool. It can be used to create something beautiful, or it can be used to destroy that which is beautiful. Which one depends upon the person wielding it.

-Book of the Unveiled

Nightshade, in her Amberley form, sat in front of the fireplace in Mordecai's great room. Her shapely legs were curled underneath her and she sipped wine. It had only been a day since she had adapted this body to stay 'incognito' and was still adjusting to its idiosyncrasies. While she very much enjoyed wine, she was perplexed with the subsequent liquid expulsion from her body. Mordecai told her this was normal for mortals... and that she should use the "facilities"... a room specifically designed for that purpose. He said the door to this small room should be closed when she "conducted her business", as he called it. She'd never understand the need for the privacy mortals required when doing that which was natural.

      Mordecai walked into the room and went to the bar. Without saying a word, he poured himself a glass of whiskey and joined Nightshade on the sofa.

"So, how did it go?" Nightshade purred.

Mordecai glanced at the demoness and scowled. "We don't have the Navy. The Queen rejected the council recommendation."

"As I told you she would," Nightshade said. She set her crystal glass of wine down on a nearby table, uncurled her legs from beneath her, and faced Mordecai. "You should've been more serious getting your people set up in their hierarchy. This is an island nation, Mordecai, and her Navy is the finest on the known world of Aster. You'll need them when you go against the Queen. It's the only escape she has. How could you not have planned for that?"

Mordecai sipped his drink and didn't answer.

Nightshade considered. She wouldn't tolerate mistakes, but decided to let this plan of Mordecai's go a bit little further before she stepped in and took charge. "I'll kill their admirals," she said. "As first councilor you'll have the Queen's ear in their replacements."

"No, at least not yet," Mordecai replied. "As much as I want the Navy and its Marines to back me, I have General Narmolanya and the Army. That'll do for now." Mordecai looked at Nightshade. "If high-level officials start disappearing, it'll look too suspicious. The Queen's not an idiot, and she's surrounded herself with smart, loyal people. She'll know almost immediately something is wrong."

"She's going to know regardless," Nightshade countered.

"Yes, but right now I control the timing. InnisRos will be mine soon enough, but we must move carefully. And when we do, I want no one to doubt I'm her legitimate successor. Then my true plans come to fruition." Mordecai laughed. "And I'll be able to deal with Goram," he said.

Nightshade smiled. That sounded more like Mordecai. She hoped, however, that she didn't have to spend much more time keeping him on track. "I have everything ready. What do you want me to do now?" she asked.

Mordecai looked at Nightshade and laughed. "There's one of the Queen's lackey's who's had it coming for quite some time." He looked at Nightshade. "Are you ready to kill?" he asked.

"Really, Mordecai, you must learn to take care of these things yourself," Nightshade replied.

"I am, my dear. That's why I summoned you from the Abyss."

Erin Mirie, Second Councilor to the queen, smiled as she made her way home from the council chamber. Mordecai's attempt to have the armed forces placed under his control, though approved by his lackeys on the council after a long and emotional debate, was rebuffed by the Queen. Though the Queen was a very strong believer in majority opinion, she had the same suspicions concerning Mordecai that her deceased father, Martin, held. Besides, the Queen wasn't obtuse. She saw his argument made little sense. Queen Lessien was the commander of ALL the armed forces. By implying they should be Mordecai's to lead for the sake of centralized control was, in essence, a covert insult to the abilities of her monarchy and an obvious attempt to seize power within the realm. "Would he be brash enough to try to take down the Queen?" Erin thought. Her smile turned into a frown. She wished she had insisted Horatio tell her everything he knew when last they spoke. To hell with the cover of 'plausible deniability'… the Queen may be in jeopardy.

As Erin walked home thinking upon affairs of state, she didn't concern herself too much with her own security. She understood there was always a threat from Mordecai, but even still, she felt safe on the streets of Taranthi. The law-keepers were always patrolling, and her own personal bodyguard followed at a discreet distance. If that wasn't enough, she also knew a few of Horatio's rangers, who seemed to have eyes and ears everywhere, shadowed her. She knew they were there, and they knew she knew they were there, but neither would acknowledge it. Erin smiled. Horatio was a mother hen when it came to people he cared about.

As she stood at the entrance to her city quarters, she suddenly felt a chill. Winter was still in the air, but there was no wind. "That's strange," she thought... but shook her head and discarded it. She whispered a command word to release the magical wards that were on the door and inside the building. She then glanced down at the locket she wore around her neck, a gift from the Queen, to check to see if it glowed. It didn't, so she knew no evil awaited her inside. When she touched the door knob, however, she gasped as terrible cold penetrated her gloved hand. The locket briefly flashed red and then darkened as its magic became inert. Erin clutched her chest and turned to face the street. Her always present guards rushed to support her as she fell… but when they got to her side, she was unconscious. By the time they had her sitting up and leaning with her back against the door, she was dead. The commander of Erin's guard sent runners to get a healer and to notify the palace. As the messengers sprinted to carry out their orders, they noticed Horatio's rangers had already cordoned off the entire block around Erin's home. But all was quiet. A comprehensive search didn't reveal even the slightest hint of anything amiss.

Though late, Queen Lessien was still awake, sitting at her desk in her private quarters taking care of administrative paperwork. While there were plenty of crown functionaries who could fulfill these duties, Lessien, as her father before her, studied each document before placing her signature and mark of office on it. As he once explained, sometimes it was the only way to get a complete picture as to how the kingdom was running.

Finally she finished. Arranged on her desk were two tidy stacks of vellum, those she had signed, and those she felt needed either revision or further investigation. Both stacks, particularly the latter, would keep her staff busy the following day. After rubbing her eyes, she drained her cup of tea. It had gone cold. Her bedroom beckoned, but first she got up from her desk and slipped into a luxuriously comfortable chair in front of the fireplace and poured herself half a glass of whisky. As the liquid slid down her throat, warming as it did, she laid her head back, closed her eyes, and cleared her mind. The peace and quiet of the night always offered an almost magical elixir against the ills of the day.

Her peace and quiet was short-lived, however, as her mind raced to her many concerns. She didn't like that her First Councilor, Mordecai, and Father Goram, shared such an animosity towards each other. Father Goram once told her to keep a keen eye on Mordecai, but let him stay first councilor as long as he showed no hint of treason. He told her Mordecai, despite his basic untrustworthiness, handled the day-to-day administration of the realm competently. Even though Lessien would like nothing more than to wipe that smug smile off Mordecai's face, she had to acknowledge he was very good at his job.

As far as Father Goram goes, though they were close at the start of her reign, they had a falling out over her insistence he formally vow allegiance to her as his queen. At the time he argued she already had his allegiance as her friend, and that the island, regardless of who the ruler was, always held his allegiance. He asked why a formal, public display was necessary. Lessien knew her father hadn't demanded this of the priest, but she felt a ceremony would show those who would threaten her rule that the fortress monastery was her ally. Her instinct was correct, but she bungled her handling of Father Goram… and she knew it. Since that time, though Father Goram would still do anything for her and InnisRos, there was a distinct rift between them that neither seemed willing to close.

Now she feared Mordecai's move to detail a battalion of her Army to Calmacil Clearing would further enhance the distance between queen and priest. Lessien sighed. She wanted to make her peace with Father Goram, but she knew to do that, she needed to settle the dispute between him and Mordecai... or choose sides, something she wanted to avoid at all costs.

There was a light rap on her apartment door. "Your Highness, are you awake?"

Lessien recognized the voice of Colonel Carl Van-Gourian, her commander of the palace guards. "Please come in, Colonel," she called out.

She watched from her place in front of the fireplace as one of her guards opened the door to let him in. Odd... though he only wore tunic and pants, his sword and battleaxe were belted to his side. He was followed into the room by his Sergeant-of-the-Guard, who stopped and stood at attention in front of the now closed door. This didn't escape Lessien's attention, but she ignored it. "Please have a seat, Carl."

"Thank you, my Queen."

"Have a drink," Lessien said.

Carl shook his head. "I'm afraid not, Your Highness. I'm on duty."

Lessien nodded. "I figured you were... why else would you show up in the middle of the night. Tea then? Or perhaps coffee? I have both."

"Thank you, My Queen. Coffee would be most welcomed," the colonel replied as he got up, grabbed a mug from a nearby decanter set, and poured from a pot that had been kept warm by a simple magical spell.

"We have a situation, Your Highness," he said without preamble as he sat back down. "Second Councilor Mirie is dead."

Lessien straightened in her chair. "When did this happen?" she asked.

"About an hour ago, Your Highness," Carl said.

Lessien waved her hand. "Please Carl, let's dispense with the formalities… go on."

Carl nodded. "Her bodyguard reported that as she was entering her home, she suddenly paused, then clutched her chest. We have the body here in the palace and our preliminary investigation shows no markings on her whatsoever. Our healers are leaning towards a finding of death by natural causes… probably her heart."

Lessien didn't believe it. "Come on, Carl! When was the last time an elf as young as Erin died of a heart attack. I know it happens with the humans all the time, but not our race… at least not until we're very old."

"Based upon witness statements and the lack of any traumatic injury to the body, it's the only conclusion we can rationally make," Carl replied.

"Have you checked where she died for any residual magic?" Lessien inquired.

Carl cleared his throat and suddenly looked very uncomfortable. "Yes, Lessien, we did. The door… her entire house… came out clean."

Lessien stared at Carl. "But…"

Carl looked away.

"Carl!" Lessien barked. "What do you not want to tell me?"

"Your Highness," he said, "did you give Councilor Mirie a magical necklace that detects the presence of evil?"

Lessien noted the shift in Carl's attitude and studied her guard commander. "Yes, Carl, you know I did. It was a birthday gift given only a few days ago. Why?"

Carl's stare never wavered. "Our sorcerers have found evidence the magic of the locket exploded in a burst of energy. Our healers have confirmed such an explosion that close to her heart could have caused it to stop without leaving damage to either the skin or surrounding tissue. How could such a thing have happened, Your Highness?" Carl asked.

"You can't possibly believe I had anything to do with poor Erin's death, do you?"

"Of course not, Your Highness," Carl replied as he shook his head. "But you have enemies… particularly Mordecai… who could use this as an excuse to weaken your position as Queen. Even after all these years, many still consider those of us who came from the Alfheim as outsiders." Carl stared at Lessien. "Child," he said, "regardless of all the good you've done here as the Queen of InnisRos, your rule is not, nor has it ever been, secure." Carl had dropped all formality. Now he was speaking as her Uncle Carl. "The Army is clearly with Mordecai. I think we still have the Navy and its Marines, but after what happened today with Mordecai's attempt to place our entire military under his command, it's obvious he's setting up everything he needs to gain power. I think he's planning a coup."

"Impossible!" Lessien bristled.

"Think it through, Lessien. Even Erin didn't have the council votes today to block Mordecai's maneuvering. You had to step in and forbid it. Now look what Erin got for her loyalty to you." Carl decided a drink of whiskey was called for after all. Lessien didn't object and the liquor calmed his building anger. "Mordecai has collapsed another roadblock to the crown," he continued. "What happened to Erin might call you into question. I don't know if it'll threaten your rule or not... probably not. No doubt he knows that. My concern is what else he might have on his agenda."

"You don't think he'd try assassination, do you?" Lessien asked.

"Of course he would," Carl said. "But not yet. First, he'll try to isolate you by removing your supporters. Then he'll look for a reason to remove you legitimately. If he maneuvers it correctly, the people will be screaming for him to take power. He'll of course acquiesce with great reluctance, maybe even promising free elections, or another search for one with the royal bloodline. But I guarantee you, once he has control of the kingdom, he'll never let go."

Lessien stared into the fireplace, thinking. Blinking to break the mesmerizing spell of the elaborate dance being performed by the flames, she looked at Carl. "My people, my supporters, my friends, are in imminent danger, aren't they?"

Carl nodded. "I'm afraid so," he replied as he too stared into the fireplace. "Not that it would be any different if you were deposed. Your allies are with you because of who you are... what you represent. Those values, those morals, don't go away if the focal point of those principles… you… were to disappear. They'd continue to fight and sacrifice."

"Then I should be no different," Lessien exclaimed. "As queen I have a responsibility. I will not shirk from it."

"Of course you shouldn't, Lessien. But you should also have a contingency plan in place should the need arise."

"I do, Carl… my death," Lessien stated.

Carl shook his head. "That's not acceptable. I made an oath to your father to protect you. I'll not break that promise."

"My father is dead, Carl. I'm your Queen and you follow MY orders," Lessien replied with steel in her voice.

"And how many of your supporters have to die because of your stubbornness!" Carl fired back. "Do you want civil war?"

Lessien looked at Carl with distaste. "Do you recommend I abdicate? Give Mordecai everything he wants without a fight? What about those principles you mentioned just a few moments ago. Should I turn on them when my supporters will not? Should my sacrifice be any less?"

Carl calmed himself. "Forgive me, My Queen. I've clearly spoken out of order. It may not come to that, but we should plan for it. War should not be our only alternative. Right or wrong, you're not in a position to win."

"And you don't think I should fight and die, if necessary, for my people?" Lessien countered.

"No, my Queen, I don't. The people aren't being threatened. Do you think the merchant will be bothered by your death if business is still good? How about the planters if their crops are still growing? Or the city dwellers if law and order is maintained and jobs are still plentiful? The academia? They're already preaching for a change to the monarchy in favor of… whatever they think will keep them in their cushy jobs."

Lessien stood, went to the hearth, and threw wood onto the fire. As the embers exploded, they flashed briefly before going out, to land as dirty ash on the stones in front of the hearth. Lessien wondered if her rule was going to end like those dying embers… cold and lonely.

Carl snapped Lessien out of her melancholy. "As I said, it may not come to all that. We may still be able to counter Mordecai if we can find out what he has planned. But as a precautionary measure, I believe we should get Father Goram involved."

That got Lessien's attention. "Go on," she said.

"We've both been to his monastery. While it's true that was many years ago, things have changed little. If anything, the monastery has gotten stronger," Carl answered.

Lessien looked at her guard commander. "How do you know that?"

"I'm not just the commander of the palace guard. I keep my eye on what's happening on the entire island both politically and militarily. Father Goram has been marshalling and strengthening his power base and those of his allies for quite some time. His reach, with respect to operatives, extends all over the island. I've no doubt he has people in the city and already knows about Councilor Mirie's death."

"Why is he doing it, Carl?" Lessien asked. "Does he think I pose a threat? Does he have the same ambition as Mordecai?"

Carl shook his head. "No, Lessien, nothing like that. He does it to counter Mordecai who, as you know, is doing the same thing. I don't think, however, that Father Goram can win in a head-to-head confrontation with Mordecai. I don't think you can either. But that monastery, from a defensive standpoint, is a thing of beauty. I'd wager it'd take the entire army of InnisRos to breach its walls."

Lessien turned her attention back to the fire, deep in thought. She saw the logic in Carl's argument. "Very well, Carl… but only as a contingency. Let me write a letter to Father Goram expressing my shared condolences for the death of Erin Mirie and present our proposal to him."

"Lessien, I've no doubt he'd appreciate the letter of sympathy, but I've already taken care of the request for sanctuary," Carl replied. "Should the need arise, of course," he hastily added.

Lessien stared at Carl and then smiled. "Of course you did."

Father Goram felt a cold, wet tongue run down the length of his face. It was early… too early… and it had been a late night. Why was his sleep being disturbed? Opening one eye, he saw a huge face in front of his, its tongue lolling out to the side. The breath coming out of the mouth, besides smelling of raw meat, tickled his nose.

Findley, one of two dire wolves their pack leader, Ajax, insisted stay with Father Goram when he couldn't be there himself, was staring intently into the priest's eyes. "Surely you're not hungry again?" Father Goram commented as he got up and swung his legs over the edge of the bed, his feet landing in soft, warm furs. He looked at Findley, who sat down and was patiently waiting, and put his fingers to his lips. He saw no reason to wake Autumn just yet.

Father Goram donned his thick robe, added a couple of logs to the bedroom fireplace, and slipped out of the room, silently closing the door behind him. Razor, the other dire wolf maintaining guard, was sitting half-way down the hallway which led from the master bedroom to the rest of the apartment. "What's going on, guys? It's not even dawn yet," Father Goram asked. Then he heard a knock on his door.

Magdalena and Landross were sitting on the sofa sipping coffee as Father Goram, with his own mug of coffee on an end table, read the message. He closed his eyes and let his hands drop to his lap, still clutching the piece of vellum. He looked up at Magdalena imploringly, but didn't speak.

"I'm sorry, Horatio, but I confirmed Councilor Mirie's death with Mother Aubria through a communication crystal," Magdalena said. "She had rangers trailing the Councilor's movements as you requested, and they gave her a firsthand account."

Landross looked at Magdalena. "Who's Mother Aubria?" he asked.

Father Goram answered Landross for Magdalena. "She's the revered matriarch of Magdalena's family. All the rangers at Magdalena's disposal in Taranthi - aunts, uncles, cousins, nieces, nephews - report to Mother Aubria. She also has other... contacts... that sometimes come in useful." Turning back to Magdalena, Father Goram asked, "What does she make of Colonel Van-Gourian's claim that Erin was murdered?"

Magdalena shook her head. "She didn't have an opinion one way or the other. She's not privy to the results of the Colonel's preliminary investigation... but she said everything seemed to point to an unnatural death. It's only been a few hours, but there's been rumors that the Queen was somehow implicated in a murder of a high-ranking official."

"Bah!" Father Goram spat. "If Erin was indeed murdered, Mordecai's the one who had the deed carried out. Of this I have no doubt." Father Goram got up, stepped around two dozing dire wolves, and placed a log in the fire. "I'll make him pay," he swore silently before turning back.

Autumn walked into the room, yawning. "I thought I heard voices out here. What's going on?" she asked with concern.

Magdalena and Landross abandoned the sofa in favor of their hosts. Father Goram handed Autumn the message he held in his hand. Autumn, legs curled underneath her as she sat on the sofa, looked up after reading it. "I'm sorry, Horatio," was all she said.

Father Goram took Autumn's hand and nodded. "Landross," he said. "What do you think about the Colonel's sanctuary request? Do you think the Queen's in agreement?"

Landross shook his head. "I don't really know the Colonel except by reputation. He's been here once or twice in attendance with the Queen, but I never really got to know him." Landross played with his goatee as he gathered the rest of his thoughts. "But he takes his duty to the Queen very seriously, as he did with her father. But, considering the Queen might be somehow connected to the Councilor's murder, if indeed that's the case, and therefore subject to the rule of law, the Colonel's planning for the day when the arrest warrant is issued. As long as the Queen doesn't actually get served, his honor is satisfied."

"That's where you're wrong, Landross," Father Goram interjected. "He'll throw his honor out the window if it will save his Queen, arrest warrant or no arrest warrant."

Landross nodded. "Anyway, I don't think the Queen knew about this particular communiqué. If she did, I'm sure her letter of condolence would have been sent as well."

"Agreed," Father Goram said. "It's not a secret that Mordecai has his generals controlling the Army. If the Queen leaves without at least answering questions about the Councilor's death, he wins by default. And with the might of the Army behind him, he'll overrun the entire island. If she doesn't leave, he'll have her thrown in prison or worse. Either way, he gains control."

"Of all except our monastery," Autumn said.

"Yes, Autumn," Landross replied, "we're a most formidable barrier, and he knows that. But to neutralize our power, he only has to do is surround us. Horatio, perhaps we can reason with the Navy? I don't think he's been able to infiltrate them as of yet."

"He doesn't have to if he can convict the Queen of murder. What choice will they have then? He'll be their lawful commander-in-chief." The conversation lapsed as each visited with their own thoughts. Father Goram ended the silence after a few minutes. "It would seem that Mordecai has more on his agenda than just taking Kristen and Emmy. I think he intends to rule not only the Svartalfheim, but InnisRos as well. Perhaps even all of Aster. Magdalena, are Arthon and Gunthor out front?" Father Goram asked.

Magdalena nodded.

"Good," Father Goram replied. "Please have them go wake up Cordelia and Cameron. I want them to join us for breakfast. Autumn, be a dear and put on a new pot of coffee while I cook bacon and eggs. Landross, please get a couple of steaks out of cold storage for our friends lying in front of the fireplace." Father Goram looked at each before they left to do his bidding. "We've got a lot of planning to do."

The portal between Aster and the Alfheim, created by the *Ak-Samarië* shard, was kept open by the *Ak-Séregon* stone. This magical stone, attuned to the shard, was necessary for mortals to travel safely through the portal. If removed from its magical resting spot on the Aster side, the portal was, though it still existed, closed to travel between these two worlds. The portal entrance between InnisRos and the Alfheim was only rarely opened, and even then almost exclusively for the transmission of messages.

The twelve elven guards surrounding the portal on the InnisRos side were anticipating their relief. It had been another long, uneventful night... and the guards were ready to return to their families for companionship, food, and sleep. Each soldier knew pre-dawn is the best time to attack the portal entrance... but complacency had set in long ago. Even still, when the six black-robed assassins attacked, the guards fought well, killing three of the assassins before they themselves were all slain.

The objective of the assassins was to steal the *Ak-Séregon* stone. Two of the three remaining assassins were killed by the protection wards surrounding it. The last assassin, barely alive, was killed after delivering the stone to his employer. His guild, however, was paid handsomely for the services rendered and, notwithstanding the death of its assassins, was very pleased with the outcome.

A constant vigil was kept at the entrance of the portal in the Alfheim by a subordinate sorcerer and several dozen warriors. Rarely did anyone, or anything, pass through the portal from either world... but Queen Angelus-Custos insisted upon a strong guard nevertheless. When the portal flashed closed, runners were dispatched within seconds... and the entire sorcerer community had been instantly notified through magical communication. Within the hour an investigation team of powerful sorcerers and clerics were on-site. It didn't take them long to determine the nature of the problem. The *Ak-Séregon Stone* on Aster had been removed.

Mordecai was dozing in his downstairs summoning chamber. He had spent the night putting together plans for the case against the Queen for the murder of Councilor Erin Mirie. Since the First Councilor's position also served as the realm's chief prosecutor, Mordecai knew there'd be pushback... for he'd become king should she be convicted. Some people would call for judicial disqualification. But he wouldn't recuse himself. And any call to remove him from the case would be soundly defeated by his highly placed henchmen. Mordecai, and all who followed him, considered himself above the rule of law, placing his lust for power beyond all other considerations.

Startled awake, Mordecai looked up to see Nightshade, as Amberley, sitting across from him. As he came alert, he studied her face. It was like looking at a statue… no expression... her eyes as soulless as the Abyss from which she came. Mordecai had to remind himself, once again, that he had made a pact with a creature far more evil and deadly than anything he had ever dealt with before... except maybe Aikanáro, the demon he had summoned to assassinate the Queen's father. Aikanáro, however, was fairly incompetent. The same couldn't be said about Nightshade.

"What time is it?" he asked as he rubbed his eyes.

"Just past dawn, Mordecai," Nightshade replied.

"Is it done?"

Nightshade nodded. "It went… what's the expression you mortals use… oh, yes… it went 'picture perfect'. The Councilor has been eliminated and the evidence against the Queen planted."

"You were subtle?" Mordecai asked.

Nightshade laughed. "Of course," she said with amusement. "Only a fine prosecutor such as yourself can link together the delicate shreds of proof I left... particularly since you already know what the evidence is. Within a few hours the Queen should no longer be a concern, and you, dear Mordecai, will have the entire might of InnisRos at your disposal to hunt down and capture your empath and her bonded guardian."

"Excellent," Mordecai said as he smiled. He pointed to the opposite side of the room. In a cage a terrified human male, chained, looked at the First Councilor and Nightshade as he shook his head in denial of what he was seeing.

Nightshade stood and turned into her demon form as she walked over to the cage. The man's eyes bulged. Opening the cage, she stood before her victim, basking for a moment in his fear. As the eight spike-tipped arms entered his body, he opened his mouth and tried to scream, but couldn't. His tongue had been ripped out and nailed into his shoulder.

Afterwards, her hunger satiated, Nightshade and Mordecai talked about many things. Never once, however, did she mention her theft of the *Ak-Séregon* stone.

THE STRUGGLE FOR INNOCENCE

CHAPTER FIVE

Elanesse

When involved in a fight for life, the wise person will accept help from every corner, from every direction, even from past adversaries. But in doing so, the wise person should also understand the penalty that might someday have to be paid.

-Book of the Unveiled

Mariko neatly sidestepped the on-rushing arrow as it screamed towards her. She then deftly snatched it from the air as it flew past and let it fall to the ground at her feet, its power spent. It happened so quickly no one saw her catch the arrow... and realized what she had done only after the arrow clattered on the stone street. The silence that followed was palpable. Mariko put her hands at her side, palms outward, and said, "I know you have no reason to trust me, but I offer a truce."

"WOW! Did you see that!" Max shouted in disbelief.

Elrond grabbed Max's shoulder. "Simmer down."

"But Elrond, she grabbed an arrow out of the air. How can you not be impressed?" Max replied. There was awe in his voice.

"We're impressed, assassin, but we've seen that before," Tangus said as he stepped forward, forcing Jennifer to lower her bow as he walked past her.

"You're familiar with assassins," Mariko said. "Good… I don't have to waste time explaining myself."

"Since you tried to kill two us, I think maybe you do," Azriel blurted. His voice was dripping with venom.

"Tangus," Safire said. "What…"

Tangus held up his hand. "In a moment, Safire," he said before redirecting his attention back to the assassin. "You're from the assassin's guild in the city of Alverno... on the Spiral Islands. We've had past experiences with other members of your guild. It didn't go so well for them."

"Obviously, since you're still alive," Mariko replied. "I'm another matter altogether. If I wanted you dead, I'd now be standing over your decaying bodies."

"Or ours yours!" Azriel shouted.

Mariko looked at the dwarf. "Perhaps," she said. "For now I don't want your deaths, and I can be valuable helping you get the empath out of Elanesse safely."

Azriel took a step forward. "I don't believe you. I'm…"

Lester grabbed the dwarf's shoulder. "Restrain yourself, friend Azriel. Let's see where this goes, first."

Azriel shrugged Lester's hand off his shoulder. "Bah!" was all he said… but he made no further effort to engage the assassin.

Tangus breathed easier. He didn't want to fight the assassin just yet. "What do you know about the empath?" he asked.

Mariko shrugged her shoulders. "Just that my employer wants her to stay alive… and that's all I care about. Now we're wasting time. At this very moment mercenaries are marching this way. They want the empath as well."

"My name is Esmeralda, Mariko." Emmy said as she slipped out of Kristen's grasp and made her way through the distracted adults to stand in front of Tangus. Kristen was not far behind. "Emmy!" she said, concerned.

Mariko, stunned that the child knew her name, stared in silence. The priestess, Kristen, who she was ordered to protect as well, had put herself in front of the child, as did the ranger referred to as Tangus. But other than a passing glance, Mariko paid little attention to them. It was the child that drew her complete attention. The child's long, silky blond hair framed a perfectly proportioned face. The eyes that met hers were the most beautiful deep blue… and the depth within them astounded her. She felt herself being drawn in by their intensity... as if some type of enchantment had entrapped her. "This child was much more than I would have thought possible," she thought. "No wonder the guild was paid so handsomely for her safe capture."

Mariko found herself irritated the two adults blocked her view of those glorious eyes. When next she saw them, however, though still exquisite, they didn't have the same impact. But Mariko knew she'd somehow been forever affected. Though still fifty feet away, Mariko dropped to her knees so she could be at eye level with Emmy.

"How did you know my name, child," she asked. "It's a well-guarded guild secret."

"I dreamed of you, Mariko," Emmy replied. "Please call me Emmy."

"Very well then. Emmy it is. What did…?" Mariko said.

Tangus interrupted. "That's enough, assassin. If you're here to help us, say what you have to say and be gone. We'll not trust one such as you."

"Agreed," Azriel shouted out. "You'll never harm or take Emmy… except over my dead body. And dwarves are hard to kill." Azriel raised his battleaxe, showing the glow of its strong magic.

"Put that down this instant, dear Azriel," Emmy said. "Mother, father, she can be trusted. She no longer walks the path of the assassin."

Both looked down at Emmy, then at Mariko, who was still on her knees and staring at Emmy. Mariko shook her head to dislodge such foreign thoughts. "You're wrong, little girl. I'll never break my obligation to my guild." But Mariko wasn't as sure as she sounded. The child had looked into her soul and yet still accepted her. As she stood up, she said, "Come, we need to go quickly."

Tangus still didn't trust the assassin, but he trusted Emmy. In just the few hours since her release from the stasis field, he'd come to realize she was, in some respects, as mature as anyone he'd ever known… including his father-in-law, Horatio. "We can't leave the city. There're things here we must still do… a great wrong that must be righted or else Emmy shall never be safe."

Mariko looked at Tangus, then Emmy, and nodded.

"Let's go," he said as he helped Kristen and Emmy up onto Arbellason before mounting Smoke. He looked at Elrond and Max. Both nodded and took their usual place at the rear of the column, though this time they didn't lead the pack horses. That responsibility fell to Safire and Jennifer. They would be ready to intervene should the assassin prove false.

Tangus then looked down at Mariko from atop Smoke. "I don't need a horse," she replied to his unasked question.

"And if we need to ride hard to escape?"

Mariko smiled. "If it comes to that, then I'll delay them with my bow and catch up later... part of my training. For now, I'll lead you south out of the Gypsy Quarter, then up and into the eastern part of Elanesse. For an inexplicable reason the mercenaries or treasure hunters won't go there... though I've heard talk that it's haunted."

"Even more so than the rest of the city?" Kristen asked.

Mariko looked at Kristen and diverted her eyes to Emmy, who was sitting in front of her. The child seemed to know her darkest secrets.. her greatest weaknesses. "Yes, from what I've come to understand," she replied demurely as she looked away from Emmy.

"Bah! Ghosts!" Azriel said. "They can't hurt anyone."

Jennifer, riding alongside the dwarf, punched him in the shoulder. "You mean like Angela's ghost? Didn't she put a stake through Lukas' chest?"

Azriel smiled. "Aye, lassie, she did, didn't she... or so I've been told. Still wish I could have seen the look on his ugly face."

Without further comment, the party rode south with the assassin in the lead. Before long they were out of the city and in the Forest of the Fey. The pursuit Mariko said was coming never materialized.

Sergeant Warfel's years of experience had given him the ability to read the emotional state of men before going into battle. He recognized fear, anger, calm, rage, and empty… the look a man gets when he feels his time to die has arrived. He didn't like the look in Lieutenant Arnish's eyes. They had the look of a madman. Sergeant Warfel dreaded this most of all, for the loss of rational thinking, particularly in a battlefield commander, was the path to disaster.

The column of mercenaries entered a small intersection. Arnish raised his hand to stop his command. All around them lay dead men and women... treasure hunters... butchered. At the center of all this death an unmoving black clad form was sprawled out on the street with an arrow in his neck and leg. Assassin! Warfel could see, as he studied the bodies, how the battle had progressed. He quickly realized not all the treasure hunters could have been killed by one person. At least two, if not three, had been involved. There were more assassins out there... and they represented an immediate threat.

Warfel grabbed Arnish's shoulder roughly and spun him around. "You've been withholding information from me since the beginning of this campaign. You must tell me what we're pursuing and what we're up against! I need to know NOW!"

Arnish shrugged off Warfel's hand. "Never touch me again!" he screamed. Sputum flew out of his mouth. "You'll follow my orders or I'll find someone else who can!"

By now all the men had gathered around the two and watched them intently. Even the treasure hunters, who had been following the mercenaries, turned their attention from the slaughter in the intersection to the confrontation.

Warfel stepped back as he looked at Arnish. The Lieutenant's eyes were unfocused, as if he was hearing a silent call to the exclusion of all other outside influence. "I'm relieving you of command," Warfel said. He turned back and looked at his corporal, "Take the Lieutenant's sword..." Warfel's breath suddenly exploded when the sword slid through him. Blood gushed out of his mouth and his eyes bulged open as the shock of the pain consumed him. When he fell to his knees, the sword slid back out, causing another round of excruciating pain. Warfel looked at the Lieutenant and saw his eyes had turned black. Drool dripped from Arnish's mouth and landed on Warfel's face... the last humiliation before death. Arnish kicked Warfel's body to the side. "Anybody else want to question my orders?"

A few of Sergeant Warfel's friends did.

"There's a small river to the east," Mariko said after they were out of the Gypsy Quarter of Elanesse and under the canopy of the forest. "If you wish, we can divert our course to water the horses and re-stock water skins. Besides, if we follow it north, we'll end up back in Elanesse, anyway. It's not far."

Tangus nodded. "You've been true to your word so far, assassin."

"I'd appreciate it if you'd refrain from using that term," Mariko said.

"That's what you are, isn't it?" Azriel replied. "Pretty much the lowest of the low. A backstabber." There was an uncomfortable silence. Both Lester and Jennifer spoke softly to the dwarf, trying to calm him... but the look of contempt never left his face.

Mariko had no answer for Azriel's challenge. In many ways he was correct. She had approached targets from the rear, but she never used a knife. She always used a garrote under those circumstances. Nevertheless, she understood it would be a mistake to make that distinction under the present circumstances.

"Friend Azriel," Lester said, "each of us have layers upon layers that, like the onion, have to be peeled away if we're to understand someone's motivation and reaction to life's many moments. Sometimes we control what we want others to see, sometimes we don't. Sometimes we allow our life experiences, our emotions, to dictate what layers we expose, sometimes we're able to control what others see. It's a matter of perspective, and, I suppose, discipline."

Azriel threw up his hands. "By the gods, Lester, can't you just say what you mean without all that flowery mumble jumble?"

Lester smiled. "Friend Azriel, don't judge a book by its cover."

"I don't need to see all her 'layers' to know she's an assassin, Lester. By nature, assassins can't be trusted... especially if they've already tried to kill you once!" Azriel replied. "Tangus, how do we know she's not leading us into a trap?"

"Good question," Tangus thought.

"Azriel," Kristen spoke to Azriel's question before Tangus could. "Do you believe in Emmy?"

Azriel started to say something but shut his mouth. Kristen walked Arbellason over to the raging dwarf. Emmy eyed Azriel from her perch on the large warhorse, smiled and nodded. She reached down and placed a small hand on his gauntleted arm and said, "Peace."

Azriel sighed and placed his other hand over Emmy's. "Of course, child."

Tangus turned his attention to Max. "Drop behind and see if you can spot any pursuit." Max nodded and within a few moments he and his horse had disappeared into the trees. Tangus looked at Azriel.

"Lead the way, laddie," Azriel responded to Tangus' unspoken question.

"Let's go, Mariko," Tangus called as he moved Smoke back to the head of the small column. Arbellason, with Kristen and Emmy, returned to their position at his side.

They reached the river after an hour of threading their way through the trees and the dense brush of the forest. The river offered a brief respite for the horses and their riders. Tangus decided to wait for a few minutes for Max to return from his scouting foray. They desperately needed information about the mercenaries. But after ten minutes, Max still hadn't returned.

"We need to go," Tangus said.

"What about Max?" Jennifer asked. "Shouldn't someone go back to see if he's okay?"

Elrond laughed. "He'll be fine, Jennifer. Max doesn't allow himself to get into trouble he can't handle. Even still, Tangus, I think we should take a few more precautions."

"Agreed, Elrond," Tangus replied. "Mariko... you said we go north?"

"Yes. There's a breach in the walls where the river runs into the city," Mariko replied.

"And beyond?" Kristen asked.

Mariko shook her head. "As I mentioned earlier, I don't know what awaits us except to repeat I've heard it's haunted. My employer refused to go there... and there was very little she feared."

"That's not making me feel very good about this whole thing," Safire remarked.

"Right now it's our only option," Tangus said. "Keep cover between you and the river. I don't want our position exposed to the other side. Bitts and I will travel parallel to you about two-hundred yards. Lester, you and Safire bring up the rear. Any questions?" There were none. Tangus looked at Kristen. "You're in the lead, sweetheart."

Kristen nodded and said, "Be careful."

"Tangus," Mariko said before the ranger rode off. "There are things out here... strange things. Be wary."

"Don't worry about me," Tangus replied. "Just get my people safely into East Elanesse. If you've been deceiving us, I'll kill you." He still didn't entirely trust Mariko.

"She won't betray us, father," Emmy said.

Tangus looked at Emmy, then at Mariko, before disappearing into the forest. Emmy's guarantee did little to satisfy his unsettled feeling.

Nigel Smythe watched in fascination as the mercenaries turned against each other and fought a pitched battle right before the treasure hunter's eyes. Not one of the civilians watching the bloody fight occurring in front of them had any intention of interfering.

Those men loyal to Sergeant Warfel were outnumbered and, after a few minutes of ferocious mêlée, succumbed to the overwhelming numbers. Half their number were either dead or wounded... and the remaining disarmed. Lieutenant Arnish, wounded slightly in the brief skirmish, faced the subdued men.

"You're all traitors! I should have each of you executed on the spot," he screamed. He took a deep breath to regain his composure and looked at each of Warfel's men. They had given a good account of themselves... about half of Arnish's loyal troops were also casualties. "However, I'll forgive you this one indiscretion... but only provided you abandon your feelings for Warfel and follow me."

The prisoners looked at each other, but each knew this was their only chance to live. Reluctantly, they agreed to a man.

"Superb," Arnish said as he smiled. He turned to a corporal standing next to him and ordered, "See to the wounded. I want to be on our way again as soon as possible. You men," Arnish said as he pointed to the treasure hunters. "You'll be accompanying us."

One of the treasure hunters yelled, "I'm not following some idiot who can't even control his own men!"

"Who said that!" Arnish roared.

A huge, muscular man stepped out of the crowd of treasure hunters and looked down at the lieutenant. "You going to stop me?" the man challenged as he looked around at his friends. He laughed. "The little man's going to stop me!" he called out.

Three arrows suddenly thumped into his chest. The man didn't stand a chance. Arnish went over to the sprawled out body, side-stepped the growing pool of blood, and looked into the now vacant eyes. "Yes, I'm going to stop you," he said.

Nigel Smythe realized the strange compulsion that drove him to Elanesse was leading him down the road to perdition. He worked his way to the rear of the crowd of treasure hunters and, unnoticed, disappeared into a building. At dusk he ran for his life.

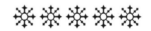

Worgs are smaller, vicious, evil versions of the proud, mighty dire wolf, that inhabit most of the forests of Aster. Very early in Aster's history, they were hunted to near extinction because of the threat they poised to both man and livestock. Consequently, though preferring solitary living, worgs were forced to evolve and attain a pack mentality to survive. This allowed their breed to rebound and become the dominant predator in some of the forested areas of Aster. Since the fall of Elanesse, the Forest of the Fey had become the hunting ground for several large packs of worgs. Each pack normally comprised twenty to twenty-five creatures.

When Emmy's presence was finally revealed to the Purge, it redoubled its efforts to control sycophants for her search and capture. The minds of the worgs were easily overpowered, and soon all the worgs who called the Forest of the Fey home were converging upon a little girl and the companions who guarded her. Though territorial, this one single imperative united all worgs to a common purpose.

"Duty!"

"What? Duty?" Tangus replied.

"Do your duty!" the voice said. "Your duty as a ranger!"

"I do my duty as a ranger. Who are you?" Tangus asked.

The voice was even more insistent. "Do your duty to Elanesse! It is imperative to the survival of the city."

Tangus, confused, nevertheless felt a compulsion to obey. "What threatens Elanesse?" he asked guardedly.

"That doesn't matter. DO YOUR DUTY!" the voice ordered, the force of which drove Tangus to his knees.

Holding his head between his hands, he struggled to talk. "What do you want me to do?"

"Bring the empath to me!" the voice replied.

"The empath to you... yes... of course," Tangus replied woodenly.

Then images flashed through his mind. Innocent people - adults, children - being butchered by men and women dressed in the browns and greens that most rangers favored. Some wore rings and amulets of Aurora... but the gemstones they contained had turned from multicolored to black. Aurora no longer favored them. Screams upon screams assaulted Tangus as the genocide was carried out, until there was only one left, hidden away and protected by the goddesses' Althaya and Aurora. Her name was Emmy.

Her name was Emmy...

Her name was Emmy...

My daughter!

"NO! You can't have my daughter!" Tangus, on his knees next to his horse, Smoke, screamed to the heavens as he raised a fist. "You can't have my daughter! Do you hear me!"

From behind him, Tangus heard a growl. He turned slowly to look over his shoulder. He recognized the growl and desperately wanted to avoid what was about to happen. But he knew he couldn't. Unsheathing his dagger as he pivoted, he stared into the mad eyes of his beloved Bitts just as the elven dog pounced.

Max was making his way as quickly as he could through the forest to catch up with the rest of his companions. In a stroke of good luck, he learned the mercenaries had a falling out which not only delayed their progress, but reduced their strength at the same time. It didn't look like they'd pose a significant threat for at least another day or two. But Max wasn't thinking about that at the moment. He had other concerns in the form of several dozen worgs hot on his heels. As much as he didn't want to lead them back to Elrond and the others, he'd die for certain if he didn't get some help.

As Max pushed his horse harder, he could hear the howling of the worgs behind him, not more than a couple hundred feet. He glanced over his shoulder to take a quick look... and didn't see the low-hanging tree limb that swept him off his horse to land hard on the ground. As Max shook his head to clear the cob-webs, arms grabbed and helped him up.

"Get up, you dope," Elrond said as he and Lester strong-armed Max to his feet.

"Worgs..." Max sputtered as he was being supported between the two. Except for Tangus, everyone was accounted for. They had established a defensive half-arc perimeter with the river on one side.

"We heard them, Max," Elrond said. "We just didn't know you were the cause of their displeasure."

By now Max had recovered from being unceremoniously dumped on his behind. As he pulled out his sword, he remarked, "Hell, Elrond, they were already pretty pissed off even before I ran into them!"

"The Purge must have them," Lester said. "We shall spoil their ambitions."

Max and Elrond looked at each other and suddenly laughed. "Spoil their ambitions, he says. I'll never get used to having a knight around," Elrond said. But soon enough there wasn't time for humor as the worgs burst through the brush. The deadly business of keeping Emmy alive and safe took their complete attention once again .

Tangus sat on the forest floor cradling the head of Bitts in his lap. He knew the Purge had attacked. He felt it himself when it tried to gain control of his mind. Unfortunately, Bitts didn't have the same capacity to resist. Perhaps if Tangus had been able to hold off Bitts for a time until the elven dog could fight off the urge, things could have gone another way. But in the end there wasn't a chance... it was kill or be killed. Just before Bitts died, the Purge released its hold. Tangus saw confusion in his beloved dogs' eyes before they closed for the final time. Tangus' heart lurched at the memory. "He thought I betrayed him," Tangus thought as his tears streamed down his face.

Tangus gently laid Bitts' head to the side as he stood. He called Smoke over and had him go down on both front knees. Though he struggled with the weight, Tangus succeeded in getting Bitts secured on Smoke's back. He would not leave his friend to the carrion eaters.

As Tangus led Smoke back to his wife, daughter, and the others, he heard the howling of worgs coming from their direction, followed by the crackle and thunder that accompanied one of Elrond's bolts of lightning. Tangus could smell the sizzle of burned flesh as the bolts hit their target. They were in a fight without him. Pushing his melancholy aside, Tangus rushed to join the fray.

As he made his way through the brambles and trees, the howling, growling, grunting, and groaning from elf and beast reached a crescendo. He heard Kristen shout "SUCCENDENT IN INFERNUM", and her *Spiritstrike* spell encapsulated its victim. The horrific braying of the worg caught in the spell's fiery enchantment was cut short as an arrow from Jennifer's bow put it out of its misery. Another thunderous bolt of lightning was released by Elrond from his sorcerer's staff. Dropping the reins of his horse, Tangus sprinted the final yards, attacking the surprised worgs from behind. Two died a quick death from his scimitars while a third dropped to the ground behind him with an arrow in his heart. Jennifer was already selecting her next target.

When considering the terrain, the defensive position they chose for the battle with the worgs was about as good as could be expected. The river was at their backs. This allowed them to build a much stronger curtain of defense since they didn't have to worry about getting attacked from the rear. Elrond, Jennifer, Kristen, and Emmy were in the approximate center of the formation. This tactic allowed Elrond and Kristen to cast spells without being interrupted while Jennifer used her bow to deadly effect. The front perimeter of Azriel, Lester, Mariko, Max, and Safire had thus far been un-breached... a wall of dead and dying worgs slowly building itself in front of their feet. Tangus, instead of working his way to his companions, remained where he was to protect Smoke... although he felt as long as the worgs were under the spell of the Purge, his horse wasn't in much jeopardy. Their target was Emmy.

The worgs were being slaughtered. Even so, they didn't relent. Their attacks remained vicious... their morale steady. Tangus estimated at least fifty were in the original group, but now only ten remained, and none of them were paying attention to him. As he observed the mêlée with a practiced eye, he knew the remaining worgs were going to be dispatched before they could get to Emmy. As the din of the battle was winding down, Tangus heard new howling from all around. More worgs were coming. Tangus turned to retrieve Smoke when he heard Romulus snarling and Emmy cry out, "Mother!" He turned back around just in time to see a huge, purple iridescent bird as it carried off Emmy and Romulus in its two claws.

CHAPTER SIX

InnisRos

*An ancient parable, handed down from
generation to generation, tells the story of a mountain
climber who, upon reaching the summit after a long day
of struggle, proudly looked up to the heavens and cried,
"Look what I've done!" In his victory, he lost sight of
the things he had accomplished to succeed. He slipped,
fell backwards, and within a few seconds his body lay
at the base of the mountain, broken and lifeless. The
moral of this parable? The journey to reach the
pinnacle takes time and is filled with difficulty and
danger. Once there, however, care must still be taken to
sustain yourself... for the journey back down can be
sudden and deadly.*

-Book of the Unveiled

"Your Highness, we need a ruling," the prosecutor
chided.

Lessien re-focused on the trial. It was a capital
case, and as her father before her, Lessien insisted on
adjudicating the process to make sure the accused
received a fair hearing. "I apologize, Prosecutor
Telrúnya. It's been a long day and my mind's distracted
with other affairs of state."

"Perfectly understandable, Your Highness. No
doubt the death of Councilor Mirie has taken an
emotional toll on you," Telrúnya replied.

"Perhaps that's it," the Queen agreed. "Regardless, I can't concentrate right now and that's not fair to the accused. Let's hold this case over for one week. I'll rule on it then."

"Very well, Your Highness," Telrúnya said as he bowed. He watched the Queen leave the courtroom for her chambers. "If you're still Queen, that is," he said under his breath as she disappeared out of the courtroom.

Lessien slipped through the door and leaned her back against the other side. Two startled handmaidens stopped their flirting with the two guards, who at once came to attention, and rushed to her side.

"Are you feeling ill, my Queen," one of them asked.

Lessien sighed. "I'm returning to my quarters," she said as she started towards the door at the opposite end of the courtroom antechamber. Both guards saluted as she passed. She stopped suddenly and turned to one. "What's your name?"

"Patrick, My Queen," the guard replied.

"Patrick, please go ask Colonel Van-Gourian to report to my chambers," she ordered.

"I'll go," the other guard said.

Lessien looked at him, was puzzled. "Your name?" she asked.

"Nicholas," the guard replied.

Lessien stared at the elf.

"Begging your pardon, My Queen," he said, "but I have to use the facilities."

Patrick snorted in derision but quickly reigned in his mockery. The two handmaidens giggled.

"Very well," Lessien said as she nodded.

As Lessien, the remaining guard, Patrick, and the two handmaidens walked through the corridors, Lessien noticed none of the guards she would normally expect to see were standing on post. Treason within the palace guard? Uneasy, she drew out her dagger. With her other hand she motioned for the two handmaidens to get behind her. They did as their Queen required, pulling out their daggers as well.

As they rounded a corner in the corridor, several guards marched towards them from the opposite end. Nicholas was in the lead.

"Nicholas, what's the meaning of this?" Patrick asked. "Where's the Colonel?"

Nicholas ignored his friend's questions. "My Queen," he said with a slight bow. "You're under arrest for the murder of Councilor Erin Mirie. The First Councilor has ordered you be detained. I'm to escort you to your chambers until First Councilor Lannian has had a chance to interview you and present his evidence." He turned to a guard next to him and said, "You'll be provided counsel afterwards to help prepare for your trail. Please give me your dagger."

The handmaidens suddenly moved in front of the queen, brandishing their own daggers.

Lessien shook her head. "Thank you, ladies, but please sheath your weapons. I want nobody hurt."

As Lessien handed over her dagger, hilt first, she said, "Surely none of you believe these false charges."

Nicholas studied his liege. "We're but soldiers doing our duty, My Queen."

"But you have an opinion," Lessien persisted. She wanted to gage the mood of her military... even if it was only a small segment.

Nicholas shook his head. "No, My Queen, I don't. But my opinion means nothing."

"It means something to me," Lessien replied.

"I don't know what you want me to say, Highness," Nicholas responded. "If you're innocent, the truth will come out in the trial and you'll be vindicated. The rule of law must be maintained."

"And if the rule of law is warped? Or perverted?" Lessien retorted. "What if this is nothing more than a ploy by the First Councilor to gain power?"

"That, my Queen, isn't for me to decide," Nicholas replied, though he didn't appear comfortable with his answer.

"Isn't it?" Lessien countered. "Do you not have a conscience?"

The guards looked uneasy in the silence that followed. Lessien removed two jewel-encrusted hair-pins from her long hair and turned to her handmaidens. "I'll no longer be in need of your services. Please take these as a token of my thanks for your service. You're free to return to your families." Both handmaidens bowed deeply. As they did so, they each kissed Lessien's ring of office.

After they left, Lessien turned to Nicholas. "Do your duty, soldier," she said.

Nicholas stood silently and didn't move.

Lessien sighed and removed the Mantle of the Sovereign from her shoulders and handed it to Nicholas.

The escort surrounded Lessien and together they marched to her chambers. The normally busy hallways

were deserted. Her guards had already cleared the way...
presumably to spare her further embarrassment. Though
Lessien didn't really care, she appreciated the courtesy
nevertheless. As they made their way through the
corridors, many thoughts flooded Lessien's mind... the
foremost of which was what, if anything, had happened
to Carl Van-Gourian and his Sword Masters.

    Father Goram and Autumn had enjoyed a late,
quiet supper. Ajax was there as well, and this time he
brought his mate, Cassandra, along for the large chunk
of venison steak Father Goram always offered his four-
legged friends. The day had been long with little chance
to rest as plans were made to accommodate the Queen's
request for sanctuary... should the need arrive. The
request, added to the death of Erin, meant things were
spinning out of control in Taranthi, and Mordecai had
finally decided to take steps to gain control.

    For the moment, however, Father Goram and
Autumn sat on the sofa together, warmed by the fire,
and sipped mulled wine. Neither spoke, preferring
instead to doze in the comfort of each other's arms.
Ajax and Cassandra suddenly sprang up from their own
peaceful slumber and rushed to the apartment entrance
door, startling both Father Goram and Autumn. A few
seconds later there came a knock.

    Father Goram shook his head. "This is how my
day started!" he exclaimed as he went to answer,
followed by Autumn. "Back," he ordered. The two

massive beasts backpedaled into the great room and sat down. They remained vigilant for any threat that might present itself.

Outside the door the stood Magdalena. "Please come in, Maggie," Autumn said. "Coffee? Or perhaps warm wine?"

"Coffee please, Autumn. Thank you," Magdalena said as she brushed past Father Goram. "Horatio, there's been a new development in Taranthi."

"You've received a message from Mother Aubria?" Father Goram asked, although he already knew the answer.

Magdalena nodded. "Yes... and it's not good, I'm afraid. The Queen's been arrested for the murder of Erin Mirie. She's currently restricted to her quarters until Mordecai can put together a mock trail."

"We know where that's going, I'm afraid. Any word on the Queen's Sword Masters?" Autumn asked as she brought three mugs of coffee. "Maybe they can get her out."

Magdalena took a sip, then shook her head. "They've been executed as traitors."

"What!" Father Goram exclaimed in disbelief. "How..."

"Military, Horatio," Magdalena said. "A different set of rules. They were captured, a military tribunal established, found them guilty, and marched them to the gallows."

"Not even an appeal?" Autumn asked.

Magdalena shook her head. "Mother Aubria indicated battlefield rules are in effect... at least for Taranthi."

"Battlefield rules?" Autumn queried.

Father Goram sat back down in front of the fireplace, desperately trying to shake off the chill that now ran up and down his spine. "Dear, it means habeas corpus has been suspended and Mordecai can legally remove all his opponents with just an arrest warrant... as long as he has the power of the military behind him. He doesn't need proof. Damn... I never thought Mordecai would go this far!" Father Goram turned to Magdalena who had taken a spot on one of his easy chairs. "I'd also have thought Colonel Van-Gourian would've been smarter than to let himself be taken like that," he said.

"We don't know exactly what happened, Horatio, except to say that their execution has been confirmed," Magdalena replied.

There was another knock on the door.

"I hope you don't mind," Magdalena said, "but I sent Arthon and Gunthor to wake and brief the others. That should be them."

"Good," Father Goram said as he got up to answer the door. "It'll save time. We have much to discuss."

Lessien was tossing and turning in her sleep. Her meeting with Mordecai and his assistant, Amberley, didn't go well and only lasted about five minutes. Without preamble, he told her she was to go on trial for the murder of Erin Mirie the following day. He also told her of the execution of Colonel Van-Gourian and her entire personal bodyguard, the Sword Masters, for high treason. They had tried to stop the arrest warrant from being served and now they were dead because of it. It was a debt Lessien was afraid she couldn't repay.

From the open doorway between Lessien's bedroom and her great room, a glowing light appeared. Lessien knew as soon as she saw it magic was in the air. Getting out of her bed and slipping on a robe to ward against the evening chill, she cautiously approached the door and peered into the adjoining room. In the fireplace only glowing embers remained, so all Lessien could see was the outline of a figure standing in a hallway where a wall once stood.

"Who are you," Lessien asked.

The figure made a few contortions with its hands and whispered a cantrip. A small fire appeared in the palm of one hand. The figure, who Lessien now knew to be a woman, placed the flame in a nearby wall sconce. When she removed her hand, the flame grew and lit the entire room.

"I know you," Lessien said. "You're Mordecai's assistant, Amberley."

Amberley strolled into the room. "You're correct, though I'm much more than that, Queen."

Lessien watched as Amberley approached. The woman's beauty and grace were evident, as was the intelligent gleam in her eyes. Amberley stopped a few feet from Lessien and looked back over her shoulder. "It's a good thing I found that secret passage. Did you know it was there?" she asked.

Lessien shook her head. "No. Neither did my father or else he would have mentioned it. What do you want?"

Amberley studied Lessien for a few moments. Lessien soon became extremely uncomfortable and looked away. There's something more in those eyes other than intelligence... like a predator sizing up its prey. Lessien wondered if the woman was her executioner.

"I've come to rescue you, Queen." Amberley said.

Lessien looked back at her visitor. "Why would you do that? Surely this isn't Mordecai's wishes."

Amberley laughed. "No. I think Mordecai will be rather upset when he discovers his 'prize' has disappeared." The humor in Amberley's eyes faded and became hard. "I've no love for you, Queen. But nor do I hold any particular animosity. But I hate Mordecai. That's all the reason you need. Now change quickly. Don riding clothes if you have them. I have your horse ready for you. Once you get outside the palace walls, people will be waiting to escort you to the monastery at Calmacil Clearing. After that, your fate is your own."

Lessien, though she had a thousand questions, held her tongue and rushed to change clothes, gather a few valued possessions, and strapped on *Ah-RahnVakha*, her father's magical sword, now hers, to her hip. She smiled as she thought how much Mordecai wanted the blade... but failed to find it even though he had thoroughly searched her chambers. Even the sorcerers couldn't find it with magic.

While Lessien was getting ready, Amberley whispered a few guttural commands and a small window opened in the air in front of her. She reached in and withdrew a black blade. Amberley walked over to the main entrance door into the Lessien's chamber, took her free hand and ran it along the door, stopping at two spots. Satisfied, she took the black sword and rammed it through the door twice, in quick succession. From the other side she heard bodies drop to the floor. She took the sword and replaced it in the floating window. With a mental command, she willed the window to close.

Lessien came out of her bedroom shortly thereafter, dressed and ready to go. Amberley noticed the gleaming sword now sitting on the queen's hip and smiled. She knew how much Mordecai wanted that sword. Both women left the great room through the opening to the secret hallway. After they had left the wall became solid once again. There was no trace of their escape... except the blackened husks that laid outside the queen's quarters.

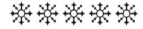

Instead of staying in Father Goram and Autumn's apartment, the council moved to the "war room", as Landross liked to call it. This was a massive room with a polished oak table and soft, comfortable chairs. The huge fireplace had been stoked by acolytes who also stood ready to satisfy any additional needs of the monastery command staff. Off an adjoining hallway was a fully staffed kitchen. Everyone was enjoying freshly baked bread with butter and jam. Also available, as always, was plenty of coffee.

Outside the door of the conference room stood four of Landross' knights. Arthon and Gunthor had taken their normal place beside the door inside the room, while two more of Landross' knights stood their posts in opposite corners... a customary practice whenever the monastery is on alert. Ajax was there, but Cassandra had gone back to the den to warn and prepare the pack for a possible move into the walls of the monastery.

"We need to neutralize Balthoron's battalion," Cordelia, Father Goram's second in command said. "He could make things very difficult for us if so ordered."

Father Goram nodded. "Agreed. Landross, can you contain Balthoron with your knights?"

"Certainly, Horatio... if it comes to that. Let me talk to Balthoron first. He's very loyal to the Queen and might join forces with us," Landross replied as he wiped jam from his mouth with a napkin.

"Why would he do that?" Cameron asked.

Landross shrugged. "I'm not really sure. But when the conversation drifted to the Queen, he insinuated there was a debt owed to her father by his family."

"Enough to commit treason?" Autumn asked.

"Probably," Landross replied. "One can learn much just walking through an encampment if you know what to look for and how to listen. I don't understand the nature of the psyche like Cameron here, but I understand honor. Balthoron has as much honor as any knight I've known. If he sees a wrong, he's obligated to make it right. I'm sure he'll see through Mordecai's attempt to take down the Queen. That mind-set translates downward to his troops as well. They love their commander."

"I'm impressed," Cameron remarked.

"That's why Landross is my chief of security, Cameron," Father Goram said. "Let's move on, shall we? Magdalena, did Mother Aubria give any hint as to her future plans?"

Magdalena nodded. "Only that the family needs to go underground. Mordecai's well aware of her alliance with you and no doubt will try to eliminate her as a threat."

"Good that Mother Aubria's taking steps to protect her people," Autumn replied. "Horatio, Mordecai's going to come after us as well."

Father Goram was sitting back in his chair, tapping his fingers on the table, deep in thought. He nodded in agreement with Autumn's observation. "I know," he said.

A slight hum broke the silence that followed. Magdalena pulled out a communications crystal from a belt pouch. "Excuse me," she said as she stood. "This is Mother Aubria." She went to an unoccupied corner of the room so she wouldn't disturb the others.

Father Goram watched his chief ranger retreat, deep in thought. "Since Mordecai's made his move to capture the throne," he said, "I assume he's garnered plenty of support. Otherwise, it'd be him facing treason charges. Landross, do you think he has the Army behind him?"

"Indeed I do," Landross replied. "Not the hearts of the men... but most certainly that of the generals. I suspect his hold is still somewhat tenuous or he'd just overthrow the Queen. Instead, he needed trumped-up charges to show she broke the law. The men will accept that."

"How about the navy?" Father Goram asked as he looked at Cordelia.

"He doesn't own them... at least not right now," she replied. "That'll probably change if the Queen is convicted of murder."

"How do you know?" Autumn asked.

"I spent time in the Navy as a healer before coming here to the monastery. I still maintain friendships within the fleet." Cordelia smiled as she thought about those past times. "Autumn, scuttlebutt in the Navy is a refined art. It has tentacles everywhere. I would've heard something if anything out of the ordinary was happening."

"We'll take you at your word..." Father Goram was saying when Magdalena interrupted him.

"It appears someone's helping the Queen escape the palace," she said without preamble. "And if she's successful, she'll be coming here."

Father Goram had his chair turned and was scratching behind Ajax's ears with both hands. He stopped and looked at each person around the table. "Who?" he asked.

"Mother Aubria doesn't know. She said she's acting on an anonymous tip."

Father Goram continued to scratch behind the ears of his big dire wolf friend. "That presents a whole new set of problems," he remarked. "I doubt she could get out of the Taranthi's harbor... and she'll know that. She'll head overland. Maggie, put together a force of your rangers... your best bowmen... and go southwest to intercept the Queen and cover her retreat... if she makes it that far. But be discreet... kill only if you have to.

Remember, any troops chasing her are doing their duty. They're not the enemy."

"How about some of Landross' knights?" Cameron asked. "I'd wager that'll put a stop to any pursuit."

Landross shook his head. "No, my friend, for several reasons. I couldn't get there in time. There's nothing discreet about a column of knights. And then there's Balthoron and his battalion to consider. He'd know for sure something's happening if I took my knights out in the middle of the night. We need to see where he's going to align himself first."

"Get going, Maggie," Father Goram said. "If the Queen's coming, bring her here safely."

"Yes, Horatio," Magdalena said. "Arthon, Gunthor, you're with me."

Father Goram rubbed his eyes and sighed. "I suspect sleep's going to quickly become a scarce commodity."

The two women exited the secret passage into a small, out-of-the way courtyard that Lessien had never seen before. Her heavy warhorse, Bristol, was saddled and ready to go. There was an unnatural fog in the air, cold and unyielding, which masked visibility past ten feet. Lessien looked over at Amberley.

"To help cover your escape, Queen. The longer you avoid guards, the better chance you have of making it out of the palace walls and the city beyond."

Amberley reached into her cloak and produced a communications crystal. "In case I need to get a message to you. Guard it closely. And don't get any ideas you can use it to track me. I've placed certain... shall we say... safeguards to prevent you or anyone else from doing so."

Lessien took the crystal and nodded. She climbed onto her familiar perch on Bristol's broad back. "If Mordecai finds out what you did tonight, he'll come after you," she said. "Be careful."

Amberley barked out a short, inhuman laugh. "If you only knew, Queen. Remember, you'll meet people outside the walls who'll help with your escape from the city. Now leave."

Lessien kicked Bristol forward when a gloved hand grabbed her arm. Lessien stopped her horse and turned to look down into Amberley's beautiful eyes. "One last piece of advice, Queen," Mordecai's courtesan said. "InnisRos is no longer yours. Leave as soon as you can for the mainland. But satisfy yourself knowing that, though he doesn't yet know it, InnisRos won't be Mordecai's for much longer either." Amberley slipped back into the fog. As Lessien was leaving the courtyard, a thick, black miasma rolled towards Mordecai's dwelling... easily distinguishable from the magical fog that had settled down upon Taranthi. The dark demon Nightshade smiled. She loved nothing more than manipulating mortals. Fools every one!

Lessien made her way carefully through the fog, weaving here and there in what appeared to be a maze, but unlike a maze, there was only one direction she could lead her horse. After fifteen minutes, Lessien came to a wall. She looked right and left, but there

185

wasn't anywhere else to go. She was at a dead-end. Lessien dismounted and approached the wall. Acting on a hunch, she stuck her hand out. At first the wall felt solid... but then a curious thing happened. There was a shimmer as if the wall was reacting to some type of stimulus... and suddenly Lessien could pass her hand through to the other side. Magic attuned to her! Though inquisitive why this would be, she shook it off, remounted her horse, and nudged him forward and through the wall.

On the other side, the fog didn't allow her to recognize any landmarks which would tell her where she was... only that she was outside the palace walls and in the streets of Taranthi. Behind her the wall re-solidified and left no trace of her passing. Not sure where she needed to go to meet the people Amberley mentioned, she 'clicked' Bristol onward, drawing the reins to the left as she did. The fog muffled the sound of her horses' metal horse shoes on the cobblestone, but what noise they made sounded empty and lost. Before Lessien had gone more than half a city block, two figures on horseback appeared in front of her. As Lessien drew closer, she recognized distinct markings that told her they were rangers and followers of the goddess Aurora.

"Queen Lessien?" one of them spoke, a female elf.

Lessien nodded. "And you are?" she asked.

The female shook her head. "Names aren't important. We're to lead you out of the city so you can escape to Father Goram's monastery at Calmacil Clearing. We need to leave before your absence is noted."

"One moment, please," Lessien said. "Who told you I had escaped and where to find me? For that matter, who told you I had even been arrested? Was it Mordecai's assistant Amberley?"

The second elf, a male, spoke for the first time. "That information came from... well, let's say it came from different sources in a very unconventional way."

"In other words, you don't know who it came from, do you," Lessien replied.

"No," the female responded. "We didn't even know if it was true... but Mother Aubria decided to send us just in case. I don't know if it was this Amberley person you spoke of. Perhaps. Mother Aubria didn't say."

"Enough conversation," the male ranger interrupted brusquely. "We need to leave now. Follow us," he said to Lessien.

After about an hour of travel, as they were entering the farmland surrounding the city, they heard bells ringing behind them. "They know I'm gone," Lessien said.

The three riders kicked their horses into a gallop, hoping to reach the cover of the forest west of the city before they were discovered.

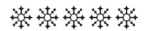

"What do you mean the Queen's escaped!" Mordecai roared at the Army generals standing uncomfortably in the foyer of his home. He had just been awakened by a night-servant, his hair was disheveled, and he wore only a plush robe. Behind him stood Nightshade as Amberley. She looked as beautiful as ever.

"The two guards are dead, their bodies blackened and burned," one replied. "Of the Queen there's no sign."

"And..." Mordecai asked.

The generals looked at each other, bewildered. Nightshade sighed but remained quiet. "This is what happens when you put incompetent fools in positions of authority," she thought. "Mordecai should have listened to me and won over the Queen's men... her Sword Masters. What a shame they had to be destroyed. Things ARE working out nicely, however."

"Raise the damn alarm!" Mordecai shouted. One general ran out to do his bidding. "And see what the sorcerers can do!" he yelled at the back of the hastily retreating general. "About time to see if they know anything other than parlor tricks."

Mordecai then pointed to another general. "Get the naval Commander-in-Chief here within the hour," he directed. "She may not like me, but with the Queen in the wind, she must accept her guilt and obey me as the lawful ruler of InnisRos. I want this island blockaded. No ships in or out." Turning to his Chief-of-Staff, Mordecai then ordered the entire Army be put on alert.

After everyone had left, Mordecai looked at Nightshade and shook his head.

"What are your plans, Mordecai?" she asked.

"Only one person has the power as well as the audacity to pull this off. We march on Goram," he replied as he clenched his fists at his sides.

Nightshade smiled.
War!

Once Lessien and her elf companions crossed the threshold into the forest, they pulled back on the reins of their horses and proceeded slowly. The pre-dawn light made it nearly impossible to negotiate the bushes, brambles, and low-hanging tree branches safely.

As they made their way deeper into the forest, Lessien remarked, "There's plenty of open farmland between here and Calmacil Clearing... and the Maranwe River to cross. What's your plan?"

"We don't have one," the male elf replied before moving his horse forward. He didn't want to engage the Queen in this conversation.

The female elf stopped and looked at Lessien. "I'm sorry, Your Highness. Our orders are to get you out of the city and into the forest. Anything more puts our entire family at risk."

"You mean I'm to make my way to Calmacil Clearing alone?" Lessien exclaimed. "There's no way I can do that!"

"The political landscape has changed considerably, Your Highness..."

"Indeed," Lessien interrupted, her indignation unmistakable in her response.

The ranger grimaced at the Queen's reprimand. She untied a large sack from her saddle and handed it over. "Inside are food, extra clothes, bedding, and gold for expenses. Mother Aubria also provided a cloak that will impart invisibility upon the wearer provided the correct command word is spoken. That command word is 'Finduilas'. But remember... it can only be used once per day... and the effects of the magic only lasts for two hours."

"Such is the way of magic. I understand," Lessien said as she opened the sack and removed a pouch containing the gold and the cloak. She attached the pouch to her belt and put the cloak over her shoulders.

From a few yards away the male elf said, "Hurry! We have to be back before the full light of day."

"One other thing, Your Highness. Father Goram's aware of the your escape and will send help. Please stay safe until then."

Lessien looked at both rangers. Now she understood the male's anger... he didn't think it was right to leave her on her own. Neither of them did. "Please thank Mother Aubria on my behalf," she said as she turned her horse northward. Within moments the forest had swallowed her as she moved forward alone.

Later that same afternoon, Lessien stood next to her horse as she looked at the Maranwe River from the safety of the thick forest undergrowth. In a span of thirty minutes, she had seen two river barges pass by with soldiers on-board, scanning the countryside. They were undoubtedly involved in the hunt for her. Though she was now wearing the clothing of a simple farmer's wife, she knew, upon close inspection, she'd be quickly recognized. There was also the problem of Bristol, her warhorse. She needed him to escape, but he was almost as well-known as she.

As she watched barges move up and down the river, a plan formulated in her mind. If she could get to a large enough barge, she might be able slip aboard, hide, and then disembark on the other side. If she remembered her geography of InnisRos correctly, there was a dock next to several grain warehouses where barges frequently stopped on their way upriver. However, before she could put that plan into effect, she had to travel across open country for several miles. But what other choice did she have? The forest was quickly filling up with searchers and wouldn't keep her safe for long. "I hope this damn cloak works," she said aloud.

Father Goram, Autumn, Cordelia, and Ajax were at Calmacil Clearing's sprawling hospital complex doing what they could to help sick and injured patients. Besides being the location of one of the most formidable monasteries on Aster, Calmacil Clearing was also home to a large farming population. As a consequence, the hospital had its share of sick and injured people which, at times, exceeded the expert healing provided by the permanent hospital staff.

Father Goram was sitting on the bed of a human female child who had the measles. She was out of danger, but her parents hadn't been so lucky. Though they'd survive, they were in another wing of the hospital and still quite sick. At the moment he was entertaining the child with a stuffed dire wolf, sewn together by Autumn, that looked remarkably like Ajax. The girl had one small hand on the real Ajax's ear while she watched as the stuffed Ajax marched up her belly and tickled her under the chin.

Cordelia stepped into the ward and motioned for Father Goram. Handing the stuffed Ajax over to Autumn, he got up from the child's bed, kissed her on the forehead, and walked over to Cordelia, briefly stopping at the bedsides of other sick and injured children to exchange words and encouragement.

When Father Goram stepped into the hallway, he was met by Cordelia, a miserable-looking Landross, and an openly angry Balthoron... who gulped and backed away when he saw Ajax following behind the priest. His uncertainty didn't last long, however.

"How long have you known about this!" Balthoron demanded as he passed over a message scroll to Father Goram.

Father Goram unrolled the scroll to read it, though he was fairly sure he already knew what was in it. What he read confirmed his suspicions. It contained information concerning the Queen's arrest, her subsequent escape, and Balthoron's orders to keep a close watch because there was little doubt Father Goram's assistance had been instrumental in her flight. If the Queen were to show up, Balthoron was to secure her until Mordecai's arrival. That Mordecai was marching in-force on the monastery also didn't surprise Father Goram.

"I'm surprised you'd show me this," Father Goram said as he raised an eyebrow. "Surely you don't want to be seen as consorting with traitors."

"I don't think... that's not the point! If you knew, if you helped her escape, you should've told me. Unless, of course, you consider me the enemy," Balthoron replied. There was uncertainty in his voice.

"I don't know what to think," Father Goram said. "That the Queen would be arrested for the murder of Councilor Erin Mirie is preposterous... even though when I heard I wasn't surprised. I know Mordecai's been eyeing the crown for some time and no doubt arranged the evidence to point to her guilt. But Commander, I had nothing to do with her escape."

Balthoron looked at Father Goram. He didn't entirely believe him.

"All right... maybe I helped a little," Father Goram admitted. "Or I should say allies of mine in Taranthi helped. But not at my direction. And only after the Queen had already gotten out of the palace. Up to that point I don't know who assisted her." Turning to Landross, Father Goram asked, "Why didn't you speak with the Commander about this earlier?"

Balthoron held up a hand to stave off Father Goram's displeasure with Landross. "That was my fault, I'm afraid. I told Landross I couldn't see him until later and invited him for dinner in my tent."

"What are you going to do?" Father Goram inquired.

Balthoron shook his head as he crumpled up his orders. "Well, I'm certainly not going to go against the

Queen," he said. "It's not treason if you don't believe the Queen committed murder. In fact, I have a duty and an obligation to see to her safety until this whole misunderstanding has been sorted out. I can vouch for my troops as well."

"And Mordecai's spies?" Cordelia asked.

"Identified and neutralized. That's why I couldn't meet with Landross earlier," Balthoron replied. Then he paused a moment and looked closely at Father Goram. "Are you going to give her sanctuary if she asks?"

"We haven't been on the best of terms for quite some time, but I liked her father very much," Father Goram said. "I have no doubts with regards to her devotion to InnisRos. And Lessien's an exceptional ruler... wise beyond her years, good common-sense, and compassionate towards our people. So yes, I'll do whatever I can to aid her against this obvious travesty of justice and keep her on the throne."

Balthoron nodded. "You're her only chance, so she'll be heading this way," he said, then smiled. "I think I must take my battalion south to effect her capture and make sure she remains safe for the trial. I'm sure it's what Mordecai would want me to do, don't you think?"

"Why yes I do, Colonel," Father Goram replied. "You need to follow your orders in every respect."

Balthoron nodded to each and turned to leave.

Father Goram stopped him. "I almost forgot. During your march, don't be surprised if a few of my rangers shadow you. I'll let them know where you stand."

"Excellent!" Balthoron said. "I can always use a few more well-placed perimeter scouts." He turned serious and frowned. "I believe the future of InnisRos is at stake, Father. Saving our nation is going to be hard... and dangerous."

"I know." Father Goram replied grimly.

As night fell on InnisRos, the Queen of InnisRos prepared to make her dash from the forest, hoping to board a barge going upriver without attracting attention to herself. From behind she could hear the distant braying of the dogs that were hunting her.

As night fell on InnisRos, Mother Aubria's entire organization had finished preparations to leave Taranthi. She knew it was only a matter of time before Mordecai discovered her involvement in the Queen's escape and take his retribution. Before the moon had reached its zenith, they would be on a ship heading to Listern Island, north of InnisRos. This island was mostly unsettled and only had one major city, Tasartir. Mother Aubria hoped it'd be far enough away to offer safe harbor from Mordecai's revenge.

As night fell on InnisRos, Mordecai was meeting with his military commanders and coordinating the search for the missing Queen. He learned that the sorcerers had a nasty surprise in store for the Queen at dawn's first light. The newly fashioned gold and gem encrusted crown resting on his head, however, was giving him a headache.

As night fell on InnisRos, Nightshade, in her mortal form, sat in front of a swirling mist she had conjured. "How much longer must I play out this charade?" she asked. The mist, in the form of a hand, reached out and caressed her face. "Not much longer, my daughter."

As night fell on InnisRos, a female elf, dressed in pure white, stepped out of a magical doorway and onto the soil of InnisRos. As the doorway dissolved behind her, she threw a staff she carried up into the air. Instead of falling back to the ground, it hovered and spun until it pointed southwest. The staff returned to its master as she walked in that direction.

As night fell on InnisRos, Father Goram stood atop the battlements of his monastery. He had his arms around Autumn, who was standing in front of him, and together they watched the sunset. "Things will never be the same again," he whispered. Autumn laid her head back against her husband and closed her eyes. She knew he was right.

CHAPTER SEVEN

Elanesse

Can life sustain itself without hope? Conversely, if life remains, is hope ever truly lost?

-Book of the Unveiled

Tangus dropped to his knees as he watched Emmy and Romulus, gripped in the powerful claws of an enormous, beautiful bird, disappear behind the trees of the Forest of the Fey. Somewhere in the back of his awareness he heard Kristen scream her own pain and loss. It broke his spirit. His heart, so recently overcome by the loss of his ever faithful companion Bitts, now suffered the pain of Emmy being taken away to parts unknown. Though the child represented the hope of the world, she was first and foremost his daughter. Tangus closed his eyes and screamed to the heavens as his frustration, his humiliation, clutched his soul. How could he ever be forgiven! How could he ever forgive himself!

After Tangus had quieted and opened his eyes, he could no longer see beauty. He could no longer see the majesty of the trees, smell the fragrance of the flowers, or feel the comfort of the sun's warm rays. His fury had become all-consuming. Standing and clutching his scimitars, he turned to face the worgs who were surrounding him and his companions. Life didn't matter... only their deaths.

Kristen looked with terror at the retreating bird. Within its grasp were two whom she held most precious. Disregarding the killing madness going on around her, she stood paralyzed as she looked up at the now empty sky and remembered Emmy's call for her mother. Someone pulled Kristen's arm, trying to get her to move, but she stood fast. She wanted to imprint into her mind every exact detail, every color, every smell, every emotion she felt, for the revenge she would have should anything happen to her daughter. The rage that built within her quickly matched Tangus'. Only killing would calm the ache and emptiness she now felt. This foreign, all-encompassing desire to kill had consequences, however. Kristen's ire strangled and blocked the bond between her and Emmy.

Emmy watched as the ruins of east Elanesse passed by below her. She was being gently, yet firmly, held in the claws of a massive, brilliantly colored bird. Romulus, just a few feet away and clutched in the other claw, was struggling to bite, but he couldn't find purchase. Emmy reached out to Kristen through the bond, but something blocked her. Stunned by the first failed attempt, she tried harder. Her mind recoiled at the dam of emotion that blocked the bond. For the sake of her sanity, Emmy was forced to retreat, drawing with her the bond until it closed. Emmy felt alone for the first time in over three millennia.

"You're not lost, Esmeralda. Be patient, I beg you," said a voice in her head.

"Who are you?" Emmy asked. But the voice didn't answer.

As the far eastern wall of Elanesse disappeared beneath them, and the forest once again dominated the landscape below, Emmy saw a large and robust tree about a mile from the city. It soon became clear to Emmy that this was their destination.

The tree was at least fifty feet higher than its surrounding companions, and the leaves of its branches were thicker and had a shimmering aspect to them. As they descended and came closer, Emmy could see the tree's branches open wide to accommodate the bird who closed its wings enough to make safe passage. Once they were through and Emmy and Romulus had been gently deposited on the lush, soft, thick-grassed ground, the tree branches closed. Then their length extended before Emmy's eyes until they touched the ground. Emmy and Romulus found themselves enclosed in a cocoon of tree branches and leaves.

The giant bird stood and looked down at the two. Romulus warily moved in front of Emmy, but he didn't act as if there was any immediate danger. The bird shimmered and standing in its place was a beautiful female elf. She wore a flowing purple gown and had long white hair. On her brow was a precious gem, woven within flowery tattoos that moved across her forehead. A larger match to the gem hung from a silver necklace around her neck.

"Who are you?" Emmy asked as she moved forward to stand at the side of Romulus, one hand clutching his fur.

"I'm called Sehanine StarEagle," the elf said. Her smile at once put both Emmy and Romulus at ease.

"Where am I and why did you take me away from my mother and father!" Emmy demanded. She suspected the elf woman was a goddess like her friends Althaya and Aurora. But goddess or not, Emmy was determined to get answers to her questions.

"You're under the protection of a very special tree, Esmeralda. The 'Lorin-Galaduiriel' in the old elven tongue, or 'Tree of Golden Radiance', as it was called during the time of Elanesse's vibrancy." Sehanine StarEagle placed a hand over Emmy's heart. "As your heart beats in your chest, this tree is the heart and soul of Elanesse. As you are to Kristen and Tangus, Elanesse is to me... my daughter."

Emmy didn't know what to say, but she knew Elanesse helped protect her during her "dream time" from not only the Purge but also the vampyre murderers of her birth mother, Angela. "Why did you take Romulus and me?" she whispered.

The goddess affectionately stroked the side of Emmy's face. "I did so at the behest of my daughter. What your mother and father, with their companions, will experience in the eastern part of Elanesse would be dangerous, or perhaps even bad enough to kill you. The support of your bond to Kristen may not be enough to protect you. It's a thing you're still too young to witness. It's the penance my daughter pays for an evil that occurred long before you were born."

"The Purge," Emmy said. "It seeks my destruction."

Sehanine StarEagle nodded. "Yes, the Purge. For the sake of all the healing magic in the world... for the sake of my daughter... the Purge must be destroyed."

"And I'm the only one who can do that," Emmy replied matter-of-factly. It was something she already knew.

"Yes," Sehanine StarEagle said.

"Permit me one final question, goddess?" Emmy requested.

"Of course, child. Ask as many as you wish," the deity replied.

"Why can I no longer reach my mother through the bond?"

Sehanine StarEagle paused and sighed. "That's my fault, I'm afraid. Elanesse tried to warn the half-elf traveling with your parents..."

"Elrond," Emmy said.

Sehanine StarEagle nodded. "Yes, that's his name. But he was too busy fighting worgs to hear her call. Your mother and father think you've been kidnapped by forces who mean you harm. This enraged both to the point they feel hatred... the very thing which will cause you the most pain. Your bond is blocking that emotion to keep you from harm." The goddess knelt and embraced Emmy. "Dear, it's only temporary. You'll be safe here until they come to retrieve you." She kissed Emmy's forehead. "We'll meet again," Sehanine StarEagle said as she faded away, leaving Emmy and Romulus alone... alone, yet under the protection of Elanesse.

Tangus crouched like a feral cat, studying the forest surrounding him with a practiced eye... a ranger's eye. The worgs were close, but there was still time to get back to Smoke. As he made the run, bobbing and darting around and under trees, branches, and bushes, his anger became more and more focused. Never had he felt such hate. This wasn't a ranger principle, and Aurora wouldn't approve, but Tangus didn't care. The Purge had forced him to take the life of his own beloved Bitts, taken Emmy, and now threatened Kristen, Jennifer, and his friends. Tangus decided he would be the righteous vindicator who would destroy this evil... or he'd die. No other possibility existed for him in his current state of mind.

He reached Smoke just as three worgs broke through the brush. Tangus cut the rope securing Bitts' body to Smoke, relieving the mustang of that burden, before turning to meet the charging worgs. Within seconds two lie dead and bleeding. Smoke, trained for combat, had kicked another's skull in. But this wouldn't be enough. Already the two were surrounded by another dozen worgs. But, having witnessed the quick deaths of the first three, took their time to coordinate the attack instead of blindly rushing in. In the back of Tangus' mind he understood this wasn't the usual attack strategy of the worg. He pause to consider his own tactics. In doing so, he regained control over his incensed state. Slamming his scimitars into their sheaths, Tangus ran and jumped onto the back of Smoke. "Just a couple hundred yards, my old friend," he said before putting the reins in his mouth and drawing his bow. As Smoke scrambled through the trees, Tangus found plenty of worg targets for his arrows.

Kristen's anger only saw the worgs as they attacked. Her friends, her companions, her loved ones, forgotten as she concentrated on her revenge. "SUCCENDENT IN INFERNUM" she screamed, commanding a *Spiritstrike* spell against two worgs. Before the screams of the burning worgs had died away, Kristen shouted, "MALLEUS DEUS." A large, glowing hammer appeared before her which she directed with her mind to attack even more worgs. She laughed in satisfaction as each head was crushed, as each evil worg hit by her "hammer of god" was sent to whatever hell awaited it.

When the spell had at last died out, Kristen drew her mace from its place on her belt and started forward... towards the front of the defensive line her friends had created to protect her, Emmy, and the horses. She heard the howl of the worgs. She smelled their blood and wanted to bathe in it, as if that simple act would cleanse her soul of the emptiness she felt. Kristen's hate and anger boiled up from a part of her she never knew existed... and at the moment she didn't care.

Someone grabbed Kristen by the shoulders. She heard that person talking to her, but the voice seemed very far away. "Kristen! Kristen! Snap out of it!" the voice yelled. Kristen looked away from the dead worgs and saw Safire standing in front of her, holding her shoulders... preventing her from moving forward. Kristen put a hand on her brow. "By the goddess, what have I become?" she asked herself, feeling shame and disgust at the primal urges that had ruled her behavior.

Safire shook her head. "It's natural, Kristen. It's called battle lust. No doubt brought on by Emmy being taken away."

"Emmy!" Kristen screamed. Then her shoulders slumped, and she looked at the blood soaked ground. "I've lost her," she said quietly. "I can't feel the bond."

Safire raised Kristen chin so she could look into her eyes. "Listen to me. Emmy is fine. Elrond told me Elanesse is keeping her safe under the Tree of Golden Radiance... whatever, or wherever, that is. East Elanesse, where we're heading, isn't safe for her."

Kristen studied Safire's face looking for any hint of duplicity. "True?" she asked.

Safire nodded.

As the last vestiges of hatred and anger drained away, the bond tentatively re-established itself. Kristen and Emmy were once again bonded. With its return came understanding. Kristen knew why the bond had been blocked... her anger. Inwardly she vowed that would never happen again. "I love you!" Kristen whispered knowing, now that the bond was once again connecting the two, Emmy would feel the warmth and depth of Kristen's affection.

"We have to move," Mariko said. "I don't think we can hold out much longer."

"I'm not leaving without my father!" Jennifer countered angrily.

The howls of worgs were getting closer. Each person knew the next wave would arrive within minutes and it appeared to be even larger than the one they just fought.

"Mariko," Kristen said. "I stand with Jennifer. We'll not leave without Tangus." Looking around, Kristen added, "Though the rest of you are free to do as your conscience dictates."

"I'm not leaving," Safire said. Lester shook his head as he grabbed Safire's bloody hand.

Azriel looked to Elrond. "You're sure the child is safe?" he asked.

Elrond nodded. "Safe as long as Elanesse lives." Elrond then directed his attention to Mariko. "I don't how it's done in the world of the assassin, but until we know about Tangus, none of us are leaving. It's what we do for family and friends."

Mariko nodded. "I've never had family before, unless you count the guild... and they'd cut your throat at the slightest provocation. But I'm with you. Do we go look for him?"

"If we're going to go, let's be quick about it," Max said.

Smoke suddenly broke through the bushes and jumped the wall of dead bodies. Both he and Tangus had been clawed and bitten. Smoke's right eye was gone, and an ear bitten off. Both of Tangus' legs were a bloody mess. They were clearly exhausted. Of Bitts there was no sign.

As Tangus was helped off Smoke by his friends, he asked, "Emmy?"

"She's fine, my love," Kristen said as she took charge of the two. She was in her element now. "I'll explain later. Bitts?"

Tangus closed his eyes. "Dead. Worgs all around," he managed to say before grimacing at the pain.

Kristen turned to Elrond. "Buy me five minutes to get Tangus and Smoke back on their feet, then get us the hell out of here!"

"Yes ma'am," Elrond said as he turned to the others. "Suggestions?"

"Can't you just do that thing you do with your staff?" Max asked. "You know, open up a door in the air and step to someplace else?"

Elrond shook his head. "Can't use a dimensional doorway into Elanesse. The disruption in this dimension would cause her too much pain."

Mariko stuck the point of her katana in the dirt. "We're here," she said as she marked an 'X'. She then draw a line up and marked another 'X'. "The river goes up and into the eastern part of Elanesse. We can we swim for it."

"Worgs can swim," Azriel remarked.

"Yes, but they can't swim faster than our horses," Jennifer answered.

"She's correct," Mariko said. "If we can reach the city, we should be safe... at least safe from the worgs. They won't enter. To be honest, I don't really want to either."

Elrond nodded. "Kristen?" he shouted.

It was Tangus who replied, however. "She's almost done with Smoke. I overheard and agree with Mariko. It's our only chance. We can't fight our way through. There's too many of them."

Max tugged Elrond's sleeve. "You sure horses can swim?" he asked.

Elrond nodded.

"Good, because I can't."

The worgs on the western bank of the river were reinforced by worgs on the opposite side. They didn't bother to enter the river, though, preferring instead to run alongside its banks to make sure none of the swimmers could go to either bank for rest from the strenuous exertion it was taking to stay afloat.

It was nightfall by the time they reached the walls of east Elanesse. As they swam through the rusted and broken grate beneath the fortification, their worg escort disappeared into the forest. Mariko was correct, they wouldn't enter east Elanesse. Climbing onto the bank, everyone, except for Tangus, Jennifer, and Safire, collapsed. The three rangers, as their training dictated, made sure the horses were okay before they allowed themselves to rest.

As night fell, so too did the temperature. Kristen and Elrond both used magic to keep everybody warm. But it soon became clear they'd have to move further into the city to seek shelter. They needed sleep and staying in the open was far too dangerous. Mariko's reticence to enter the city, as well as the worgs absolute refusal, had everyone anxious and on-edge. It was impossible to know what they might encounter. Even Elrond, in constant communication with Elanesse, couldn't get an exact picture of the threat. But as they moved deeper into the city, no menace materialized and the night remained quiet.

Since this was Elanesse's business district, there was no lack of various-sized warehouses from which to choose for shelter. They ended up choosing a warehouse large enough to bring the horses in, but small enough to easily protect. The extra heat generated by their bodies made a large fire unnecessary. As midnight approached, only Lester and Safire remained awake, alert for anything that might threaten their sleeping friends. An occasional piece of wood kept the small fire fueled. At midnight, the screaming began.

Emmy was lying against Romulus' side. He had curled himself around her to give not only protection but also warmth against the night chill. Emmy, her bond with Kristen restored, was content as she drifted off into sleep, although she still worried about the dangers her parents and friends faced... dangers that the goddess, Sehanine StarEagle, said would kill her. But the steady beating of Romulus' heart put Emmy at ease, and she slept... and she dreamed:

Emmy was in a large pyramid, floating and looking down. Though the pyramid was several stories tall from the surface up, it also extended deep into the ground. Ten levels burrowed into the ground. Ten square balconies went around each level, with metal, spiral stairs connecting each. Magnificent wooden doors were interspersed along the walls of each level. Every door gleamed as it released the magic that had been cast upon it.

At the bottom of the pyramid was a ten foot diameter circular depression in the stone floor. Glowing magical runes surrounded the hole. At the bottom of the hole there appeared to be a black, thick liquid. Emmy thought it might have a metal quality about it. Occasionally an obsidian hand reached out of the liquid, grasping but only clutching empty air.

Next to the pit several elves in robes, who Emmy recognized as priests, surrounded another elf in the livery of either a very wealthy person or a ruler... gold and silver-lined robes, jeweled rings and gauntlets, and a magical scabbard with sword on his hip. Though he didn't wear a crown, all but one priest deferred to him.

"Are you sure this'll work," the richly dressed elf asked. "The King expects much."

The high priest nodded. "Yes, Amroth, it'll work, provided your rangers have the stomach to carry out their duties."

"Don't worry about my rangers," Amroth snapped. "They'll do their job or I'll have them exiled." Several of the priests cringed. As Emmy watched this exchange, she suddenly understood banishment out of Elanesse and into the world of humans, dwarves, and halflings was a punishment sometimes considered

worse than death itself to an elf. She wondered why that would be. "So explain how this works," Amroth asked, bringing Emmy's attention back to the conversation.

The high priest laughed. "You think you could ever hope to understand the complexity of the magic used to do this?" he said. "Or the sacrifice?"

Amroth puffed up." Now you listen to me..." But he didn't get the chance to finish.

"Do you think I fear some popinjay who's been feeding off the teat of his mother since the day he was born?" the high priest said. Emmy could hear the power, the arrogance, and the disrespect for Amroth in the high priest's voice. Though she knew she was witnessing what had happened over three thousand years ago, it was as if the priest's malevolence had spanned that gulf of time... momentarily leaving her breathless. It was at that moment Emmy came to understand the hate that birthed the Purge.

Amroth had been completely humiliated by the high priest. He knew, as did everyone in the room, there wasn't anything he could do about it. The high priest smiled.

"You see," the high priest continued as if nothing had happened, "it takes an empath to destroy an empath." He clapped his hands together one time. A door opened and two guards appeared with a struggling human girl between them. She was about twelve years old. The fear in her eyes broke Emmy's heart.

As the other priests surrounded the liquid filled hole and chanted, the girl was brought before the high priest. Without pause, the high priest drew a ceremonial dagger and slashed the palm of one of the girl's hands. The girl cried out in pain. Taking the palm, he licked the blood that streamed from the deep wound. He then produced a golden chalice and let the blood flow into it before the empath's natural ability to heal herself closed the wound. Going to each chanting priest and using the girl's blood, he made a blood mark on their forehead. By the time he had finished with the last one, their chanting had reach a fevered pitch.

The high priest nodded to the guards, who dragged the empath over to the pool. A black hand extended out towards the girl. The guards picked her up and threw her to the waiting hand. Her screams ceased as she was immersed in the liquid metal. With a suddenness that startled Amroth and the guards, hands exploded out of the pool and grabbed each of the chanting priest's. They disappeared into the murky liquid as well.

Amroth kept quiet as the high priest began his own mantra. After just a few seconds he finished. Complete silence followed. The high priest then clapped his hands, and the guards exited through the same door they had entered with the empath.

"Well?" Amroth asked.

The high priest smiled. "It's done."

Amroth looked confused. "But nothing is..."

With unexpected speed a black, swirling column suddenly ascended from the pool and reached the top of the pyramid before coming back down. As it retreated from the pyramid top, the other end also ascended from the pool on the floor and together they formed a black swirling sphere floating in the air. Smaller globes, equal in number to the priests that had just been consumed, broke free and circled the parent *for a few seconds before falling back in. At the point where they merged back into the larger orb, black tentacles reached out and extended through the walls of the pyramid in every direction. Emmy knew these black appendages were how control of Elanesse's rangers came to be. Emmy stared in horror. She had just witnessed the creation of the Purge.*

Suddenly a face appeared in the side of the churning globe. It was the face of the empath used to help create the Purge. The face looked through the span of years directly at Emmy. "I'm so alone," it said.

Lester and Safire didn't have to wake the others. Everyone rose from exhaustion-induced sleep in response to the screaming. Within moments all stood at the huge warehouse door watching what transpired before them.

"We need to help!" Jennifer said as she took a step towards the door threshold.

Azriel grabbed her arm just as she started to draw her sword. "Lassie, there's nothing we can do," he said gently.

"There's always something the strong can do to help the defenseless, Azriel. We have to at least try," Jennifer pleaded.

"No, Jennifer. Azriel's right," Tangus said. "Sweetie, we're watching something that happened a long time ago. I believe this is the first night of the Purge being played out before our eyes."

The scene being displayed in front of them was horrendous. Everywhere, groups of people were running for their lives, being hunted by rangers on horseback. Men were trying to defend their families, but provided little protection against the Riders of the Purge. Blood flowed in the streets. The cries of babies for their dead mothers could be heard over the din of pain-filled shrieks. All too soon those cries were silenced as well. Some of the doomed empaths, watching their deaths charge towards them on horseback, dropped lifeless before they were even assaulted... their bodies twitching on the streets. These were stabbed, hacked, and slashed anyway.

The black eyes of the executioners gleamed in the torchlight that lit the streets. In them there was no concern, no remorse, no compassion, no sympathy... just hate. What drove that hate mattered little to the innocents who were being slaughtered.

Each deadly strike the rangers of Elanesse used to commit murder upon the empath made Elanesse convulse in waves of pain. At first imperceptible, a groan rose from the city. This groan traveled through space and time to reach the ears of those witnessing the events of that night so long ago.

They continued to watch in revulsion as carts, pulled by horses and followed by raggedly-dressed gypsies, followed behind the path of destruction and cleaned the streets of bodies.

"Emmy would never have survived this, even with the support of our bond," Kristen said. "Elanesse was right to get her out of harm's way."

Elrond took a deep breath. "This is what Elanesse dreams every evening," he said. "She still feels the hate and the horror of those first few hours."

"You mean we're witnessing the dream of a city?" Max asked.

Elrond nodded. "She won't forget until she's been forgiven," he said.

Max frowned. "But who can forgive her?"

Elrond shook his head. "I don't know."

Emmy awoke with a start, her dream still vivid in her memory. Romulus leaned his head in as Emmy clutched his fur. She scratched behind his massive ears with two small hands to re-assure him. "Althaya was wrong, Romulus. I'm not the last empath," she said. "And I know how to defeat the Purge." Still very sleepy, Emmy didn't stay awake for long. But before she drifted off for a second time, she whispered, "We forgive you."

Neither Emmy nor Romulus heard the great and audible sigh that came from the heart of Elanesse. It sounded like the gentle breeze of warm spring air coursing through the leaves and branches of a tree. It was the breath of freedom from guilt. For Elanesse, the forgiveness that Emmy bestowed upon her meant the nightmare of that night so long ago would never again be relived. Tears, in the form of sap, ran down the massive trunk... and Elanesse, for the first time since the creation of the Purge, truly rested.

As quickly as it began, the ghastly spectacle transpiring within the city of Elanesse ended and the quiet of the night returned. Crickets began to chirp once again and occasionally the deep base of bullfrogs could be heard coming from the river's bank. The torchlight from the Riders of the Purge was replaced with starlight, and the streets no longer ran with the blood of the innocents. Instead, a great peace prevailed.

"What happened?" Jennifer asked.

Kristen shook her head. "I don't know, dear. Everything stopped."

"The dream," Elrond said. "It's over. Something happened to finally end it. Do you think it was Emmy?"

"Of course it was Emmy," Azriel replied. "She's the hope of the world."

Tangus cocked his head. "Do you hear that?" he asked.

"I don't hear any... wait... now I do, friend Tangus," Lester said as he drew his sword.

Soon everyone heard. With the haunting of east Elanesse finally broken, so was the fear that it had instilled.

The worgs were once again on the prowl.

The Purge was frustrated. It had lost the empath once again. "How could that be?" it wondered. "She was so close."

Then the all too familiar whispers of the voices in its head began their mantra. *"You must redouble your efforts,"* they implored. But a smaller voice... a voice that came from the heart... followed with a plea of its own. *"No, don't listen to them. Cease your attacks and go back to sleep."*

"Damn the universe for my creation," the Purge silently roared.

CHAPTER EIGHT

InnisRos

The soldier raised his sword to strike, but a stony hand grabbed the blade from behind and snapped the sword like kindling. Turning, the soldier gazed upward into the face of my earth elemental. The glare of an angry, animated, twenty foot tall piece of stone and earth can be quite disconcerting. The soldier ran away.

-From the Journal of StarSinger Nefertari Arntuile

Lessien waited at the edge of the forest as long as she dared. She shivered uncontrollably from the cold, and wished it were spring and the full moon was hidden behind clouds. As it was, she'd be easily spotted if the invisibility cloak given her failed to function as promised. And if it did, how much attention would a riderless horse draw? And the tracking dogs... they relied on scent, not sight. How long could she stay in front of them?

Lessien took a deep breath and kicked Bristol into a gallop. She hoped to put as much distance as possible between her and the dogs. It felt good to feel the cold air whip against her face and through her hair.

217

Though she was running for her life, a sense of exhilaration overpowered her. For the first time in a long time, she felt free. She giggled like an excited, adolescent child as Bristol ran.

After about two miles her enthusiasm came to an abrupt end. She'd seen a small, shallow ravine to her right and thought a small stream probably ran along the bottom. If she traveled in the stream, it might throw off her scent and momentarily confuse the tracking dogs behind her. Lessien directed Bristol over to it. Neither she nor Bristol noticed the pride of Nighthunters until it was too late. These wolf-sized, black and brown cats came up and over the edge of the ravine, surprising both Lessien and Bristol. Though there were seven, a trained warhorse with a competent rider weren't helpless, even if taken unaware, and could readily defend themselves. But as Bristol rose on his hind legs to stomp one of the big cats, an arrow released from the soldiers tracking them hit him from behind and pierced the main tendon in his left, back leg.

Bristol came crashing down and Lessien was thrown over his head and into the ravine where she splashed into the murky water at the bottom. Hurt as he was, the Nighthunters dispatched the big warhorse quickly... though not before one of their own had its head crushed. The force of Bristol's kick launched it into the air where it landed next to Lessien. She stared into the Nighthunter's eyes as death claimed it. As she shook off the effects of being thrown, she knew the sounds coming from above meant Bristol was lost.

Lessien crawled to the opposite bank and took stock of her condition. The water had helped to break her fall, but it was shallow and rocky. Her dominant arm had been wrenched to where she couldn't raise it... which made it almost impossible to defend herself. She had other minor bruises and abrasions, but no broken bones. Her supplies, tied to Bristol's saddle, were lost... though she still had her sword, cloak, and the gold. She took a brief refuge under the magical cloak to regain her senses... but she couldn't stop shivering from the cold of the night made worse by her wet clothes. Fortunately, the Nighthunters were too busy enjoying their hard-earned meal to pay Lessien much interest. Even still, Lessien knew it was only a matter of time before they'd turn their attentions to her. Though she was invisible, animals had other means of tracking prey. Teeth chattering, she dragged her sore body up and over the edge of the other side of the ravine and crawled several feet to a small bush.

As she gathered her strength to make a run for it, she again heard the braying of the tracking dogs. They were closer than she thought. From her vantage point, she saw the Nighthunters suddenly raise their heads and stare. They slinked away from the carcass of her horse and disappeared into the night. It wasn't long before Lessien heard the growls of the big cats as they attacked, the whimpering of the over-matched dogs, and the curses of surprised soldiers. Lessien got up from the bush and bolted like a rabbit in the opposite direction, heading towards the Maranwe River.

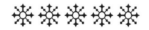

It was early morning and the sun had just peeked over the eastern horizon. Autumn had gotten an early start and, along with Cordelia, was coordinating efforts to prepare the hospital for the potential battle and siege of the monastery. Father Goram was sitting at his desk in his small study off the great room reading intelligence and monastery status reports. From these he garnered the Queen was still free and on the run, but her exact location remained unknown. That wouldn't help Balthoron or Magdalena and her rangers, but Father Goram was sure the Queen could be found as long as she remained free from Mordecai. Landross was preparing his knights... knights required a lot of time to get ready for battle... but it was well worth the wait. Cameron had gone to see if he could enlist the young sorcerer, Eric the Black, and put him on the monastery payroll. They would need sorcerer magic to help counter what Mordecai's forces would bring to bear. Father Goram hoped Eric the Black was as good as everyone said he was.

Father Goram's concentration was disturbed by a tentative knock on the front door. He looked up from the papers strewn across his desk, irritated. "Who could that be?" he asked himself. Then he remembered it was cleaning day... his housekeeper, Sandis, must be here. Father Goram looked around the apartment. "It needs it," he said as he got up to let the girl in. Ajax, snoozing by the fireplace, suddenly rose on all fours and growled as he darted forward to stand in front of the priest. "What is it, Ajax," Father Goram asked as he laid a hand on the dire wolf's back. Using his own clerical ability to detect evil, Father Goram reached out with his senses. "By the goddess!" he exclaimed as he took a step back. "An obsidian blade!"

"Father, please let me in," Sandis pleaded as she rapped on the door with more force. "I need your help. Father! Please!"

Father Goram sighed. He didn't really have a choice... the girl was in terrible trouble if she had an obsidian blade. He stepped past Ajax and opened the door. Sandis collapsed in Father Goram's arms, the hilt of the blade sticking out from between her shoulder blades. "I couldn't use it on you," she said before blacking out.

Father Goram carefully inspected the wound without touching the hilt. Buried as deep as the blade was, the fact his young housekeeper wasn't already dead was a miracle. His experience told him she was probably bleeding inside unless the blade itself was stemming the flow of blood. Regardless, she had little time. Written on the hilt was a glowing, magical rune, "Maglor Telperiën", or "Black Death". Ajax whimpered. "Don't worry, my friend, I know the danger," Father Goram said to calm the huge dire wolf.

Father Goram reviewed what he knew about obsidian blades. They're used primarily against clerics, though as poor Sandis now could attest, the blades don't care whose flesh they devoured. If a cleric were to touch the hilt, it would instantly drive him or her mad. The blade itself didn't have to pierce the skin of a cleric to kill. And there's one other thing that made the obsidian blade so dangerous... they're possessed by demons.

The blade moved on its own, first swaying back and forth, and then it slowly rose from Sandis back. The wound, now unsealed, spewed blood. Father Goram faced the dilemma every cleric feared and knew the price that would be paid for failure. If Father Goram saved Sandis' life, his would be forfeited. She only had seconds to live... seconds the blade wouldn't give him. But if he chose to save his own life instead, he'd be turning his back on his clerical vow to Althaya. Father Goram gathered his will and laid his hands on Sandis' wound, the blue light of his magic working to repair severed or damaged skin, muscles, blood vessels, and internal organs. As the healing magic coursed through Sandis, the floating obsidian blade rotated so that the point aligned with Father Goram's heart.

Lessien reached the Maranwe River just as the sun was chasing away the dark. As she bent over, hands on her knees, catching her breath, she listened for any signs of pursuit. She could hear or see nothing. The Maranwe River was two miles wide and flowed south into the Bay of Sorrow. Though she was an excellent swimmer, the distance, and the current made it impossible for her to even entertain the notion of swimming across. Her best hope to slip aboard a barge was still a few miles to the north where the northern Aranel River joined with the Maranwe. The magically enchanted cloak Lessien was using to make her invisible wouldn't last much longer, so that'll be a problem.

As she traveled north along the bank of the Maranwe, staying under the cover of trees that lined the river's path, she noted several military barges moving along the river in both directions. This in and of itself wasn't too disconcerting. It was common practice for the Army to patrol the rivers of InnisRos. But she also understood they'd be on the lookout for anyone who matched her appearance. Her heart sank, however, when she saw a freight barge stopped on its way downriver and searched. She'd soon be boxed in on the wrong side of the river.

By mid-morning Lessien had arrived at the confluence of the two rivers, but her plan to sneak aboard a barge going north on the Aranel was immediately dashed. Army patrols were everywhere. The two large villages nestled along the banks of the Maranwe had armed guards checking every man, woman, and child... every locker, basket, barrel... every wagon, cart, carriage... as well as every dock, barge, and boat. Lessien studied the situation from her covered perch in a tree. She could see there wasn't any real expectation of success, at least not without using the magic of her cloak. Because of its limitations she'd have to stay hidden for the rest of the day and well into the night before she could use it again. As she watched the garrison establish complete control over who and what entered and left the villages, she saw signs the Army was going to push out its perimeter, conducting a thorough search of the immediate area as it did so. It was standard search and rescue... and the Army was being very efficient. Lessien saw how well her father had trained them and grimaced at the irony. That training would probably be the death of her.

Mordecai didn't sleep that night as he waited for the news his prize had been re-captured. If she did get to Goram, he might never root her out... and as long as she remained alive, she was a threat to his rule. By morning's light, he was sleeping on the sofa in his great room. Empty bottles of wine and whiskey lay on the floor. The warming fire had long ago been reduced to ashes.

The front door to his mansion opened and Nightshade, in her Amberley form, walked in, took one look at him, and motioned for one of the guards. "Bring me a bucket of cold water."

As the guard ran to do Nightshade's bidding, she stacked logs in the fireplace, waved her hand to start a fire, and sat on the padded arm of an easy chair. As she stared at the unconscious Mordecai, her disgust that he'd allow himself to turn to alcohol became palpable. Didn't he understand too much of it muddled the mind and made smart mortals weak and stupid? She'll tolerate neither. The fool! At the moment, she wished nothing more than to eat his black soul.

There was a loud rap on the entrance door and a guard entered with a bucket. Nightshade pointed at the end of the sofa. As the guard set the bucket down, she thanked him and told him Mordecai would be ready within the hour.

"I want all the sorcerers and his generals in the palace conference hall by that time," she ordered. "His

Highness will wish to discuss what they have planned to capture the rogue Queen."

The guard bowed deeply and backed out of her presence. As he ran to his headquarters to communicate Amberley's orders to his superior, he shook his head. "Rogue Queen indeed!" he thought, still refusing to believe Queen Lessien was guilty of murder. Among the men in his platoon, none would disagree with his assessment.

Nightshade took one of the wine glasses Mordecai used and lowered it into the bucket of water. She smiled... it was ice cold. Taking the now filled glass, she leaned her head over it and allowed saliva from her mouth to drop into the water. It immediately began to sizzle and then turned slimy green. Nightshade set the glass down and dumped the bucket of cold water on Mordecai.

Sputtering awake, filling the room with curses, Mordecai glowered at Nightshade, who by now was now sitting in the chair. "You drunken idiot!" she admonished as she watched him shake his head and rub his hands through his wet hair. "We've got a long day ahead of us. Drink that," she said as she pointed to the glass.

Mordecai stared into the glass and sniffed it, immediately wishing he hadn't.

"The stronger the hangover cure, the better it works," Nightshade said smiling. "Disgusting stuff... but, all things considered, you deserve it. Now drink!"

Mordecai looked at Nightshade angrily, but did as she asked. He clutched his stomach and threw up all over himself.

Nightshade watched without emotion. "Now go clean up. We've a meeting to attend with your sorcerers and generals." As Mordecai disappeared, she yelled, "And don't linger!" to his retreating back.

Mordecai stormed into the conference room with Nightshade following closely. He was angry... and bothered once again by the effects of his alcoholic binge. Nightshade's disgusting home remedy for a hangover had stopped working, for his headache returned as soon as he put his crown on. The sorcerers and Army generals rose at once and stood at attention.

"Oh sit down," Mordecai said as he took his place in his throne at the head of the table. Mordecai now had thrones at strategic places all over the palace... at great expense to his personal finances. He had been planning his eventual control of InnisRos for quite some time... and spared no expense. Besides, he'd soon be able to refill his vault with the island's wealth.

"Where's the Navy?" Mordecai asked.

"As you can see, Your Highness, they didn't bother to heed your summons," General Maglor Narmolanya, InnisRos' Army commander, replied. "They mentioned something about critical fleet maneuvers."

Mordecai sighed. He now understood firmer measures would be required to bring the navy under control. "Where are we in the search?" he asked.

"Still nothing, Your Highness," General Narmolanya said. "We've established strongholds all over the island and from these we'll conduct systematic searches. The Queen..." that got a stern look from Mordecai, "the fugitive won't be able to run free for long. No stone will be left unturned."

"And the loyalty of your men?" Nightshade asked.

Several of the generals looked at each other. "I have to admit, there have been rumblings, Your Highness," one of the generals said.

Mordecai slammed his fist on the table. "You'll execute any soldier not doing his duty!" he screamed, spit flying from his mouth.

Nightshade laid a hand on his arm and leaned over. "You're being too extreme, Mordecai," she whispered. "You don't want an insurrection."

Mordecai calmed. "As always, your counsel is wise, my loyal advisor," he acknowledged. He decided to offer the Generals an olive branch. "Perhaps I misspoke. Have any of your soldiers who still hold allegiance to the Queen arrested and detained. We'll see if they feel the same after the trial. If they're still loyal to her, they'll be exiled to the mainland. I want no more unnecessary bloodshed."

Mordecai rubbed his forehead. "Narmolanya," he continued, "where do we stand in preparations for our march on Calmacil Clearing."

General Narmolanya looked at Mordecai. "Your Highness, as I've mentioned, the monastery there presents a somewhat large, tactical challenge. I have Balthoron keeping close tabs on the comings and goings of the keep, but I can't guarantee he'll know when, or even if the Queen... excuse me... the fugitive, actually arrives. Neither will he be able to determine the monastery's duplicity in her escape. In his acknowledgement of orders he indicated that nothing out of the ordinary had thus far occurred. Your Highness, he doesn't have the strength to contain the keep's military if they decide to sortie. We'll need the entire Army to do that. Even then I'm not sure we can succeed."

Mordecai stared at his Commander-in-Chief, but Narmolanya didn't back down this time. "It could mean civil war, Your Highness. I think it best to put the fugitive on trial, even if it's in absentia, and prove her guilt. That way, Father Goram will be forced to give her up."

Nightshade was surprised General Narmolanya would show this much backbone... and concerned Mordecai might display some discretion. She didn't want that. "Even if found guilty, he won't give her up," she said. "We have no choice but to march. She's a murderess and the law must be followed, or the island will fall into anarchy. General, do your secret operatives in Balthoron's battalion have anything to add?"

General Narmolanya shook his head. "I haven't heard from them."

"Then we must consider Balthoron compromised," Nightshade remarked to Mordecai. "Yet another reason we must march on Goram."

Mordecai nodded. "Yes, we must. Generals, see to your duties. I want the Army ready to go by dawn's light tomorrow... unless we have her captured by then. We'll still march, but it'll be after the trial and at my

228

convenience." Mordecai looked around the table to see if there were any questions. None of the generals felt the compulsion to ask anything, so Mordecai waved his hand. "You're dismissed."

After the generals had left, Mordecai shifted his attention to the sorcerers. "Now then," he said, "what do you have planned for our little renegade?"

Ajax leaped over the kneeling Father Goram just as the obsidian blade streaked forward. The blade moved much too quickly for Ajax to snatch in his jaws, but he slightly changed its trajectory with a lightning fast swipe of one of his massive paws. The push sent the blade spinning as it whizzed past Father Goram's face. It buried itself into the wall next to his right shoulder. As the demon possessed blade worked to free itself, Father Goram pulled an unconscious Sandis into the great room. Ajax had positioned his body between the wall-captured blade and the priest.

Father Goram used the time Ajax had bought him well. He magically dissolved the poison from the blade coursing through Sandis and then healed the wound itself. Satisfied that she wasn't going to die, he looked up just in time to see Ajax grab the blade hilt in his strong jaws as it worked its way out of the wall. Though Ajax refused to let go, his strength was no match for the demon within the blade. He was slung around the room by the blade as if he were a ragdoll. What had been a messy great room was now a shambles as Ajax was continually slammed against furniture and stone walls.

After moving Sandis into a corner and behind a chair, Father Goram rushed into his study. As he was searching his collection of magical and religious tomes and scrolls, he smelled smoke coming from behind him. Turning, he saw that the fireplace screen had been knocked over and searing hot coals were scattered on the floor, igniting a rug. The tip of Ajax's tail was also burning. Pointing a finger at the fire, Father Goram concentrated and whispered, "NEBULA AQUAE FRIGIDAE". A dense mist of cold water appeared over the fire and snuffed it out. Father Goram cursed because the fire and water had ruined the rug.

The fire on Ajax's tail started to become a serious concern. The water spell, good only for stationary fires, ended the moment the flames had been extinguished and the burning coals cooled. Father Goram needed to extinguish the flames that were slowly making their way up Ajax's tail. Again using his finger, Father Goram tried to follow Ajax around the room as he was being led by the blade. He didn't think Ajax was feeling any pain yet because of the adrenaline rush fighting the blade... but that'd change soon enough if he couldn't stop the tail from burning.

Suddenly the blade broke free of Ajax's grip and flashed towards Father Goram. He grabbed a thick tome from his bookshelf and raised it to intercept the blade just as it reached him. The blade careened off the tome, glance off a wall, and buried itself into his wooden desk. Father Goram raised an eyebrow and looked at the tome... *"Demon Possession: A Thesis on the Identification of a Demon Possessed Object and the*

Means by Which the Demon can be Exorcised". It was the tome Father Goram had been searching for. Father Goram contemplated this amazing coincidence when Ajax whimpered. "Oh! I'm so sorry, my friend," Father Goram said. "EXSTINGUERE DOLOR," he whispered. A white sphere appeared around the burning portion of Ajax's tail and the fire was extinguished. When the sphere disappeared after a few moments, there was a barely audible 'pop' as air rushed in to fill the once airless space around the tail.

After casting the spell to help Ajax, Father Goram looked over at the blade. It was already about half way free from its wooden prison. He opened the tome. "Great!" he said. "No Table of Contents!" As he looked once again at the blade, Father Goram had an inspiration... though there wasn't any guarantee it would work. He closed the tome and slammed it down on the hilt of the blade, driving it back into the wood of his desk. He looked underneath and could see the animated tip sticking out, trying to work its way back up through the wood. Father Goram took the tome, laid it flat on the underside of the desk with the back binding facing the blade, and slammed the tome forward. Once, twice, three times. The tip of the blade had been bent parallel to the bottom of the desk. "That should hold you for a while," the priest said as he straightened back up and opened the tome.

Father Goram frowned. He had little time, and the tome was large... perhaps a thousand pages. There came a disturbance from across the room. He looked up and saw Ajax chasing his tail. It would've been funny if it wasn't so damn serious.

"Come here, Ajax," he said.

The dire wolf walked over to the priest. The burn on his tail didn't look grave, but all burns are painful. "MEDICAMENTUM MAERORUM," Father Goram said as he laid a gentle hand on the furless and blistered tail. A rich blue light arched from the priests' hand and ran up the tail and encompassed Ajax's entire body. The burn healed as well as all the bumps, bruises, scrapes, and cuts Ajax had suffered in his tussle with the obsidian blade.

Father Goram scratched behind one of Ajax's ears and said, "Watch over our young guest." Ajax left to do the priest's bidding. Father Goram ran his hands through his hair. "How am I going to find what I need in time?" he asked himself as he leafed through the enormous tome.

"Magic," he exclaimed out loud as a thought came to him. "Yes, magic!"

Father Goram closed the tome. "But what's the key to unlocking your powers?" Then he remembered how the tome seemed to appear just when he needed it the most. "That couldn't have been a coincidence," he said. The tome glowed slightly for but a moment... but that was all Father Gorman needed to confirm his suspicions. At least he hoped he was right. If not, he was dead.

The entire desk began to move back and forth as the obsidian blade increased its efforts to free itself. Father Goram slid his chair back and picked up a marble cheese tray, sweeping the forgotten food to the floor, to act as a shield... just in case. As the blade moved more and more violently, the tome exuded power. The intensity of the tome's magic grew as the blade worked its way free. After a few moments, the blade rose, unhindered, and turned its now straightened point towards Father Goram.

Determined the priest wouldn't get away this time, it wasted no time flashing forward. But the tome was faster. Father Goram watched in fascination as the tome opened, flew up, engulfed the obsidian blade, closed, and slammed back down onto the desk.

"Yes!" Father Goram yelled as he pumped his fist into the air. "That's how you exorcise a demon, by the gods!" Then he collapsed back into his chair, closed his eyes, and took a deep breath.

Cameron knocked on the open entrance door to Father Goram's apartment. "Anybody home?" he called out. "Horatio, I've brought someone to meet you. It's the sorcerer, Eric the Black, and he's agreed to help. Can we come in?"

Father Goram opened his eyes. "Certainly, Cameron, the doors aren't going to stop you."

Cameron entered the great room, followed closely by a tall, dark-haired elf dressed in homespun clothes but with an elaborately decorated cloak. Cameron stopped and looked around. "Horatio, you really do need to talk to your housekeeper," Cameron said. "This place is a mess."

Ajax growled. Father Goram quickly got up and rushed over to place himself between the snarling dire wolf and the two newcomers.

Lessien awoke with a start. It was late afternoon. The long, sleepless night and a physically demanding morning had proven to be too much for her. She had fallen asleep. Lessien closed her eyes and took a deep breath. She was sore, tired, hungry, thirsty, and cold... the things her father tried to ensure she'd never have to experience. Times had changed, however, and Lessien wouldn't let a little discomfort stop her. Above all else, she was her father's daughter. Above all else, she was a queen.

Lessien suddenly had the sensation she was being watched. Lessien opened her eyes and looked over her shoulder. A floating eyeball was staring at her. She looked around and saw hundreds of eyeballs in her tree, and each of them were also staring at her. Lessien knew this was a sorcerer's spell... just as she knew her hideaway in the tree had been discovered. She looked out from her perch and saw a squad of cavalry ride out of the village on her side of the river and head in her direction. Lessien looked over her shoulder. A barge had landed just downriver and was unloading troops.

"I'm trapped," she whispered.

The white-clad female elf walked through a well-maintained field of corn. Draped over her shoulders was a spectacular cloak which seemed to be all colors yet none. Around her neck she wore a necklace that resembled an eight-sided star surrounded by a field of smaller four-sided stars. Like her cloak, the star symbol changed colors as well. The effect of this color change, however, made it seem like rays were radiating outward from the center and intersecting the other, smaller stars.

The stalks of corn had grown to about eight feet... a remarkable yield, yet not too surprising considering the richness of the earth. As the figure carefully moved through the rows of corn, careful not to damage any of the plants, she was drawn to the center of the field. It was off her present course, but she was curious and it wouldn't take much time to investigate her intuition.

In the center of the field was a large boulder. The priestess studied the rock. The corn had been planted around the boulder, and with good reason... it wasn't a rock. It was composed of an unusual metal... denser than any other material on this world except for diamond. It was too heavy by far for manual removal. She surmised, as she used her hand to examine the boulder, it'd be highly resistant to sorcerer's magic. "Not from this world," she whispered. "But then again, neither am I."

The boulder suddenly shivered. The priestess backed up a step, then tentatively placed her hand back on the surface. It was now warm. "A creation stone," she whispered, amazed.

The priestess stepped back even further and released her staff, which hovered in the air by her side. She made symbols in the air... symbols that materialized as small points of light. The boulder glowed with a brilliant white luminosity. "ESSE UNUM CUM UNIVERSE ITERUM," the priestess chanted. "CONVERTERETUR UNUSQUISQUE A SOMNO." The points of light slowly drifted down and landed on the boulder.

The boulder lifted out of the ground. Though very heavy, it wasn't as large as its weight would indicate... roughly twenty feet in diameter. Several two foot long appendages, shaped like the triangle blades of a large knife, appeared around it. After it had risen above the ground, it began to spin quickly. The sharp appendages disappeared in a whirlwind of speed... all that could be seen was an outline around the boulder. The spinning stopped, and a mouth appeared on the boulder.

"I'm Maedhros Nénmacil," it said.

The priestess bowed. "And I'm..." she said.

"You're Nefertari Arntuile," Maedhros Nénmacil interrupted. "I've been waiting a long time for you to make your appearance, StarSinger."

CHAPTER NINE

Elanesse

The nature of evil: insidious and cunning with the capacity to ride the ebb and flow of time. It's not real in that it has physical form or substance... but it exists nevertheless in the hearts and minds of both mortal and immortal souls. Evil's transcendence is not always guaranteed, however... for righteousness will never give up its place in the hierarchy of the spirit.

-Book of the Unveiled

"It appears the city is no longer our refuge," Mariko said as she listened to the sound of worgs howling.

"Indeed," Azriel agreed.

Elrond closed his eyes and drifted into a momentary trance. "Elanesse can protect us," he said. "Even as she does Emmy and Romulus. But first we need to get to the 'Lorin-Galaduiriel'. The worgs won't go there."

"The what?" Tangus asked.

"The Tree of Golden Radiance," Elrond said.

"Where?"

"Out of the city," Elrond replied. "Northeast and back into the forest."

"But..." Max said.

"It's our only chance, friend Max," Lester said. "At least until we've rested. From the sounds of it, there's far too many worgs even for the likes of us... at least in our present exhausted condition."

Tangus nodded. "Everybody mount up!" he shouted. "Mariko, ride behind Kristen. Arbellason's big and strong enough to carry the both of you."

"I can run," Mariko said.

Kristen shook her head. "No, not this time."

Mariko looked at Kristen and Tangus. She could tell Tangus didn't like the idea even if he was the one who had suggested it. He probably would've preferred she run as she suggested, but Kristen had made her wishes known and he wouldn't contradict his wife in this. Besides, Kristen was correct. She didn't stand a chance against the number of worgs converging on their position. Though she knew she had forfeited her life the moment she chose Emmy over Nightshade, now was not the time to make that sacrifice.

Mariko nodded. "Very well."

Tangus approached her as everyone else mounted their horses. "If you do anything to hurt Kristen, I'll not hesitate to destroy you."

Mariko scowled. "My destruction will come soon enough, ranger," she said.

Tangus stood where he was for a few seconds after Mariko walked away. "I wonder what she meant by that?" he asked himself.

When the party made their escape from the warehouse, the worgs were already in the east side of the city. The nearest group was only a few hundred feet behind. As the worgs pursued, they howled to their brothers and sisters. Answering howls came from all around.

"They're going to intercept us," Tangus yelled over the beat of the horse's hooves on the hard-packed dirt.

"It's as if they have a strategy," Lester shouted back. "Most unusual!"

"How can the forest support this many worgs?" Jennifer asked.

"It can't, lassie," Azriel called back.

The two packhorses were released to buy time, but most of the worgs passed them by... and those that didn't only stopped long enough to kill the horses and rip the supplies apart before beginning their pursuit once again. Not too unsurprisingly, the horses initially didn't appreciate being coaxed by their masters to run away. Each mount had been trained for war. They were proud, unafraid, and willing to show their prowess against the evil wolves... their main adversary since the dawn of time. But when they caught the scent of the sheer number of worgs chasing them, they were more than happy to obey their master's commands to run. And run they did... literally flying like the wind. For the next few moments no one made a sound as the horses and their riders made the mad dash to avoid the worgs.

As they rounded the corner of a large building, they saw the northeast gate. But what they saw next turned their relief into trepidation. Streaming from an open gate and into the city was a group of fifteen saber cats... and from an opening in the city's walls on the north side a pack of nine mountain wolves. The saber cats were four feet tall at the shoulders, weighed on average six hundred and fifty pounds, and had two twelve-inch long, razor-sharp front canines. They were quick, deadly, and fearless predators. The mountain wolves were even more impressive. Though not quite as big as the dire wolves of InnisRos, they weren't far from it... four and a half feet at the shoulders and five hundred pounds. Both species could only be found in the mountains. Unlike the worgs, however, these newcomers weren't known to be evil or aggressive against the civilized races of Aster... until now.

Tangus held up his hand to stop everyone. They had been cornered. "Elrond, can Elanesse give us a hand?" Tangus asked.

"The cemetery. It's sacred ground and not far east," Elrond responded.

Tangus didn't wait for an explanation. It was their only option at this point. That... or death. "Move! Move! Move!" he yelled as he slapped Arbelleson's rump. No one argued, but Tangus could see they wouldn't be fast enough to avoid the saber cats coming from the northeast gate. They were simply too fast and agile. As he had done the previous day, he put Smoke's reins in his mouth, grabbed his bow, and placed an arrow in the first saber cat's eye, bringing it down for good. His next two arrows, however, missed the nimble saber cats. As Tangus reached back into his quiver, he came up empty. Fortunately, the death of the first had made the others more cautious. They slowed their approach.

As Smoke sprinted towards the cemetery, trailing the others, Tangus replaced his bow with two scimitars. In front of him was Azriel. His horse, not as fast as a mustang, was lathered already falling behind. Tangus watched in horror as one of the saber cats got close enough to jump on the horse and slide both its long, front canines into the back of the neck. The bite severed the horse's spine and Azriel, his horse, and the saber cat crashed down in front of Tangus. As Smoke ran past, Tangus extended an arm, careful to keep the scimitar pointed towards the ground, for Azriel to grab. But Azriel was too busy killing the saber cat with his battleaxe to notice.

Tangus whirled Smoke around to make another pass at Azriel... but Max's horse ran past him towards Azriel. Max was hunched low in the saddle with his arm stretched out. A volley of three arrows fired by Safire, Lester, and Jennifer killed a saber cat and wounded another. It had given Azriel and Max a few more seconds of precious time.

"Grab my arm, you hard-headed son of a mountain goat!" Max screamed as he rode up to Azriel.

Azriel was untying a saddlebag. "Damn it! It killed my horse," he cursed. "I liked that horse!"

"That's not all they're going to kill," Max yelled back as he brought his horse to a stop.

At that moment the worgs came out of the darkness like a rolling tidal wave. As Tangus moved Smoke forward to cover Max and Azriel, a ball of fire erupted above the first few worgs. Several were incinerated and several others set on fire. The saber cats stopped, startled. But they didn't hold for long. Tangus, momentarily blinded, squinted his eyes just in time to see Max and Azriel ride up to him. As they did so, they slowed just enough so Azriel could grab Smoke by the halter and lead him and Tangus back to the others. Everyone broke once again for the cemetery. Elrond trailed slightly behind and used his enchanted staff to summon more deadly magic. When they rode into the cemetery, they found themselves immersed in an unnatural fog.

"Attack! Attack! Attack!"

"Don't listen to them. You must go back to sleep."

The Purged cringed. The voices that had been beleaguering it ever since awakening after thousands of years of sleep had become shrill and unwanted. The voices in its mind didn't need to encourage... it knew what was important. As for the voice in its heart... it served as a counterbalance. As a result, a war raged inside the Purge. It was the same war that raged in every conscious being. It was a war engrained in the very psyche of the universe... good versus evil. The Purge knew without doubt which side of the war it fell... evil. The imperative to murder empaths was intrinsic, the intended by-product in the formulation of its creation. But the Purge sometimes wondered what it would be like to listen to the voice in its heart instead.

The Purge redoubled its efforts to retrieve the last empath. But now it didn't want to kill her. It wanted her to meld with it... to let her join with the other already in its heart. Perhaps the last empath could show the way to peace. The Purge, after three thousand years, was tired and wanted to rid itself of the conflict inside.

Then everything changed. There was a different 'feel' to the reality it had known since that first night when the empaths were slaughtered. Something had occurred to free the city of Elanesse from its self-imposed prison. Elanesse had been unchained from her guilt. Even more disconcerting, however, was that the Purge felt a strong, potentially lethal, new threat emerge. Though uncertain, the identity of this new danger seemed somewhat familiar. But regardless of its confusion, one thing was unmistakable... the Purge knew this new menace would soon be coming. For the first time since it was created, the Purge felt the need to defend itself. For the first time, the Purge felt afraid. Forgotten was the peace the Purge briefly thought it wanted. It called on its human and animal thralls to return and defend it against this inevitable attack.

The fog in the cemetery engulfed them. As soon as they entered, everything went silent. Visibility was only about ten feet. Everyone dismounted and carefully led their horses around gravestones and small sepulchers.

"Elanesse says the fog will stop our attackers from sensing and hearing us," Elrond said. He kept his voice low. "It won't stop them from entering, however. The 'Lorin-Galaduiriel' is over the city wall bordering this cemetery and about a mile north by northwest."

"A mile through the forest, the natural habitat of the worg," Max replied. "Wonderful."

Tangus stopped. "Elrond, is there a gate through the walls?"

Elrond paused. "Elanesse says no."

"Then we've only managed to box ourselves in," Safire exclaimed, "unless we leave the horses behind."

"I'm not too keen about that," Kristen responded as she patted Arbelleson's neck.

"It may be our only alternative," Mariko said. "That, or find a place to hide. I don't think our adversaries will leave anytime soon, so hiding will only delay the inevitable."

There was silence as each person thought about the problems they faced. Finally Tangus broke the stillness. "Let's move forward and see what we can find."

But other than gravestones and mausoleums, there was nothing to distinguish this graveyard from any other. The wall that bordered the very eastern point of the city... and the end of the cemetery... were fifteen feet high with a turret raising another ten feet above that. The three-story turret was empty except for vines that had infiltrated through narrow arrow slits which faced outward and into the forest.

"Elrond, can you use magic to get over the wall?" Tangus asked.

Elrond nodded. "Aye, my staff can do that. And I have other usable magical spells as well. But I can't get the horses over... at least not from here. They're simply too large and too heavy. What we need is a hole through the wall. I can do it... but it's very powerful magic and Elanesse warned against that. She said there are... spirits... in this graveyard that wouldn't appreciate the disturbance."

Tangus shook his head. "I don't care," he said. "We need to get out quickly. We don't know how much time we have or where the worgs are. With this fog, they could be as close as ten feet."

"You don't understand, Tangus," Elrond replied. "These spirits will be worse than any worg, wolf, or saber cat." Tangus stared at Elrond. "Look," Elrond continued, "we've faced all kinds of phantoms in our lives - ghosts, wraiths, spectres - but none of that could even remotely prepare us for what lies here if disturbed. Elanesse gave me a mental picture. It scared the life out of me."

"This city's full of surprises. Why didn't you say something sooner?" Max asked.

Everybody looked at Elrond. "I didn't want alarm anyone unnecessarily," he replied. "It's not about awakening spirits. That's only how Elanesse interprets it. But rather, it's about the deceased and their demons. I don't understand how, but something about how elves consecrated this ground when they built Elanesse caused a link to be formed. It's a connection between this world and the dead who are buried here... or something akin to that." Elrond shook his head. "The consequences if those creatures I saw in Elanesse's vision were ever unleashed... well, I don't even want to think about it."

"Creatures?" Jennifer said. "We all have personal demons, Elrond, but they're not real to anyone but ourselves."

"I think what Elrond is trying to say, lassie, is that they ARE real here," Azriel responded.

Elrond nodded.

"That makes sense, dear," Kristen agreed. "My clerical senses have been assaulted ever since we walked in, but I couldn't quite place my finger on it until I heard Elrond's warning."

"You led us into a dangerous dead end, Elrond," Tangus said.

Elrond grimaced. "It's our only choice, Tangus. We barely made it as it was."

Tangus drove his two scimitars into the dirt and drew his bow. Jennifer handed him a fist full of arrows which he put in his quiver, less one. "Next time, Elrond, be a bit more forthcoming," he said. "Be ready to get Kristen..."

"Tangus, no!" Kristen said.

Tangus looked at Kristen. "Not this time, love. Emmy needs you too much. Elrond, be ready to use your magic to get Kristen out of here if this starts to go badly for us."

Elrond nodded.

As the sun rose in the eastern sky, the fog created by Elanesse lifted. Everyone stood ready as they awaited the imminent attack... but nothing happened. The worgs, wolves, and saber cats were nowhere to be seen.

Lester approached Tangus. "Perhaps I should take a little stroll and see what's going on."

Tangus shook his head. "I'd prefer you didn't, Lester. We need stealth. That armor makes you slow and noisy. And though it might keep you alive against three or four, you wouldn't stand a chance against what's out there." Tangus turned and looked at Elrond and Kristen. "Either of you two have a suitable spell?" he asked. "Kristen, maybe your doves?"

"Do that thing where you use an eyeball, Elrond," Max said excitedly. Turning to look at Kristen, he said, "Usually it's me that gets to do all the scouting. I'm pretty much everything Lester isn't."

Azriel laughed. "Aye, Max... everything Lester isn't, that's for sure. He's a knight and you're a thief!"

Max shook his head. "Ignore him. Anyway, Elrond learned this new magic spell where he makes this eyeball appear and then uses it to see what's ahead. It's quite remarkable."

Kristen smiled at Max's enthusiasm. "I think we should see the eyeball at work," she said as she winked at Max. "My doves are sweet things, but they tend to be a bit scatterbrained and easily frightened. Besides, I can't see through their eyes." Kristen looked back at Max and whispered conspiratorially, "I really only conjure them during certain ceremonies. It's impressive but mostly just for show."

"Very well," Elrond said as he opened one of his book of spells.

"I thought you knew it," Tangus commented.

Elrond nodded, but didn't take his eyes off his spell book as he turned pages. "As Max said, I only just learned it a few weeks ago. I need to verify the incantations. Don't worry, it's all here. Ah... got it."

Elrond studied the spell and then closed the book and put it away. He handed his sorcerer staff to Max and chanted while making symbols in the air with his very nimble fingers. Loose dirt rose from the ground and coalesced into a small sphere. Elrond finished the spell and waved an open hand over the floating ball of dirt. It turned into an eyeball, winked at Elrond, and left to do its creator's bidding.

No one said or did anything to interrupt Elrond as he concentrated on his connection with his spell. Suddenly Elrond said, "Well I'll be damned."

"What do you see?" Tangus asked.

Elrond focused on Tangus. "I think you need to see this. It's like a migration," he said as he took the reins of his horse and walked towards the cemetery entrance. Everyone else did the same.

Elrond was correct... it was something that had to be seen to be believed. Worgs were streaming in from the eastern gate and going west. They were quiet and moving with no apparent will of their own... like automatons. Even at this distance everyone could see the eyes of the worgs had rolled back into their heads to a point that only the whites showed.

"That's a lot of worgs," Jennifer remarked.

"They're under the control of the Purge," Kristen whispered, fearing that any loud noise might break the trance that had the worgs under its power. "It calls them to it." Kristen looked at Tangus. "How do we fight through so many worgs?"

"We'll figure that out when the time comes," Tangus replied as he stared at the unusual procession. "First things first. When this, whatever it is, is finished, we need to make our way to the 'Lorin-Galaduiriel' and find Emmy. Then sleep. We're all dead on our feet."

As they moved through the city, they came across a few stragglers. Like the others, each straggler was under the control of the Purge and paid them no heed. Outside Elanesse's walls, the forest was completely devoid of other animal life. As hard as the three rangers searched, none of them could find any sign that animals, such as deer, rabbits, and squirrels, were in the area.

"It looks like we'll be living on nuts and berries for a while," Safire said. "The animals living here before the arrival of the worgs have long since left for a safer domain."

"We can live off the fruit of the 'Lorin-Galaduiriel' for a time," Elrond said.

"Oh great!" Max grumbled. "I don't like fruit or berries."

Lester laughed. "Except for peaches, friend Max."

Max nodded and smiled. "Yes," he said wistfully. "Except for peaches."

The 'Lorin-Galaduiriel'... or 'Tree of Golden Radiance'... was a short hike away through a deserted forest. When it appeared, it became clear why it bore the name. The leaves were a spectacular golden shade and shined brilliantly in the mid-morning sunlight. It rose two hundred feet into the sky, easily eclipsing even the tallest trees in the forest. Like the willow, its branches filled with glistening leaves bent downward to the ground. The branches were thick enough to conceal everything within its perimeter.

"Elanesse wishes us peace and tranquility," Elrond said.

The branches before everyone shivered and several parted. Emmy, with tears in her eyes, and Romulus, were standing in the opening.

It had been about six hours since the party found refuge with the 'Lorin-Galaduiriel'. True to Elrond and Elanesse's word, they were safe and secure... though Tangus still felt the necessity of maintaining a guarded vigilance. The fruit of the magnificent tree was plentiful, delicious, and nourishing. Max decided he liked it even better than peaches. There was also a small spring of cold, pure water that bubbled up at the base of the tree. The only thing missing was coffee. Elrond wouldn't allow a fire to be built so close to the tree.

The reunion between Kristen, Emmy, and Romulus was heartfelt and emotional. But it was a bittersweet moment... the loss of Bitts keenly felt by all. For a while Emmy stayed near Tangus, holding his hand and comforting him as best she could. Though she didn't know the story, she knew he was hurting.

Without the rush of battle awareness to sustain him... without the need to keep his mind focused on the survival of his loved ones and friends... Tangus' mind turned to Bitts. Tangus knew he needed to work through his grief. Wide awake, he took the first watch, using the time alone to process his feelings and put them into perspective. By the time Tangus finally slept, the pain had been packaged up and placed in a compartment in his mind. For Tangus, this helped to dull the pain. It also allowed the memory of Bitts to roam free with all the other memories of those Tangus had lost during his lifetime... memories that were a great comfort to him.

After everyone had rested, they used the next few hours to 'feel normal', as Lester so succinctly put it. Kristen approached Tangus and sat beside him. They both watched silently as Azriel tried to bounce Emmy on his knee. Emmy was none too pleased. It only took a couple of hard yanks on his beard to restore her dignity, much to the delight of everyone else.

"Do you want to talk about Bitts?" Kristen asked.

Tangus looked at her and took her hand. "There's really not much to talk about. The Purge turned Bitts against me and I had to kill him."

Kristen leaned her head on Tangus' shoulder. "I'm so sorry."

Tangus shrugged. "What I killed wasn't Bitts. He was already gone."

For a few moments there was only silence between the two as they watched the others. The few hours of rest they were able to catch seemed to buoy everybody's spirits.

"Sweetheart," Tangus said, "I'm coping with it."

"Sometimes we need a little help," Kristen said. "I know I did when my mother died."

Tangus kissed Kristen on the top of her head but said nothing else.

The Purge had Lieutenant Arnish pull his men back instead of continuing their pursuit of the last empath. Like a rabid animal, Arnish was insane with the desire to slaughter whoever stood in his way... but the Purge wouldn't give him free rein to do so. Instead, it ordered him and his human ensemble to establish a defensive perimeter around one of the many structures in west Elanesse. Arnish was too far gone in his madness to question or wonder why.

The predator worgs in the Forest of the Fey, as well as worgs, wolves, and saber cats from the surrounding mountains and forestlands, had also been influenced by the Purge and were by now inside the city proper, deployed by the Purge in strategic areas throughout the city. The Purge knew the last empath would come, and it now had eyes and ears everywhere. The Purge wouldn't be taken unaware.

"Attack! Attack! Attack!"

"Don't listen to them. You must stop your war on the empath and go back to sleep."

The voices still pleaded their case, still attempting to draw the Purge in one direction or another. The Purge became angry... it had reached the end of its patience with those inside that would tell it what to do. But it couldn't quiet them. They were as integral to its nature as the black tar-like metal liquid that made up its body.

"Attack! Attack! Attack!"

"Don't listen to them. You must stop your war on the empath and go back to sleep."

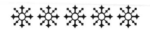

"Laddie, that's a huge problem!" Azriel exclaimed. "If the Purge can force Bitts to turn on you, his lifetime friend and master, what chance do you think we'll have against those other critters that answered its call? You saw them... they were marching like a four-legged army. Enough to blanket the city. And they don't feel any constraint."

Tangus looked at Azriel. "Bitts showed no constraint either," he said.

"Maybe, maybe not," Azriel replied. "Maybe Bitts delayed just long enough to give you the opportunity to end him before he ended you. Those worgs we fought at the river were like... well, I guess more vicious than any worg I've ever encountered. They were absolute killing machines." The more Azriel talked, the more animated he became. "They held nothing back! No worg will attack after being cut up so badly it can barely stand! They run! But not these! And did you see their eyes? Completely white! It gave me the creeps! No laddie, what you propose is suicide."

Everyone else had remained silent as Tangus and Azriel discussed strategy. Both were right. No one had a better option than Tangus... but everyone also knew it would be extremely dangerous.

Tangus had drawn a rough map of Elanesse, with the help of Elrond and his bond to the city, in the dirt. "Azriel, we don't have to cover a lot of ground," Tangus said as he used a stick to point. "We come in from the forest south of west Elanesse. The Pyramid of the Purge is right there... maybe a few hundred yards. Azriel, it's the closest we're going to get without going through the city."

"That's so, Tangus. But we have to move through this open area," Azriel said as he used his own stick to point. "Not to mention this whole area will be extremely well guarded. The Purge has to know that's where it's most vulnerable to attack."

"Perhaps if I ran interference?" Mariko said.

"And me," Max added.

Mariko looked at Max, surprised. He smiled back at her in return. "Yes... and Max," she said. "We could come in about... here... from the east next to this group of buildings and create a diversion," she said as she pointed to the dirt map.

"That's the healing complex," Elrond said. "And it might be too close to the Purge to draw enough of them off."

"Don't worry about that, Elrond," Mariko said. "I... Max and I will have them thinking a whole army is coming."

Kristen shook her head. "Tangus, I don't like it. Emmy is far too exposed. And even if Max and Mariko draw enough off for us to make it, what do you suppose the Purge has inside the pyramid to oppose us. A lot, I suspect."

"What do you suggest, Kristen?" Safire asked.

"That's just it... I don't have a better idea," Kristen replied. "But I agree with Azriel. This plan is too dangerous by far."

Tangus sighed as he and everyone else studied the map in silence. Suddenly Max said, "Tunnels!"

"What?" Azriel said.

"Every city we've ever been to has had an underground sewer system," Max said. "But some of them also had tunnels BELOW the sewers... some so aged they've been forgotten. As old as Elanesse is, I wonder if there's a system of ancient tunnels below her."

"You might be on to something," Tangus said.

"Aye, laddie," Azriel agreed.

Tangus directed his attention to Elrond... but by the blank look in Elrond's eyes, Tangus and everyone else could tell he was already communicating with Elanesse. When Elrond broke contact with the city, Tangus asked, "Well?"

Elrond nodded and smiled. "Elanesse said there's so many tunnels below her it's a wonder she hasn't collapsed."

THE STRUGGLE FOR INNOCENCE

CHAPTER TEN

InnisRos

Any adversary will remain dangerous as long as it lives in darkness. It must first be exposed to the light of familiarity before it can ever be truly subjugated.

-Book of the Unveiled

Father Goram sat at his desk in his study and stared at a large tome...*"Demon Possession: A Thesis on the Identification of a Demon Possessed Object and the Means by Which the Demon can be Exorcised"*... the very same tome that had saved his life just a few hours before. His apartment had been cleaned and the only signs of the morning struggle was the scorched rug lying before the fireplace.

Autumn had come home as soon as she learned of the assassination attempt on her husband. Though relieved everything appeared to be in order, she wasn't in a very good mood. At the moment she was in a guestroom with Sandis. Ajax, his dignity only a little damaged, left to be with his family. He had, however, sent Findley and Razor back to keep an eye on things. Both of the dire wolves kept a close watch on the entrance door instead of their normal practice of snoozing in front of the fireplace. Even the smell of venison stew, which was cooking in the kitchen, didn't disturb their vigilance. Ajax made sure they both understood the severity of the situation.

Father Goram looked up as Autumn walked from the back of the apartment. "How is Sandis?" he asked.

Autumn went over to the kitchen to check the stew. "She'll be fine. She just needs rest. I still think she should be recovering in a dungeon cell."

"Relax, dear. She was used by Mordecai."

Autumn sat down on a chair by the side of Father Goram's desk. "Yes, Horatio... used to attack you," she said. "What other secrets might she have learned?"

Father Goram looked up and smiled. "She's just the housekeeper, Autumn. I guard my secrets much closer than that."

Autumn looked none the happier.

Father Goram took her hands in his. "Okay, here's what I believe," he said. "Sandis was recruited by Mordecai for one purpose... to kill me. I'm not sure what hold he had over her, but I'm fairly certain she wasn't bought with money or promises of power like Vayl. In the end, she couldn't do it and almost paid with her life. That speaks to her character. We'll find out more when we interview her."

Autumn nodded.

Father Goram continued. "Ordinarily Mordecai would never have made such a brazen attempt... too many things could go wrong and he'd risk being implicated. The queen wouldn't hesitate to put him on trial..."

"But with the Queen charged with murder and on the run, he no longer has that concern," Autumn finished for her husband.

"Exactly," Father Goram replied. "If she were still in custody, he probably wouldn't even bother with me. He's about to be the king. But with her in the wind, he understands he must get her back to stand trial. That's the only way he'll be able to legitimize his reign. He also has to know the monastery is the Queen's last refuge... and I'll fight to keep her and put her back on the throne. I have many allies... enough to bring about civil war. It makes sense he'd try to assassinate me in the hope the monastery could be brought back in line without further complications. Hell, that's what I'd do if I were him."

"No you wouldn't," Autumn said flatly, as if she were stating a mere fact.

Father Goram laughed. "Well," he said after he reached over and kissed Autumn on the forehead, "perhaps I wouldn't. Then again, don't underestimate what I'm capable of in the defense of my loved ones... or the innocent."

Autumn reached over and ran her hand over the gold and silver-plated front cover of the tome. "Where did you get this?"

Father Goram opened the tome and leafed through pages. "It's curious you should ask. I've been trying to work out that very thing for the last hour. It seems like I've always had it, yet I can't quite remember how I actually got it. Strange."

"Yes it is," Autumn answered. "I think this requires a bit more... what's wrong?"

Father Goram stared at the open book. "The Maglor Telperiën," he whispered.

Autumn, confused, looked at the page Father Goram had the book opened to. On it was an extremely lifelike sketch of a black dagger. As she watched, it seemed to move, as if it was real and trying to escape from the pages of the book. It reminded Autumn of a fly fluttering its wings in a desperate attempt to break away from the web of a spider. Mesmerized, Autumn reached toward the blade. Father Goram quickly snatched her hand away. "No, no, no, my dear," he said. "You must never touch the obsidian blade. It's death for a cleric."

"But it's only a picture," Autumn replied.

Father Goram shook his head. "No, it's more than that. That's the same obsidian blade that attacked me. I don't think the tome destroyed it, but rather captured it."

"Are there other pictures in the tome?" Autumn asked.

Father Goram nodded. "Yes... but none of them move."

"Does that mean they're not dangerous?"

"I don't know, but it definitely calls for more research," Father Goram replied. "Off hand, I'd have to say the magic of the book captures demon possessed items and engages the demon within until expelled, making the item inert." As both watched, it appeared the obsidian blade was struggling less.

Autumn stared at the blade on the page of the tome. While she watched, it made one last effort to break free, and then was still. Before she could stop

Father Goram, he reached down and tentatively touched the picture. Her heart stopped. But nothing happened.

"As I suspected," he said. "The blade is no more... nothing but a picture in a book."

Autumn was angry... angry and frightened out of her mind. "How could you take such a chance!" she railed.

Father Goram was taken aback by Autumn's vehemence. "I didn't mean to frighten you, my love, but I was certain it no longer poised a threat."

"You shouldn't be taking such risks," Autumn replied.

Father Goram didn't respond. He knew Autumn was right... it WAS a huge risk. But something about the tome assured him there was no danger. Father Goram wondered how that could be. He closed the tome, tucked it under his arm, and got up. "Let's secure this in the bedroom wall-safe. Then I think it's time to question Sandis."

Mordecai was anxious as he made his way to the council chamber. The demon Nightshade/Amberley walked at this side.

"What troubles you, Mordecai?" Nightshade asked. "We have the Queen and tomorrow she'll be back to stand trial. Her escape was just a momentary inconvenience. Everything is once again going to plan," she told him while thinking she must be more proactive the next time she helps the Queen to escape. The Queen must be with Goram when the monastery's finally taken. As long as she remains alive, Goram won't capitulate and war will be inevitable. Only a war between Mordecai and Goram would suffice if her and her father's plans are to be successful. Nightshade smiled at the thought of the bloodshed this will cause.

Mordecai stopped and looked at Nightshade. "That meddling priest is going to be a problem," he said.

Nightshade shook her head. "We knew that from the beginning. That's why we march on the monastery, is it not?"

"I've been having second thoughts about that," Mordecai remarked.

"Really," Nightshade replied, though her voice hid her true feelings.

Mordecai nodded. "Goram has allies," he said. "Lots of allies. Marching on him could spark civil war."

"So what, Mordecai," Nightshade exclaimed. "Once the Queen's convicted, you'll be the rightful king of InnisRos. He won't have a legal right to challenge or deny your ascendency to the throne. If he attempts to stop any part of that, or if he attempts to whisk her away again, he'll be a traitor. Would his allies still stand behind him then? Remember, many of the allies Goram has were also allies of the Second Councilor. Will they stay with Goram and the Queen if they think she was responsible for Erin Mirie's death... particularly if we fabricate evidence implicating that he and the Queen colluded together? You must march on Goram. If you don't, he'll be a constant thorn in your side. You'll never be able to secure your rule."

"And if you're wrong, Nightshade? I don't want to rule a kingdom that's in ruins because of civil war," Mordecai replied.

"It's just cutting off the deadwood," Nightshade responded. "Goram has to go."

"But..."

Nightshade stopped Mordecai with a slap across the face that sent him flying off his feet. Mordecai's back slammed against the opposite wall and he slid down until he was sitting on the floor. His jaw was broken and the breath knocked out of him from the impact. Nightshade stood over Mordecai as he struggled to breathe.

"Remember we have an agreement, Mordecai," she hissed angrily. "This will be my kingdom as well as yours. Don't let your mortal weaknesses cloud your judgment." Suddenly she smiled as if nothing had happened. Nightshade reach a hand down and caressed his jaw, healing it. "Is there anything else you wish to discuss?"

Mordecai carefully got back on his feet. His head was still ringing from the force of the blow... and though Nightshade healed his jaw, his whole body still ached. "You do that again, Nightshade, and I WILL banish you," he said. "In this realm I'm your master. You had best keep that in mind."

Nightshade bowed. "Certainly, Mordecai. I don't know what came over me. This mortal body is so... emotional."

Mordecai stared at Nightshade for a few moments and then turned on his heel and walked away.

Nightshade didn't follow immediately. Inside she raged with the desire to strip the soul from his body and suck it dry. She had nothing but pure and unadulterated hatred for him. "Your day of reckoning is soon upon you, Mordecai," she whispered to herself before following him into the council chamber where the council awaited. "You'll feel my wrath and beg for a quick death. But it's too late for that. Too late by far."

At Olberon Naval Base, the Commander-in-Chief of Her Majesty's Navy, Admiral Tári Shilannia, was sitting at her desk reviewing fleet disposition orders when she heard a sharp rap on her door. Marine Commander-General Aubrey Feynral walked in. "Care for a drink, Tári?" he said as he went to the bar and poured two glasses of whiskey.

Admiral Shilannia looked at the documents scattered about her desk and nodded. "I could use a break," she replied as she got up and went over to sit in one of the padded chairs in front of her huge marble fireplace. General Feynral handed one of the drinks to her before taking his own seat. Admiral Shilannia raised an eyebrow... both glasses were full.

"To soften the blow?" she asked, indicating the full glass of whiskey.

General Feynral frowned. "Perhaps," he responded as he raised his own glass. "Salute," he said.

After the toast, General Feynral got down to business. "They captured the Queen," he said without preamble.

"I know," Admiral Shilannia replied as she took a sip of whiskey. "She's being held upriver at Ashakadi."

General Feynral wasn't surprised at this admission. "Do you think she's guilty?"

Admiral Shilannia shook her head. "Of course not, Aubrey. Regardless of the evidence, what's her motive? Councilor Mirie was the Queen's strongest ally on the council. I've also seen the two together. They didn't relate only as subject to sovereign... but also as friends. And even if you were to remove all of that, the Queen is as noble and honorable as her father. She wouldn't have anyone murdered. No, my friend, she is being framed by Mordecai."

General Feynral nodded. "That's pretty much the same conclusion I reached," he said as he reached inside his tunic, pulled out a folded parchment, and gave it to Admiral Shilannia. "My new orders."

Admiral Shilannia placed her drink on a table and read. "I'm not surprised. He wants your five thousand Marines." The Admiral re-folded the parchment. "I received orders as well."

"What are you going to do?"

"I've already done it... I threw them into the fire," Admiral Shilannia replied as she did the same to the General's.

"But..." he said.

"Relax, Aubrey. I take full responsibility," Admiral Shilannia said as she took another sip of her drink. "I'll not let Mordecai issue orders to MY Marines until he's formally sworn in as king... and maybe not even then."

General Feynral frowned. "This puts us in a very precarious position, Tári," he said. "As First Councilor he has the right to order any or all of InnisRos' military contingent. Refusal would be considered treason."

"Not if Mordecai's orders are no longer valid," Admiral Shilannia replied. "Not if Mordecai is himself the traitor."

"That's not for us to decide."

Admiral Shilannia gulped down the last of her drink. "Then who, Aubrey? Who gets to make that decision? The Army? Please... their generals belong to Mordecai. I have it on good authority he pays them quite handsomely." Admiral Shilannia leaned towards General Feynral. "Aubrey, you're a warrior... the best InnisRos has to offer. That's what you're so very good at. But I'm the Naval Commander-in-Chief at least partly because I have a knack for politics. I see things... nuances... that many miss. I keep myself very well informed. It was something Martin... our lost King... insisted upon."

General Feynral looked confused. "You have... you use Naval Intelligence for that? To spy on your own people?"

Admiral Shilannia sat back in her chair and studied at the General. She tapped her fingers on the end-table next to her. "Aubrey... I AM Naval Intelligence. The King and I set it up decades ago and I reported directly to him. When he died, I continued on for the Queen... with her knowledge, of course."

"It didn't do the Queen much good," General Feynral remarked.

Admiral Shilannia winced.

"Tári, I'm sorry. That was uncalled for," General Feynral said.

"But nevertheless true. I didn't see Mordecai's plan. I had prepared for an assassination attempt, not a frame-up." Admiral Shilannia smiled. "I'll fall on my sword tomorrow. As for today, we need to help the Queen."

"You're provoking civil war," General Feynral said.

"No, Aubrey, I'm not," Admiral Shilannia replied. "Mordecai did that. It's up to us to stop it."

"How?"

Admiral Shilannia frowned and looked away. As she watched the flames in the fireplace, her mind quickly evolved several different scenarios... all of which she discarded. "I really don't know," she admitted. "We'll wait to see how things play out. I expect the Queen will be brought back to Taranthi sometime tomorrow. Mordecai will make the trial public and follow the letter of the law. He wants no one to doubt his legitimacy or the Queen's guilt. So we have maybe a week before we need to move on the Queen's behalf. In the meantime, send one of your best officers to check on her."

General Feynral nodded. "I have just the person for that."

"Thank you."

"I can't believe we're having this discussion," General Feynral said sadly. "Do you think the Queen will be sentenced to death?"

"She has to be," Admiral Shilannia replied. "Though I suppose Mordecai could find compassion and banish her to the mainland."

"I doubt that," General Feynral said.

"So do I. For now, cancel all leaves and get your people back to their bases," Admiral Shilannia ordered. "I've already put the entire fleet on alert until further notice."

"Including units up north in the archipelago?"

Admiral Shilannia nodded. "Keep that quiet, Aubrey. Few know of their existence. Martin had me put that force together in secret and I want to keep it that way... at least until I'm ready to use it. And there's an Army general... General Singëril... "

"The Screw!" General Feynral exclaimed. "He's up there?"

"Yes," Admiral Shilannia replied. "His army's currently engaged with pirates. He detests Mordecai. He knows about our units, but, according to my information, has said nothing to his superiors in Taranthi."

"Surely he'll notice when they leave."

"They have orders to be very discreet," Admiral Shilannia said. "If they sail at night it might at least buy us a few hours."

General Feynral nodded. "I understand, Tári," he said as he got up. He looked at his empty glass and thought it would be good to share another drink, but the Admiral was clearly ready to move on to other things. Instead he came to attention and saluted. "I'll report to you later this evening."

Admiral Shilannia stood and returned the general's salute. "Very good," she said. As General Feynral walked out the door, the admiral called after him. "Are we ready for war, Aubrey?"

General Feynral stopped and turned around. "We are if necessary, Tári. But I don't want to send my Marines against our own people."

"I appreciate that and completely agree," Admiral Shilannia replied. The two locked eyes for a few moments. "You're dismissed, General."

"Yes ma'am."

Nefertari Arntuile sat on a small hill overlooking the junction of the Aranel and Maranwe rivers and studied the villages on the both sides. At one point it appeared they were simple river villages... but no longer. Both villages had been turned into military bastions.

"Well, Maedhros Nénmacil, what do you think?" she asked her large companion.

The creation stone rested by Nefertari's side. It looked like the priestess was sitting next to a boulder. The sharpened appendages around its body were the only things that distinguished it from other, more ordinary boulders... or, as Maedhros Nénmacil liked to call them, 'the silent majority'.

"I didn't know rural communities were so well protected, StarSinger," the creation stone replied in a deep, grating voice.

Nefertari smiled. The creation stone turned out to be a good companion. During the last few hours she had found Maedhros Nénmacil to be charming, of quick wit, and sometimes very amusing. But it wouldn't answer her queries regarding its motivation and why it was on this world waiting for her... except to say, "I'm your foundation."

"It's well protected because they have something precious," Nefertari replied to the creation stone's remark. "They have my sister."

The creation stone rose a few feet off the ground and spun around for a several seconds before settling back down. "Does she need to be rescued from forces of evil?" Maedhros Nénmacil asked.

"I don't know, my friend," Nefertari replied as she continued to watch the villages. "I'll decide that when I ask." She then threw her staff into the air. It orbited her head before pointing to the village on the western side of the river junction.

Nefertari stood. "I don't think it'd be wise for you to go with me," she said.

Maedhros Nénmacil laughed. It was deep and rich, and the surrounding ground vibrated as if a small earthquake had struck. "The world will have to learn of me someday, StarSinger. But perhaps you are correct... maybe today isn't yet that time. I will play dead." Maedhros Nénmacil slowly dropped and settled onto the ground, contracting his razor arms as he did so. "You need but to call upon me when needed, StarSinger," the creation stone said.

Nefertari smiled. It was good to have a friend, even if that friend was a creature beyond her comprehension. As she started down the hill, Maedhros Nénmacil became an innocuous boulder, one of many that littered the countryside.

Nefertari needed a barge to get to the other side of the river... which she had little trouble finding. Though there was a strong military presence throughout the entire area, none of the soldiers gave her cause to worry. In fact, just the opposite. She was treated with both respect and great deference. Nefertari supposed it was because of the holy symbol she wore around her neck. She was reminded of the discipline her father instilled in those he commanded in the Alfheim all those decades ago. It would appear her sister expected much of these same qualities of her own men-at-arms. These soldiers were not the enemy as much as they were simply doing what their country required. "It will matter little if they try to hurt my sister," she thought.

As the river-barge made its crossing, Nefertari engaged the barge owner, who sat at the tiller. He was a human named Aberdeen.

"May I sit with you, Master Aberdeen?" Nefertari asked in the language of the humans.

Aberdeen indicated a wooded deck chair off to the side. "It would be my pleasure to have your company, Mistress," he said in Elvish. "Though the journey be short."

Nefertari took the proffered chair. "Master Aberdeen, sometimes it's not the length of the journey that's important. Your Elvish is very good. I could detect no accent."

"I've had much practice, Mistress, living on InnisRos as I do. There's not much call for speaking in my native tongue since most of the population is elf." Aberdeen smiled. "Besides, even though I'm human, I can still appreciate the beauty of the language."

Nefertari returned Aberdeen's smile. "The true beauty lies in the meaning of the thoughts conveyed," the priestess replied. "I'm new to InnisRos. What's the name of these two villages?"

"We just left A'el Ellhendell and are going to my home village, Ashakadi." Aberdeen suddenly waved at a passing barge. "Ahoy and good day, McAllister!"

Turning to Nefertari, Aberdeen apologized for his outburst.

Nefertari shook her head. "There's no need, Master Aberdeen. But you can answer one more question for me before we part company on the other side."

"Certainly, madam."

"Is it normal for there to be so many warriors here?" she asked.

Aberdeen shook his head. "No. The Queen always maintains a small contingent here to help keep the peace, but this is unusual. Something's been going on for the last few days, but no one knows what except the soldiers... and they're not talking."

As the barge gently snuggled alongside the dock, Nefertari noticed one of the larger buildings in Ashakadi had an high number of guards surrounding it. Inside the guarded perimeter and sitting off to one side of the structure was an elaborately decorated coach. Several soldiers were attaching bars to the windows and heavy slide-locks on the outside of the door.

"Madam?"

"Yes, Aberdeen? Oh, I'm sorry," Nefertari said as she reached into a pouch hanging from her belt. She pulled out a gold nugget and offered it to the bargeman.

Aberdeen shook his head. "Oh no, madam, I couldn't take that. It's far too much for a simple crossing."

Nefertari smiled. She genuinely liked the man. "Please, Aberdeen, take this. It is what the passage, and the conversation, was worth to me."

Aberdeen looked at the gold. It'd help him considerably... new coats for the family, fresh meat for the stewpot, needed repairs to his barge... but he didn't feel right about it.

"Do you know how much that nugget is worth?" he asked.

"Of course I do," Nefertari replied, though she didn't really have a clue about the exchange rate on this world. "Take it."

Aberdeen took the nugget out of Nefertari's open hand and bowed. "You humble me, priestess."

"Nonsense, Aberdeen."

The human climbed out of the barge onto the dock and extended his hand. Nefertari took it and allowed him to help her off the barge.

"Blessings to you, Aberdeen," she said.

Aberdeen put his hands together and touched his forehead. "Blessings to you as well, mistress."

"Bargeman!" a soldier called. "Can you cross over my men?"

Aberdeen smiled at Nefertari, who nodded. As she walked away, she heard Aberdeen and the solder dickering over payment for his services.

Ashakadi was much like the villages Nefertari was familiar with in the Alfheim... except for the bivouacked warriors. There were well maintained homes, shops and markets, a library, taverns, inns, and stables. Though the number of soldiers could easily outstrip the villages' resources, Nefertari saw no sign the village was being taken advantage of. Far from it...

the arrival of the Army provided the village with an unexpected boon. Soldiers paid well for the goods and services the village offered. Everything was well organized... not a hint of pandemonium anywhere to be seen. And from the interaction Nefertari observed between villager and soldier, it's obvious respect went both ways. "Lessien has done a good job as Queen," Nefertari thought. "InnisRos seems to be a good, safe place to live."

Nefertari bought a meat pie from a street vender and took it to the park situated across from the heavily guarded building. As she sat on a wooden bench, she broke her fast with the hot, tasty treat and studied the building. It was two stories tall and made of smoothened stone. "Only a cleric could do that," she thought to herself. It had the look of government... pillars by the front entrance, an obvious peacekeeper's office, and a small hospital... all in one location. A large number of soldiers patrolled the adjoining grounds. "My sister's in there," Nefertari said to herself, "Is it against her will? And if so, why?"

Nefertari finished her meat pie and was about to get up to go find Lessien when she noticed several riders approaching from the south. There was no mistaking their bearing or attire, they were without doubt military... but their uniforms differed from those of the guards. Nefertari settled back onto her bench to watch the reaction of the soldiers to the new riders.

Lessien stared out the window of a second-floor room in the back of the building. The sun was descending below the horizon. Its rays of light reflected off clouds which gave the denizens of Aster another spectacular sunset. There were so many beautiful things in the world, and each one she welcomed... for when one took the time to pause and consider, those sights would put the mortal spirit at ease.

Since her capture, Lessien had been treated with the respect and courtesy due a queen. Though they relieved her of father's sword, the magical cloak, and the gold coins she'd been given, her captors hadn't shackled her. She was fed, given plenty of cold spring water as well as an excellent vintage of wine to drink, and harbored in a comfortable room. She was still a prisoner, however. Armed guards stood in front of her door... and she'd be forced against her will to return to Taranthi in the morning for Mordecai's mockery of a trial. As much as she wanted to live... to shrug off the shackles of her imprisonment... she understood the reality of her circumstances. She understood that if she had been successful in her attempt to escape, those loyal to her would go to war to keep her free and return her to the throne. It would tear the kingdom apart.

Lessien opened the window. She wrapped a towel around her hand and, while supporting the back of a windowpane with another towel, carefully broke it. Without hesitation she slashed her wrist against one of the broken shards still secured to the window. Turning and slipping to the floor, she watched as her blood expanded in a pool on the floor.

"Father," she whispered before losing consciousness. "I'm sorry."

THE STRUGGLE FOR INNOCENCE

CHAPTER ELEVEN

Elanesse

Sometimes the best approach to a crisis is to expose what's not there rather than what is.

-Book of the Unveiled

"Where, Elrond?" Kristen asked. "Where's the entrance into the tunnels?"

"Elanesse says the only entrances into the tunnels are at the Grand Palace in west Elanesse and some place called the 'Mii-Enyalie Regis' in the old tongue, or 'In Memory of the Kings'," Elrond replied. "It's a monument southeast of here." Elrond shook his head. "No, that's not right. It's not really a monument but rather a mausoleum. But this one is for the dead kings and queens of Elanesse."

Max sighed. "I don't like the sound of tunnels or old tombs."

"Have no fear, laddie," Azriel laughed. "You have a dwarf amongst you. I'll not allow you to get lost in the tunnels. As for the tomb... " Azriel shrugged his shoulders.

Tangus knelt next to Emmy, grabbed her by the arms and gently turned her so he could look into her eyes. She's much more than a little girl... or even an empath. Tangus knew that. She had perception abilities that sometimes exceeded what should be possible.

277

Maybe she could use that talent to provide information about what might lie in the tunnels.

At first she wouldn't meet his gaze. Tangus thought that was curious. Kristen knelt down behind Emmy and wrapped her arms around the child. Through the bond she felt something wasn't right.

"What's wrong, sweetie?" Kristen asked.

Emmy looked away and to the side. Tears were flowing down her cheeks though she made no sound.

Tangus took her chin and tenderly forced her to look into his eyes. Through the tears he saw fear... understandable... but also a great sadness. "Tell me," he whispered.

Emmy bowed her head... and for a few moments she didn't say anything. By now everyone else also saw Emmy's reticence and waited for an answer. When Emmy raised her head again, she looked resigned, yet still determined.

"Mr. Elrond, you can't go with us," she said.

Elrond was taken aback by this announcement. "What do you mean, I can't go? You'll need my help to defeat the Purge. Besides, it's the only way I can be sure Elanesse is no longer threatened."

"It's because of Elanesse that you can't go," Emmy said.

"Explain, sweetie," Kristen coaxed.

"The Purge isn't something that can be easily destroyed," Emmy said to Elrond. "The magic that brought the Purge to life drew in and used the evil purpose within its creator's heart. When we get close, and if the Purge feels threatened and sees no other path to its survival, it'll look for a host to dominate. The only possibility is Elanesse. Mister Elrond, she'll need you to be here to help fight the Purge. If you don't and the Purge is successful, then our sacrifice to neutralize its influence will be for naught."

Everyone was silent. They believed Emmy... each of them had experienced her cognitive talents first hand.

"And if Elanesse and I succeed?" Elrond asked.

"Then the Purge cannot escape and will be destroyed if we're victorious," Emmy replied. "It'll need a host if it wants to continue to live. Like the mighty oak that dies, collapses, and returns to the earth, the Purge will have its essence torn apart and returned to the heavens if it doesn't quickly find a refuge."

"There's something else, Emmy, isn't there," Kristen asked. "Something that distresses you greatly."

Emmy looked away. "Mother," she said quietly, "I don't know how or why I know this. I wish I didn't. I wish I was just an ordinary little girl." Emmy looked back up at Kristen. "But I'm not."

Tangus laid his hand on Emmy's shoulder. "To us you are. But you must speak to the rest of your knowledge."

Emmy nodded. Everyone standing around Emmy, Kristen, and Tangus, leaned in closer. "The tunnels below have been abandoned for a reason," Emmy said. "When the elves from the Alfheim built Elanesse three thousand years ago, they unknowingly did so over a great and ancient race of beings. In fact, this whole world serves as a prison for creatures of unimaginable power. Creatures who's purpose was to serve as guardians over this world... creatures who demanded purity and considered the mortal population nothing more than a parasite to be destroyed... creatures that challenged the hierarchy of the old gods... and almost succeeded in destroying them. Aster was their home... and now it's where they're banished, deep in the earth and surrounded by imprisonment magic that even the new gods don't understand."

Max shook his head. "Child, that's the story of the boogeyman. It's not real."

"Not so fast, laddie," Azriel interrupted. "My people have tunneled deep below the surface. We have legends of... something... that lives at a certain depth. Something that only has to touch you, and all of your flesh melts away and your bones are turned to stone. Our 'boogeyman', as you call it, Max, is known by my people as the 'Caligo Terroris'... the 'Mist of Terror' in the common tongue."

"It's real," Emmy said. "While your description, Azriel, may be an exaggeration... know the real creature is just as dangerous as you say. It's down there. And it will kill someone. One of us."

Everyone stared. They knew the quest to destroy the Purge and save the last empath would be dangerous... indeed, Christian and Euranna had paid with their lives... but this declaration was a death sentence for one of them.

"Please forgive me," Emmy pleaded. "I wish I could've kept this information to myself... but you're my friends... my family... and deserve to know."

Kristen put her arms around Emmy. "It's not your fault, sweetie."

Emmy shook her head. "Fate is cruel, mother. The reason someone will die is because Mister Elrond has to stay behind to keep Elanesse safe."

The horses were left behind under the protective umbrella of Elrond and Elanesse. The 'Mii-Enyalie Regis' was only a short distance away... but the thick brush of the forest made the hike difficult. After an hour of travel, the forest gave way to an open field. Standing at the center was the 'Mii-Enyalie Regis'. The necropolis was the size of a small castle. It was surrounded by a circular, stout, gem encrusted crystal wall with a simple opening rather than a door. A large helmeted cupola tower stood in the center and was bracketed by an additional four towers that duplicated the center tower except for their smaller size. Short, soft grass carpeted the grounds... and unlike Elanesse, this structure looked to be perfectly maintained.

"Some sort of protection magic is keeping this structure looking so pristine," Kristen remarked. "I can't even begin to understand its complexities. It's so... intricate. Such a light touch, yet very powerful. Amazing!"

Tangus stopped anyone from entering as he looked over the grounds. "It seems innocuous enough," he said. "Elanesse said the entrance to the underground tunnel complex is at the approximate center of the larger tower."

"I don't see a door," Max observed.

"We need to move closer," Azriel said. "Tangus?"

Tangus shrugged and nodded. Azriel led the way and after a few minutes they were standing in front of the tower.

"It's got to be at least a couple hundred feet in diameter," Max said as he stepped closer to examine the base. "It's made of pure crystal!" he exclaimed.

"Can you find a door?" Tangus asked.

Everyone waited Max searched for a door. "There has to be one here somewhere," Max said to himself. Suddenly everyone heard a soft "click". Max turned and shouted, "Get down!" as he flung himself facedown onto the soft grass and closed his eyes. Before the stunned party could react, a section of the tower disappeared, revealing a doorway. Max opened his eyes and looked up to see everyone staring at him.

"It would appear you were successful finding a doorway, friend Max," Lester said as he helped Max back on his feet... a slight smile the only sign he found the whole thing somewhat amusing. Azriel, however, was openly guffawing.

"Kristen, what do you make of this?" Tangus asked as he looked into the doorway.

"It's completely dark," Mariko exclaimed. "No light from the outside seems to penetrate it."

Kristen peered in and tried to pierce the darkness. "Magical... magical darkness," she said.

"So we're going in blind," Safire remarked.

"I'll go first," Mariko said as she drew her two katanas.

Azriel leaned his great axe against his leg and spit into his hands. "I'll be going in with you, lassie," he said as he rubbed his hands together. "I want to know what's there before little Emmy walks in."

"Be careful, Mariko and Azriel," Emmy called from behind Kristen. "The darkness holds the light out for a purpose."

"What purpose, child," Mariko asked.

Emmy shook her head. "I don't know, my Mariko," she replied.

Mariko tilted her head as she tried to decipher the endearment in Emmy's response, but put it aside as she turned and entered the darkness with Azriel following closely. Both came out a few minutes later and were visibly shaken.

"What did you see?" Safire asked.

Mariko looked at Azriel who nodded. "A huge room," she replied. "At the center was a crystal sarcophagus that looked to be grown from the crystal floor."

Azriel interrupted. "It was solid diamond... and it WAS grown from the floor."

Mariko nodded. "Around the room were thrones upon which sat dead kings and queens. The thrones were made from precious stones. But not lots of individual stones worked into a base metal of the throne. Each throne was a solid gem. Ruby, topaz, emerald..."

"I've never seen such craftsmanship!" Azriel exclaimed. "My people can't do that! Not a tool mark to be seen. Flawless execution! Astounding!"

"Yes, all very astounding," Mariko said, "until each one of the kings and queens sitting on the thrones opened their eyes. Then it got rather strange."

"And damn frightening, I don't mind telling you," Azriel added.

Mariko shivered. "They looked at us. They knew we were there."

"But they did nothing... just sat there and stared at us," Azriel added. "They watched us with their eyes."

"Did you find the entrance to the tunnel?" Tangus asked.

"Aye, laddie, we did," Azriel replied. "It's under the sarcophagus. We'll probably have to tunnel underneath the throne to get to it."

"What's the floor made of?" Kristen asked.

Azriel looked at her and Emmy who were standing together. "Stone, lassie. Why do you ask?"

"I know a magical spell that allows me to shift stone as if it were dirt," Kristen replied.

Mariko shook her head. "Tangus, I don't know if those kings and queens will allow any disturbance in the crypt," she said.

Azriel nodded his head. "That's a fact, laddie. It felt like they were waiting for us to do anything that might disturb... the peace, shall we say." Azriel sighed. "There's power in there. Even a dwarf like myself can feel it... and my axe glowed like the sun, just itching for a chance to take them all on. Stupid axe... always wanting to challenge strong magic. It's going to get me killed one of these days."

Kristen grimaced. "Azriel, who was in the sarcophagus?" she inquired.

"I see where you're going with this, friend Kristen," Lester observed. "Undead protecting its own."

"Yes, Sir Knight," Kristen concurred. "Who lay in the sarcophagus, Azriel?"

"A queen, Kristen," Azriel said. "But not just any queen. She was perfectly preserved and more elaborately dressed then the others. It's a good thing

Elrond's not here. He'd have a stroke seeing all that treasure and knowing it can't be touched."

"And you don't think I won't?" Max said.

Lester laughed. "Discipline, friend Max, discipline."

"She has to be Elanesse's first ruler," Kristen said, ignoring the banter. "Husband, we may not make it out of there alive if we're not extremely careful. There will be severe consequences if we're viewed upon as grave robbers."

"We don't really have a choice," Jennifer said, speaking up for the first time. "Unless you want to re-consider going through the city."

"That might almost be preferable, lassie," Azriel said. "Tangus, really, it's dangerous in there. The hairs on the back of my neck were standing straight up."

"We'll take our chances," Tangus said. "Jennifer, maybe you, Romulus, and Emmy should stay..."

"I will not, father," Emmy blurted.

Jennifer moved to Emmy's side and placed an arm around her shoulders. "Neither will I," she said. "I go with my family."

Tangus looked at Kristen who nodded. "All right then, let's go," he said.

The chamber was as Azriel and Mariko had described. Max walked to the center of the room and stared at the diamond sarcophagus. No one said a word, but all could see the 'thief' in Max was salivating.

The eyes of the queen lying in the sarcophagus suddenly opened and the lid vanished. The eyes of the other lesser kings and queens opened as well. Everyone stared as this ancient, but still beautiful, elf floated out of her burial coffin to stand in front of Max. Complete silence enveloped the room. One of the seated corpses, a king, pointed its finger at Emmy. "An empath!" it hissed.

Emmy winced and went to a knee. Though Kristen had taken the bulk of this cold, black hatred for Emmy through the bond, enough of it seeped through to momentarily stun the young empath. Kristen put herself between Emmy and the undead king while Emmy regained her balance against this mental assault.

The king rose from his throne. "Now I understand why the Purge did not retreat," it said. "Empath's still existed even though I was assured by that priest all had died. You and your companions did not choose wisely coming here."

Romulus growled and rushed to pounce on the undead king. As he was flying through the air, his snarling snout and fangs aimed at the throat, the king held his hand out, palm forward, and stopped Romulus mid-flight. With his other hand, the king flung Romulus away. Romulus slammed hard against the far wall and didn't move.

The king then placed both hands together, palms pointed outward, thumb to thumb, and unleashed a multi-colored ray of power at Emmy. Kristen made a swirling motion with her hand and shouted "OBICE DEFENSIONIS". A shimmering wall of light appeared in front of Emmy and her. When the ray of power hit the wall, it was absorbed in a flash of brilliance, momentarily stunning everyone.

A blue streak of lightning from the undead king caught Azriel, who had somehow stumbled in front of Emmy, and dropped him like a stone. He lay on the floor smoking and jerking as the lightning wrapped him in its embrace for several seconds. A part of the lightning then arched and struck Lester. His steel armor attracted and served as no defense for this insidious power. By the time everyone had regained their senses, both Azriel and Lester lay motionless at their feet.

The undead king smiled. "No one else need be hurt. Give me the empath."

Kristen didn't waste any time responding to the undead king. "Tangus, distract him if you can," she whispered.

Within moments arrows from Tangus, Jennifer, and Safire struck the chest of the king while Mariko charged, screaming her battle cry, with Max close behind.

Kristen planted both feet in front of Emmy and cast a spell. Her arms flailed in a seemingly random pattern, but were actually the precise arm movements needed for the magical spell she was casting.

Mariko slashed the king, scoring several deep cuts along his torso, while Max came underneath and cut at the legs to disable him. The king struck both with a closed fist. The force of the blow was tremendously magnified by magic. Mariko's head snapped around and she went down, her katanas rattling on the floor. Max was thrown off his feet and back several feet. There was an audible 'whoosh' as the air was driven from his lungs when he hit the floor. Neither moved .

As another round of arrows streaked forward, the air around the king became thick and the arrows stopped mid-flight. They dropped to the floor when the king released his spell.

"Give me the empath," the king repeated.

A blue diamond appeared in front of Kristen. She cried "TE EXPELLO, DAEMON VILIS, IN ABYSSUM PROFUNDISSIMUM TARTARI". The blue diamond rushed forward, penetrated the king's magical defensive wards, and buried itself into the king's chest. From the impact point blue tendrils extended outwards to cover the king. The tendrils then contracted until there was only a blue diamond floating in the air. It then disappeared without a sound. The king never had a chance to express his surprised displeasure.

Everyone who had been harmed in the mêlée with the undead king were shaking off their injuries and getting to their feet. Romulus was limping badly, Lester had scorch marks on his armor, and Azriel and Max, though still shaken, looked to be fine except for some serious bumps and bruises. Mariko, however, still didn't move. Max bent down to help her, but at once called to Kristen.

Kristen and Emmy rushed over to where Max was kneeling next to the prone assassin. Mariko was lying on her stomach and Max started to turn her over.

"No, Max," Emmy screamed as she knelt next to Mariko's head. Bending over, Emmy put her hand on Mariko's neck as she listened for breath sounds. Mariko was conscious and breathing, but only just barely.

"Emmy," Mariko whispered. "There's something I need to tell you."

Emmy brought her mouth close to Mariko's ear. "Shhhhh, my child. Why you came to us no longer matters. You're going to be fine."

Straightening up, Emmy looked at Kristen. "Her neck is broken, mother," she said. "Mariko's starting to lose all function below her shoulders... her heart, her lungs. She only has a minute or two to live."

"Emmy, you can't heal a broken neck," Kristen replied. "It'll kill you."

Emmy nodded. "I know... at least not alone. Do you remember how we healed Euranna?"

"Yes, sweetie. What do you want me to do?"

Emmy took Kristen's hand and placed it on Mariko's neck. She took Kristen's other hand and placed it on her heart. "Close your eyes and pray for your healing spells," Emmy said.

Kristen closed her eyes and reached deep inside her soul for the power of healing. Unlike her other magical spells which required the contortion of fingers and arms, as well as certain magical words said precisely and with the exact inflection, healing spells required absolute devotion to the magic being sought. Her father taught her that magical healing depends upon the willingness of the cleric to sacrifice for another.

With her eyes closed, Kristen saw into Mariko's neck. She saw Emmy's power as it gently held several strands of nerves. She heard Emmy say, "When I touch two ends together, you must fuse them."

Kristen did as asked, but the nerves remained inert. "It didn't work," Kristen said with concern.

"New pathways must be created through the spot where the nerves are joined," Kristen heard Emmy say. "Can you do that?"

Kristen nodded as she sent magic coursing through the nerves, which at once pulsated into life.

"Mariko can now breathe again without difficulty," Emmy said. "Her heart beats slowly... but it's getting stronger. You did well, mother. Now I must heal the broken neck."

Kristen resisted. "It's too dangerous!" she cried. "We can splint her neck and take her back to the 'Lorin-Galaduiriel' to let it heal naturally. Elrond will watch over her. We can't lose you."

Kristen felt a calm come over her through the bond with her daughter. "I know how to do this, mother," Emmy said." I'll be in no danger. Besides, we need her to be with us."

Kristen felt it was more than that... perhaps Mariko is more important to Emmy then she was letting on. Regardless, Kristen had no counter-argument... they did need Mariko. "I'll watch you closely, dear heart," she said. "If there's any problem, however, I WILL stop you."

"I love you too, mother."

An empath mends by taking the injury upon herself. She then relies on her body, which is exceptionally gifted with the ability to repair itself in a very short period of time, to mend the damage. There are limitations, however. An empath cannot re-grow parts of the body such as an arm or a leg, nor can an empath bring back someone from the dead. If a wound will lead to imminent death, the empath can die if her body cannot heal itself in time. This was Kristen's concern.

Emmy started healing Mariko's fractured neck. Bit by bit she joined the broken parts of the neck vertebra together and healed them. Kristen saw what Emmy was doing and relaxed. Emmy's own healing gift could absorb and mend each small fracture to her own neck as it transferred to her. Through the bond Kristen could feel the pain each healing caused Emmy... but Kristen deflected a good portion of it. After a few minutes Mariko's fractured neck had been restored completely.

Mariko awoke and felt her neck... then looked at her arms, relieved that she could move them again. Emmy was kneeling over her and Mariko looked into her eyes. "My lady..." Mariko said.

Emmy put a finger to Mariko's lips. "Rest for a few minutes, dear Mariko."

Kristen watched the brief exchange between her daughter and the assassin and wondered again at its implications. There's more to the relationship between the two than she understood... which wasn't acceptable. Looking over at Tangus, Kristen started to call his name, but saw his attention had been drawn to something else. The queen from the center sarcophagus was gliding over to them.

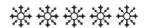

The Purge once again felt the presence of the empath... and at once wished it hadn't. The empath had, beyond the Purge's ability to understand, become aligned with the same power the Purge believed was coming for it. No! In a spark of precognition, the Purge suddenly understood the empath WAS the power coming for it.

"Attack! Attack! Attack!"

"Don't listen to them. You must stop your war on the empath and go back to sleep."

The Purge cringed. The voices in its mind and heart kept to their prattle. There was no escape.

"Attack! Attack! Attack!"

"Don't listen to them. You must stop your war on the empath and go back to sleep."

The Purge didn't comprehend fear, but it could judge when there was a threat to its existence. But the voices wouldn't free it to think, to comprehend, to take action.

"Attack! Attack! Attack!"

"Don't listen to them. You must stop your war on the empath and go back to sleep."

Something in the Purge snapped. It was no longer the focused creature of before. It could no longer rationalize... it could no longer put two coherent thoughts together... it could no longer find itself. The Purge had become lost in a pool of its own madness.

Everybody prepared themselves for another battle as the queen drifted silently over to them on a cushion of air. Though her eyes were animated, the rest of her body remained motionless. Kristen, joined by Romulus, stood in front of Emmy and Mariko and prepared to fight in defense of the two. Mariko grasped her katanas and tried to rise, but Emmy kept her down with a hand. Surprised by the weakness that prevailed throughout her body, Mariko offered no resistance.

The queen stepped in front of Tangus, who was standing nearest, flanked by Lester, Safire, and Jennifer. Azriel and Max stood close behind. There was no sign the queen meant harm. Her eyes studied the gathered assembly with curiosity. The queen raised and extended her arms. A calm came over the entire chamber and the dead kings and queens sitting on their thrones closed their eyes.

Satisfied, she moved forward. Reassured by the queen's demeanor, Tangus and the others made a path while keeping themselves and their weapons ready to defend against any deception. The queen stopped in front of Kristen and Romulus. Neither were willing to stand aside.

"She doesn't mean to harm us, mother," Emmy said.

Kristen's eyes never left those of the queen as she said, "Sweetheart, how can you know that? The Purge will stop at nothing to see you captured or murdered."

"You killed the last king of Elanesse, mother," Emmy replied. "It was he who ordered the Purge to be brought to life. He was the only connection between this place of rest and the Purge."

Emmy walked between Kristen and Romulus. "Your Majesty," Emmy said.

The queen looked down at the child. Stunning everyone except Emmy, the queen dropped to her knees to accept Emmy's blessing. Emmy put her hand on the queen's forehead and then took the queen's hands in hers and bid her to rise. The queen did so with a smile. She turned and pointed to her sarcophagus. It quietly slid several feet to reveal a dark tunnel. The queen turned back to Emmy and bowed her head.

Emmy reached up and cupped the queen's face with her small hands. "After we've left, Your Majesty, return to your sleep knowing you'll never again be disturbed."

The queen looked at Emmy. "I'd gladly awaken again to give counsel should you ever have a need," she said.

Emmy nodded. "I suspect I will. What is your name?"

"I was called Gabriella of Dorthanion," the dead queen replied. "I was born on the Alfheim and came to Aster with the first wave of settlers. When Elanesse was in its infancy, we cherished the human empaths. What happened during the last generation... the Purge... has put a black mark over all our heads. My people were not like that."

Emmy nodded. "I know they weren't. Rest without shame, Gabriella of Dorthanion."

CHAPTER TWELVE

InnisRos

In a monarchy, the case for war is rarely taken before the very people who will suffer the outcome most grievously. Therefore, it's incumbent upon those who decide such things as to whether or not the means justify the ends.

-From the Letters of Father Horatio Goram to His Daughter, Kristen

Sandis sat in a chair facing Father Goram and his monastery staff---Autumn, Cordelia, Father Goram's second in command and a very experienced priestess in her own right, Cameron, the director of the monastery's health component and hospital, Landross, a noble knight and the commander of the monastery's military arm, and newcomer Eric the Black---in the war room. Magdalena, with most of her rangers, were still out in the field with Balthoron's battalion. With the possible exception of Father Goram, everyone looked angry. Even the huge dire wolf, Ajax, snarled a couple of times.

Autumn had asked her husband if she could conduct the interview. Father Goram reluctantly agreed after he received Autumn's assurances she wouldn't frighten the girl too much.

"We need answers, Sandis," Autumn admonished. "We can detect lies, so it won't do you any good to answer untruthfully. Do you understand?"

Sandis nodded. "Yes ma'am. But I'd never lie to you," she said. "What I tried do to Father Goram weighs heavily on me."

Father Goram glanced at Autumn. "Yet you didn't in the end," he interrupted. "Instead, you choose to refuse Mordecai and suffered as a result."

Autumn looked sternly at her husband. "Horatio, please."

Father Goram held up his hands. "Yes, ma'am."

Autumn nodded and directed her attention back to the nervous housekeeper. "What was your arrangement with Mordecai?"

Sandis sighed. "It was actually Vayl who approached me on Mordecai's behalf... after he... seduced me. I feel so foolish, but at the time I would've done anything for Vayl. He gave me the dagger with instructions to leave it on Father Goram's desk. Then Vayl disappeared and I didn't know what to do. Was the dagger important?" Sandis took a deep breath. "After hearing the rumors of Vayl's treachery, I began to suspect the dagger was actually meant to harm Father Goram and that Vayl had lied." Sandis looked at Father Goram. "Father, you've been so good to me! I didn't want to see you hurt."

Landross shook his head and said angrily, "There's no honor to any of this, Horatio!"

"Quiet, my friend," Father Goram said. "We'll deal with Vayl soon enough."

"If we can ever find the rogue," Landross mumbled under his breath.

"Why would you even entertain such an idea?" Autumn asked Sandis, unperturbed at Landross' outburst.

Sandis looked away. Tears were falling down her cheeks.

Autumn got up from her chair and gave Sandis a handkerchief. "Tell us, child. So you didn't want to hurt Horatio. What changed your mind? Was it really infatuation? Or gold? Maybe a promise of power?" Autumn paused and bent over in front of Sandis, placing her hands on the arms of the chair with her face just a few inches away. "Or maybe revenge. Tell me, do you have a grievance against my husband?" Autumn's voice was hard. Father Goram suddenly realized she'd make a great prosecutor.

Sandis retreated into her chair as far as she could. "I've already told you I didn't want to harm Father Goram!" she exclaimed. "Vayl left and I... I realized how foolish I'd been. But even though he had vanished, others knew of his plans for Father Goram and the dagger. I was attacked because I hesitated. A simple prick on the arm was all it took. For several minutes my arm felt like it would melt away. Then the pain... vanished. I had been poisoned. I never truly saw him... the one who poisoned me... for he was cloaked in the haze of magic. He told me he had the antidote, but first I must deliver the blade to you." Sandis shrugged her shoulders and then looked at the priest. "What's the life of a simple housekeeper worth compared to yours, Father?"

Father Goram's heart tightened up. "Dear child," he thought. "If you only understood that I'm YOUR servant."

Sandis continued her narrative. "I tried to destroy the blade with a hammer. But it came alive. I didn't know until it was too late it had a mind of its own. After the blade attacked me..." Sandis looked away. "I was in so much pain, Father! So much pain! I couldn't deal with it. I'm sorry... but I didn't know where else to go."

That caused Autumn to pause and look at Father Goram, who was already getting out of his chair. He put his hands on Sandis neck as he felt her pulse while using his healing abilities to find and identify the poison.

"I treated the poison from the Maglor Telperiën, but... wait... there it is." Father Goram stepped back. "The poison from the obsidian blade camouflaged the second poison. I should've seen it."

"What is it, Horatio?" Cordelia asked.

Father Goram looked down at the distressed Sandis. "It's called Nilafinwë," he said. "The more common name is Frostheart. It's originally from the Svartalfheim."

"How did it get here?" Cameron asked.

"Probably through the Alfheim," Eric the Black said. "We know of many battles between the Elves of Light and the Elves of Dark for supremacy of the Alfheim. I wouldn't be surprised if that poison was used during one or more of those forays by the Elves of Dark. If it was in the Alfheim..."

"Then it could've made its way to our world," Cameron said, finishing Eric the Black's thought.

"I know I don't deserve it, but can you help me?" Sandis pleaded.

Father Goram bracketed Sandis' face with his hands. "Nonsense, child. You were forced into these actions by those who would do great harm for the sake of power and greed. No blame rests with you. We'll have you healthy in no time. Now rest here while I consult with my friends."

"Father Goram, she was lied to. There isn't an antidote for Frostheart," Eric the Black whispered as soon as the group had moved away so Sandis couldn't hear. "At least none I'm aware of."

"I know," Father Goram replied.

Cameron raised an eyebrow. "It's in some documents Martin brought from the Alfheim," Father Goram replied in answer to Cameron's unasked question. "Those documents are accessible from the Royal Library."

Father Goram then looked over at Sandis who was patiently waiting. She shivered uncontrollably from her fear. "It slowly stiffens the heart muscle until it can no longer pump blood. In the latter stages it becomes quite painful."

"How long," Autumn asked.

Father Goram shrugged his shoulders. "It depends upon many of different factors... the strength of the dose, how concentrated it is, the size and hardiness of the one poisoned, the actual amount injected. From what I've read of the symptoms, Sandis looks to be in the very early stages. She has maybe a few hours."

"And there's nothing we can do?" Autumn asked. Her hard expression moments ago had turned to genuine concern for the young elf.

Father Goram shook his head. "Nothing except make her as comfortable as we can."

"Forgive me, but maybe you're wrong," Eric the Black said.

Everyone looked at the sorcerer. "Explain," Landross said.

Eric the Black looked puzzled. "Isn't it obvious?"

"Apparently not!" Cameron replied.

The sorcerer shook his head. "Think! There's a new player in the game."

"This is a game to you!" Landross roared.

Father Goram held up his hand to quiet Landross and to hold off any further comment. "Please go on," he said. "Who's the new player."

Eric the Black rolled his eyes. "The empath," he said.

Cameron looked at Father Goram. "He's an arrogant bastard, but he does make a valid point. Do you think she might have a different way of looking at this?"

Father Goram nodded. "Perhaps. Kristen and I have a matching set of communication crystals. I'll contact her and ask. In the meantime, Cordelia, please escort Sandis back to my apartment and make her as comfortable as possible."

"I'll go too," Autumn said.

Father Goram nodded as he pulled a crystal out of a belt pouch and set it on the large conference table. Taking a seat, he activated the magic.

"Father?"

"How are you, dear?" Father Goram asked.

Everyone could hear Kristen's pain. *"We've lost a couple of friends as well as Bitts. It's been a hard road, but we're determined."*

"I'm sorry for your losses... especially Bitts. I don't have to tell you to be careful, but I will anyway... be careful." Father Goram paused as he organized his thoughts. "There's so much I want to tell you, but the crystal's power drains quickly. Since we have little time, I'll be brief. Does Emmy know anything about the poison Frostheart?"

A strange voice replied. *"You mean Nilafinwë?"*

"Who was that?" Father Goram asked, surprised.

"It's Mariko, father," Kristen replied. *"She's a new friend who has, shall we say, certain credentials which I don't think you'd approve."*

"On the contrary, Kristen... as long as she's on your side," Father Goram answered. "Mariko, what can you tell me about Frostheart? And make it quick. This crystal's about to run out of power."

"I can tell you there's not an antidote this side of the portal between Aster and the Alfheim," Mariko replied. *"However, there's one thing you can try. Mind you, I've only heard of this... I have no idea if it actually works."*

"I guess it's either that or let her die," Father Goram replied.

"Very well," Mariko said. *"Magic healing won't work. At the onset of the final stage, you must open the chest and gently message the heart. This will keep the poison from taking hold and hardening the heart while maintaining blood flow. The poison acts rather quickly at this point, so if the timing is correct, it'll run its course in a minute or two and the heart will no longer*

be in jeopardy. Then you should be able to heal the incision with magic."

Father Goram nodded. "It makes sense," he thought to himself. "Mariko, how do you know about this?" Father Goram asked. His curiosity was peaked.

There was a long pause at the other end. *"My line of work necessitates I keep abreast of... all kinds of things relating to..."*

"She's no longer in that line of work, father," Kristen said. *"My crystal has little power left before I have to recharge."*

Father Goram nodded. "Thank you, Mariko. Kristen, all my love."

"Love you, grandpa..." and the crystal went dead.

"That must've been Emmy," Father Goram thought. "Grandpa... I like the sound of that!"

"Horatio... are you with us?" Cameron asked.

Father Goram returned his attention to the here and now. "Sorry. Cameron, you come with me. Landross, I want you and Eric to reach out to your people to see if anyone's been acting suspicious. Talk to Sandis' friends. Maybe they can identify anyone new in her life."

"I don't understand. Why so much trouble for a simple housemaid?" Eric the Black asked. "Surely we can ferret out the assassin without her help."

Landross started to object with his sword but Father Goram stayed him with a wave of his hand.

"That's not how we do things around here, Eric," Father Goram replied. "We don't judge people by the value they have to our political aspirations. Here, all life is sacred. It's the governing precept of our beliefs and we'll not compromise on this point." Father Goram studied the sorcerer. "Do you understand?"

Eric the Black looked at Father Goram. He could see the priest, though in complete control of his emotions, was deadly serious. Landross still had his hand on the hilt of his sword. He then shifted his gaze to Cameron, who nodded.

Eric the Black bowed. "Of course. Please forgive me. I've been forced to give up much human interaction in pursuit of my study and practice of the arcane art. My sense of... propriety... is somewhat lacking."

"Indeed it is," Landross remarked. But his hand was off the hilt of his sword when he said it.

Father Goram looked at the two. "Are you going to be alright together?" he asked. Both nodded. "Very well. Let's see to our responsibilities, gentlemen."

Marine Colonel Daeron Tirion and his warriors arrived in Ashakadi at dusk. The pickets surrounding the village offered nothing but salutes as he rode past without slowing. Under normal circumstances Colonel Tirion might've stopped and reprimanded the Army guards for their sloppiness... he should've been held up by the guards and questioned regarding his intentions... but he wanted no delays to his mission to check on the Queen.

The colonel and his small contingent of Marines stopped in front of the Army's two-storied headquarters building and dismounted.

"Sergeant!" Colonel Tirion said as he took off his gloves and tucked his riding crop under his arm. He hated the thing and never used it on his horse, but it seemed to add a certain tough, no fooling around aspect to his persona. "Take care of the horses and secure accommodations for you and the men."

The sergeant snapped a rigid salute. "Yes, sir!" he bellowed.

As the colonel walked into the building, he stopped, turned, and called out, "Oh, and Sergeant. I want to leave at first light. Keep the men in check."

The sergeant pulled a half-smoked cigar out of his mouth. "You mean no drinking, sir?"

The colonel smiled at his second in command. "No, you can drink. Just don't let it get out of control. I want everyone looking sharp in the morning."

"You mean 'we're the Marines and you're just the Army', type of sharp, sir?"

Colonel Tirion smiled. "That's part of it, Sergeant. But I also want you to leave enough beer for me."

The sergeant laughed. "Understood, Colonel."

The soldiers guarding the front entrance came to attention and rendered salutes as the colonel approached.

Colonel Tirion returned their salutes. "As you were, gentlemen," he said as he stepped through the doorway. Inside the building he was met by more guards. A sergeant sitting at a desk stood as soon as the colonel walked in.

"I'd like to speak to your commanding officer, Sergeant."

The sergeant shook his head. "Sorry, sir, but the General left strict instructions he not be disturbed until daybreak."

"Then who's in charge?"

"I am, Colonel," said a captain as he came down the stairs from the second story. "How can I be of assistance?"

Colonel Tirion reached into his tunic and produced a rolled scroll. "I've orders to see how the Queen fares."

The captain studied Colonel Tirion as he unrolled the parchment and read. "This is signed by your Marine General Feynral," the captain remarked. "I'm under no obligation to..."

"As a courtesy, Captain?"

The captain re-rolled the scroll and handed it back to Colonel Tirion. "We've given her the best quarters we could find in this dirt water town. She's eating and drinking better than any of us... maybe even better than the General himself. I can assure you every courtesy has been extended, Colonel. She is, after all, an escaped prisoner wanted for murder."

Colonel Tirion took the proffered scroll back and replaced it in his tunic. "Captain, there's the presumption of innocence, is there not?"

The captain looked away. The conversation had taken an uncomfortable turn. "You're right, Colonel. I suppose it won't hurt to look in on her. I'll give you five minutes."

"That should be more than then sufficient," the colonel replied.

The two warriors climbed the stairs and approached a guarded door. Both guards came to attention.

"As you were," the captain said. "Any problems?"

"No, sir. Everything's quiet," one of the guards replied.

The captain removed a key from a belt pouch and rapped on the door several times. "Your Highness, you have a visitor," he shouted.

There was no answer.

"Your Highness?"

Still no answer.

"Perhaps she's retired for the evening, Colonel," the captain remarked. "Maybe you could come back at dawn?"

"No, Captain, that won't be acceptable," Colonel Tirion replied. "Please open the door."

The captain nodded and did as he was asked. After he unlocked the door, he slowly opened it and called out, "Your Highness?"

It was Colonel Tirion who first spied the Queen, slumped on the floor in front of a broken window, and sitting in a widening pool of blood.

Nefertari was just about to get up when she notice a sudden burst of activity coming from the building where her sister was held. Several soldiers frantically ran out the front entrance and down the stairs from the front porch while another soldier stood at the top of the stairs and bellowed orders.

"Find a cleric!"

"Notify the General!"

"Send a message to Taranthi!"

Nefertari had a sinking feeling in the pit of her stomach. "Something's happened to Lessien!" she thought as she rose.

"Maedhros Nénmacil, I may have need of you," Nefertari said as she walked towards the well guarded building.

"I'm at your service, StarSinger," he replied in her mind.

Nefertari nodded as she strode forward with purpose. With a wave of her staff, she brought to life an air elemental which surrounded her and created an invisible barrier. Because of the chaos surrounding the building, none of the guards noticed her until she was at the perimeter of the landscaped hedgerow that encircled the entire structure.

"Halt!" one of the guards shouted as he ran over to confront Nefertari. "This area is off-limits to civilians."

Nefertari stopped. "I couldn't but help to overhear the call for a cleric," she said. "I'm at your disposal."

"Well..." the guard said as he looked around for someone of rank to make the decision for him. Nefertari saw he was unsure how he should proceed.

"How badly injured is the person?" Nefertari asked, hoping to provoke the soldier into a decision.

All caution left the guard's face. "Very, mistress," he said. "Please follow me."

The two hurried across the yard, up the front stairs, and into the entrance unmolested. There were no soldiers on the bottom floor, but Nefertari could hear the noisy pounding of booted feet coming from the second floor above her.

"Please remain here, mistress, while I get the captain," the soldier said.

Nefertari shook her head and rushed up the stairs. The soldier tried to grab her arm as she passed, but was turned away by Nefertari's air elemental companion. As she got to the top of the flight of stairs, several soldiers looked at her from outside a room.

"Madam, what..."

"Stand aside, soldier!" Nefertari ordered. She didn't bother to slow down and, again with the help of her elemental, bulled her way into the room. Inside, the scene was frenzied. Nefertari pushed her way through the crowd of onlookers.

"Captain, get me that cleric!" she heard someone yell. "And get your soldiers out of here. I don't like the Queen being gawked at so!"

Nefertari broke the ring of soldiers just as a soldier, presumably the captain, stood. Another soldier, dressed in a different uniform, remained kneeling next to a still form.

"My sister!" Nefertari screamed inside her head as she stared. Though Lessien was only a young child when last Nefertari saw her, there was no mistake as to her identity.

The soldier kneeling next to Lessien had bandaged her wrist and applied a tourniquet. But Nefertari could see it might be too late... so much blood had already been lost. Nefertari banished her air elemental as she knelt beside Lessien and felt her pulse. It was very weak... the heart was on the verge of stopping. Nefertari next put her ear to Lessien's chest... breaths were almost nonexistent.

"Who the hell are you!" the kneeling soldier said as he brusquely moved her aside. In response to his outrage, two other soldiers grabbed her by the arms and dragged her back and onto her feet.

With surprising strength, Nefertari shrugged out of the soldier's grasp, but didn't try to run. The soldier Nefertari recognized as the captain drew his sword.

"Madam, I don't wish to harm you or cause further damage to your dignity, but you don't belong here," the captain said.

"Do you wish for me to come, StarSinger?" Maedhros Nénmacil asked in Nefertari's mind.

"Not yet, my friend," she replied to the creation stone. Aloud, she said, "My dignity be damned, sir. You," she pointed to the kneeling warrior. "I'm that cleric you've been screaming for... and the Queen rests on the precipice of death. If you don't let me attend her, she'll surely go over."

The warrior blinked. "How do you... "

"Come now, everyone knows the Queen," Nefertari said as she cut short his question. "Now let me help."

The warrior nodded, and Nefertari immediately knelt next to her sister and called forth her healing power. The warrior gave Nefertari room to work.

"I'm Colonel Daeron Tirion. May I ask... "

Nefertari shook her head. "Shh," she said as she concentrated her healing magic on Lessien's heart. It must be propped up and supported immediately or it was going to stop beating. As Nefertari's mind went into the faraway place that all clerics visit when performing their healing craft, she felt the room and its occupants vanish, to be replaced by magical energy... energy that was in all things, even the air itself. It was the energy the initiated used to perform miracles. Nefertari found strands of blue colored healing magic. They danced and sang to her. They invited her to shape and mold them as she saw fit. Nefertari used her clerical talent to carefully pull the blue from all the other colors of magical energy. She tapped into their power and directed a portion into Lessien's heart, which, reinforced, began its work anew.

She then re-directed the blue healing magic to Lessien's deeply lacerated wrist, closing skin, muscle, tendons, and veins. Finally, Nefertari used her will to reach into the surrounding magical energy field and pull stands of green growth magic... which she applied to Lessien's blood. Within moments Lessien's body was restoring blood at several times the normal rate.

Nefertari's mind returned from the directed focus of its labors. She checked Lessien's breathing and her heart-rate. Both were normal. Next she inspected Lessien's wrist. The grievous wound was closed, leaving nothing behind but new, pink skin. In a few hours it would be as if nothing had happened.

Nefertari stood and re-called her air elemental. The sleeping Lessien was gently lifted up and placed in the room's only bed. None of the soldiers moved to interfere. Nefertari walked over and placed a blanket atop the recumbent Queen. She then sat on the side of the bed and turned to address Colonel Tirion. "She'll need warmth until all her blood returns. Please have the fireplace re-stoked."

Colonel Tirion nodded. "As you wish, madam. Captain, if you please? Oh, and Captain, please have the window repaired. There's a cold draft outside."

"Certainly, Colonel," the captain replied. Within seconds men were rushing to carry out their orders. Each were now breathing sighs of relief because the Queen had apparently been saved.

"No need to worry about the window, Captain," Nefertari said. Her air elemental now covered the broken glass, preventing any air from entering. The captain frowned, but nodded.

There was a sudden commotion from outside the room. "Make way for the General," someone ordered. "And return to your posts!"

Nefertari turned to see several figures emerge from the quickly disappearing mob of soldiers. The general and his aides made their way to the bed. Colonel Tirion and the captain both came to attention and saluted. The general didn't even acknowledge them. He was fat for an elf, with a belly that saw far too many rich and sugary meals. His uniform, however, belied his physical appearance. It was extremely well maintained and spotless, with medals covering most of the left side of his chest. His black, beady eyes revealed both intelligence and cunning. "A pompous ass with a brain," Nefertari thought. "He's going to be trouble."

The general looked over at Colonel Tirion. "What are you doing here, Colonel?"

"Sir, I was dispatched by Marine General Feynral... "

"I know who sent you," the general said.

"Yes sir. Anyway, I was sent to check on the wellbeing of the Queen," Colonel Tirion replied stiffly.

"You mean you were sent by Feynral and Shilannia to spy on us," the general shot back. "We know the Navy and her Marines don't stand with First Councilor Mordecai. Perhaps you might even think to steal the murderess away from her just punishment."

"General..."

"Quiet!" the general shouted before turning his gaze upon Nefertari. "What matter of priestess are you?" he asked. "I don't recognize your holy symbol. A pagan god?"

Nefertari rose from the bed. But she didn't allow the general to bait her into anger. "I come from far away," she said. "I'm visiting Ashakadi and heard the call for a cleric. Of course I'm bound by my goddess to help a person in need."

The general looked at her slyly. "Who do you visit?" he asked.

Nefertari wasn't ready for that question. "The bargeman... Aberdeen," she said after a pause.

The general nodded... but Nefertari knew he wasn't satisfied with her answer. "And how does the Queen fare?" he asked.

"She's stable, though she needs rest to recover fully," Nefertari replied.

The general looked between her and Colonel Tirion, then turned on his heel. "Arrest them," he said as he walked out of the room. "And the Colonel's Marines as well."

Father Goram came out of the main monastery building and took a seat on a bench in front of a small spring. The stars in the night sky sparkled like diamonds. Though the temperature was crisp, spring was in the air and soon would be upon them. Father Goram looked at his bloody hands... spring wouldn't come for Sandis. She'd never again feel the warmth of the sun or see a flower bloom. Father Goram sighed.

Autumn sat next to him. She had rags and a filled washbasin of water. She took one of his hands and washed it. "You did everything you could, dear," she said.

"I know," Father Goram replied as he took the rags Autumn had brought and cleaned his own hands, thinking upon how much he loved her for the gesture. "Perhaps Kristen could've saved her. She has more of a knack for physical healing."

The two sat in silence for a few minutes. Then Father Goram rubbed his hands through his long, silver hair. "Another young innocent lost... made to pay with her life for the ambition of an adult," he said.

"She'll be avenged," Autumn replied.

"There you are!" Landross said from behind. Autumn and Father Goram turned as Landross and Eric the Black walked across frost-covered grass to join them.

"What'd you find out?" Father Goram asked.

"Nothing," Eric the Black said. "Either Mordecai's spy is extremely well hidden, or the girl is lying and acted on her own."

"But why would she give herself poison?" Autumn countered.

The sorcerer shook his head. "I guess we'll have to interview her more carefully."

"That won't be possible. Sandis is dead," Father Goram said as he and Autumn stood.

Neither Landross nor Eric the Black seemed surprised.

"Can't clerics speak to the dead?" Eric the Black asked.

Autumn looked at him with distaste. "We can. But here, at this monastery, we prefer to allow the dead to rest in peace. It's a sign of respect."

Eric the Black narrowed his eyes. "Madam, I have no such... "

"Eric, I think we need to let this pass," Landross said as he grabbed Eric's arm and pulled him back a step.

Eric the Black shrugged off the grasp of the big knight and looked at him. "Even if it's to save lives?" he argued. "To hell with honor and... and... reverence for the dead. We need information."

Though it had appeared Landross and Eric the Black had reached a truce during their mission together, it wasn't deep enough to prevent Landross from placing his hand on the hilt of his sword. "I don't much like your tone, sorcerer," Landross said.

"Enough!" Father Goram shouted, bringing the disagreement between the two to an abrupt halt. More calmly, Father Goram looked at the sorcerer. "Eric, you don't know what it's like to talk to the dead. It's very traumatic for us to expose ourselves to that experience. A conduit between two worlds must be opened. We... we feel the blackness between. And when we call to the deceased, if the dead soul has found eternal peace, it's often angry at the disturbance. If the soul hasn't found peace, it's angry as well, but for a much different reason. Either way, we must then bend the dead to our will... none answer willingly. It's... distasteful."

"I didn't know it was so involved," Landross said.

Father Goram nodded. "It has to be. A call to the dead has lasting consequences not only for the cleric but also for the dead soul called. You see, Landross, though the magic exists to do such a thing, it's not something mortals should do. That's true for many things. Eric, I'd be remiss in my responsibility to Althaya and the clerics I lead if I either did or allowed them to do such a thing. I understand your point, but for us, another way must be found." Father Goram looked away. "Sandis said the person who poisoned her was cloaked in a 'haze of magic'. I wonder what she meant by that."

"There's a magical spell known to a few sorcerers that causes the subject to appear as a blur," Eric the Black said. "I suppose one could call it a haze. That'd certainly hide a person's identity."

"So we're looking for a sorcerer," Landross said.

Autumn shook her head. "Not necessarily," she said. "Some spells can be written down on scrolls... or potions can be made to mimic the effects of certain spells. It could be anybody."

"And they'll probably try again, Horatio," Landross said. "We know Mordecai was behind Vayl's treachery. Now, if poor Sandis is to be believed, Mordecai has just tried to murder you. I rather think he's declared war on us."

"For once I agree with the knight, Father," Eric the Black said.

Father Goram, with Autumn at his side, began to walk back to the main monastery building. He stopped and turned to Landross and Eric. "Gentlemen, let's not lose sight of Mordecai's ultimate goal... to capture both Kristen and Emmy to take them to the Svartalfheim. He intends to rule the land of the Elves of Dark, and, eventually Aster. Being the legitimate king of InnisRos gives him a firm foothold in this world. I don't think he wants a civil war which would weaken his power-base here... just me out of the way. That being said, he may decide to march against us if he can't eliminate me... or any of us who would carry on in my stead."

"They'll never take this monastery!" Landross exclaimed.

"Perhaps not, my friend," Father Goram said. "But a lot of people will suffer, and die, in the attempt. Is that really acceptable to you?"

Landross fell quiet.

"It's not acceptable to me, either," Father Goram said.

"Then what are we to do, Horatio?" Landross asked. "We can't..."

Silence.

Eric the Black rolled his eyes. "What Landross is trying to say..."

Father Goram held up a hand. "I know what Landross is trying to say, Eric," he said. "He's correct, we can't desert our people. But here's the dilemma. If we stay, Mordecai will send the Army against us... particularly if the Queen escapes and make her way here. That will have a brutal effect on the people of InnisRos. But if we run, Mordecai's rule will essentially mean the same thing. I've seen him in the Council. He's iron-fisted."

"So what are we to do, Horatio?" Autumn asked.

Father Goram shook his head. "I don't know... yet. If the Queen successfully flees Mordecai's clutches and presents herself here, I don't see how civil war can be averted. However, if she's convicted and Mordecai becomes the king, we have another problem altogether."

Landross nodded. "Aye. We'd be honor-bound to follow our lawful king... or become renegades against the realm."

Father Goram put his arm through Autumn's and started forward again. "I'm going to see how Maggie and Balthoron fair. While I'm doing that, Autumn, show Eric the sorcerer section of our library."

Eric the Black raised an eyebrow.

"This wasn't always a monastery, Eric," Autumn said in response to his unasked question.

"That's correct," Father Goram remarked. "We have a number of sorcerer's tomes stored away. Obviously, I don't have a need for them... but I still recognize their value. See if there's anything that might help us in a war."

Eric nodded eagerly.

Father Goram continued. "Landross, see to your men. Then get your staff together and come up with a battle plan. If we're going to fight a war, we may as well be ready for it."

Landross saluted and sprinted off.

Eric the Black laughed. "That got his juices flowing!"

Father Goram shared a smile with Autumn. "Indeed it did, Eric," he said. "Autumn, after you've shown Eric where the sorcerer's wing of the library is, please tell Cordelia and Cameron I'd like to see them in the war room."

Autumn reached up and kissed Father Goram on the cheek before she moved off with the sorcerer in tow.

Father Goram took one last look at the peaceful and starry sky before going back inside.

Magdalena joined Balthoron for an early breakfast. Magdalena's rangers had joined with Balthoron's battalion a few hours after nightfall of the previous evening. In a testament to the skill of Magdalena and her rangers, they worked through Balthoron's perimeter guard of soldiers and into the camp of the bivouacked battalion before anybody noticed. Balthoron was visibly upset... but Magdalena managed to settle him down before he disciplined the guards. The guilty did have to pull a double shift, however.

"I heard from Father Goram last night... or perhaps I should say early this morning," Magdalena said around a mouthful of biscuit and bacon jerky.

"And?" Balthoron said as he poured Magdalena a second cup of coffee.

Magdalena blew on the hot brew and took a sip. "He doesn't want us to expose ourselves yet." Magdalena set her coffee down and looked at Balthoron. "I probably should have mentioned this last night, but you had already retired and I didn't want to disturb your sleep. Mordecai tried to assassinate Father Goram."

Magdalena noted that Balthoron didn't react like she expected. "You don't seem surprised," she said.

Balthoron shook his head. "Not really," he said. "Don't get me wrong. I'm grateful the attempt was unsuccessful, but it makes sense. Since the Queen escaped, Mordecai's probably hedging his bet against the possibility she makes it to the monastery. Without Father Goram's leadership, he most likely figures it'll be easier to convince us release the Queen back into his custody without a fight." Balthoron frowned. "Seems to me I heard there's bad blood between the two."

Magdalena nodded.

"Then Mordecai's also trying to kill two birds with one stone," Balthoron said as he chomped on a piece of bacon jerky. "No doubt there's plenty of other... political reasons... Mordecai had for the attempt. But I'm just a simple soldier, so what do I know."

Magdalena stared. "Simple soldier? Yeah, right," she thought.

Balthoron had finished his plate of food and sat back in his field chair. He took out a cigar, bit the end off, and spit it on the floor. He grabbed one of the lit candles on the table and puffed, enticing the cigar to light. Satisfied, he blew out a ring of smoke, grabbed his coffee and took a sip. "Did Father Goram have anything else to say?" he asked.

Magdalena nodded. "He doesn't want us to do anything to provoke Mordecai. Just exactly how we proceed without provoking Mordecai he left up to us."

Balthoron, with the cigar in his mouth, cleared away the dishes from the small breakfast table. When he had finished, he pulled out a leather pouch from his open tunic, withdrew a vellum sheet, and spread it out on the table. It was a map of InnisRos.

As cigar smoke swirled in the air, he pointed to the forested area southwest of Calmacil Clearing. "We're approximately here," he said as he pointed to their location on the map. "About a half mile from the forest edge. I think we should keep the main body of my battalion in the forest... but closer to the outskirts. The Army uses sorcerers who have magical means by which they can do long range reconnaissance. So the cover of the forest should prevent us from being spotted."

"Unless they're actively looking for us," Magdalena said.

Balthoron needed. "If it comes to that, no one on InnisRos can hide for long. So we don't want to give them a reason to look in our direction."

Magdalena agreed.

"Good," Balthoron said. "I think we should send some of our rangers into the foothills of the North Spire range. Find a place with cover that gives us a broad view of the farmland below and wait."

Magdalena studied the map. "We should place a scout or two in this little village on the Aramel River. It's straight due west of the foothills. If the Queen stays on the river going north, this is the most likely place she'll disembark for the trek to Calmacil Clearing."

Balthoron concurred. "Makes sense. Not too many barges go further north and into the mountains. How about the coast?"

Magdalena shook her head. "Highly unlikely. The Queen escaped inland. To get to the coast, she'd have to cross the Maranwe River first. She can't swim the river and that close to Taranthi there aren't any barge crossings."

"Unless she went to the west coast," Balthoron said. "But that doesn't make sense. We both know she'll run to Calmacil Clearing."

Magdalena and Balthoron fell silent as each studied the map.

After a few seconds Balthoron pointed to the villages of Ashakadi and A'el Ellhendell. "I think you and I should go here," he said. "My gut tells me the Queen will try to escape overland and not use the rivers. She'll judge, rightly, that it's better to go incognito through farmland. We both know the Army will be patrolling the rivers extensively. Besides, even if we don't run into her along the way, we'll gather necessary intelligence."

Magdalena nodded. "Are we forgetting anything?"

Balthoron took a puff of his cigar and then a sip from his coffee cup. "No, I don't think so," he said. "Then again, there's a saying I learned at the Academy... 'the unexpected has sharp teeth'. We plan knowing we can't plan for everything. It makes us officers a bit paranoid."

Magdalena smiled. "Paranoid, perhaps. But also wise," she said. "Rangers also have a saying... 'trouble is but a tree away'. So... are we ready?"

Balthoron, in response to Magdalena's question, finished his coffee and got up out of his chair. "Let's get 'em going and move 'em out."

Mordecai was sitting behind his desk in his dungeon. Across the room, a soldier who hadn't shown proper respect earlier was chained to a stone altar. He was unconscious. Mordecai was stripped to the waist, sweat and blood mixing as they ran down his torso in rivers. The sweat was Mordecai's... but the blood was that of the soldier.

Mordecai, though happy the Queen had been re-captured, worried about the Marine colonel who had appeared to check up on her... though in retrospect it was probably a good thing, since the colonel discovered the Queen before she died from a slashed wrist. But the colonel's presence also meant the Navy and Marines weren't going to capitulate easily... and that concerned him. This frustration drove Mordecai and his victim to the dungeon.

The soldier on the altar moaned as he slowly regained consciousness. Mordecai smiled.

CHAPTER THIRTEEN

Elanesse

There are many forms of darkness... the darkness of evil, the darkness of despair, the darkness of death, the darkness of the unknown. Who chooses which is worse? Each person has their own definition of true darkness based upon their most innermost fears... except below the surface of Elanesse. To that darkness, everyone agrees. There is nothing worse.

-Mariko, Former Assassin

"Romulus, I'm sorry, but I have to send you back to Elrond and Elanesse," Tangus said. "You can't negotiate ladders."

Romulus whined. This obviously disturbed him. He didn't want to vacate his responsibility... nor did he want to leave those he loved. The vacant spot in his heart where he held Bitts still weighed heavily.

Kristen went to Romulus and wrapped her arms around his huge neck. "Wait for us, our loyal guardian," she said as she kissed him on the forehead.

Kristen stepped away as Emmy approached. Romulus bowed his head so the diminutive child could be at eye level with him. Emmy embraced her wolf tightly... then whispered into his ear before letting go. The wolf looked closely into Emmy's eyes, nodded, then bolted away and out of the mausoleum. A few seconds later everyone heard Romulus howl.

Tangus, surprised, looked at Emmy. "What did you say to him?" he asked. Everyone looked at the two as they waited for Emmy's answer.

"I told him he needed a mate." Emmy smiled.

"Oh, lassie... you're much too young to be thinking about such things," Azriel remarked as he laughed.

"Indeed!" Lester said as he joined in on the banter. "Friend Tangus, Friend Kristen... seems like you'll have your hands full with this one."

Kristen wasn't laughing, however. "Sweetheart, Romulus isn't like other wolves."

"I know that mother," Emmy replied. "But it'll be all right. Besides, Romulus needs this. He's put his life on hold ever since you were a baby."

"Who are you, child, that you would know such things?" Tangus asked.

Emmy looked confused. "I don't know what you mean, father. I'm just Emmy." But she did know what her father meant... and she didn't understand exactly who she was either.

Tangus looked at Kristen who shrugged. "All right," he said as he walked over to the exposed, and very dark, hole underneath the queen's elaborate sarcophagus. "Let's get going. Pretty dark," he said as he looked down.

"There's a ladder," Max observed as he, along with the others, joined Tangus. "I need a light source."

"Max... my responsibility to go first," Tangus said as he took hold of Max's arm.

"But I'm the thief," Max replied. "I can recognize traps and pitfalls far better than you. It's how we've always done things."

Tangus nodded. "I know, my friend. But this isn't the same and you know it."

Max shook his head. "Yes it is, Tangus... though the motivation is different, the skills and methods are exactly the same. You need me to do this."

Tangus gestured towards the hole with his arm. "Very well. But please be careful."

"I always am," Max replied. "Azriel..."

"Aye, laddie, I'm already getting it," Azriel said as he dug through his backpack. "Here you are my little jewel."

Azriel pulled out a battered and well worn metal helmet. It was elegantly decorated with carved symbols that had meaning to the dwarven race. Attached to the center of the helmet was a small cylinder with a lever which allowed the wearer to open and close the end. Azriel wiped the helmet off with a cloth and then opened the end of the cylinder. Brilliant light escaped... but not in all directions. The cylinder caused the light to be directed as if it were a beam... only exposing that which it touched.

Azriel closed the cylinder. "Magical light," he said to no one in particular. "Dwarves use these all the time when mining. Don't forget to use the chinstrap, Max." Azriel warned. "I don't want to take the chance of my helmet falling off your hard noggin like it did the last time. Thought I was never going to get it back."

"My word," Max said as he took the helmet and strapped it to his head. He turned to Tangus and gave him a mock salute. "Reporting for duty, sir," he said before he looked into the hole. The light on Azriel's helmet didn't show the bottom. Straightening, he looked over at Azriel. "Remind me. What's the approximate range on this thing?"

"About one hundred feet," Azriel replied.

"That's pretty much what I remembered," Max responded as he got on his knees and looked back down into the hole. "No bottom. But at least there's a ladder." Max grabbed the top rung and studied it. "Solid metal... no rust. Wait a minute..."

"What is it, friend Max?" Lester asked.

Max had his head in the hole and was looking at the opposite side from the ladder. "There's some writing chiseled into the wall." Max raised his head out of the hole. "It's in an elven dialect I'm not familiar with."

Kristen knelt next to Max and looked at the writing herself. "My father made sure I'm skilled in many languages and their variances. This is very ancient and no longer written or spoken... at least as far as I know. I don't think I can... "

"It's the language of the first elven settlers to this world," the queen said in a sweet, melodious voice which startled everyone. She had been quiet and the hole had captured everyone's attention. They had forgotten she was there. "Unknown to the histories of this world, my people traveled from the Alfheim to find freedom. We are... were... a sect of warriors devoted to the maintenance of the peace in the Alfheim. But our methods were somewhat... brutal... for we had no tolerance for rehabilitation. The Alfheim didn't approve of the way we dealt justice. They felt we were too... uncivilized. When a pathway to this world was discovered, we were granted 'permission' to leave with the others who sought the adventure Alfheim couldn't provide."

Everyone stared at the queen.

"This world was rather primitive at the time... at least by elven standards," she continued. "But we learned to curb our passions and had no desire to interfere with other civilizations. We built Elanesse and strove to live in peace with our neighbors. We even accepted a small number of other races to live within our city, including roaming bands of human gypsies." The queen sighed and bowed her head to Emmy. "The empaths were honored members of our society back in those days. As I have mentioned, I'm repulsed by the genocide later perpetrated upon them."

"How do you know what happened?" Kristen asked.

The queen smiled. "I've been a willing audience to Elanesse's cry of loneliness over the millennia. We didn't know what we had wrought when we built... that's not correct... when we gave birth to Elanesse. Unknowingly, we relegated her to the same status as, say, a rock. But now I know even some rocks have a spirit." The queen paused and looked at Emmy. "She spoke of you often, mistress. I am sorry for the mistakes of my people."

Emmy took the hand of the queen. "Elanesse will once again become a thriving city... a city filled with empaths... a city that will be a centerpiece of healing... a city that will accept all who come to her with peaceful intent." Emmy's expression suddenly grew hard. "But I'll never allow what happened to the empaths of yesteryear to happen again."

Emmy stopped and looked around at the faces staring at her. She realized something extraordinary had happened during her long sleep. Emmy reeled as she was flooded with unbidden knowledge. It was knowledge she didn't understand... yet. There was also a sense that something lay inside her... something just out of reach and layered beneath her consciousness... something that would explain her recent capacity for precognition. Emmy knew she was meant to be more than just the last empath. And she knew others, like the elven queen, already knew and accepted it.

Kristen approached Emmy from behind and loosely draped her arms around the child. Kristen addressed the queen. "Your Majesty, please interpret the writing on the wall for us."

The queen nodded and glided over to the opened entrance to Elanesse's underbelly. "It's a warning," she said. "Seek thee not the darkness below, for within lies an appetite that will never be quenched." The queen looked up. "I have memories of this. It's a malevolence that came up from the very bowels of this world. It will not tolerate intrusion."

"We have no choice," Tangus said. "We must defeat the Purge. Only then will Emmy be safe and the future of the empaths secured. Below Elanesse is our best course... if we can avoid this 'darkness' you've warned us of."

"You cannot," the queen said.

Everybody stood in silence.

"Maybe we should re-think this whole approach," Max commented.

Tangus looked around at the faces of his friends and loved ones. There was concern and uncertainty in everyone's eyes. "We know our options and it looks like going underground may be as dangerous as an assault through the city," he said. "Maybe we should put this to a vote." Everyone agreed the direct assault alternative was too risky.

"I guess we go down," Max said.

Emmy and the long dead queen locked eyes. The queen pulled a ring off her finger and reached out to Emmy. "The malevolence below will seek you out as it has sought all innocence since before the dawn of time. Take this ring. It has the power to ward off evil, though I don't know if it will be an effective barrier against that which waits beneath. One last bit of information before I return to my sleep. The exit from the tunnels is in the Grand Palace. However, we sealed it off with mortar and powerful magic to keep the darkness from gaining access to the surface. It may be impenetrable."

"Great," Azriel whispered.

"We'll deal with that problem when we get to it," Tangus said.

Emmy nodded to the queen. "Rest well," she said as she put the ring on her finger. It flared with a brilliant light as it adjusted itself to Emmy's smaller size.

The queen smiled. "You're coming into your own, mistress."

"Attack! Attack! Attack!"

The Purge could no longer hear the singular voice of reason that had been warring with the voices of hate. A chasm of madness now engulfed the Purge and the sanity of its heart had been cordoned off. The Purge drank in the rage it felt for the empath.

The voices of hate altered their chant. Their new mantra, which changed to take advantage of the Purge's current state of psychosis, became even more demanding.

"Kill! Kill! Kill!"

The Purge couldn't wait for the last empath to show herself before satisfying its wrath. She no longer mattered. Only mortal bloodlust would gratify its depraved hunger.

The voice of the heart, now silent, realized she'd lost. She must now hide to protect herself from the madness that had taken root in the Purge. Even still, she knew it was only a matter of time before she'd be rooted out and destroyed. She could no longer take refuge in what little compassion was left in the heart of the Purge... for that compassion, as small as it had been, no longer existed.

Lieutenant Arnish surveyed the carnage outside the walls of the Grand Palace. The non-believers... those interlopers who had stayed hoping to fatten their money pouches with treasure that rightfully belonged to the Purge... had been gathered up and butchered like the carrion they were. As he watched, the worgs that had filled the city were now gorging themselves on the fresh meat of humanity.

Lieutenant Arnish shook his head. "A sad waste," he thought. "Oh well... plenty more where those came from." Lieutenant Arnish had not yet fallen into the madness that held his men and those treasure hunters still alive. He didn't know, however, that his tenuous hold on sanity would be brief.

Max was tired. He had climbed down the ladder for approximately one hundred feet and still the floor had yet to show itself. "Wish I could see the damn bottom," he mumbled. "Now that I think about it, why didn't I just borrow that magical ring from Elrond so I could float down. What a minute... what's this?" Ten feet below Max, the magical light from the helmet no longer penetrated the darkness. "That's strange," Max wondered. "Magical darkness?" A tendril of the darkness suddenly exploded up and towards Max. Surprised, all he could do was watch as the black appendage pierced his leg and dragged him down with incredible strength.

From the surface, Max disappeared in the darkness as he made his descent... except for the light shining from Azriel's helmet strapped to Max's head. But even that light began to fade as Max continued his journey down the ladder. Without warning, the light from below flickered and disappeared. Max's scream of pain and terror climbed upwards and out of the hole.

"Ho, Max!" Azriel bellowed with obvious concern.

Silence... followed by a burst of activity as everyone responded to the obvious danger Max faced. Azriel and Mariko were already climbing down the ladder, while Tangus and Safire quickly pulled two long ropes that radiated magic from their backpacks and spiked the ends of each into the concrete floor of the mausoleum. They both attached spiked crampon straps to their boots and connected carabiners to their belts.

"Safire and I are going to rappel down the sides of the hole," Tangus said. "It'll get us down faster than climbing the ladder." Tangus looked at Jennifer. "When we're at the bottom, I want you to follow. It'll be just like rappelling down one of the mountains in the North Spire back home. Take it slow and easy. Remember... these ropes are spelled so they'll never be too short." Tangus then reached over to Kristen and Emmy had hugged both. "Sweetheart," he said to Kristen, "we've practiced this, so it shouldn't be a problem. When I give the signal, pull the ropes up and tie yourselves off before climbing down the ladder. Lester, make a sling so Emmy can ride on your back. Remember... listen for my 'all clear' first."

Kristen nodded. "Be careful," she said.

Tangus gave her and Emmy a quick kiss on their foreheads. He then looked at Lester. No words were necessary... Lester understood what Tangus expected. Lester would defend both with his life.

Max was nowhere to be found. Azriel's helmet, battered, lay on the coarse stone floor of the tunnel at the base of the metal ladder. The light from the helmet illuminated the floor. Blood had pooled in several cracks and crevices. Red drops went down the tunnel until they disappeared into the dark.

"There's not enough blood to believe Max is dead," Kristen said. "But there's enough to tell me he's bleeding copiously and will be dead soon if he doesn't somehow manage to stop it."

Azriel bristled. "Damn it! Well... at least we have a trail to follow."

"And it appears to be heading in the direction we want need go, friend Azriel," Lester replied.

"Father." Emmy said as she stared into the darkness. "It's out there, I can feel it."

Tangus turned first to Emmy, then Kristen. "Can you feel it through the bond as well?" he asked Kristen.

"No, she can't," Emmy replied for Kristen. "I won't let her."

Kristen turned Emmy around and kneeled so she could look into the child's eye. "Honey, why?"

Emmy shook her head. "Mother, I don't want you to suffer the depravity of what this thing did to Max."

Kristen pulled back. "I'm supposed to protect you," she said. "Not the other way around."

Safire joined the two and put a hand on Kristen's shoulder. "My dear Kristen... have you not been paying attention?" she asked.

Kristen looked at Safire. "What do you mean?"

"What Safire means," Emmy said, "is that, while only a little girl in your... and everybody else's... eyes, I'm still over three thousand years old. I've found that my... talents... have evolved much quicker than the norm since being released from Althaya's stasis spell. Surely you can feel that through the bond."

Kristen closed her eyes and nodded. "I've been denying it. I've wanted so much for you to be dependent upon me. No, that isn't true. Not really. We've had so little time together. I only wanted you to be my little girl."

Emmy hugged Kristen. "I'll always be your little girl," she whispered.

"We need to leave," Tangus said.

The tunnels deep below Elanesse had been there since before the creation of the city. They branched here and there in many random directions. Great cavern rooms, each large enough to house a small city, served as the joining point for most of these passageways. The underground complex was cold and damp, but perhaps the most telling aspect was the all-encompassing dark from which there was no escape. It boxed everyone in. Only the light from their magical stones defined the outer limits of the world of sight. Past this boundary lie the unknown. Past this boundary lie the culmination of everyone's greatest fear.

It wasn't long before the blood trail disappeared. Azriel used the underground abilities of his race to walk the party through each niche and cranny, each tunnel offshoot, each false channel. Azriel's expertise, combined with the tracking abilities of the three rangers and each person's grim determination, kept them on the right track.

After several hours of drifting through the world of rock, stalactites, stalagmites, and the never-ending impenetrable night, they came upon a huge cavern. Florescent lichen lit up the cavern floor and walls while small florescent creatures skittered here and there. A large waterfall at the opposite end kept the cavern damp and chilly. The noise it projected was deafening. Dotted in the walls all around the cavern were dark-filled holes... representative of tunnels that went in different directions.

"What the hell do we do now," Tangus yelled above the din of the crashing water.

Azriel studied the cavern. "We study the floor for any sign of tracks or blood," he shouted back at Tangus, but loud enough so everyone could hear. "We check each tunnel entrance for signs of the same thing."

Tangus nodded and turned to face everybody else. "We'll search for Max," he yelled. "But it's more important we confront the Purge... which means finding the correct tunnel out of here."

"I'll do that while you conduct your search," Azriel said.

Tangus nodded. "We need to split up. Kristen, Emmy... I want the both of you to stay over there, next to that large stalagmite," Tangus pointed to the approximate center of the cavern." Kristen nodded. "Mariko, do you mind staying with them?"

"Certainly not," Mariko replied.

"Love, we can take care of ourselves," Kristen remarked... but her plea fell on deaf ears. Emmy tugged Kristen's sleeve and shook her head. "Let it go," she said.

Tangus looked at Lester. "Jennifer will go with me to the left. Lester, you and Safire inspect the tunnels on the right." Tangus waited for questions... but there were none. "Let's get at it, then."

After an hour of searching, Tangus, Jennifer, and Azriel converged on the stalagmite sheltering Kristen, Emmy, and Mariko.

"No luck. How about you, Azriel," Tangus asked.

Azriel nodded. "I think I found the tunnel that'll take us in the direction we need to go," Azriel replied with a cringe. "The only problem is I can't tell if it makes any false turns deeper in."

"Any other possibilities," Mariko asked.

Azriel shook his head. "No."

About that time Lester and Safire returned. Both looked very disturbed. Safire at once went over to Kristen and hugged her close. "Grant me strength, Kristen," she whispered.

Tangus could read the look on Lester's face. "Max?" he asked.

Lester nodded.

"Is he... ?"

"Dead? Yes," Lester said, vocally acknowledging what everyone already knew.

"Damn it to hell, Max," Azriel bellowed. "Why did you have to go and do that, laddie."

Tangus looked at his feet and sighed. "I never thought this day would ever come," Tangus said. "Take me to him."

As Lester, Azriel, Mariko, and Tangus walked away, Kristen and Emmy started to follow. Safire grabbed Kristen's arm and brought her to an abrupt stop. "Leave Emmy with me, Kristen. She shouldn't see what's in there."

But Emmy resisted. "No Safire, I need to see it. Max died for me. At least allow me to honor that sacrifice."

"Maybe Safire's correct, dear," Kristen said. "I would spare you if I could for as long as I can."

"Mother," Emmy replied, "this isn't just a journey to destroy the Purge. It's also a journey of discovery... a journey of enlightenment. I must be a witness to the death of a dear and brave soul."

As Kristen, Emmy, and Safire approached, Tangus and the others were staring into a small space off the main cavern. The illumination from their magical light-spelled stones exposed a scene straight from hell itself. Max didn't die an easy death. His skin had been cut whole from the rest of the body and mounted on a stalagmite. The skinned body had been discarded off to one side. The muscles, tendons, and bones, exposed to the wet atmosphere of the cavern, looked fresh and gleamed in the light. It was difficult to fathom the precision of the cuts necessary to keep the skin intact... and the suffering Max must have endured.

Azriel knelt and fought the urge to vomit. Though he was a survivor of many skirmishes and a witness to many of the things that can be done to the physical body, he still wasn't prepared for this. As

Azriel stared at the cavern floor, fighting to control the need to retch, he became furious. His magical battleaxe flared in response to the rage that burned in the belly of the dwarf. Very deliberately, Azriel got up and turned to the horrified Tangus.

"My brother, keep your family away," he said. "They shouldn't see such a thing. They shouldn't remember Max like this."

Tangus re-directed his attention from the body of Max to Azriel. "I don't know if I can."

"Give me but a few minutes, laddie."

Tangus finally nodded and turned to intercept Kristen and Emmy.

Lester put his hand on Azriel's shoulder. "I feel your pain," he said. "Indeed, it is my own. How can I help?"

Azriel grasped the big knight's arm. "My friend, I'm not tall enough to take Max's skin off that stone pillar. Would you be so kind?"

Lester nodded. He looked at Mariko and held up his hand as he followed Azriel into the room, silently telling her to stay back.

Azriel stood next to the pillar and waited for Lester. "C'mon!" he said impatiently. "Before the wee lassie sees this!"

Lester reached up and removed the skin with great reverence. He gingerly carried it over to the rest of Max's body and draped it over the remains. He took off his heavy cloak and covered everything. Pulling his great sword from its scabbard over his back, Lester planted the tip on the floor, knelt on one knee, and said a knight's prayer to the fallen.

A great 'clang' rang out as Azriel, using his battleaxe, cut though the blood-stained pillar. It offered little resistance. As he did so, his tears fell to the floor. With a loud crash, the pillar toppled over. Azriel then turned and walked out of the room. His companions who had, by now, crowded the entrance of the room, silently gave way so he could pass.

Lester followed Azriel, but stopped at the entrance. "Friend Azriel grieves heavily."

No one said anything as they stared at the retreating back of the dwarf. Azriel stopped by the pool of water at the base of the waterfall and took a long, deep drink.

"Kristen, would you please bless our friend?" Lester asked.

"Of course," Kristen replied.

But Lester wasn't finished. "As a priestess, you have certain abilities to magically shape stone. Do you think you could close this small room... Max's final resting place... so he is properly entombed?"

Kristen nodded.

Lester smiled. "Thank you, Kristen. Tangus, Max once told us that if he ever died... "

"That he wanted us to raise a toast to him and then get roaring drunk," Tangus said. He looked back into the room at Max's cloak-covered body. "He said the same when I was running with him and Elrond." Tangus shook his head. "What say we go over and see if Azriel needs anything."

Lester nodded, and the two walked over to stand with Azriel.

Emmy slipped her hand into Kristen's and pulled her away until they could speak in private.

"Mother, we can't kill this creature," Emmy said. "I'm so sorry, but I should've realized this before Max went down the hole."

After all that had recently happened regarding Emmy, Kristen wasn't surprise the child had insights concerning this newest threat. She knew Emmy had access to knowledge which eclipsed even that of the wisest scholar. It scared Kristen. "What do you mean, sweetheart?" Kristen responded.

"It's not a being... or a god... as we know of such things. It's not even malevolent as the queen said. This creature is something very ancient... and perhaps the only one of its kind." Emmy looked at her father, Azriel, and Lester, as they talked at the base of the waterfall. "They only see a need for revenge. Mother, we have to stop them."

Kristen frowned. "So you mean we can't kill it... but not because it's not within our power to do such a thing, rather because..."

"... it doesn't deserve to die for simply acting on its nature. It's not evil, mother, just very territorial," Emmy said. "I don't understand the ecology here, but we're in its lair. It's only protecting its home."

Kristen shook her head. "Perhaps it should be destroyed. I didn't see what it did to Max, but from the way everyone was acting it was gruesome and Max suffered horribly. Such a thing below Elanesse is a serious threat, especially should it ever decide to come to the surface."

"It won't come out of its lair, mother," Emmy replied. "I'm not saying we shouldn't defend ourselves, but let's not hunt it... just leave before it's forced to kill again."

Kristen sighed. "You should probably be the one to speak to those three over there," she said as she pointed to Tangus, Azriel, and Lester. "I suspect they'll be much more receptive if you made the plea rather than me. For now, however, would you help me consecrate Max's body and tomb?"

Emmy nodded. This was a gravely serious last rite which would help to settle and bring peace upon Max's soul. More importantly, however, it would reassure and help soothe the grief all felt over losing a member of their family.

As the two walked into the chamber, followed by Safire, Jennifer, and Mariko, one of the dark doorways in the cavern wall slid onto the floor, leaving a solid wall in its wake. The undulating, swirling mass silently moved towards them along the floor.

Lieutenant Arnish and two of his men stood before a large pool of thick black-red liquid. The tar-like gruel moved constantly. The Purge spoke inside the minds of Lieutenant Arnish and his men.

"Report!" the Purge ordered.

"Most of the treasure hunters have been disposed of," Lieutenant Arnish replied. "Our worg allies are, as we speak, getting rid of the bodies."

A part of the pool rose twenty feet and towered over the three men. It took on the appearance of a murky demon... wings grew from its back and orange, swirling eyes stared down. It opened its maw and black-red slime dripped from foot-long fangs.

"And the empath?"

The lieutenant hesitated. "We still haven't located her," he said reluctantly.

The demonic, insane face of the Purge lowered until it was at face level with Lieutenant Arnish. "How can that be? Even now I can feel her presence. She's within the city."

Lieutenant Arnish backed a few steps away... but the face of the Purge followed.

"Well?" the Purge said. Its breath stank of sulfur.

"My... my Lord, the empath is not within the city. Perhaps... maybe underground?"

The swirling eyes of the Purge abruptly turned from orange to silvery metallic. With speed impossible to fathom, the head engulfed one of the two guards in its maw. The guard screamed as the Purge's jaws clamped shut, piercing the man with its terrible fangs while supra-heated saliva burned from the inside out. The purge viciously whirled the guard around before throwing the body away.

"KILL THE EMPATH!" the Purge screamed. "SHE MUST NOT FIND ME!"

Lieutenant Arnish bowed and, along with the other guard, backed away. The Purge returned to the pool which bubbled and hissed. As they walked away, Lieutenant Arnish cuffed the guard. "They have to be coming from under the city. Find the entrance. Check every damn building, every alleyway, every nook and cranny. Go below and into the sewers. I don't care what you have to do, just bring me the head of the empath!

Because if you don't, we're going to end up like poor Traskerly."

The guard saluted and sped away. Lieutenant Arnish watched the back of the retreating man as he disappeared from sight. Things were starting to fall apart and the survival instinct of the lieutenant momentarily overpowered the Purge's control of his mind. "I need to leave," he thought.

"You will die in my service," the Purge countered in the lieutenant's head. It had read his thoughts and answered the question as to which impulse was stronger.

Lieutenant Arnish ran after the guard with newfound vigor.

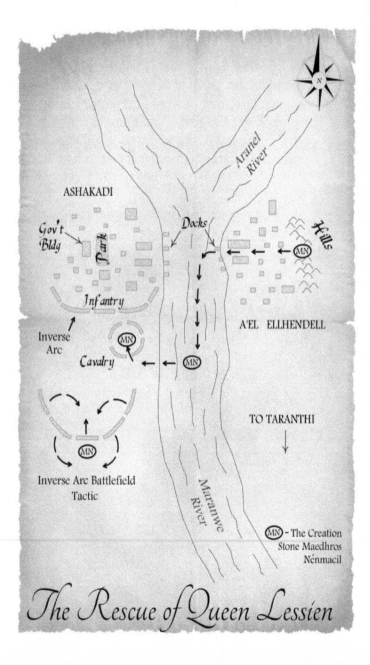

The Rescue of Queen Lessien

CHAPTER FOURTEEN

InnisRos

It was my first real combat experience with a creation stone. I asked Maedhros Nénmacil if he would help rescue my sister, Queen Lessien. In retrospect, perhaps I should have affected her escape on my own. Who knew a creation stone could be so destructive!

-From the Journal of StarSinger Nefertari Arntuile

All barge traffic on the Maranwe and Aranel Rivers was temporarily suspended as elements of InnisRos' Army moved up-river on military barges and speedy riverboats. A thundering herd of cavalry, well-armored knights riding horses of outstanding size and speed, flanked the barges on both sides of the Maranwe River. Following the knights came the slower supply train wagons and several huge siege weapons - the catapult, the battering ram, the ballista, the siege tower. In all, seven thousand infantry and mounted warriors had left Taranthi and were traveling to lay siege to the monastery at Calmacil Clearing. General Maglor Narmolanya, InnisRos' Army commander, rode at the head of the mounted knights. His orders were to capture Father Goram and take possession of the monastery. He was to use his own discretion regarding the followers of the priest. Mordecai had strongly hinted that he didn't care if the priest was taken dead or alive.

In the capital city of Taranthi, Mordecai had declared martial law. Two thousand knights and infantry patrolled the city streets and alleyways to enforce the edict. Violators were detained, questioned, registered, and escorted back to their homes with strict instructions to abide by the curfew. Second offenses resulted in confinement. The council was disbanded and those council members aligned with the Queen were placed under house arrest. The remaining council members were nothing but menial sycophants whom Mordecai used to do the mundane things he no longer deemed important. City administrators were working overtime to stem the tide of summons, registrations, arrest warrants, judgment documents, and sentence recommendations. The rule of law was, for all intents and purposes, abandoned. In a very short period, Mordecai had complete control over InnisRos... with the exception of Calmacil Clearing, controlled by Father Goram, and the waters surrounding the island which were controlled by the Navy. The Army would handle the monastery... but Mordecai knew the Navy would be a monumental stumbling block to his plans to rule.

Mordecai, the architect of the island's state of emergency, sat on the throne and rubbed his forehead. Every time he put the crown on it gave him a terrible headache... something that had been happening from the first moment he usurped the throne. No craftsman could discover why this was... the crown fit Mordecai's head perfectly.

The only other person in the room was Nightshade in her Amberley guise. Mordecai wouldn't seek nor accept guidance from any other. Nightshade sat to Mordecai's right in an ornate chair which had been placed in the throne room specifically for her. Mordecai now saw her as someone other than his concubine and advisor. In his mind she was, for all intents and purposes, his queen.

"Do you think I've sent a large enough force to secure Calmacil Clearing?" Mordecai asked the demon.

Nightshade frowned. "From all accounts, it's well fortified and equipped to handle a long siege." Nightshade looked at Mordecai. "That is if Goram doesn't sortie his own knights and warriors to beat your forces off."

"He might be able to do just that," Mordecai replied.

"Perhaps, but I think not," Nightshade said. "He'll not want to be the cause for what would undoubtedly be a high cost in life. The priest has... a conscience, I believe. Besides, you can always send reinforcements. Goram doesn't have that option."

Mordecai tapped his chin. "Once the Queen is back in Taranthi, tried and found guilty, I can negotiate with him. He'll accept exile if the Queen is allowed to go with him."

Nightshade looked at Mordecai. "I thought you wanted Goram dead? And you'd allow the Queen to leave?"

Mordecai shrugged his shoulders. "I want a kingdom left to rule, Nightshade. A long, drawn out fight with the priest will tear it apart." Mordecai frowned. "Keep your focus on our long-term goal. We need the empath and her bonded priestess. The more time I spend dealing with this uprising, the greater chance those two will find a hole in which to hide. I don't want to spend years ferreting her out."

"Don't forget my assassins, Mordecai," Nightshade responded. "You won't need an army to retrieve the two."

Mordecai looked unconvinced. "And the Purge? From what I know, it's a serious threat."

Nightshade shook her head. "You know my assassins have infiltrated their little group. They report that the empath's in good hands and her protectors will most assuredly eliminate that particular threat." Nightshade didn't have a clue concerning what was actually happening on the mainland with the empath. Her assassins hadn't been in contact with her for several days. But she didn't care. The empath wasn't important to her plans... only that there was war on InnisRos. And that could only be accomplished if Father Goram had the Queen.

Mordecai stood. "I need to meet with the magistrate," he said. "I have a trial to prepare and begin once the Queen is returned. You?"

Nightshade smiled. "Oh, I have 'demon stuff' to do," she said aloud while thinking there was something Mordecai wasn't telling her.

"Later?" Mordecai said... an invitation for her to spend the night in his mansion.

"We'll see," Nightshade replied as she thought, "Never again, you fool!"

It was morning and the sun, as it rose, covered the landscape of InnisRos with its brilliant beams of light and warmth. Magdalena and Balthoron, with two of Magdalena's rangers, approached Ashakadi and A'el Ellhendell. Riding up to a huge boulder sitting atop a hill over-looking the two villages, the four studied the scene unfolding below them. Barges and riverboats filled the river. Half of the barges were disembarking their cargo of troops while the other half continued further north up the Aranel River. Further to the south a cloud of dust could be seen on the horizon. Both Magdalena and Balthoron knew from experience what that represented... mounted knights... usually accompanied by light cavalry.

"They're coming for the monastery," Magdalena said.

Balthoron looked over at her. "Indeed," he said, "though I never believed Mordecai would actually take such a course... especially since we don't have the Queen."

Magdalena, still looking below, said, "The Queen's no longer on the run. They have her. Notice that two story?"

"Aye," Balthoron replied. "Their command post. What of it."

Magdalena pointed. "Look just to the right. See that wagon?"

Balthoron took a few moments to study the wagon. "Sharp eyes," he said as he pulled out a single-lens spyglass and directed it at the wagon. "You're right... prisoner transport wagon. Bars, and... " Balthoron said as he handed the spyglass over to Magdalena, "it's being readied for royalty."

After taking a few moments to study the wagon, Magdalena handed the spyglass back to Balthoron. "So the Queen's back in the hands of Mordecai... yet he still marches on us."

Balthoron shook his head. "It makes little sense," he said. "Why do this before he consolidates his position as king? He can't really claim that title until the Queen has gone to trial and found guilty... at least not legally. Pushing an attack on the monastery seems premature. Father Goram has too many allies in Taranthi."

"Unless they've been neutralized," Magdalena said. "I need to get word to Horatio. Let's get back before we're detained and questioned."

Balthoron nodded as he pulled on the reins of his horse. "Agreed. Nothing we can do right now."

Magdalena pointed to a couple of higher hills slightly to the north. "Sarah, Kerrick... go over there and keep an eye out," she told the two rangers who had ridden with them. "Give me hourly status reports using your crystal."

As the four rode off, the huge boulder they were next to rose out of the ground. Razor sharp appendages sprouted out of the body as the boulder spun... only the outline of the appendage tips could be seen. Unknown to the warriors in and around the villages of Ashakadi and A'el Ellhendell, the creation stone and follower of the StarSinger Nefertari Arntuile, Maedhros Nénmacil was about to descend upon them in a cascade of death and destruction.

Admiral Tári Shilannia was eating her breakfast in the wardroom of Her Majesty's Ship the *Felicidade*... or *Felicity* as she was more affectionately known by her crew. Though the Felicity was not the largest warship in the fleet, she was one of the fastest. For that reason, Admiral Shilannia often made the Felicity her flag ship when she went to sea.

During the night the Admiral had overseen maneuvers in which the entire east coast fleet had set sail and were now heading for the tip of the "Arrow". Though First Councilor Mordecai had ordered her to stand down, Admiral Shilannia feigned a problem with her crystal. Unfortunately, Mordecai, perhaps expecting a breakdown in communications, had sent a personal representative to personally deliver his orders. Admiral Shalannia smiled. She had taken great pleasure in having that pretentious ass thrown in the brig while his credentials were confirmed. Regrettably, that had taken all night.

Admiral Shilannia was interrupted from her reverie by a Marine walking to her table. "Madam, I have the First Councilor's representative waiting outside per your instructions," the Marine captain said.

Admiral Shilannia nodded. "Thank you, Captain. Please escort him in."

The Captain saluted and retreated to do her bidding. Soon enough a disheveled figure, flanked by four Marines and led by the Marine captain, approached.

"I most strenuously protest the treatment I've been forced to endure. This won't go easy on you, Admiral!" the prisoner said.

"And you are?" Admiral Shilannia asked as she looked over the brim of her coffee mug.

The elf snickered. "Don't play games with me, Admiral. You know very well who I am."

Admiral Shilannia smiled. She loved baiting politicians. "Actually, sir, I don't," she said in all seriousness. "Though your papers seem to check out, documents can be easily forged. For all I know, you could be a spy for the Army. They're pretty serious about the Army-Navy competition coming up in a few weeks."

"That's ridiculous!"

The Admiral attitude grew somber. "Enough banter," she thought. "It's time to end this charade." Unfolding vellums she had in front of her, the Admiral said, "Your papers say you're Second Councilor Fingolfin Celebrindal." She looked up at the elf. "Please forgive me, but I thought Fingolfin Celebrindal was only a Third Councilor."

The elf got even angrier then he already was... if that was possible. His face turned a light shade of red as he puffed his chest out. "Again, I protest this treatment!" he said. His voice had become high-pitched. This self-important minor government agent of Mordecai's sickened Admiral Shilannia... and she was ready to throw him overboard.

"Why are you here?" she asked, although she already knew the answer.

"You have my papers. Among them are your orders to drop anchor and await his Highness... I mean Lord Mordecai's pleasure," Fingolfin Celebrindal replied.

Admiral Shilannia shook her head. "Impossible. We're at sea."

"I know that! I'm not an idiot!" Fingolfin Celebrindal said.

"Oh?"

Fingolfin Celebrindal clenched his fists. "Lord... No... His Highness King Mordecai orders you to turn around," he said haughtily. "As Second Councilor, I demand it!"

Admiral Shilannia rose out of her chair with cat-like agility and slapped the elf across the face, sending him staggering and then down on his backside. Walking over to the prone Fingolfin Celebrindal, she stood over him, drew her sword and placed the point on his neck. "YOU make demands of ME!" she said calmly, but there was steel in her voice. "I'm not aware the Queen had gone to trial and been found guilty of murder, Councilor. Until such time, deferring to Mordecai as our liege is treason." Turning to the Marine captain and his four guards, who were still in the wardroom, Admiral Shilannia nodded.

"Ma'am!" the captain said as he walked over.

"Please be so good as to escort Mr. Celebrindal back to the brig."

"Aye, ma'am," the captain said as he saluted. Already the guards were manhandling Fingolfin Celebrindal to his feet.

"You won't get away with this!" the councilor screamed. He was cuffed across the back of the head.

"Careful, Councilor," the Admiral Shilannia said. "Since you're on a Navy vessel, I could have you court-martialed under Navy regulations. That wouldn't go well for you." Fingolfin Celebrindal smart enough to keep his mouth shut as he was dragged away.

The admiral turned to the Marine captain. "Please tell the ship's captain I wish to see him here in the ward room."

"Ma'am!" the captain said as he saluted.

As she watched the retreating Marine, Admiral Shilannia sighed and sat back down. She didn't want to declare the Navy's loyalties so soon, but Mordecai forced her hand. Despite how she came across, she wasn't prepared to murder one of his councilor's to conceal that fact. "Our fate is sealed with the Queen," she said aloud to an empty room. "May the gods help us all."

Razor and Findley were lounging around Father Goram and Autumn's apartment, occasionally looking up at Father Goram and Autumn to make sure all was right. Ajax would be most put out if anything should ever happen to either of the two elves. Every once in a while one of the two would get up from his warm spot in front of the fireplace and walk through the large dwelling, sniffing and seeking anything that might be out of the ordinary. Both wolves loved Father Goram and Autumn, as did the entire pack... but they were particularly keen on this guard duty because it always meant a large chunk of meat at the end of their watch. What self-respecting wolf would ever turn down a chance to fill his belly? Both Razor and Findley's ears perked up as they sensed a change in Father Goram's attitude. The fireplace was obscured as the two huge dire wolves sat up and watched their benefactors.

"I really thought she'd get away," Autumn said.

Father Goram stared at the communications crystal sitting on the table. "I'm not very surprised. The whole attempt was problematic from the start. I just wish there was something we could've done to help."

Autumn shook her head. "It unfolded much too quickly for us to do anything."

Father Goram nodded. "At least now we know Mordecai has her... again... and that the Army's heading our way. That's good intelligence. Now we need to plan and act accordingly."

"We're doing everything we can to prepare for a siege," Autumn said. "You've told Maggie and Balthoron to shadow the Army and to keep an eye out. We're storing food and those who chose to stay are inside the walls. You and Landross have a solid strategy to defend the monastery." Autumn paused and took a breath. "We have to keep Mordecai bottled up on the island so he won't be free to capture Kristen and Emmy."

"I know," Father Goram said. "But the number of lives that will be lost could be high. The soldiers we must kill aren't the enemy... they're only following orders. And the innocents we'll have here within these walls... they don't deserve the life we'll be offering."

"Most of the people of Calmacil Clearing have already made their choice, so it's not as if we'll be the ones determining their future," Autumn replied. There was harshness in her voice. More softly she said, "No, Horatio, their future is not in your hands... and you'll not be responsible for their decision to stay." Autumn paused. "We don't really have any better alternatives, love. We may not be able to stop the Queen from being convicted... but we can keep Mordecai's attention focused on us as long as possible. We must fight. Otherwise, Mordecai will have a clear path to Kristen and Emmy."

Father Goram nodded. "You're right, of course," he said dolefully. "Though I might force the civilians to leave for their own good. All walls fall eventually. Even a simple priest like me understands that much."

Autumn shook her head. "There's nothing simple about you, dear."

Father Goram smiled. "Except my love for you." The affectionate expression Father Goram had given Autumn changed and he became distant.

"Horatio?" Autumn inquired.

Father Goram looked at Autumn. "I just had a thought," he said. "We'll go to war... but maybe we can do some things that will reduce the number of casualties. Maybe we can change soldiers minds... convince them to rally around their Queen instead of blindly following orders. Get into their heads. I need to talk to Cameron."

"What can I do?" Autumn asked.

Father Goram's fingers were tapping the table. "Take a few of Landross' knights and go find Maggie. I want her to rely a message to Mother Aubria." Father

Goram stood and nodded at Findley to stay with Autumn. "I think it best Maggie hears this from one of us. She probably wouldn't believe it otherwise. And by the goddess, don't tell Landross or any of his knights."

Autumn nodded and also stood. "Mother Aubria's on Listern Island," she said.

Father Goram draped Autumn's cloak around her shoulders, then put his own on. "I know, but that hasn't stopped her from keeping her hand in the pot, so to speak."

"So what message do you want me to give Maggie?" Autumn asked. "What's so secretive you don't want Landross or any of his knights to know?"

Father Goram gave Autumn a kiss on the forehead. "I want Maggie to tell Mother Aubria that I need assassins."

Nefertari and Marine Colonel Daeron Tirion were put into adjoining, windowless cells for the night. Nefertari's magical staff had been taken while the guards removed Colonel Tirion's sword and several other weapons. As to the fate of Colonel Tirion's men, neither could hazard a guess, but Colonel Tirion speculated either they had been rounded up and imprisoned as well, or the Army didn't consider nine Marines a serious threat. If the latter was true, the Army should've known better.

Neither of the two slept, instead preferring to converse... each trying to garner as much information from the other as possible. During these discussions, Nefertari learned much about what was happening on the island of InnisRos, both politically, and militarily... at least from the perspective of a Marine colonel. She learned that other than her sister, the main players were Lessien's First Counselor, Mordecai Lannian, whom the Colonel disliked and was the cause of their current incarceration, Father Horatio Goram, a priest of the goddess Althaya and 'one of the good guys' as the Colonel put it, Naval Chief-of-Staff Admiral Tári Shilannia, Marine Commander-General Aubrey Feynral, and a host of Army generals who the Colonel felt was in league with Mordecai to usurp the Queen's throne.

Nefertari, though open and responsive to the Colonel's many questions, hid the fact she was Lessien's older half-sister and that she was from the Alfheim... among other places. The Colonel was particularly interested in her ability to control the elements and wondered why she couldn't break them out of their confinement. Nefertari explained she needed her staff, which was only a half-lie. While the staff served as a focal point for her power, she could still harness the elements without it if necessary. But Nefertari wasn't ready to expose her command over the five elements to her captors.

The more the two talked, the more they both felt a solidarity of purpose. By the end of the long night their common interests made them allies. As morning dawned, Nefertari and Colonel Tirion had agreed to search out the Queen and spirit her away to safety. As morning dawned, Nefertari told Colonel Tirion to ready himself... the method of their escape would soon be upon them. Nefertari had no idea what Maedhros

Nénmacil was going to do... but she felt whatever it was it was going to be spectacular.

Lessien awoke from a deep, healing sleep before the sun had risen. She was dreaming of her sister, Nefertari. It seemed so vivid. She could still smell Nefertari's scent... still feel the warmth and comfort of her touch... still feel the strength of her presence. Though Lessien knew it was impossible... her sister had been lost to her many years ago... she took refuge in her remembrance of this simple dream. With its help she realized the terrible mistake of suicide. And even more appalling she saw it as an attempt to abandon her people. That brought shame.

Lessien got out of the soft, comfortable bed and went over to a washbasin. She rinsed the sleep from her eyes and straightened up her disheveled appearance in front of the wall-hanging mirror. By the time she was through, she once again looked every bit the Queen that she was--royal, confident, commanding. Even if she was bound by fate to meet Mordecai's headsmen's ax, Lessien was now prepared to do so in a manner befitting her father. She won't allow Mordecai to break her into a fearful, sniveling little child.

Lessien walked over to the door and sharply rapped on it. It was opened immediately by a guard. He and his hulking companion just looked at her.

"You will kneel to your Queen," Lessien reminded them.

They looked at each other, confused.

Lessien understood their dilemma.

"Gentlemen," she said. "Am I convicted? Or only suspected of murder? Though under arrest, I've not been tried and found guilty. I'm still your sovereign and demand the courtesy that goes with it."

The soldiers now looked uncertain and only needed one more small push.

"And if I'm found not guilty?" Lessien asked.

That resonated. After exchanging a momentary glance, both guards went down on a knee. "Yes, Your Highness. How may we be of service?" one of the two replied.

Lessien smiled. "You may rise. I'd like breakfast served."

"Of course."

"And a fresh change of clothes."

"We'll see to it, Highness."

"And my sword." Lessien said finally.

Both men became very still. "Excuse me, Highness. Did you just ask for your sword?"

Lessien nodded and then laughed. "Oh, come now... surely you don't think I present a threat!" she said. "Gentlemen, it belonged to my father as I'm sure you both already know. Since we've established I'm still the queen until found guilty, I should be allowed to maintain at least part of the trappings of my station."

The bigger of the two guards looked at Lessien suspiciously. "Highness, with all due respect, I've seen what you can do with that sword on the practice field." The man shook his head. "I'm not even sure our captain could best you in a fair fight... and he's the best we have out here."

"I've no intention to use it on anyone," Lessien said. "My word on it. But perhaps I'm being unfair. This shouldn't be a decision you have to make. Please get your commanding officer."

"I see nothing wrong with that, Highness," the smaller of the two said. "I'll talk to the Captain and be back shortly with your breakfast and change of clothing."

Lessien smiled. "Thank you," she said. "Oh, before I forget, do you think you can retrieve my cloak? There's a chill out this morning and the trip back to Taranthi will probably be uncomfortable."

The guard bowed. "Very well, Highness."

Lessien closed the door and leaned back against it. "I hope my gambit works," she thought. "I have little time."

Young Jasper was skipping stones across the surface of the Maranwe River. He snuck away from school because of all the exciting things happening on the river. Troop barges full of soldiers constantly moved up river, or made landfall at either Ashakadi or his home village of A'el Ellhendell. As barges passed, Jasper waved, hoping the soldiers would throw him things... such as candy or copper pieces. He was correct. The Army of InnisRos was usually very generous with children, and Jasper had accumulated a small fortune... for a child.

Jasper was a mile south of A'el Ellhendell on the east side of the river. He was smart enough to understand the farther away he was, the longer it would be before his parents or school officials tracked him down and return him to the prison of reading, writing, and mathematics. As he skipped a stone across the water, he heard a commotion coming from the north. The troops on the barges were ignoring him... most pointing to something up on the hill overlooking the two river villages. Jasper looked in that direction and saw a huge boulder as it flew down the hill, spinning at incredible speed. As Jasper watched, the stones in his small hand slid through his fingers and to the ground. Jasper turned and ran as fast as his legs could carry him, hoping to get to his mother and father before the strange flying boulder did. His young mind didn't understand what was happening... only that it scared him. He couldn't know a child would never have reason to fear a creation stone. That wasn't true for some grown-ups, however.

The unexpected arrival of Maedhros Nénmacil in the village of A'el Ellhendell panicked the citizens and the bivouacked soldiers in and around the village. Reaction was swift as Army troops ran to confront the threat. But they soon realized there was no answer for the spinning blades or the imperviousness of the boulder itself. Arrows were useless because they couldn't penetrate the spinning blades before being turned to dust. The steel of swords? Fruitless as they were ripped from hands by the force of the blades, leaving the swords bent, mangled, or broken.

Though to observers it appeared the boulder was making a mad rush forward toward the river, Maedhros Nénmacil was taking every care to avoid direct confrontation. When that became impossible... when a soldier barred his path and refused to relent... Maedhros Nénmacil stopped spinning and, in a deep, rumbling voice, ask the offending person to remove himself from harm's way. The surprised soldier would usually back away... but other times the soldier was so stunned they would freeze in place. This allowed Maedhros Nénmacil to harmlessly avoid the roadblock with no harm done. It wasn't long before the warriors defending the village determined they didn't have the necessary weaponry to stop the creation stone. They cleared a path and formed a barrier so Maedhros Nénmacil could move forward unimpeded without posing a threat to the village populace. He entered the water and disappeared.

Maedhros Nénmacil's progress towards the river through A'el Ellhendell didn't go unnoticed on the other side. General Tathar Ciryatan, the officer commanding the forces in the area... the same general who had Nefertari and Colonel Tirion arrested... shouted orders to his troops across the river to stop what he called "that abomination". Those commands fell on deaf ears, however, despite the general's promise to court-martial each soldier for desertion in the face of the enemy.

Silence fell over the two villages after Maedhros Nénmacil entered the waters of the Maranwe River. Everyone dropped everything they were doing and watched. The only noise heard was the creaking of armor as soldiers positioned themselves for combat. General Ciryatan was determined he wasn't going to give up the Ashakadi side of the river without a fight. He didn't understand the nature of this enemy, but he reasoned its objective... the Queen. He'd sacrifice his whole command to make sure she was returned to Taranthi. Better to die here by the blades of that thing than face Mordecai's particular brand of displeasure.

Five minutes passed, but there was no sign of the creation stone. By now, soldiers were griping their weapons nervously as they stared into the river. Civilians had strengthened their resolve and became willing spectators to the battle soon to come. They sat on the hill overlooking A'el Ellhendell on the east side of the river and lined the docks and the river bank on the Ashakadi side. They too began to fidget in the quiet.

The civilians sitting on the hill, because of their vantage point, were the first to notice a disturbance in the water three hundred feet downriver. Standing, they pointed and shouted as a whirlpool developed in the center of the Maranwe. This strange vortex increased in size as it moved closer to the western bank of the river. Within a few seconds, Maedhros Nénmacil was out of the water and spinning toward Ashakadi. He headed straight toward the government building housing the Queen.

As soon as General Ciryatan saw Maedhros Nénmacil reappear, he ordered his infantry to form an inverse arc in front of the government building. This battlefield tactic created a line of troops that bowed outward... similar to a half-circle. If deployed successfully, when the enemy made contact in the center, the two ends would collapse inward to reinforce the point of impact while other points on the line break and surround the enemy. As his soldiers rushed to obey their orders, General Ciryatan, with his cavalry, charged to intercept, engage, and delay the creation stone as long as possible.

It soon became clear to Maedhros Nénmacil that he wouldn't be able to release the StarSinger from her imprisonment without a regrettable loss of life. Having been forced to make this unfortunate decision, the creation stone was determined to use brutal force to guarantee the outcome. He'd withhold nothing until those who opposed him surrendered to his will. Maedhros Nénmacil stopped spinning, contracted his many razor-sharp arms back into his body, and settled to the ground.

General Ciryatan and his riders surrounded the still boulder. The general cautiously pricked the boulder with his saber. "What the hell should I do now," he said himself.

The general backed his horse up a few paces and looked at his cavalry commander. "I don't like this," he said as he turned his horse around to leave. "Keep this thing surrounded while I get the Queen on her way to Taranthi."

The officer saluted. "How do I stop it if it decides to move?" he asked the general. "It's a damn rock!"

General Ciryatan pulled on the reins to stop his horse. "I don't care how you do it," he said as he looked back over his shoulder. "Get in front of it to slow it down. Dig a hole to drop it into. Jump on it if you have to. Just buy me some time!" As the general rode away, he shouted, "I'll send you the sorceress. Maybe magic can stop it. About time she earned her pay."

That was the last thing the general would ever say as hundreds of small shards exploded out of the boulder in all directions. The fighters manning the inverse arc formation stared, stunned, as the entire cavalry unit, including horses, hit the ground... each visibly holed in several locations on their body... each very much dead. As the witnesses to this devastation gaped, still trying to process what had just happened, the corpses jerked and thrashed about as the shards violently withdrew and retreated back into the boulder. No words were spoken... only the sound of the wind and the gentle call of the morning dove broke the silence that ensued. The boulder rose off the ground. Two eyes appeared and looked over what it had wrought. Then it looked over the line of soldiers nervously waiting. The eyes were angry. They deliberately made contact with each warrior standing in the formation before him. After a few minutes the eyes closed, the blades once again extended from its body, and the boulder began to spin. The soldiers didn't run like craven cowards, however. Despite the fear each one felt, they were much too disciplined. But neither did they relish a fight, either... for they knew they were outclassed and out-muscled. They opened a hole in the line to allow the boulder passage.

Maedhros Nénmacil's eyes reflected the truth. He was angry... angry that he had to kill to achieve his objective. But he was also satisfied. His grim and deadly demonstration had served its purpose. Perhaps he wouldn't have to take another life this day.

CHAPTER FIFTEEN

Elanesse

The vast depths of loneliness and despair will warp the thoughts and feelings of even the most rational being. For some, the expanse of this abyss is simply too great to recover. For others, however, a simple act of kindness will save their soul.

-Book of the Unveiled

The jet-black mass grew... ten, fifteen, twenty feet... until it blocked the doorway just inside the room entrance. From outside the room everyone heard Tangus give warning "Behind you!"... but by then it was too late. The only way out was blocked. At once Safire, Jennifer, and Mariko took fighting stances in front of Kristen and Emmy.

The madness staring down at them, however, made no attempt to attack. From outside the room, Tangus, Azriel, and Lester were rapidly approaching, the hard soles of their boots slapped the stone floor of the cavern. The standoff continued as the "thing" appeared completely unconcerned about either the warriors facing it, or the warriors approaching from behind. Its whirling eyes shifted from one color to another until it showed the colors of the rainbow before starting anew. The overall effect was beautiful and mesmerizing.

The tension in the room was palpable. Mariko looked at this strange threat, then over at the cloak-covered remains of Max, and knew they couldn't defeat this ancient horror. That thought, though sobering, could never overcome her resolve, however. But even still, she didn't want to attack until it was necessary.

The creature attacked first. Part of it moved with incredible quickness and went under Lester's cloak covering Max's body. Everyone stared as the cloak began to rise. When the cloak slipped to the floor, the creature was standing before them, dressed in Max's bloody skin. Jennifer retched while everyone else stared in horror. The moment between heartbeats when each hesitated, stunned, was enough to give the advantage to the creature. A part of it had slithered between the feet of Tangus, Azriel, and Lester and came up behind them. As it did, razor-like blades sprang out of the thick, black ichors. With brutal efficiency, all three were down and bleeding from numerous wounds before they could defend themselves.

Mariko, Safire, and Jennifer didn't share the disadvantage of having the creature behind them. Mariko and Safire charged the Max skin, swords held high and ready to strike, while Jennifer aimed her bow, deadly arrow notched and ready to fly.

Kristen positioned herself in front of Emmy and raised her arms in supplication to her goddess Althaya and asked for her mistress's indulgence. A blue beam of light pierced the underground cavern from above and collated to a point centered between her outstretched arms. "MANUS HABENT CURATIONUM," she whispered. Three blue-glowing hands appeared over Tangus, Azriel, and Lester. Each enchanted hand touched their intended target and discharged their healing magic. All cuts and slashes caused by the creature's blades were healed, leaving not a single blemish. The blood lost to the injuries was replaced... hearts were beating stronger than before. The three warriors stood, refreshed and completely cured of their battle wounds, and rejoined the fray.

Kristen felt faint and dropped to a knee. She had used a good part of her magical resources to create the powerful healing spell required to restore her husband and friends. She needed a few moments to recover... moments she knew she didn't have. Kristen stood and surveyed the battle. Despite the best efforts of her companions, it didn't appear swords, arrows, or axes were having much of an effect on the creature. If it didn't block sword strikes or arrows with its own blades, successful attacks only slipped through the creature's body causing no apparent harm. The attacks from the creature, however, caused quite a bit of damage. What appeared to be hundreds of blades always struck accurately and with a quickness that couldn't be matched by even the most well-trained warrior.

Kristen's friends were once again absorbing a tremendous amount of injuries. Blood, mixed with a few pieces of Max's skin which had been hacked off, ran in rivers. This affected everyone's footing as well as their grip on weapons. The creature seemed undaunted. As Kristen watched, trying to think of effective magic to use on the creature, her companions were again falling one by one. In only a matter of minutes everyone was prone and, if not already unconscious, moaning as their life drained from their bodies.

The creature ignored Kristen and Emmy. It moved to deliver the *coup de grâce* to each of the wounded and dying. Kristen felt helpless. It was as if she were in another world... as if the battle being played out in front of her was happening from far away. Kristen cried as her hopes and dreams were being snuffed out. She clutched her mace and started forward, hoping to at least slow the slaughter of her beloved husband and friends... and to join them in their journey to the world of the dead. A small hand checked her movement. "My Emmy!" she thought as she shook off her anguish. "What was I about to do?!"

Emmy looked up at Kristen and shook her head. "Mother, brute force won't work against this ancient creature," she said.

"What will?" Kristen asked.

"I don't know," Emmy replied. "The creature's protecting its lair. To it, we're the invaders... and a threat to its existence. Perhaps it has a family hidden somewhere. Who knows?" Emmy watched the creature. It had stopped its attacks and became still... as if it heard Emmy's words. "Mother, maybe it can understand us. If we can communicate with it... show it we mean no harm and are only passing through... perhaps it'll relent."

"How do we do that, sweetie," Kristen asked. "We have little time... your father and the others are dying."

Emmy shook her head and walked towards her friends... the people who would give up their lives to keep her safe... her family. The creature turned and looked at her, but made no overt move to intercept.

Lester stirred and looked up at the creature towering above him. In the background he heard Kristen and Emmy talking, but he couldn't understand their words. All around his friends were laying still... only the occasional groan told him they were still alive. Mustering every ounce of strength he had left, he slowly sat up. His armor was bent, creased, and sliced open. His helmet lay several feet away... it was damaged beyond repair. He remembered a severe blow to the head. He felt tired. Each movement a struggle against exhaustion. Getting to his knees, he reached down and picked up his sword. Placing the tip on the floor in front of him, he leaned his head against the hilt and said a prayer. Slowly he stood. He wobbled before he found his footing... and even then he couldn't stand straight. His whole body trembled. He didn't have the strength to lift his sword. Lester just stood there and looked at the creature defiantly.

But the creature didn't strike.

Following Lester's example, one by one each of the others stood. Like Lester, none of them had the strength to continue the battle. Each could've been blown over by a wisp of air. But that didn't matter... only that they die bravely.

Still the creature didn't strike.

Emmy took Kristen's hand and looked up at her. She didn't speak... but she didn't have to. Both knew that neither would leave voluntarily.

Still the creature didn't strike.

Kristen, crying as she watched the courage and bravery displayed by her husband and friends, led Emmy to stand with them. The fate of the world could now rest in another's hands... for now they would die together.

Still the creature didn't strike.

Lester toppled over, his heavy armor hitting the stone floor with a crash. Safire used the last bit of energy she had to kneel and cradle his head in her lap. Kristen, letting her nurturing impulse take over, rushed to Lester to heal him as best as she could. Both Kristen and Safire were acting on instinct and love, never once considering that death might be a blessing.

Still the creature didn't strike.

With Lester stabilized, Kristen and Emmy went among their friends and loved ones, dispensing healing magic to each.

Still the creature didn't strike.

"What do you think it's waiting for?" Jennifer asked.

Tangus shook his head. "I don't know. It's a bit disconcerting," he replied.

"Creepy is more like it, lassie," Azriel remarked.

Jennifer persisted. "But why isn't it attacking?"

Mariko sheathed both of her katanas. "We can't run fast enough, we can't defeat it, and we can't ignore it. It knows that all too well. It wants something else. Something having nothing to do with our deaths."

"How... " Azriel said.

Emmy interrupted him. "Mariko is correct. It doesn't want to kill us any longer." Emmy shook her head. "But I can't fathom what it does want."

"We know better than to doubt our young charge, here," Safire said.

"Indeed!" Lester exclaimed. "Mistress Emmy does seem to have an uncanny ability to read emotions and intent." Lester then looked suspiciously at Mariko. "Apparently Lady Mariko has this same aptitude as well."

"Of course she does, dear Lester," Emmy explained matter-of-factly. "She belongs to me."

"She..."

"That's enough, folks," Kristen said, hoping to drive a wedge between Lester and his questioning thought. If what Kristen suspected was true, now wasn't the time to have this conversation. "We have other things to worry about."

Tangus watched the exchange between Emmy, Lester, and his wife. "Something's going on with Emmy," he thought. "First when Elanesse's dead queen bowed to her and now this. I need to speak to Kristen... though I know she's going to make fun of me because I'm probably missing the obvious." Tangus frowned. "Mariko accepted that she belonged to Emmy," he said to himself. "What does that even mean? Strange."

Azriel moved forward toward the creature. "I don't know about the rest of you, but that thing killed my friend," he barked. "I'm going to kill it and I'd appreciate your help."

"No!" Kristen shouted.

Azriel stopped and turned to face Kristen... his eyes burned with fury, though everyone who saw them didn't know if it was because of the creature or Kristen. "Lassie," he said with barely controlled rage, "that thing's going back to the hell that spawned it, or, by the gods, I am."

Azriel attacked the creature before any of his friends could stop him, screaming dwarven invectives as he did so. Time after time his battleaxe struck, the magic of the weapon flashing its magic each time he did so. But for each stroke of the battleaxe, the creature countered with a defense of its own which effectively negated everything Azriel tried to do. To the amazement of all, however, the creature only shielded itself. It didn't harm Azriel.

Azriel's arms were heavy and his battleaxe felt like it was two tons of steel. He roared at the top of his lungs and made one last attack. In the brief exchange that followed, his battleaxe was knocked from his hands and it flew through the air. It hit the cavern floor, skidded and crashed into a wall. Azriel stood in front of the creature, forcing air into his lungs. He turned to his friends.

"Well, are you going to just stand there?" he asked. "Or are you going to help me bring this monstrosity down?"

"Azriel," Tangus replied, "look at yourself. Not a scratch on you."

"Aye, laddie," Azriel remarked as he looked at Tangus. "That's because I know how to defend myself."

Kristen shook her head. "It's more than that, Azriel," she said. "The creature doesn't seem to want our lives anymore. Lives, my dear friend, that it can take if it so chooses. We can't defeat it with swords and battleaxes, and I don't think I have enough experience to defeat it with magic... even if I had the magic left to do so. I need rest."

Azriel looked at his friends.

Tangus understood. "Azriel, we'd die with you," he said. "You know that. But we didn't step in because the creature wasn't fighting back. We were ready to intercede, but we didn't want to force it into a corner. Kristen's right. We can't survive this encounter."

Azriel looked up at the creature before him. It was just standing there... its colorful, whirling eyes studying Azriel with interest. Azriel nodded to the creature. He started to retrieve his battleaxe but stopped and sat down on the floor. Reaching into his vest, he took out half a cigar, as much a victim of the creature as was his sliced, torn, and bloody vest. "Max gave this to me," he said. "He told me to smoke it on a special occasion. I guess this qualifies." As the cigar smoke swirled around him, he lowered and shook his head. "Max wouldn't want us to die to avenge him, anyway."

"What do you suppose it wants?" Safire asked.

Emmy had a ready answer. "She wants to go home."

"Attack! Attack! Attack!"

"Kill! Kill! Kill!"

The mindless, mad followers of the Purge flooded the sewer system... seeking the entrance to the labyrinth below it. To a man they were willing to rush to their death as they sought the pleasure of the Purge. They didn't care. Neither did the Purge.

"Attack! Attack! Attack!"

"Kill! Kill! Kill!"

"You can talk with it... her, sweetheart?" Tangus asked.

Emmy shook her head. "Not so much talking with her as understanding her needs on a more... emotional level," Emmy replied. "Though I suppose that's certainly a form of communication. She also understands me... or, I guess, my feelings." Emmy hesitated. "Father, the myth of her evil is just that... a myth. She's neither good nor evil. She simply... is."

"Seems to me if she wasn't evil she wouldn't have killed Max, lassie," Azriel remarked.

"Fear, Azriel," Emmy responded. "One of the strongest, if not the strongest, of all emotions. It can force us to do terrible things to survive... to feel safe again. The only response she knows is to fight until the fear she senses is no more."

Azriel snorted. "Fear... bah! Max wasn't a threat to no one!"

Emmy nodded. "She understands that now," she replied. "But at the time she saw him as an invader. She didn't know until it was too late that Max was just as frightened as she was."

"Max... afraid?" Azriel said as he shook his head. "By the beard of my forefathers! Nothing scared Max! If he was so spooked, why'd he put himself up front all the time?"

"Friend Azriel," Lester said, "Max was always in the front because of his special thieving skills. How many times did he save our lives by finding and disarming deadly traps?"

"More times than I can count," Azriel replied. "He was the best thief in the business."

"And he knew that," Lester admitted. "He was also the most conceited individual I've ever met. He was extremely confident of his abilities. But unknown situations and dark places terrified him."

Azriel looked at Lester. "How do you know that?" he asked.

"Friend Azriel, we spent many hours on the keep battlements watching the sun go down," Lester replied. "Hours that led to discussions of many different things. Discussions... and confessions."

"Then why'd he do it?" Azriel asked harshly. "Why'd he put himself in the very places that he feared so much?"

"Because of us," Tangus said as he nodded to Lester. "Azriel, he did it to protect us. You see, my friend, he feared our death even more than his own. We were his family."

Azriel looked dejected. "Did everybody know this except me?"

Neither Tangus nor Lester answered.

Kristen broke the uneasy silence. "We should see Max properly buried. Then we need to see if we can help this... whatever she is," she said as she pointed to the creature.

"She's a sylph," Emmy said.

"I've heard stories of such creatures," Safire said.

"They're not stories, Safire," Mariko replied. "The sylph is a creature of the world below ours. Occasionally one awakens from the deep sleep forced upon them by the ancient gods and loses their way... only to find themselves stranded up here on the surface."

"And you know this how?" Azriel asked suspiciously.

Mariko smiled. "Relax. I'm not in league with the devil. We've procured very old and precious texts that tell the story. My guild actually has a plan in place to capture a sylph the next time one surfaces. They'd make excellent assassins. Though after what we've just experienced, I don't think my guild leaders have a true sense of the... challenges... offered by the sylph."

"No kidding," remarked Jennifer.

"Indeed!" Lester said. "I suspect it'd mean one less assassin's guild."

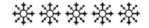

Kristen performed a "field funeral" for Max... so named because this burial is carried out on the battlefield, or the "field of death," as the ancient elven bard Eöl Tolommaitë described in his epic song, *Lost Reason*:

> *"Winter night, long and cold.*
> *Blankets the warriors, oh so bold.*
>
> *Mothers and fathers could not shield,*
> *their sons and their daughters sprawled on the field.*
>
> *Winter night, long and cold.*
> *Blankets the warriors, oh so bold.*
>
> *This field of death, oh so still.*
> *Carrion eaters devour their fill.*
>
> *Winter night, long and cold.*
> *Blankets the warriors, oh so bold.*
>
> *Kings and Queens sacrifice the brave,*
> *for power or greed, whatever they crave.*
>
> *Winter night, long and cold.*
> *Blankets the warriors, oh so bold."*

After Kristen had completed the memorial service for Max... and everyone had made peace with his departure... she sealed the entrance to the small chamber by magically fusing the adjoining stone together to create an airtight tomb. The sylph waited patiently.

The sylph led them through a maze of dark tunnels until finally stopping at a large hole in a much larger cavern. Unlike the rest of this dark, damp underground world, which had remained untouched for thousands of years, this cavern showed obvious signs of a disturbance... probably from a small earthquake. Stalagmites were broken and overturned, while stalactites had fallen from the ceiling of the cavern far above. Their crumpled remains reduced to chunks of stone littering the floor.

Tangus took a hand-size rock and dropped it into the hole.

"From the time it took to hit bottom, I'd say maybe about a hundred feet deep," Azriel commented as he stared into the darkness of the hole. Turning to Emmy, he asked, "Is this the way to her home?"

Emmy nodded.

"So I guess the sylph got trapped here by an earthquake that occurred thousands of years ago," Tangus said.

Kristen nodded. "Long enough ago for the sylph to become a legendary creature in Elanesse who, herself, has been dead and abandoned for several thousand years."

"Elanesse isn't dead, friend Kristen," Lester gently reminded the priestess.

Kristen shook her head. "No, my dear friend, she isn't, is she."

Safire whistled. "The sylph must be incredibly old!"

"She's almost immortal, Safire," Emmy stated. "Her kind has lived, and will live, as long as the world of Aster lives. They have no natural predators or diseases. They don't know how to hate. They don't experience greed, jealousy, or the need for power... so they don't murder."

"So they live in a perfect little utopia," Safire remarked.

Emmy looked at Safire. "Nothing's perfect," she said.

The look in Emmy's eyes took Safire's breath away, and she stepped back. She saw enormous depth... wisdom and knowledge all wrapped up into one little girl. Emmy's stare reverted back to that of a child. Safire didn't know what to think... but she understood Emmy had, with a simple look, entrusted her with something that was important. "I wonder if anyone else has questions about Emmy?" she thought to herself. "Vague references about Mariko... that thing with Romulus needing a mate... Elanesse's first Queen showing obeisance to her. I need to talk to..." but Safire was jolted out of her reverie by Azriel.

"Laddie, you mean we take time to excavate?!" Azriel said with disbelief.

Tangus smiled. "We have complete faith in your dwarven ability to work the stone," he replied. "Of course we'll help."

"Dwarves are short, in case you haven't noticed," Azriel remarked. "I can't just step in the hole with pick and hammer to clear the obstruction. Laddie, you first got to get me down there, which should be easy enough. Then we need to figure out how to get the stone out of the hole. Do you have any idea how many feet of stone I'll have to tunnel through?"

Tangus shook his head.

"Of course you don't," Azriel replied wryly. "It could be one foot or twenty. How long do you suppose it'll take to bring that much loose stone out of the hole?"

Tangus stuttered. "I... ahhh..."

"And what if that thing... that sylph... has buddies waiting on the other side?" Azriel continued.

"Surely not after this much time," Tangus replied weakly.

Azriel threw his hands up in the air. "Not after this much time? Tangus, the damn thing's immortal, at least according to Emmy. It doesn't CARE about time! If it's got angry friends on the other side, we're all dead."

"And if we don't help, THIS sylph might kill us," Kristen replied.

That stopped Azriel's rant. "Aye, lassie, you're probably correct."

Jennifer edged over to the hole, giving the sylph a wide berth, and looked down. "Why don't we just punch a hole through the rock. Seems a bit easier than digging it all out."

Everyone stopped talking and stared at her.

"I mean, you've seen what that thing can do. It moves like a fog." Everyone continued to stare. Jennifer gulped, but didn't let the silence stop her. "It could just... seep... through a hole. Couldn't it?"

Azriel nudged Tangus in the side with his elbow and nodded. "Pretty smart kid you got there. But I've known that all along." Azriel moved over to Jennifer, grabbed her hands, and pulled her down slightly so he could give her a quick kiss on the forehead. "Aye, lassie, you said it. A damn sight better than digging it out."

Turning, Azriel rubbed his hands together. "Now we're talking. Emmy, lassie, you tell that sylphie thing to just hold her horses. We'll get her home. Tangus, I need rope and a long pick."

Tangus shook his head. "A long pick?"

Kristen smiled. "Don't worry, honey. I have just the thing." She pulled out a short, steel rod. It glowed with magical enchantment. "A gift from Vayl... long before he turned traitor," she remarked. Kristen closed her eyes and whispered several words under her breath. The steel rod flashed and in her hand was now a six-foot long, steel quarterstaff. "Will this do?" she asked Azriel.

"You know how to use that thing?" Azriel asked Kristen.

Tangus laughed. "Of course she does. Kristen, give Azriel a demonstration."

Kristen smiled as she whirled the quarterstaff. Her movements with it were graceful, fluid, and precise. She directed all her concentration on her dance with the quarterstaff. It was stunning.

When she had finished, Safire clapped. "I've never seen you use a weapon with so much beauty and grace," she remarked.

"Vayl taught me... mostly in private," Kristen replied. "He was extremely accomplished with the quarterstaff."

"Okay... let's get me hooked up to some rope and get this done," Azriel said as he took the quarterstaff from Kristen. "Let's hope I don't have to defend myself with this."

Azriel took the one hundred foot long rope offered to him by Jennifer and tied one end into a large hangman's knot. While he was doing this, Tangus hammered several spikes into the stone floor of the cavern. He then tied the other end of the rope to the spikes. Looking at Azriel and Lester, Tangus nodded.

Azriel fitted his end of the rope around his rear to use it as a chair. He made sure he had a solid grip on Kristen's quarterstaff and then nodded that he was ready. Tangus and Lester grabbed the rope and slowly lowered the dwarf down. It was quiet for the next several minutes as Tangus and Lester lowered Azriel deeper and deeper into the hole.

"I didn't notice this from above, but, starting about twenty-five feet down, the walls are covered in a moss-type plant which gives off a dim, greenish glow," Azriel called. "Slight... but enough that I can use it to see."

"Have you spotted the bottom yet?" Lester called down to the dwarf.

"Laddie, I've only just barely started," Azriel replied.

Several more minutes passed in silence. On top of the hole, only Tangus and Lester made noise as they strained to keep Azriel's descent from becoming a free-fall. Suddenly, everyone heard the distinct sound of metal striking stone, followed by Azriel shouting, "Oh, crap!"

"Attack! Attack! Attack!"

"Kill! Kill! Kill!"

Thirteen men scrambled down an old tunnel. They felt no fear or pain. They had become animals... far more dangerous than any thinking, rational being. As they rushed headlong into the tunnel, the stone beneath their feet cracked. With each step they took, the crack became deeper and longer. With each step they took, the crack fractured into many other cracks until finally the floor could no longer sustain the weight of the men. It collapsed into a chamber below with a crash and a rumble. None of the thirteen men survived the one hundred foot drop to the floor below. The tremor of the collapse reverberated for miles throughout the lower burrows.

Minutes later several ropes dropped down and torchlight filled the emptiness of the cavern. Soon men were climbing down the ropes.

"Attack! Attack! Attack!"

"Kill! Kill! Kill!"

"What's wrong?" Tangus shouted down the shaft at Azriel. He and Lester had stopped lowering the dwarf.

"Didn't you feel that?" Azriel replied. "It felt like a small earthquake."

Tangus looked around. Everybody shook their heads. "No, nothing up..." Tangus stopped and looked back. "Where's the sylph?"

Suddenly the rope moved violently and slipped through Tangus and Lester's hands. Safire, Jennifer, and Mariko each grabbed a part of it and lent their strength to brace and stabilize the unexpected jerky contortions Azriel was putting on the rope.

Azriel suddenly screamed. "Get me out of here!"

CHAPTER SIXTEEN

InnisRos

"Holy crap!"

-Exclamation from an unknown soldier after seeing what a flying boulder did to a legion of mounted cavalry.

The creation stone, Maedhros Nénmacil, watched as the soldiers opened their line of battle to allow him to pass. "It would seem," Maedhros Nénmacil thought, "they've learned the lesson I have just taught." He moved forward cautiously with the knowledge they could actually be setting a trap. But nothing happened as each soldier watched him pass. Maedhros Nénmacil wasn't an expert in mortal behavior, but as he moved through the long line of soldiers, he didn't see fear in their eyes... but instead what looked like relief.

Maedhros Nénmacil knew where he was going... he could feel the presence of the StarSinger... and was soon in front of a large and heavily fortified building. A flesh and blood ring surrounded the structure, led by a young lieutenant who seemed intent upon defending what was inside with the lives of the soldiers under his command. The lieutenant broke through the line of soldiers and warily approached the creation stone. He stopped twenty feet away.

"Do you understand me?" he asked.

Maedhros Nénmacil did. He understood and spoke all the languages of the world of Aster. "Yes," he rumbled.

Even though the lieutenant had come to parley, he hadn't expected the boulder to speak. Though briefly taken aback, he recovered quickly. "I'm afraid I can't allow you to take the Queen," he said.

Now it was Maedhros Nénmacil's turn to be taken aback. "A queen?" he thought. "Do they think the StarSinger is their queen?"

"Even as we speak you're being surrounded," the lieutenant boldly continued. "Don't doubt our resolve... we'll stop you. I give you this one chance to leave peacefully."

Maedhros Nénmacil looked around. He had indeed been surrounded. But these soldiers, the same soldiers who had let him pass, looked like they were only interested in seeing what was going to happen... not to try and stop him. The creation stone laughed... a deep low rumble that shook the surrounding buildings. He then extended his blades and spun. As one, the soldiers moved back. But Maedhros Nénmacil didn't move forward. Instead, he went straight up.

Lessien was just finishing up a warm and fulfilling breakfast when she heard a commotion coming from outside her room. Soldiers were running up and down the hallway and shouting excitedly. Lessien got up and, with her coffee cup in hand, went over to the southeast corner window in her second-story room. "By the gods!" she explained.

About a quarter mile away she saw a large boulder surrounded by a ring of soldiers. Even as she watched, more soldiers were being disgorged from river barges to join the encirclement. Amazingly, one soldier, probably an officer, seemed to be talking to the boulder.

When Lessien turned her gaze further to the southeast, she suddenly had to struggle for breath. Her coffee cup crashed to the floor. She saw the killing field. Two hundred cavalry soldiers with their horses lay dead. "Oh no," Lessien whispered as she backed away from the window and sat down in a chair.

A quick rap on her door was the only warning she received before it opened. The captain of her guard stepped in and walked over to where she was sitting. He was carrying her sword and cloak.

"You've seen what's going on, Highness?" he asked.

Lessien nodded.

The captain knelt in front of the Queen. "I don't know what strange forces are in play," he said. "But from what I've seen, we're in a good bit of jeopardy. Here's your sword and cloak as you requested." The captain shook his head. "I wasn't inclined to give you the sword, but..." The captain shook his head.

"What is it, Captain?" Lessien asked. She had recovered from her brief shock at his submission and listened carefully.

"Highness, I'm supposed to guard you with my life," he replied. "Not because you're the Queen, but because Mordecai ordered it. I believe the charges against you were fabricated. But if I aid you in any way to escape, I, as well as those under my command, will be executed as traitors. I have a responsibility to them. However, in the commotion, perhaps I can look away while you leave?"

Lessien remained silent as the captain got up and walked across the room. At the doorway he paused and looked back. "Unfortunately, all I can offer is a chance. There's a horse saddled and ready on the north side of the building. While we're occupied with this threat, you should be able to commandeer a barge for the crossing. Head northeast to Calmacil Clearing and ask Father Goram for asylum. There's no love lost between him and Mordecai... he'll protect you. I'll stall as long as I can to give you a head start. Safe travel, Your Highness."

As the captain turned to leave, Lessien called out. "Captain!"

He stopped.

"You're right about me," she said. "I'm innocent. As you suspect, Mordecai arranged the murder of my friend and framed me for it. I... I feel you should hear this from my own lips."

The captain nodded. "I'm a simple soldier... not a politician. I try to keep my opinions to myself and follow orders. But this whole incident has made me extremely uncomfortable... as it has my warriors." The captain sighed. "I believe you. Now, if there's nothing else, Your Highness?"

Lessien stood. "Of course, Captain. Please be careful."

The captain came to attention, clicked his heals together, and saluted. "My Queen..."

A few seconds after the captain left the room, the whole building suddenly shook violently and Lessien was thrown to the floor. The smoke and dust was so thick she couldn't see beyond a few feet. Coughing, Lessien felt along the floor until she found her sword... but the scabbard had come off and was missing. Lessien stood slowly and waited for the smoke to clear. When it did, she saw the wall... and hallway outside her room... had completely collapsed. Of the captain and the two guards there was no sign.

StarSinger Nefertari Arntuile and Marine Colonel Daeron Tirion, though they had no windows in their guarded basement cells, heard commotion inside and outside the building. They could hear the boots of soldiers as they ran across the floor... sergeants and officers giving orders... cursing and complaining about the early hour and the interruption of their breakfast. Finally, they heard the sound of weapons being readied for use.

"I presume that's the friend you spoke of coming to our rescue?" Colonel Tirion said.

Nefertari nodded. "No doubt," she replied. "Though I have no idea what he's going to do."

"Colonel!" someone called.

"Over here," the colonel shouted back.

Soon keys were inserted into the lock on the colonel's cell and the door swung open to reveal several Marines standing on the other side.

Colonel Tirion saw cigar smoke drifting in the air before Sergeant Eären Lossëhelin poked his head into the room. "You okay, sir?" the sergeant asked.

"I'm fine, Sergeant," Colonel Tirion replied. "Open the adjoining cell."

"Already done, sir," another Marine shouted out.

When Colonel Tirion stepped out of his cell, he was met by his Marines and Nefertari. "How do you fare, madam?" The colonel asked.

"None the worse for wear. Thank you, Colonel."

Colonel Tirion nodded. "Eären, the guards?"

"Sleeping like babies, Colonel," the sergeant replied. "They'll have a headache when they regain consciousness... but that's about all."

Colonel Tirion nodded. "I need my sword."

Sergeant Lossëhelin wasted no time in sending one of his men to the guardroom. Soon the colonel's sword was resting in the sheath hanging on his side... back where it belonged.

"And the lady's staff," Colonel Tirion said.

"No need," Nefertari replied as she extended her hand. Her staff flew through the open door of the guardroom and alighted in her outstretched hand. The Marines watched in amazement as streaks of multi-colored light flashed from Nefertari's hand and into the staff as she re-established her bond.

Colonel Tirion turned his attention to Sergeant Lossëhelin. "What's the situation?"

Sergeant Lossëhelin shook his head. "Well, sir, I'd say the situation is somewhat... ah... fluid at the moment. And strange. Yes sir, I'd definitely say strange."

Nefertari chuckled. "Sergeant Lossëhelin, strange doesn't even begin to cover it."

The sergeant looked curiously at Nefertari. "Pardon me... please go on," she said.

"Something big came out of the river. The General tried to contain it with his cavalry, but was massacred."

Nefertari winced.

"Stop right there, Sergeant," the Colonel ordered. "What do you mean massacred?"

"I don't know how they died, just that the General and his cavalry had it surrounded and then were all killed." Sergeant Lossëhelin shook his head. "The troops are pretty riled up, Colonel. And scared."

The whole building suddenly shook and the ceiling above them began to collapse. Everybody except Nefertari scattered and jumped for cover as a huge boulder landed a few feet away... from the top of the building, through both floors, and into the basement jail, crushing everything beneath it.

"Someone use a catapult?" one of the Marines shouted over the din of falling stone and timber.

As the smoke cleared, gasps of surprise escaped some of the Marines. Before them, the boulder smiled. "It is good to see you again, StarSinger!" it said. Its voice gravely and deep... deep enough it reverberated throughout the underground chamber. Several small stones fell on the Marines from above... forced off their precarious perches by the vibration. None of the Marines, however, seemed to notice.

Nefertari chuckled. "Colonel, this is my friend. His name is Maedhros Nénmacil."

The boulder rose slightly and tipped to one side. "It's indeed a pleasure to meet the allies of StarSinger Nefertari Arntuile."

All the Marines, including Colonel Tirion, suddenly stopped looking at the creation stone and turned to stare at Nefertari.

"Arntuile?" the Colonel said.

Nefertari nodded. "I'm your Queen's sister."

A soldier... a member of the Army host... suddenly came bolting out of a door at the other end of the hallway. He didn't get far before two Marines forcibly detained him. There was a brief calculated look on his face... followed by one of feigned panic.

"We got to get out of here," he screamed as he struggled to break the grip of the Marines holding him.

Colonel Tirion faced the squirming soldier. "Stop this minute!" he roared. His own Marines were used to their Colonel's rage. Though it wasn't as bad as Sergeant Lossëhelin's annoyance, Colonel Tirion wasn't a tenderfoot when it came to voicing displeasure. The soldier gulped and at once calmed.

"That's better," Colonel Tirion said. "Now, what's the problem?"

"Fire, sir. Fire in the armory down the hall," the soldier replied.

Colonel Tirion knew that wasn't the entire story. The soldier was running for his life. "And...?"

The soldier looked from Colonel Tirion to the end of the hallway and back. "We stored liquid fire in there. Several fifty-gallon casks. The earthquake knocked several torches off the walls."

"Liquid fire!" Sergeant Lossëhelin yelled. "But that's... ," Sergeant Lossëhelin paused before he continued. "You lit torches in there! Oh hell... what kind of damn fool does that around liquid fire. Leave it to the Army to screw something like this up. Idiots! Morons! Bunch of low life, no good..."

"Calm down, Sergeant," Colonel Tirion ordered as he grabbed the soldier by the front of his tunic and stared into his eyes. "Torches? Really?"

The soldier looked down sheepishly. "Well sir... actually a cigar, sir... on a bale of silk. It sort of got out of control."

Sergeant Lossëhelin yelled again. "Of all the stupidest... sir, this whole building's going to explode. Hell, probably the whole village."

"I know, Sergeant," Colonel Tirion replied as he nodded to the two Marines holding the Army soldier. As soon as he was released, he fled.

Nefertari stepped forward. "Let me handle the fire. You go find my sister and get her out of here."

Colonel Tirion nodded. "Sergeant, see to it. Also, send a couple of men to get our horses ready. And evacuate the building... or what's left of it."

Sergeant Lossëhelin saluted.

Colonel Tirion returned the salute. "Don't forget to get horses for Nefertari here and the Queen. Oh, and Sergeant, how about, at least for the time being, you stamp out your cigar. Just to be on the safe side."

Sergeant Lossëhelin, embarrassed, did as his commanding officer asked before disappearing with his Marines.

"Colonel, really, I can... " Nefertari said.

"I'm coming with you," the colonel replied, brushing off Nefertari's objection.

Nefertari nodded and started down the hallway. "Maedhros Nénmacil!" Nefertari called over her shoulder. "Please provide a distraction while we take care of this?"

"Certainly, StarSinger," the creation stone said before flying back out of the building.

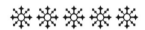

Lessien wrapped herself in the cloak and whispered the command word 'Finduilas' to activate its invisibility function. Her first thoughts were for the captain and his men who are probably buried beneath the rubble below. But she knew she had to be quick with her search, for the magic of the cloak lasted only two hours and she still needed to make her escape.

She made her way to the first floor, carefully traversing several piles of building rubble. She found the three soldiers after a few minutes of searching. They had taken cover under a pillared overhang. Though the collapse had rendered them unconscious, they avoided the worst and Lessien felt they'd be fine. As Lessien looked at the damage around her, she swore. The entire building was unstable and could give way at any moment. The decision wasn't difficult for Lessien. She couldn't leave these three soldiers behind. After all, she was still their Queen, and these soldiers were still her responsibility.

She took the cloak of invisibility off her shoulders and, looking around, found an empty backpack to stuff it into. After shrugging into the backpack, she removed debris from the trapped elves. Two of the soldiers were only lightly covered. The third, the captain, was more firmly trapped, however. "I'll need a lever," Lessien thought to herself.

Grabbing the wrists of one soldier, Lessien dragged him out of the rubble. She was well muscled and had little difficulty. She left him just outside the front door. Returning to the second soldier, she dragged him out as well and was just about to return for the captain when she heard movement behind her. Thinking she'd been caught, Lessien sighed and turned. Several Marines stood facing her.

One, a sergeant from the look of the epaulets on his uniform, saluted and said, "Your Highness, we're at your service. And right now that means getting you out of here."

Lessien pointed to the two soldiers lying at her feet. "They should be fine," she said. "Do you want my surrender?"

The sergeant drew back. "Your surrender?" he said. "Of course not. Highness, we're Marines."

"I know that," Lessien replied.

"The Navy... and by extension the Marines... don't take orders from Mordecai like the Army," the sergeant said. "We're here to rescue you." Turning to his fellow Marines, the sergeant issued commands. Several Marines worked on freeing the trapped captain, who was regaining consciousness, while the others checked the rest of the bottom floor of the building for more trapped people.

The sergeant gently took Lessien's elbow and led her toward a rear entrance. "Your Highness, my Colonel and your sister want you evacuated as soon as possible. We'll... "

Lessien stopped. "Wait Sergeant, did you say my sister?"

Sergeant Lossëhelin nodded. "At least that's what she said. And I wasn't about to argue with her."

Lessien couldn't believe it. Yes, she had distant memories of her sister Nefertari, but her father told her Nefertari was queen of the ancient elven home of the Alfheim. What's she doing on Aster?

"Take me to her, Sergeant," Lessien ordered.

Sergeant Lossëhelin shook his head. "I'm sorry, Your Highness, but I have my orders and your safety comes first."

Their argument was interrupted by a huge boulder that flew past them and out of the building.

Lessien and Sergeant Lossëhelin watched it go up. While Lessien stared, stunned, the sergeant took it in stride. He pointed at the boulder as it made a ninety-degree turn to the south. "And then there's also that," the sergeant said calmly. "A friend of your sister's."

Sergeant Lossëhelin reached inside of his tunic and produced a fresh cigar which he put in his mouth, unlit. "And I DO NOT want to piss that thing off!"

Lessien, still looking up at the now empty sky, held her hand out. "Sergeant, you got one of those cigars for me?"

Nefertari and Colonel Tirion raced down the hallway towards the closed storeroom door. Smoke was already escaping through the seams.

"Tell me about this 'liquid fire', Colonel," Nefertari asked as the two stopped in front of the door.

Colonel Tirion didn't respond right away. When he did, Nefertari could hear the distress, and anger, in his voice. "Liquid fire... other than magic, it's a soldiers worst nightmare. It's a sticky, incendiary substance that keeps burning even when water is thrown on it. It doesn't stop burning until it's either removed from the air or it burns itself out."

"How do you treat someone who gets touched with it?"

"If the soldier survives long enough, we immerse him or her in water," the colonel replied. "The liquid fire will stop burning... but it'll reignite again as soon as it's exposed to air. While underwater, we either have to scrap it off with a knife or, in severe cases, amputate the limb."

Nefertari looked at Colonel Tirion. "And if it's on the body someplace other than a limb?"

The colonel shook his head. "That person is usually dead," he said. "Liquid fire has been banned for decades. Just having it goes against treaty conventions we have with the humans and other races on the mainland."

"I can't believe my sister had anything to do with this," Nefertari remarked as she moved closer to the door and extended a hand outward.

"I'm sure she didn't," Colonel Tirion replied. "This has the smell of Mordecai on it."

Nefertari didn't respond except to say, "Don't open the door."

Colonel Tirion looked over at her and could see she was concentrating. The staff she carried glowed.

"Stone to stone, beam to beam.
Surround this danger without a seam.
Strong and formidable should be its hue.
Create a barrier, tried and true."

"DEAE FACITE UT!"

A rainbow-colored beam of power exploded out of the end of the priestess' staff and struck the wall in front of the two. The stone took on a life of its own and moved to cover the door. Within seconds the bricks, mortar, and wood of the door had fused together into a smooth barricade of stone. There was no break... no crack... no imperfection... in the facade.

"We have to go," Nefertari said as she grabbed Colonel Tirion's hand and started back down the hallway.

"What..."

Nefertari didn't stop or let go of the Marine colonel's hand. "The fire was too involved to be put out in time," she explained. "The only real choice I had was to contain it... which I did on five sides.

They had reached the stairway. "Why not all sides?" Colonel Tirion asked.

Nefertari started up the stairs. "If I had completely enclosed it, the pressure of the explosion would probably destroy most of this village. So I had to allow venting."

"Where did you do that? Hell, how did you do that?!"

"Through the floor," Nefertari replied, ignoring the second question. "I've no idea what the consequences will be. But the alternative, the ceiling, would likely create a volcano with liquid fire raining down on everyone's head... resulting in a firestorm that would definitely kill a lot of people."

Colonel Tirion shook his head. "So you decided upon an earthquake instead?"

Nefertari didn't answer.

The two were now on the first floor. "There's a door on the north side of the building," Colonel Tirion said. "Follow me."

Just as they ran out the building, there was a terrible explosion below them... strong enough to knock them off their feet. The government building, already weakened by the creation stone's small dalliance with it, collapsed into a pile of rubble.

"To the stable," the colonel shouted as he got to his feet, dragging Nefertari up with him. They made the run unmolested... Maedhros Nénmacil had drawn most of the troops away to the south. The few remaining soldiers paid no attention to the Marine officer or the priestess... they were too busy dealing with a very scared and angry populace.

When they arrived at the stable, most of the colonel's warriors were sitting on their horses and ready to ride. Sergeant Lossëhelin held the reins of three rider-less horses.

"Where's my sister?" Nefertari asked Colonel Tirion.

Lessien removed her cloak of invisibility magic and appeared behind Nefertari. "Turn around," Lessien said.

The two sisters stared at each other for a few moments until Nefertari said, "I've missed you, little sister."

Lessien suddenly started to cry and rushed into Nefertari's arms and clung to her until Nefertari grabbed her shoulders and pushed her back to arm's length.

"You've grown into a beautiful young lady... and a regal queen," Nefertari said. "Well, except for the cigar."

Lessien smiled. "Desperate times. Father told me you were to be the Queen of the Alfheim. You look more like a priestess."

"That's because I am, dear sister."

"Excuse me, Your Highness, Nefertari," Colonel Tirion interrupted. "We need to leave before they realize what's happened."

The colonel turned to Sergeant Lossëhelin who nodded and replied, "We need to cross the Maranwe. I've got a barge procured, but we need to hurry. And Your Highness... things would probably go much better for us if you were to continue using your magical cloak."

The river crossing went without incident. The barge owner had left the barge unattended to be with his family and they had little trouble getting safely across. When they reached the top of the hills east of A'el Ellhendell, Nefertari turned her horse and looked out over the two villages. Maedhros Nénmacil was keeping a large number of Army soldiers busy... and somehow was doing it without causing too many casualties.

"Maedhros Nénmacil, break off your fight and come join us," Nefertari mentally called to the creation stone. She then felt a disturbance below her feet. "Something's happening."

"What's happening?" Lessien asked.

The ground beneath their feet rumbled and shook. Large cracks appeared in the ground... streaking across Ashakadi in several directions... while sections of the village disappeared into the earth.

"Damn!" Nefertari swore. "I had hoped this wouldn't happen."

"Priestess?" Colonel Tirion asked.

"The earthquake you mentioned earlier, Colonel," Nefertari responded. "There must be a fault line close by. That's the only explanation. I should've seen it."

"Considering the other option, I fail to see how this could be any worse," the colonel said. "You did the only thing you could under the circumstances."

"I need to get down there to help my people," Lessien said as she removed her magical cloak from her shoulders.

"Your Highness... you'll be recognized," Colonel Tirion said as he grabbed the reins of the queen's horse to prevent her from riding back down the hill. "I can't let you do that."

"Colonel..." Lessien said angrily.

"He's right, sister," Nefertari said.

Lessien turned on her newly-found sister. "They suffer because of me! I'm responsible for this!"

"Your Highness," Colonel Tirion said gently. "Are you responsible for being framed for murder, hunted down and held against your will?" The colonel shook his head. "No, don't allow yourself to shoulder the blame. But the fact you feel responsible is part of what makes you such a good sovereign. You'd risk everything, even your own life, to help people in need. The Navy has believed this all along."

"Listen to the colonel, Lessien," Nefertari interjected. "He speaks the truth. Besides, I'm the one who set everything in motion. I'm the one who owes the debt. Lessien, I can help those people. You need to get to safety."

Lessien shook her head. "I won't..." The queen's eyes suddenly widened as she stared at something over Nefertari's shoulder.

Nefertari smiled. She didn't have to look to know Maedhros Nénmacil had joined them. "I won't be alone, sister."

Lessien closed her eyes and took a deep breath. When she opened them, they were composed and confident. "We need to have a long discussion, sister," she said.

Nefertari bowed slightly from her saddle. "As soon as the chance presents itself."

Lessien moved her horse over to Nefertari, reached over and kissed her on the cheek. "Be careful."

Nefertari smiled. "He keeps me out of trouble," Nefertari said as she nodded her head towards Maedhros Nénmacil.

"Most interesting," Lessien replied. "A flying boulder."

"I do much more than that, Your Majesty," Maedhros Nénmacil rumbled. "Rest assured no harm shall come to the StarSinger."

Lessien, surprised to hear a large and suddenly very intimidating boulder talk, pulled her horse back. "Ah... well, yes. Please see that you do, Sir Boulder."

Maedhros Nénmacil laugh caused the ground beneath their feet to shake slightly.

"Your Highness," Colonel Tirion said. "Before you go, I need to inform you that the Army had liquid fire stored in the building they held you in."

"What!" the queen roared. "That goes against the Articles of War we have with the humans and the other races! Colonel, I negotiated that treaty myself."

"Yes, Your Highness," Colonel Tirion replied. "No doubt Mordecai had something to do with it. Liquid fire would do much to bring down a certain monastery we both know he needs to negate."

Lessien focused her attention on Nefertari. "That's the source of the explosion?"

Nefertari nodded. "In a manner of speaking. I had nothing to do with the fire that caused the explosion... but I did inadvertently cause the earthquakes by redirecting the force of the explosion into the earth." Nefertari paused. "I didn't have time to check for fault lines. This may also set off additional earthquakes all across the island."

"In just a very short period of time, Your Highness, I've learned from your sister there's a lot I know little about," Colonel Tirion said. "But I trust her. Right now we need to get you on your way to the monastery. Sergeant Lossëhelin!"

"Sir!"

"You and the rest of the squad escort the Queen to the monastery," Colonel Tirion ordered. "Ride hard and ride fast. The Army will be here in force shortly. I'm going back with the priestess."

Nefertari shook her head. "You don't need... "

"I'm going, madam, and that's final. Unless, of course, your boulder plans to stop me."

"Very well, Colonel," Nefertari replied as she smiled.

After last-minute instructions and brief goodbye's, both parties went their separate ways. Neither knew if they'd ever see each other again.

Father Goram looked around the room. Except for Magdalena and Autumn, his advisors... Cordelia, Cameron, Landross, and Eric the Black... were seated at the table eating a light dinner and making small talk. He cleared his throat to get everyone's attention.

"I know everyone's busy, but I want to take a few minutes to update you regarding my earlier conversation with Magdalena." Father Goram waited a few seconds to make sure he had each person's complete attention. "As you know, I sent Autumn with a few knights to contact Maggie and Balthoron earlier this morning. She has done so and, via a communications crystal, reported back about half an hour ago."

"I still don't understand why you didn't just talk with Magdalena through her own crystal," Eric the Black said.

"I wanted another pair of eyes directly on the scene," Father Goram replied. He knew his cover story was weak, but he didn't have time to come up with something more plausible. Besides, his friends were smart. Sometimes a simple lie can succeed where a complicated one might not. The simplicity itself tends to be more believable.

"The Army?" Landross asked.

"Moving fast. But most of the infantry was forced to stop at the village of Ashakadi to conduct rescue operations," Father Goram said. "Along with A'el Ellhendell, these two villages bracket the junction of the Aranel and Maranwe rivers. Apparently there was a large explosion followed by several earthquakes. Magdalena reports trembling all the way up into the foothills. Those two villages have suffered a great deal of damage."

"At least the Army is helping," Landross remarked. Then he frowned. "You didn't mention the cavalry?"

Father Goram shook his head. "Still moving swiftly towards us from the south. They'll be here in a couple of days."

"Unless they're delayed," Cordelia said. "Is Balthoron going to delay them, Horatio?"

"I don't see the point," Landross answered for Father Goram. "Mordecai has to throw at least a whole Army corps against us if he wants any chance of success. Each corps has at least one cavalry division consisting of armored knights and speedier outliers.

They wouldn't have much trouble overrunning Maggie and Balthoron. A high price to pay for only a few additional hours."

"Landross is correct," Father Goram said. "I don't want needless sacrifice. Their mission is strictly one of scouting." Father Goram had stopped talking and drew a breath. Everyone knew he hadn't finished. "The Queen was being held in Ashakadi. Maggie didn't witness the actual explosion, but she doesn't believe the Queen had started her transit back to the capital before it occurred. We need to face the very real possibility that the Queen was killed."

"Then Mordecai wins," Cameron stated.

There was complete silence in the room. Father Goram didn't contradict Cameron, preferring to remain silent instead. But he didn't think circumstances were as dire as Cameron said they were.

And if they were?

"More work for the assassins," Father Goram said to himself.

Admiral Tári Shilannia stood on the quarterdeck of Her Majesty's Ship the *Felicidade*, hands clasped behind her back, and watched the coastline pass by as the warship made its way northward with the main fleet. The smaller northern fleet was coming south from bases in the Santea Archipelago. Both fleets will rendezvous northeast of The Arrow. Admiral Shilannia wasn't sure where to go after that... she had little information or reconnaissance. "I guess we'll anchor in the Bay of Eltoria," she thought. "We'll be close enough to support the Queen and Father Goram... if that becomes necessary. I wish I knew what was happening."

Marine Commander-General Aubrey Feynral climbed the ladder from the main deck and walked over to the admiral.

"What news?" Admiral Shilannia asked.

"Just spoke to Colonel Tirion on our communications crystal," General Feynral replied. "As we feared, that smoke we saw earlier came from an explosion in the river village of Ashakadi. But the Queen was able to get out safely and she's now with the Colonel's squad and heading for the monastery."

Admiral Shilannia visibly relaxed when she heard the Queen was well. Then she looked at her subordinate. "You said the Colonel's squad is escorting the Queen. Is the Colonel not with them?"

General Feynral shook his head. "This is where it gets strange."

"Oh?"

"The Queen tried to kill herself..." General Feynral said before being interrupted by the Admiral.

"What!"

"It was only by luck Colonel Tirion showed up and demanded an audience with her when he did. If he hadn't, she'd be dead." General Feynral paused.

"Go on," Admiral Shilannia prompted.

"Yes, Admiral. As Colonel Tirion was trying to save the Queen, a strange priestess bullied her way into the room and took control. She saved Her Majesty's life. The Colonel tells me this priestess wears a holy symbol unlike any he's ever seen." The General peered at the

Admiral. "Tári, Colonel Tirion's traveled the known world. He's probably seen every religious order represented."

"There's still much of the world that remains unexplored," the admiral remarked. "But I take your point." Admiral Shilannia shook her head. "Already the Colonel's story defies logic. But then again, life itself is full of unexpected twists and turns. Please go on."

"For whatever reason, after the Queen had been administered to and was out of danger, the local Army garrison commander had both Colonel Tirion and the priestess arrested and put in a dungeon."

Admiral Shilannia nodded. "Not too surprising," she observed. "I'd do the same until I had a chance to figure things out."

General Feynral continued his report. "Well, that particular Army general, along with his entire cavalry contingent, were later killed by... and this is verbatim from the Colonel... a huge, flying, intelligent boulder."

General Feynral winced when he saw the admiral staring at him as if he'd lost his mind.

"I swear, Tári, that's what he said," General Feynral protested.

"Okay, Aubrey. The Colonel's a good Marine... and I've seen and heard of stranger things... so we accept this information about this priestess and the flying boulder." Admiral Shilannia peered back at the coast as she organized her thoughts.

" Tári?"

Admiral Shilannia glanced back over at her friend.

General Feynral took a deep breath. "Colonel Tirion told me the priestess was the Queen's sister."

General Feynral shook her head. "Impossible. The Queen's sister is a queen in her own right... the ruler of the Alfheim. Martin said so himself. Why would she even be here at all... let alone in the garb of a strange priestess?"

"Why indeed," General Feynral said. " Tári, I'm only relaying what Colonel Tirion told me. But as you've already mentioned, he's a good Marine. Perhaps my best."

Admiral Shilannia went quiet, deep in thought. After a few moments, she said, "Very well, Aubrey. Finish your report."

And General Feynral did. He told the admiral how the explosion was caused by liquid fire and how the strange priestess was able to contain it... but as a result, the village of Ashakadi was experiencing earthquakes which threatened the populace. He talked about how Colonel Tirion's was going to accompany the priestess back to the village to help its people dig out from under the damage caused by the earthquakes... and the rest of the colonel's squad would escort the Queen to the monastery. At this point Admiral Shilannia interrupted him.

"He's going back into that viper's pit?" the admiral exclaimed. "Why would he do that? Surely the Army would capture him once again."

"He didn't seem too concerned," General Feynral replied. "The priestess would not leave, so he felt obligated to help. He said that between his sword, the priestess' power to manipulate the elements, and

411

that flying boulder, there wasn't a safer place on the island."

Admiral Shilannia shook her head in disbelief. "I'm very eager to meet the Queen's sister... this strange priestess and her flying boulder. Anything else?"

"Yes, Admiral. The Army is on the move and heading towards Father Goram's monastery."

"Approximate strength?"

"Colonel Tirion estimates an entire Army corps," General Feynral said.

"Damn!"

General Feynral shook his head. "It's not that bad. I've been to the monastery on several occasions and have a passing acquaintance with Sir Landross, the military commander there. The monastery is a fortress. One corps may be enough to take it... but it's not a certainty. Sir Landross has an extremely strong defensive position with which to work."

Admiral Shilannia nodded. "Very good, Aubrey. We'll anchor in the Bay of Eltoria. Begin preparations to off-load your Marines to support the monastery."

General Feynral saluted. "Yes, Admiral," he said.

"And Aubrey."

"Ma'am?"

"Make sure your battle plan includes options to cover a full retreat of the Queen and any other monastery personnel requesting safe harbor," the Admiral added. "We may need to move everyone to the mainland if this goes bad."

After General Feynral had left, Admiral Shilannia returned to her study of the coastline which was receding. The *Felicidade* and the rest of the fleet had made the turn northeast to sail up the Arrow. "If the Queen doesn't make it to the monastery and is captured... or worse," she thought, "what I'm doing is treason."

"The Queen might be dead," Mordecai said as he sat down at his dinner table.

Nightshade, sitting at the other end, couldn't believe her ears. "What do you mean?" she asked. "I thought the Army would deliver her to us later this evening?"

"Apparently there was some kind of trouble in the village where she was being held," Mordecai said around a mouthful of food. "My messenger didn't have all the details... and what he did say made little sense... but he was quite adamant the building she was in exploded. A complete loss. No survivors."

Nightshade sat back. "You don't appear too broken up about it," she stated.

Mordecai smiled. "Why should I. It gives me a legitimate reason to crown myself king of InnisRos."

"I thought you had already done that," Nightshade replied sarcastically. But Mordecai either didn't care, or he wasn't listening. He continued to eat his dinner as if nothing had happened. "Do you still war against the monastery?" she asked.

Mordecai looked at her. "Of course. Goram's a traitor."

"But his allies? It could mean civil war. You said so yourself."

"I've reconsidered." Mordecai smiled. "The Queen's death in this unfortunate accident legitimizes my succession as much as her conviction would have. Besides, Goram has honor... a disgusting trait. My guess is he'll probably turn himself in and face punishment rather than sacrifice his friends and followers. Then I'll take his head, we'll get the priestess and the empath, and I'll rule the Svartalfheim just as we planned. Nothing can stop us now."

Mordecai speared a piece of meat with his fork and looked at it. "You know," he said. "Liquid fire is damn destructive. No wonder that building exploded."

Nightshade stared at Mordecai in disbelief.

CHAPTER SEVENTEEN

Elanesse

My whole life has been spent studying the various disciplines required to be an expert assassin. I learned and became adept in stealth, endurance, speed, and all the other things that made me a successful killer. I did this to please my assassin guild masters, who were the only family I ever knew. Then I met Emmy. From that moment forward I knew I had a new family. From that moment forward my life would never be the same.

-Mariko, Former Assassin

Azriel screamed in pain. It was primal. It was horrific. It was the last thing those at the top of the fissure heard before the rope stopped jerking. Azriel's weight was still on the rope, so he was either unconscious or dead.

It only took a few moments to pull Azriel up and place him under the care of Kristen and Emmy. The injuries he had suffered were appalling. His left foot had been completely burned away and his right hand was also severely burned. Still firmly grasped in it was Kristen's steel quarterstaff... one end soft and glowing bright red, as if it had been placed in super-heated fire... or worse. The quarterstaff had been fused to Azriel's hand. In the dwarf's left hand he held his great battleaxe. The blade had struck something, that much was clear... but the glowing orange splotches on the blade were alien to anything anyone had ever seen. Like the quarterstaff, the battleaxe was also fused to Azriel's hand... though the burns were not as significant.

Azriel opened his eyes. They were lucid and showed no signs of pain. He looked into Emmy's eyes. "Oh lassie, I'm so sorry, but there's one who needs me more than you." Tears were now flowing unashamedly down Azriel's cheeks. Those tears glowed orange. "Will you forgive me?"

Emmy took hold of Azriel's face between her hands. "My dear Azriel, of course I forgive you," she said. "And I thank you for your service. But we're not done, you and I."

Azriel nodded. "Her name is Elbedreth-Ahlasim," he said. "She has been so alone."

"Who's Elbedreth-Ahlasim?" Kristen asked.

"The sylph, mother," Emmy replied.

Emmy used her thumb to gently wipe away the tears from Azriel's rough and weathered face. "Dear friend, please go with my blessing."

Azriel nodded and smiled. As everyone watched, Azriel's body became covered with an impenetrable cocoon of a glowing, orange substance. Emmy and Kristen got up, and they all backed away. The orange substance solidified for a few moments before melting away. In its place was a formless, undulating mass of a black substance. It was the same as the sylph. It was a sylph.

The new sylph... Azriel... rose up. Out of its black body Kristen's steel quarterstaff appeared, as did Azriel's battleaxe. The sylph Azriel tested the weapons. They moved with a grace that no dwarf, elf, or human could ever hope to achieve. Satisfied, Azriel stopped, and the weapons contracted back into the black of his body. Nodding to Emmy and Kristen, he turned to leave in search of his new mate, Elbedreth-Ahlasim. On the floor where Azriel the sylph had stood lay six cigars.

Emmy began to cry and was quickly comforted by Kristen and Tangus. The three of them looked so natural together... so right... it was impossible for the casual observer to believe they were ever apart. Indeed, their souls never were.

"What the hell just happen?" Safire asked.

Kristen looked up at her. "Something wonderful."

As the sylph, Elbedreth-Ahlasim, was watching the small person being lowered into the blocked entrance to her world, she felt the intrusion of more outsiders and at once left to drive them away. These invading outsiders, however, differed from the one's now trying to help her return home. Elbedreth-Ahlasim thought this curious since she had killed one of their brethren as a warning to keep them away. That the killing didn't accomplish its intended goal filled her with regret... needless death served no purpose. But these outsiders seemed to understand her nature as well as her strongest desire... and overlooked the loss of their comrade by her hands to help. Astonishing!

As Elbedreth-Ahlasim traveled the tunnels she now called home towards the other outsiders, she felt a new presence... something hauntingly familiar... yet still unknown. Elbedreth-Ahlasim stopped and extended her senses back toward the source of her bewilderment. "Another like me!" she exclaimed silently. Her form changed in and out... many different shapes... many different colors. She was suddenly very excited about what her future might hold. Maybe... just maybe... she'd no longer be so terribly alone.

Azriel felt free. He no longer had to face the physical constraints of a corporal body. His new, physical self, could roam without restriction in the underground maze that represented Elanesse's vulnerable underbelly. Now he could redirect his life to keep the city safe which, in a much broader sense, will also help to keep Emmy and Kristen safe. Azriel inwardly smiled. He had a new sense of purpose. More importantly, he wouldn't have to do it alone.

"I am now Azriel-Ahlasim," he broadcast mentally to his new mate and love. "Named in the way of my new race... our race. I'm coming to be with you... and together we shall defend our home, and the city that lies above, against all unwanted outsiders."

"Salutations, Azriel-Ahlasim!" Elbedreth-Ahlasim replied with enthusiasm. "But my love, are there different outsiders?"

Azriel-Ahlasim laughed as he moved up to stand with his mate. A black wisp extended from each as they greeted the other. "Aye, lassie," Azriel-Ahlasim said. "There is much I must teach you about outsiders."

Azriel-Ahlasim 's magical battleaxe and quarterstaff appeared. "But first, we must help my friends."

"I don't understand. What is friend?" Elbedreth-Ahlasim asked as they silently moved towards their quarry.

Azriel-Ahlasim smiled. "Next to family they're the most valued treasure of all."

Hate and murder boiled through the lower corridors beneath Elanesse in a rolling wave of humanity. The mindless horde of the Purge's army ran blindly onwards, seeking the last empath and all of her followers. Now, the only thing that now mattered to the Purge was the empath's complete and absolute destruction... at whatever cost... by whatever means.

The leading contingent of the mass didn't notice, or distinguish between, the different shades of black in the tunnel they were charging until it was too late. Azriel-Ahlasim and Elbedreth-Ahlasim tirelessly hacked, sliced, and bashed until nothing but dead bodies remained for three hundred yards.

But the sylphs weren't immune to the swords, maces, and clubs they faced. Though their incredible speed and their innate ability to shift body mass made it difficult... impossible against lesser numbers... the sheer volume of opponents guaranteed limited success. Both sylphs emerged from the battle hurt and exhausted.

"Are you badly injured?" Azriel-Ahlasim asked.

Elbedreth-Ahlasim nodded. "I've never been hurt so badly," she replied.

"How do we... ?"

"How do we heal ourselves, love?" Elbedreth-Ahlasim said. "Our bodies will mend our wounds... but I've found a special place which will accelerate the healing. It's a place of great comfort. Follow me, Azriel-Ahlasim, and I will take you to it. I call it the Silef-Sant."

"Silef-Sant?"

"Crystal Garden in the language of the outsiders."

Mariko walked ahead of the rest of the group as they made their way through the tunnel system beneath Elanesse. Without Azriel and his dwarven ability to travel unerringly underground, Tangus knew the journey to the Grand Palace through the tunnel network would be difficult... and that every misstep had the potential for disaster. Though Tangus and Lester had been through many dungeons and tunnels in the service of the Dagger Company, Mariko had an easier time traveling underground... in part because of her assassin experience... but mostly because she had a magical locket which constantly pointed in the direction of her choosing.

The journey was slow going. Mariko, though she had magical aid, nevertheless took each step with care. Though she knew they must maintain a westerly course, there were many tunnels and tunnel off-shoots that, while they looked promising, ended up curving away in different directions.

"I've never seen such a maze of underground passages before," Mariko remarked. "I know we're going in the right direction, but there's absolutely no signs to show we're using the right tunnel."

As if to illustrate her point, they came upon a three-way branch... none of the tunnels went directly west... but all three did go in a westerly direction.

Mariko knelt and studied the floor. "Arrrggghhh!" she exclaimed. "Not a single clue... wait a minute, what's this?"

Tangus came forward and knelt beside Mariko. She ran her finger along a line that appeared to be burned into the stone floor. It pointed to the left passage. "This line doesn't have the look of age to it," she said. "Freshly made, I'd say."

"Azriel?" Tangus mused.

"Probably," Mariko responded. "We might as well follow this tunnel and hope for the best."

Tangus nodded.

As they continued down the marked corridor, Jennifer moved up beside Tangus.

"Father, what happened back there to change Azriel into... into a sylph?" she asked.

Tangus shrugged his shoulders. "I don't know, sweetheart," Tangus replied. "I'm not even sure Azriel knows... if he's still Azriel, that is."

Kristen, walking beside Emmy behind Tangus and Jennifer, said, "He's still our friend. Jennifer, sometimes things happen which have no explanation... except maybe it's what the gods decided should happen. Yet possibly it's even bigger than that. It could be what fate determined should happen."

"Fate?"

"Even the gods must defer to fate, Jennifer," Emmy said before Kristen could respond. "I believe the same elven magic used to create Elanesse all those years ago formed a bond between the city and the sylph. It's a bond like the one that exists between my mother and me... or between the empath and her protector. There's a commonality about it that feels similar. Though it's what she believes, the sylph didn't come from another place... or another world or plane of existence."

Kristen continued the narrative. "This is speculation, of course, but what if she wasn't created by the elves as was Elanesse. What if the sylph has always been here. She... or her people if more sylphs exist... are actually part of the same magic the elves used to create Elanesse. Maybe even part of the same magic the elder gods used to create the world."

Jennifer stopped and looked at Kristen. "Then that makes Elanesse..."

"That makes Elanesse the sylph's sister," Kristen replied. "The bond between the sylph and Elanesse is much like the bond between Emmy and me... but different. More like the unique bond between twin siblings. Only, though Elanesse and the sylph know of each other, neither are aware the bond exists between them."

"How could you know this?" Jennifer asked.

Kristen paused. "Intuition," she replied. "My bond with Emmy has allowed me to sense... and understand... much that lies beneath the obvious."

Jennifer looked at Emmy, who smiled. "Discovery and comprehension, Jennifer," Emmy said. "We're only restricted by our ability to see beyond that which is readily observable... or as mother puts it... that which lies beneath the obvious. There are many different levels to reality. The bond allows us to see different aspects of this, just as your father, through his experience and training, can see certain nuances in animal behavior others can't."

Jennifer shook her head. "I shouldn't have mentioned it." She suddenly laughed.

"What's so funny?" Kristen asked.

"Oh, nothing really," Jennifer replied. "It's just that everything I've seen over the last few weeks makes the question of 'How?' somewhat irrelevant."

"I think we're in the right tunnel," Mariko said as she stopped. Before her lay a bloodbath. Body upon body filled the passageway as far as she could see. The smell of death was unmistakable... and overpowering. Blackish, drying blood covered the floor, intermixed with body parts... arms, legs, brains, and guts. Empty, staring eyes looked up from faces devoid of emotion on heads that weren't always attached to their bodies. "Azriel and his sylph friend... "

"Azriel-Ahlasim and Elbedreth-Ahlasim," Kristen corrected.

Mariko nodded. "Yes, of course. Anyway, they've been very busy."

Everyone stared at the carnage. Jennifer had to turn her head away.

"This will need to be cleaned up," Kristen said. Her voice sounded detached... she wouldn't allow herself to think about the pain and humiliation these men and women had endured. Her two sylph friends had no choice... these very same people wanted to destroy those she loved. But even still, Kristen never accepted suffering lightly.

"Can't we bypass this?" Safire asked.

Mariko shook her head. "No, Kristen is correct. This cannot be allowed to remain. It'll fester like an open wound if not addressed."

Kristen nodded. "Mariko understands," she said. "These human remains will poison the city and all her inhabitants... particularly if any of these contaminants were to seep into the water table. Everyone understands the health concerns of a rotting corpse." Kristen shook her head. "There's so much here. We can't take the chance."

"But the only inhabitants of the city above us want to kill or capture Emmy," Jennifer remarked.

"For future generations, sister," Emmy replied. "We must clean this for future generations."

"Will you need anything from any of us, love?" Tangus asked.

Kristen shook her head. "No, darling. Only that everyone stand back."

Once everyone was behind her, Kristen gathered her will. As a priestess who's skill was healing, she understood what was needed to render the dead harmless... which in this case was fire. The magical power inside her rose from the depths of her soul. Kristen raised her arms into the air, each of her hands engulfed in a burning conflagration. The power inside her continued to climb and augmented that which was already being held in her hands. The escalation of magic forced everyone else to turn away, unable to look into the brightness any longer.

"Praecipio tibi ignem purgantem, hic munus fungatur tuom officium", Kristen whispered as she brought her hands together, fusing two brilliant balls of intensely hot infernos into one.

"VERUM ARDEBIT!" Kristen shouted as she pointed her locked hands toward the gory hallway. A long, white-hot fire filled the tunnel before her and raced forward, disintegrating everything in its path. As long as there were human remains to keep the magical fire alive, the business of cleansing continued.

When at last the fire died out for lack of fuel, Kristen and everyone else stared at the tunnel. Of the human body parts and blood, nothing remained. The tunnel, however, stood in silent witness to the heat of the magical fire. For as far down the tunnel as anyone could see, the walls, ceiling and floor were as smooth as ice... melted into shining glass by the terrible heat.

Kristen looked at her husband, embarrassed. "I never intended to take it this far," she said. "I was upset."

Tangus took her hand and kissed Kristen on the forehead. "I didn't know you could do that," he said.

"I didn't know I could either," Kristen replied.

"It was the Fire of the Righteous," Emmy said. "Very rare and only available to the most devoted of Althaya's followers."

No one bothered to ask Emmy how she knew that.

The death of so many followers of the Purge drove it even further into madness. Its rage resonated outward to all its mind-controlled slaves. The twenty-five worgs who now served as its personal bodyguard snarled and howled. Every human within one hundred feet grabbed their heads and screamed... then dropped to the ground, mindless husks who's only contribution now was to serve as food for the worgs patrolling throughout west Elanesse.

The death of the Purge's followers had served a purpose, however... the location of the empath. The Purge laughed manically as it ordered its remaining human followers to the spot beneath the city. Each human received final instructions... "KILL THE EMPATH! KILL THEM ALL!"

The empath held captive in the Purge cowered deep into the protective barrier she had created. She'd been defending herself from the relentless psychosis of the Purge... but something happened and for a moment the attacks ceased. She felt a faint hope that the madness of the Purge had caused attention to be focused away from her... that the Purge would forget she still existed. She had no god or goddess to help her... so she asked fate to intervene.

But fate wouldn't intercede on her behalf. The assault on her defensive shields continued once again with renewed vigor. The empath screamed from the pain. She knew she had little time left. "I'm so alone," she cried.

Mariko led them into a large cavern. On the floor near the center were thirteen bodies... broken and mangled... lying on a pile of rubble. Above the bodies was a hole in the ceiling which led to another series of tunnels above them. Several ropes hung from the opening. At the opposite end of the cavern was another tunnel.

"Now we know how they got down here," Mariko commented as Tangus and the others came up to stand next to her. She turned to look at Tangus. "Do we go up or continue on at this level," she asked.

Tangus considered the question then looked at Lester. "What do you think?"

"Going up and into the sewers will give us the advantage of choosing our exit," Lester replied. "But it also offers the highest probability of armed resistance." Lester pointed his sword at the tunnel opposite the one they came in. "I'd go that way. At least we'd know then we wouldn't have to worry about the Purge's minions." He looked at the rope and the dead bodies. "Well, probably."

Tangus nodded. "Safire?"

"I agree with Lester," Safire said as she flashed a smile at the knight. "Besides, I don't want to climb up a hundred feet of rope."

"Kristen?"

Kristen stared at the tunnel.

"What do you see?" Mariko asked.

Kristen shook her head. "I don't know. Something... I can't explain it." Kristen put an arm around Emmy's shoulders and looked at Tangus. "It's a feeling more than anything else... like something unnatural lies in that direction."

"We're getting close to the Purge," Emmy uttered.

Kristen felt a sick feeling in the pit of her stomach. The final showdown was at hand and Kristen was terrified of losing Emmy.

Emmy felt Kristen's apprehension through the bond. "Mother, we both know this has to be done," she said as she turned and caused Kristen to kneel in front of her so they were at eye level. "The threat to healing magic must be eliminated. You know that's only possible through the death of the Purge... and that I'm the only one who can kill it."

Kristen nodded. "I know," she replied. "I'm not worried if you fail... because if you do, it'll mean we're all dead as well. What worries me is what happens when you succeed?"

Emmy didn't answer. Instead, she put her hand on Kristen's cheek to calm and reassure her.

As Tangus watched the exchange, it occurred to him that the roles of child and parent had just been reversed... if only for a moment. He nodded. Kristen needed that. "We go through the tunnel," he said.

The empath, ensconced in her last refuge, fought off the attacks from the Purge for as long as she had the strength to do so... but, as she knew must happen, the Purge breached her guard and captured her... imprisoning her in the deepest recesses of its soul. Any hope for a reversal of the hate and madness that filled the Purge faded away into oblivion with the final imprisonment of the empath... the same empath used in its creation... and the last chance for the Purge to expunge the evil of its existence.

Emmy, as well as the others, was exhausted from a long, hard day of traveling. When they reached the magical barrier the long-dead first queen of

Elanesse had spoken of, Tangus, with many voices of agreement, decided to stop and rest for a few hours before attempting to bypass the obstruction. As soon as she laid down, she fell into a deep sleep. And she dreamed:

Emmy found herself in the place of dreams... a murky, convoluted backdrop to a world where everything seemed real... but wasn't. Like clouds in the sky which can be seen but never touched...you know they exist yet can offer no concrete proof of that existence. Emmy wasn't afraid, however... this is where she wanted to be.

From the shadowy depths of the dream a figure emerged. She wore simple peasant garments... tunic, long skirt, and a brightly colored swatch of cloth used as a belt. The figure moved through the dream towards Emmy. As she came closer, Emmy recognized her. She was the empath used to create the Purge...the same girl who had come to Emmy once before in another dream and looked directly into Emmy's eyes. Emmy would never forget her face nor her simple plea..."I'm so alone."

The figure stopped before Emmy and made a clumsy curtsy. "Mistress," she said. "I had thought I'd not see you before the end."

Emmy placed a kiss on the girl's forehead. "What's your name?" she asked.

The girl paused. "I'm not sure I... yes, I remember... Charity, my lady," she said.

Emmy smiled. "Charity, you've done well considering the circumstances."

Charity shook her head in denial. "Mistress, I helped to create the Purge," she said as tears rolled down her cheeks.

"You were used against your will," Emmy replied. "No blame can be laid at your feet."

"But our people... they've all been murdered."

Emmy grabbed Charity by the shoulders and looked deeply into her eyes. "Our people will return and the world will rejoice."

Charity bowed her head.

Emmy tilted Charity's chin. "Child, I'm coming as fast as I can to free you," she said. "But until I do, I want you to wear this ring," Emmy said as she slipped a ring on Charity's finger. "This was given to me by the first elven queen of Elanesse to keep me safe. It will do the same for you."

Charity protested. "No, mistress. I mustn't."

Emmy hugged the girl tightly. "Charity, I don't need it. I have a family to keep me safe."

After a few moments, Emmy held the girl at arm's length. "Now, we both must return to our separate realities," she said. "It won't be much longer, I promise. Will you stay strong for me?"

Charity smiled. "Of course, mistress," she said before fading away.

Emmy watched the shifting shadows of the pseudo reality of her dream as she thought about Charity. She wasn't sure if they'd make it in time... and that worried her.

When Emmy awoke, she heard the sounds of battle all around her.

THE STRUGGLE FOR INNOCENCE

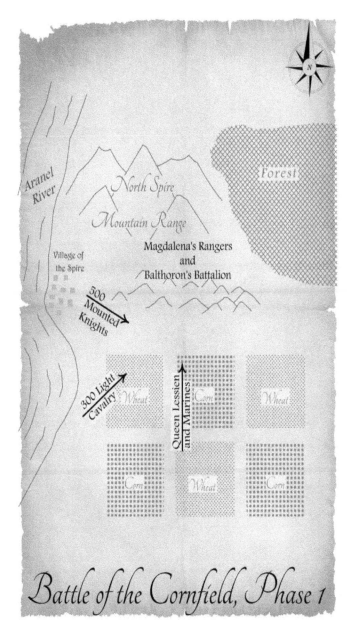

Battle of the Cornfield, Phase 1

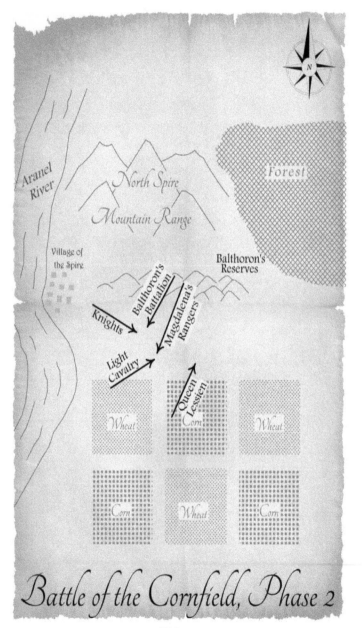

Battle of the Cornfield, Phase 2

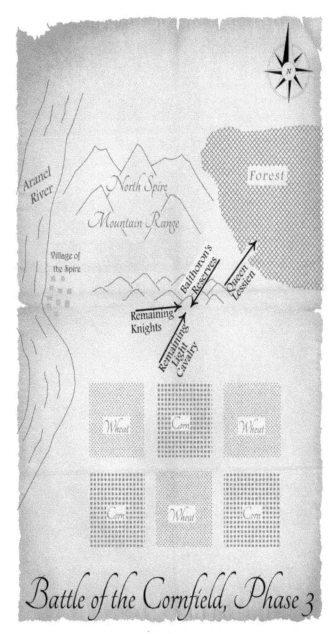

Battle of the Cornfield, Phase 3

THE STRUGGLE FOR INNOCENCE

CHAPTER EIGHTEEN

InnisRos

There are many causes in life worth fighting for... worth dying for. But losing friends to death is always difficult, regardless of the circumstances, regardless of the cause. As I write this, Autumn sleeps safely... thank the gods... but others are not so fortunate. Many friends have been lost today. Many tears are being shed. But such is the nature of war.

-From the Letters of Father Horatio Goram to His Daughter, Kristen

Nefertari, Colonel Tirion, and Maedhros Nénmacil were making their way through the village of A'el Ellhendell when they felt a deep, underground rumble come from across the Maranwe River.

"I had hoped this wouldn't happen," Nefertari said as she looked across the river at the village of Ashakadi. She had stopped running.

The village suddenly moved up and down. The movement was violent and knocked scared and running people off their feet. Great fractures appeared in most of the buildings though none actually collapsed.

"That's just a precursor," Nefertari shouted above the sound of screaming people and the earth moving. "Something much bigger is coming! We've got to get those people away!"

Colonel Tirion nodded." Right!" he shouted. "Follow me!"

The three continued their journey to the river, forcing their horses through villagers and soldiers running in the opposite direction. No one challenged them as they moved forward. On the opposite side of the river, panic had also overtaken the civilians and soldiers in Ashakadi. Most were running south while others were filling barges to cross the river to safety. Several filled barges were already on the water.

"Can Maedhros Nénmacil fly us across?" Colonel Tirion shouted.

Nefertari looked at him. "Huh?"

Colonel Tirion pointed at the river. "No barges on this side! Can Maedhros Nénmacil fly us across?"

Nefertari looked back across the river. "It's too late," she said.

"What? I didn't hear you!"

"We're too late," Nefertari shouted. "Look!" She pointed to a spot in the middle of the river.

A small whirlpool was spinning in the water. As they watched, it increased in size until it encompassed half the river between the two shores. Two barges filled with soldiers were swallowed up while several others made a hasty retreat back to the river bank. Its appetite satiated, the whirlpool closed. Of the two barges consumed in the great maw of this river demon, there was no sign.

Nefertari got off her horse and dropped to her knees. "This is going to be bad," she whispered.

Maedhros Nénmacil began to fly across the river, but Nefertari held him back with a shake of her head. "My friend, if you go, you'll also be lost."

"What's going on!" Colonel Tirion shouted as he got off his horse. "Get up, priestess, and do your duty, damn it!"

But Nefertari was doing her duty. She was praying for the souls of those who had died, as well as those she knew were going to die before this horrible tragedy was over.

Colonel Tirion gently grabbed Nefertari's arm. His demeanor had quieted considerably. "We need to get over there and help," he pleaded.

Both remounted their horses, but neither made any effort to move forward. "It's happening," Nefertari said with resignation.

The entire village of Ashakadi rose several feet before dropping back to the earth. For several seconds it appeared the worst was over. Quiet reigned and people picked themselves up off the ground, coughing and beating dust and dirt from their clothes. Then, without warning, the village disappeared into a crevice that opened in the earth.

Lessien, Sergeant Lossëhelin, and the rest of the Queen's Marine escort were moving through rich farmland... rows and rows of corn and wheat. To the west was the Aranel river. They were only a few miles away from the villages of Ashakadi and A'el Ellhendell when they felt the rumble beneath the feet of their running horses. Lessien pulled the reins of her horse to stop it.

"Another earthquake," she said. "Sergeant, I should go back and help if I can."

Sergeant Lossëhelin shook his head. "No, Your Highness. Right now your safety is paramount."

Lessien objected. "They're my people!" she said. "Sometimes my life doesn't matter."

"And this isn't one of those times, Your Highness," Sergeant Lossëhelin responded. He took the ever-present cigar from his mouth and looked at his Queen. Everyone's horses were dancing around, waiting to run once more.

"Do you think your presence will serve any purpose other than to put your life in jeopardy?" Sergeant Lossëhelin said with deliberate calm. "And what about the distraction you'll cause. The drain of valuable resources. Regardless of your status... regardless of the claims the First Councilor has made against you... you're still the Queen. You must be guarded and protected. That would mean manpower drained away from the help the people of those two villages need."

The Queen looked away.

"Your Highness, my orders are to get you to Father Goram's monastery. While it's true that, as my sovereign, you can contradict those orders... I'll not listen if you do so. I'd rather face your justice then that of my Colonel." Sergeant Lossëhelin stuck his cigar back into his mouth. "Disobeying an order from the Queen during times of war is a treasonable offense. Do you wish to take my head?"

Lessien looked at Sergeant Lossëhelin and smiled. "No, Sergeant, I don't wish to take your head."

"Very well then..."

One of the Marines called out, "Riders coming from the west... moving northeast!"

Sergeant Lossëhelin focused his spyglass in that direction. "Damn corn," he said before turning to his Marines. "The corn's too high. All I can see is a cloud of dust with an occasional glimpse of riders. I don't know how many, but they're definitely Army cavalry. Probably disembarked from barges on the Aranel."

"Do you think they know we're here, Sarge?" one of the Marines asked.

Sergeant Lossëhelin shook his head. "Doubtful... but that won't last long. In the direction they're moving, they'll intercept us. We need to ride hard for Calmacil Clearing." Turning to Lessien, he said, "Highness?"

Lessien nodded. "Your show, Sergeant. Lead on."

As they sprinted northeast, they did their best to keep the tall corn between them and the Army cavalry. They didn't notice a larger cloud of dust closing from the northwest. Neither did they notice the pair of flying eyeballs following at a discreet distance.

Magdalena and Balthoron were up high in the foothills of the North Spire Mountain Range which overlooked farmland to the south. The sun was just disappearing over the western horizon. On their right ran the Aranel River. They could see a platoon of mounted Army knights moving to the southeast from the river. Another smaller cavalry unit further south was pushing northeast. Two dust clouds were also coming from the south... but they were still a hard day's ride away. The smaller of the two outpaced the larger by several miles.

Magdalena watched the scene below... but half her interest had been diverted to something else. Autumn had ridden from the monastery to ask her to contact Mother Aubria concerning assassins in Taranthi. Of course Mother Aubria would be more than happy to put Father Goram in contact with any number of assassin guilds owing allegiance to her. After all, Father Goram paid well for services rendered. What disturbed Magdalena was why her moral compass... Father Goram... would consider such measures. She knew he wouldn't employ these types of tactics unless things were desperate... and that worried her.

"Maggie... are you with me?" Balthoron had been looking south with his spyglass, but was now staring at the ranger. "I said a division of cavalry is moving in front of the main body of infantry."

"Sorry... just wondering why the hell I can't contact Sarah or Kerrick!" Magdalena lied in feigned frustration. "They're in perfect position to give us better information."

"We must assume something's happened to them," Balthoron replied. "Maggie, let's worry about that later. Here, look at this," Balthoron said as he handed Magdalena the spyglass. "See those knights moving to the southeast?"

"Yes."

"Now look southwest to that smaller unit."

Magdalena did so.

"Anything strike you as strange?" Balthoron asked.

"They... they're moving on an intercept course," Magdalena blurted.

Balthoron nodded. "Which probably means..."

Magdalena lowered the spyglass and looked at Balthoron. "They're chasing someone."

Balthoron took the spyglass from Magdalena and studied the farmland. "There's only one person I know who'd demand that much attention from the Army."

"The Queen," Magdalena whispered. "She escaped."

"And she's heading this way," Balthoron said as he handed Magdalena back the spyglass and pointed.

Magdalena trained the spyglass on the spot and saw several mounted riders encouraging their horses to run faster. "They're not going to make it," she said.

"No," Balthoron agreed. "We need to get down there."

Nefertari, Colonel Tirion, and Maedhros Nénmacil, in the now deserted village of A'el Ellhendell, looked across the Maranwe River at the spot where Ashakadi once stood. Nothing was left of the village except a great rift in the earth... a rift which was a thousand feet across and a mile long. There were no signs of survivors. Behind them, cresting the hills above A'el Ellhendell, several Army infantry units from the Second Corps, drawn by those who fled and the earthquakes, looked down at the devastation. They were silent as each soldier struggled to accept the catastrophe and the tragic loss of life.

Colonel Tirion's horse neighed and danced around. "We need to leave," he said, "before those soldiers take an interest in us."

Nefertari didn't have her full attention on her companion. "I'm not worried about those on the hill," she responded. Her voice was vague... as if she had her mind on more important matters.

Colonel Tirion calmed his horse. "I'm more concerned about the Queen."

"We'll leave soon enough... now hush," Nefertari said.

Colonel Tirion looked over and saw Nefertari was listening for something... no, perhaps it would be more correct to say she was using her senses to detect something. He waited. Then he began to worry as the soldiers moved down the hills. The last thing Colonel Tirion wanted was a confrontation between them and Maedhros Nénmacil. "Priestess... any time, if you please."

Nefertari turned to the colonel. "Daeron, there's a child over there... barely alive. We need to save it."

Colonel Tirion sighed, but nodded assent. Several undamaged barges were docked on their side of the river. "Let's go to the docks."

Nefertari shook her head. "Not enough time," she said as she kicked her horse into a run. Colonel Tirion and Maedhros Nénmacil followed.

When they reached the bank of the river, Nefertari raised her staff into the air.

"Water's soul, hear my call.
Airless spirits, one and all.
A path of water you must pave.
For life and innocence we must save."

" EXAUDI PRECEM MEAM!"

The water began to move and churn until it had solidified into an overpass which spanned the river. Without a word, Nefertari kicked her horse forward. Though unsure about the bridge of water, the horse trusted its master enough to step onto it. The footing was firm and solid.

Nefertari stopped her horse and looked back. "Coming, Colonel?"

Colonel Tirion stared at the priestess. Maedhros Nénmacil, flying alongside her, had also stopped and was looking at him. The creation stone rumbled a laugh. "I think Colonel Tirion has seen enough of the impossible for one day."

Colonel Tirion winced at the truth in Maedhros Nénmacil words. "Coming," he said as he walked his horse forward. Within moments they were on the opposite side of the river and stood at the edge of the precipice. They could hear the cry of an infant.

Both got off their horses and peered into the gloom, using their elven talent to see the infrared heat signature radiated by all living creatures in darkness. Below them, close to fifty feet down on a ledge, was a squirming, swaddled baby resting on the dead body of what probably was one of its parents.

"Looks like the baby's parent broke the fall," Colonel Tirion said. "I'll get some rope." He stood to go to his horse.

"No need," Nefertari said as she nodded to Maedhros Nénmacil.

Maedhros Nénmacil drifted down the side of the crevice until he reached the small, moving bundle. Two stony arms appeared out of his body and gently disentangled the squirming baby from the dead hands of its parent. Cradling the baby, the creation stone started to rise... but stopped. It noticed something on the dead parent and used a third arm to retrieve it.

Nefertari took the crying infant from Maedhros Nénmacil. "My priestess, you will no doubt have need of this," the creation stone said as he handed over a water skin. "It may contain milk for the child."

Nefertari removed the stopper and sniffed. It didn't smell spoiled. Handing the baby over to a surprised Colonel Tirion, she squeezed a drop onto the back of her hand and tasted it.

"It's fine," Nefertari said as she took the baby from the colonel and sat down, putting the baby in her lap. She opened the swaddling and inspected the baby from head to toe. The baby was female. There were no apparent injuries. Nefertari then placed her hands on the baby's forehead. Rainbow colored magic flowed out and surrounded the baby. "Good. No internal injuries," she said.

Re-swaddling the child, Nefertari held the baby up over her head. "I name you Miracle," she said. "For the miracle of life will forever triumph over the horror of death." Lowering the newly named Miracle, Nefertari cradled the infant in her lap and fed her from the water skin of milk.

"Army soldiers are crossing the river," Colonel Tirion said anxiously.

Nefertari looked up at him. "Let them come. Besides, I'm sure between you and Maedhros Nénmacil we're in no danger."

Colonel Tirion nodded and looked at the creation stone. "Are you my friend?" he asked.

Maedhros Nénmacil laughed with gusto. A rumble tore through the immediate area, forcing the soldiers on the river bank to brace themselves against the possibility of another earthquake.

"I am your friend, Colonel Daeron Tirion."

The colonel nodded and smiled.

"But," the creation stone continued, "only as long as the StarSinger wishes it."

When Colonel Tirion went to confront the soldiers, the smile on his face had drained away.

"It's suicide!" Magdalena exclaimed. "You can't split your command and hope to be successful against mounted knights."

"Even with my entire battalion we don't have the strength defeat those forces," Balthoron replied. "All we have to do is delay them long enough to give the Queen a chance to get away. Besides, your engagement with the cavalry further south amounts to the same thing. They have you outnumbered at least twelve to one."

Magdalena shook her head. "We're quick," she said. "All I want to do is annoy the hell out of them... force them to stop and deal with me while the Queen escapes. You should do the same thing. Your men stand no chance in a pitched battle with that many armored knights." Magdalena threw up her hands. "What's to stop them from dividing their forces?"

"Of course they're going to divide their forces," Balthoron replied. "That's why I'm holding back a reserve. Split in two like that, perhaps we can slow them down considerably."

Magdalena was still dubious about the whole plan... but she knew she wasn't the military strategist Balthoron was.

"Did you contact Father Goram?" Balthoron asked.

Magdalena nodded. "Landross will be here as soon as he can with his knights," she responded. "But it'll not be soon enough."

"Maggie..."

Magdalena smiled and put her hand on his shoulder. "We'll be fine," she said, hoping to give Balthoran strength and encouragement. But deep down she knew that probably wasn't true.

She was right.

Lessien and her Marine escorts pulled up on their tired horses to give them a brief rest. In the receding sunlight they could see two mounted Army components, which Sergeant Lossëhelin estimated was at least a battalion strength force, moving to intercept them. Then two smaller units, whom Sergeant Lossëhelin presumed were from Father Goram's monastery, raced out of their cover of the foothills to engage the first two. The sergeant, a veteran of many battles, knew the monastery troops didn't stand a chance. Perhaps if they had used the element of surprise and ambushed the knights in the foothills. But instead it appeared the encounter was going to be fought in open terrain where the greater number and superior armor of the Army knights took away that advantage. The only chance the monastery warriors now had was hit-and-run attacks using their faster horses and bow and arrow. But Sergeant Lossëhelin knew those folks had no intention of doing that. They raced to battle against overwhelming odds to slow down the advance of the two Army units. They're sacrificing themselves to save the Queen from recapture.

Sergeant Lossëhelin lit a cigar and continued to watch as the inevitable battle took shape. He dismounted, bent down, selected several strands of grass, and called for his Marines.

"What do you intend to do, Sergeant," Lessien asked.

"Marines never run away from a fight, Your Highness," Sergeant Lossëhelin replied. "With all due respect, whoever of my men chooses the two shortest blades of grass will continue with you to Calmacil

Clearing. The rest of us... well," Sergeant Lossëhelin shrugged his shoulders.

Lessien looked at the sergeant. She knew of Marines' devotion to duty... their loyalty... and their bravery. They were the best of the best... the finest fighting warriors on all of Aster. She also knew Marines were smart, cunning, and adapted to battlefield conditions as if it were second nature. Even still, this seemed foolish.

She watched as the men drew the blades of grass from Sergeant Lossëhelin hand. The men chosen to go with Sergeant Lossëhelin were happy and grinned from ear to ear. The two who were to go with the Queen looked sad and broken.

"I understand duty and honor," Lessien said. "But my father believed... as do I... that it must be tempered with common sense. Sergeant, this isn't logical."

Sergeant Lossëhelin climbed onto his horse and took a puff off his cigar. Several other Marines were also smoking. The acrid smoke waffling around them burned her eyes. "It's perfectly logical to a Marine, Your Highness."

Lessien sighed. She knew she'd probably never see these men again. "Very well. It's doesn't appear I can stop you, so I won't play that charade."

The Marines saluted their Queen and shouted, "Fidelis usque ad mortem!" in unison.
Lessien acknowledged their salute. "Ibimus vobiscum benedictionem meam," she replied.

Sergeant Lossëhelin nodded and turned his horse.

"Oh, and Sergeant," Lessien said. "Remember, those are your countrymen you war against. Try to spare as many as you can."

Sergeant Lossëhelin smiled. "Of course, Your Highness," he responded.

Lessien watched as they rode away toward the battle.

"We must go, Your Highness," one of the two remaining Marines said.

"I know the way to the monastery," Lessien replied as she kicked her horse into a run. "Follow me, gentlemen."

The soldiers, though suspicious, weren't inclined to challenge a Marine colonel. They allowed Nefertari, the baby, and Colonel Tirion safe passage away from the devastated villages of Ashakadi and A'el Ellhendell... although all that remained of Ashakadi were a few deserted barns. Nefertari had decided it was best for Maedhros Nénmacil to once again play the part of an inanimate boulder. He'd catch up with them under the cover of darkness.

As their horses made their way up the hills overlooking A'el Ellhendell, Colonel Tirion looked over at the strange, beautiful, and powerful priestess holding the baby, Miracle. They looked natural together even though Nefertari claimed to have never been a mother. "What are your plans, Nefertari?" he asked.

"Follow my sister, Daeron," Nefertari replied. "My goddess told me she needed my help... and she was right. In more ways than one."

"Yes," Colonel Tirion said. "The suicide attempt."

Nefertari looked at the Colonel. "And war brewing all around."

They reached the crest of the hill, stopped, and looked east upon the farmland below. Crops had been either confiscated... or destroyed... by the marching Army. Cavalry and mounted knights had already passed and could be seen several miles to the north. The main body of the Army was just now marching by... though the Colonel saw that a company of infantry had branched off and were now helping the survivors of A'el Ellhendell.

"My," Nefertari exclaimed as she watched. "All this to capture my sister?"

The Colonel looked at Nefertari. "It's a little more complicated than that. Their true intent is to lay siege to the monastery at Calmacil Clearing... the Queen's strongest supporter. I've been to the monastery and talked with its military commander, Sir Landross. He's got a good head on his shoulders for war... and his superior, Father Horatio Goram, is a powerful priest and brilliant tactician. It'll take at least this much, if not more, to defeat it."

"Good. My sister will be there, so that's where we go."

Colonel Tirion nodded. "I don't really see an alternative either way," he said. "We'll be riding through a war-zone. Not a place for a child."

Nefertari shrugged and kicked her horse forward. "That's somewhat obvious, Daeron. But I'm not worried. You and Maedhros Nénmacil will get Miracle and me safely through."

"I pretty much thought I'd seen everything... then that flying rock comes along," Colonel Tirion said. "And he's... sentient. But is he really that powerful?"

Nefertari laughed. "You'd be surprised. Next time you see him, try sticking him with that sword of yours."

Colonel Tirion shook his head. "No, I'll pass on that suggestion. He's not from around these parts, is he?"

Nefertari laughed. "What an astute observation," she said. There was a tone of amused facetiousness in her voice. "Actually, I've only just met him myself. But he knew exactly who I was. He was waiting for me in the middle of a cornfield. The farmer couldn't move Maedhros Nénmacil... so he simply planted the corn around him."

"I should think enough horses..." Colonel Tirion suddenly smacked his forehead. "When I said he's not from around these parts, I was oversimplifying, wasn't I?"

"Yes, Daeron, you were," Nefertari replied. "Most of what I know about him is through what I learned from my goddess, Sehanine StarEagle."

Colonel Tirion shook his head. "I've never heard of that particular deity."

"She's one of the Elder Gods. Their followers have long since died off on Aster."

"Except for you," Colonel Tirion.

"Except for me," Nefertari agreed.

453

"Then... I know you're from the Alfheim, but it goes deeper than that, doesn't it?"

Nefertari looked over at the Colonel. "Perceptive," she agreed.

Colonel Tirion snorted. "Sometimes I have my moments. Eären... Sergeant Lossëhelin... would say they're few and far between. Anyway, you were saying about your rock?"

"Please don't call him that, Daeron. He's not too sensitive... for a boulder... but I can't really predict what his limits are. Except to say he's extremely dedicated to my goddess... and very loyal to me as her priestess." Nefertari sighed. "Sehanine StarEagle doesn't believe there are many of his ilk... and that a power higher than her fashioned and set his kind on an unknown path. I appear to be Maedhros Nénmacil's current assignment."

"He's old, then."

"As old as the universe," Nefertari responded. Miracle had fallen asleep, so Nefertari gently rearranged the baby so she could nap more comfortably. "He's what's called a creation stone. He came here from up there," Nefertari used her head to point to the sky, "and this valley of rich, dark earth is a result of his arrival."

"Like... well... like a crater," Colonel Tirion said. "We've seen the results of other rocks that came from beyond our world. Most burn up in the sky. But the ones that land..." Colonel Tirion shook his head. "Nothing as large as this valley, however."

"That's why the farmer couldn't move him... and why most of your weapons are harmless against him. His physical makeup is unique." This time it was Nefertari who shook her head. "But he's not invulnerable... though Sehanine StarEagle doesn't know what his weaknesses are."

"That's problematic," Colonel Tirion replied as he absentmindedly scratched his chin. "A good leader never wants to be in the dark concerning weaknesses... or potential weaknesses... in his command." Colonel Tirion looked at Nefertari. "Unless he doesn't care. Too many Army commanders are like that... at least the commanders on Mordecai's payroll. They don't give a damn about their troops. Only Mordecai's wishes matter."

Nefertari raised an eyebrow. "Mordecai?"

"I'll explain later. But the short of it is, he's the reason my Queen... your sister... has to run for her life."

"Then I'm sure you'll do me the favor of arranging a meeting with this Mordecai person," Nefertari said grimly. "There are certain 'aspects' of his behavior I should like to amend."

"Madam, you'll have to stand in line."

Landross surveyed the battleground before him. Thirty minutes before he and his five hundred knights, half his strength, emerged from the forest to find what was left of Balthoron's command in a desperate battle with both Army knights and light cavalry. His outlying pickets had already informed him that the Queen had made good her escape... thanks to the delaying tactics of Balthoron and Magdalena... and would soon be under the sanctuary of Father Goram and the monastery.

Landross' knights only had to eliminate further resistance by the Army. They made that happen in a most brutal and efficient manner. No quarter was given by either side... each believing their foes were traitors to InnisRos.

A blood-soaked soldier from Balthoron's battalion... a captain and one of the few survivors... slowly walked her horse over to Landross. Though bloodied, she didn't seem to be severely injured... only a shallow, bleeding cut to the forearm which had already started to close. Most of the blood was that of the enemy... or of her dying comrades.

Landross dismounted his huge warhorse as the captain approached. The captain, though obviously exhausted, stopped, went to attention, and snapped a crisp salute.

"I wish your timing had been a bit more... coordinated... sir," the captain said.

Landross studied the captain's eyes. They were familiar with battle. He then noticed three stars sewn in her tunic over her left breast. "Three combat stars," Landross said.

The captain nodded. "Against pirates with King Martin," she wearily replied. "That was many years ago."

Landross nodded. "Give me your report and then see to your soldiers, Captain... ?"

"Sorry, sir. Captain Larien Anárion."

Landross nodded.

Captain Anárion gave her narration of the day's earlier events. She told Landross that two mounted forces were closing in on the Queen as she crossed the fields below the foothills. The Queen had an escort of at least one Marine squad. Captain Anárion said both Army groups appeared to know exactly where the Queen was heading and had planned to intersect her before she escaped into the forest.

At this point Landross stopped the captain's narration. "How did Balthoron know this?" he asked.

"We were west of here on a high hill," she said. "The plain below gives up many secrets if one knows where to look and, more importantly, how to look. The Commander... "

Landross gently cut her off. "Saw what was needed and acted accordingly. What was the troop strength of the two Army units moving on the Queen?"

"Total... about five hundred knights and three hundred light cavalry," Captain Anárion replied. "The Commander took the main body of the battalion to engage the knights while the ranger force went after the lighter cavalry. Balthoron knew the knights would most likely split their forces so they could continue their pursuit of the Queen. That's why my platoon was held in reserve... to counter that certainty. I was ordered to delay them long enough for the Queen to reach the forest... after which I was to escort her to Calmacil Clearing." Captain Anárion paused and reached around her waist to grab a water skin. "With your permission."

"Certainly," Landross replied and waited for her to finish her drink of water.

"Sorry," she apologized. "Once I engaged the knights, however, I couldn't back away without losing my entire command." The captain looked across the killing filed. "But that happened anyway," she said dejectedly.

Landross put an arm around her shoulders and walked her to the triage area established for the wounded. "See the healers about your arm and get something to eat. Your day is done, Captain."

Captain Anárion nodded. "Thank you, sir."

"And Larien," Landross said as the captain was walking away. "We'll get you that fourth battle star."

Captain Anárion stopped and turned. "With all due respect, sir, I don't really care."

Landross nodded and watched the captain's back as she left. Without taking his eyes off her, he motioned for his second-in-command, who was always somewhere in the vicinity, over to him.

"Sir," he said while saluting.

Landross returned his salute. "Nathaniel, take a detail southwest. Take a healer... two if another can be spared. I want you to locate the other two battlefields. Find any wounded and take care of the dead."

"We have little time, Commander," Nathaniel replied. "The Army corps marching north will be here soon... their mounted knights probably sooner."

"Understood," Landross said. "We have scouts watching the south to give warning, but you're correct. We need to move quickly. Get the wounded treated and back here as soon as they can be safely moved. As for our dead, take their identification tags and then burn the bodies."

"Their wounded and dead?"

Landross paused. What happened to Balthoron and Magdalena infuriated him. But there was a code of war to which all knights adhered. "Help the wounded as much as possible... then leave them with the dead for their own Army comrades to find."

458

Nathaniel saluted and turned to obey his orders. "Oh, and Nathaniel," Landross called out. "Don't burn the bodies of Balthoron or Magdalena. Bring them back for a more proper burial."

Nathaniel nodded.

"This isn't easy for any of us," Landross thought to himself. "Especially Father Goram and Autumn." Aloud, he said to no one in particular, "I wish I could give Mordecai to Horatio. I wonder if Althaya would forgive her priest after what he'd probably do to that bastard if I did?"

Lessien was despondent. One of the two Marines who rode with her had taken an arrow in his back and lay dead in the grass and weeds several miles behind her. The gods only know how many more had already sacrificed their lives so she could stay free. And more death and destruction in her name was to come. She swiveled on her horse, looking at the warriors who surrounded her... the surviving Marine and two dozen knights who were part of Sir Landross' contingent... and wondered how many of those brave souls will still be alive at the conclusion of this civil war. Lessien gripped the hilt of the sword that hung at her side. "My father's sword," she thought. "I miss him."

"Highness?"

Lessien broke from her self-examination... self-recrimination... to direct her attention to the knight speaking to her. Her horse was dancing about uncomfortably and snorting.

"I'm sorry, Sir Knight," she said. "You were saying?"

The knight had positioned his horse in front of Lessien's. He moved his horse back. There, sitting patiently in the middle of the roadway, were two massive dire wolves. These were undoubtedly the cause of her horse's jitteriness.

"Your Highness," the knight said, "I present Razor and Findley. We're two miles from Calmacil Clearing and the good father has sent a wolf delegation to welcome you."

Lessien was delighted. She knew of the pack of dire wolves that that roamed the forest... and the symbiotic relationship between them and Father Goram. But it actually went deeper than that. There was a genuine affection shared by both. On the occasions when she visited the monastery, she had come to know the pack leader, Ajax, quite well.

Lessien dismounted her horse and walked over to the wolves with the palms of her hands outward so they could sniff and introduce themselves in the way of the wolf. Once past this formality, she hugged them and buried her face in their soft fur. As the two wolves sat uncomplaining, Lessien released her emotions for the first time since her rescue and cried... but only for a moment. She quickly harnessed in her feelings and stood. Lessien kept a hand on Razor and Findley's back and looked up at her escort, all of whom were still on their horses.

"Sir Knight," she said to the escort leader. "I'll walk the rest of the way with my two wolf guardians. Please have someone lead my horse."

The knight protested. "But Your Highness... "

Lessien shook her head, ending any further discussion. She wanted to reconnect with her people... to show Father Goram she hadn't been broken. She couldn't do that atop a large warhorse surrounded by armored knights. She'd walk into Calmacil Clearing in front of her escorts with the dire wolves at her side and her head held high. No more thoughts of suicide, of inadequate feelings, or that she was a disappointment to her father. It was time to win back her kingdom.

Night had fallen, but Nefertari and Colonel Tirion both kept moving. They wanted to make sure they outpaced the Army so they could reach Calmacil Clearing before the siege began. Maedhros Nénmacil had rejoined them earlier and was now flying out in front and serving as the de facto scout for their small party.

Miracle, though awake, was quiet and still. Colonel Tirion assumed Nefertari had worked a glamour on the child... but she hadn't. Nefertari, though grateful... for it made traveling with the child in her arms much easier... was concerned. But each time she inspected the babe with her clerical abilities, she could find nothing wrong. Miracle was healthy. "Was it possible for the baby to be depressed over the loss of her parents?" she asked herself. "Such a traumatic event often damages the psyche. Though a newborn's mind will recover quickly, they're not immune."

"StarSinger," Maedhros Nénmacil said within Nefertari's head.

"Yes, my friend."

"I see fires to the northwest," he replied. "They look to be funeral pyres."

Nefertari related the creation stone's message to Colonel Tirion, who reined in his horse to a stop and looked in that direction.

"I see them now," the Colonel said. "That could only mean one thing... a battle."

Nefertari looked at her companion. "Wouldn't they have buried their dead?" she asked.

"Not if there wasn't enough time." Colonel Tirion shifted in his saddle and looked behind them. He saw light shining in the sky just over the horizon. "The Army's bivouacked for the night... but I'm not sure about the cavalry. They're the Army's eyes and ears and usually ride scout. They could still be coming."

Nefertari looked back to the northwest. She was conflicted... on the one hand she had a duty to care for any wounded left on the battlefield. But she was unwilling to put Miracle in danger unnecessarily. "Maedhros Nénmacil," she said aloud. "Will you scout the pyres for me?"

"Certainly, StarSinger," he replied from above before he sped to do Nefertari's bidding.

Colonel Tirion jumped. He has yet to grow completely accustomed to the deep bass of the creation stone's voice. "Sorry," he said apologetically to Nefertari.

Nefertari had dropped the reins of her horse, letting it rest and graze, while she unstrapped the water skin containing the milk from the saddle horn. The water skin glowed slightly from a magic spell Nefertari cast to keep the milk fresh. As she fed Miracle, she looked at the Colonel.

"Daeron, about how far is Calmacil Clearing?" she asked.

Colonel Tirion thought about Nefertari's question. "Well... if we travel the rest of the night, we should be there midmorning... maybe earlier. There's a forest surrounding it. Without a guide, it'll be slow going once we enter it."

"No roads or trails?"

Colonel Tirion shook his head. "Not many... and that's the way Father Goram wants it. The forest acts as a maze... one more barrier to protect his monastery. Another thing we must consider is the pack of dire wolves that roam the forest. From everything I've heard, they can be a deadly force to reckon with. If they get it in their minds we're the enemy, I don't think we'll survive the night... though between your magic, my sword, and the flying rock, we'd no doubt put a sizable dent in the dire wolf population." Colonel Tirion shook his head. "But I don't really want to do that. Father Goram loves those dire wolves as much as they love him and he'd be particularly upset if anything should happen to them. I'd rather face the dire wolves then that priest's wrath."

Nefertari had put Miracle on her shoulder and patted her back. "If my sister has made it to the monastery with your men, they'll pass the word, don't you think?"

Colonel Tirion nodded. "Of course... if the monastery guards don't shoot first and ask questions later. No doubt everyone's on edge. And with good reason. Right now the Queen and Father Goram probably think the whole island's against them."

"Isn't it?" Nefertari asked.

"Madam!" Colonel Tirion exclaimed. "I..."

"I don't claim to understand your politics or who's on whose side," Nefertari said pointedly. "Only that my sister is in grave danger... and your island's military forces hunt her."

Nefertari studied the Colonel as she settled Miracle back into her arm. "Daeron, I trust you and your Marines... it's the broader perspective I'm concerned with. Where do your superiors stand in all of this? Who can I trust to have the best interests of my sister in their hearts?"

Colonel Tirion looked at the priestess. He couldn't see her face, but her voice had turned rigid.

"Colonel," Nefertari continued. "I don't know who Lessien's enemies are just yet. But know this... I'll do everything in my power to protect my sister and see her returned to the throne of InnisRos. Anyone who jeopardizes that will have to contend with Maedhros Nénmacil and me. And I assure you it won't be a good... "

"Shhh," Colonel Tirion whispered suddenly.

Nefertari at once stopped talking. Without thinking she put a finger into Miracle's mouth to suckle... making sure the child stayed quiet as well. Then she heard why Colonel Tirion shushed her. Horses behind them... many horses... and moving in their direction.

"Army cavalry," Colonel Tirion whispered.

As Nefertari and Colonel Tirion nudged their horses into a run, they heard a faint voice call out. The cavalry horses turned and moved toward the funeral pyres.

Colonel Tirion grabbed the reins of Nefertari's horse and came to a stop. "They've seen the pyres burning," he whispered. "Let's hold still and remain silent for a few minutes."

Nefertari nodded, though she didn't know if the Colonel could see her in the dark. As they waited, she silently warned Maedhros Nénmacil. The creation stone didn't answer... but a series of explosions lit the sky about where Nefertari thought he might be.

"Let's go," Colonel Tirion shouted. "They have sorcerers with them!"

An Army cavalryman named Jaxxam, one of many scattered in the cornfield, lay on his back and looked at the stars. The chill of the night had been driven away by the burning funeral pyre of the rebel rangers his unit had fought earlier in the day. The pain from the arrow that felled him had receded... just as the rebel clerics who healed him after the battle said it would. But he still didn't have the strength to stand on his own two feet.

He dreamed of being back in his small home, where he often sat in front of the fireplace after a supper of meat stew and bread. He'd bounce his children on his legs and entertain them with stories of trolls, ogres, and dragons while his wife cleared the table and cleaned the dishes. Then, after the small ones had gone to bed, he'd cuddle with his wife while smoking his pipe and drowsily staring into the fire. Every evening it was the same routine, over and over again... which was part of the reason he joined the Army cavalry. He had begun to feel the boredom of complacency. Now, however, he feared he'd never get that contentment back. Jaxxam told himself he'd learned a valuable lesson this day. He only hoped it wasn't too late for him and many of his wounded brothers.

Jaxxam saw stars blotted out of the sky... only to reappear. "Something huge is up there flying around," Jaxxam thought. "A dragon perhaps?" He was so intrigued by the flying object he didn't stop to realize the enormous danger he was in if it was a dragon.

The night abruptly awoke in an explosion of light and fire. The concussion knocked the air out of Jaxxam. As he struggled to breathe, he noticed a huge boulder tumbling of the sky. It was straight over him. His eyes widened as he watch it grow larger and larger.

Jaxxam closed his eyes, waiting for the death that fell from above. But it never came. When he opened his eyes, he saw the boulder spinning six feet above him. It stopped its spinning and rotated. As Jaxxam stared, two shinny eyes and a smiling mouth appeared on the surface of the boulder. One eye winked before the boulder left, flying northeast at ground level.

Jaxxam stared at the retreating boulder until the night swallowed it. To the south he could hear horses. Reaching over and grabbing his sword lying next to him, he flung it as far as his strength could manage. "I quit!" he shouted. Then he began to laugh uncontrollably. When his fellow Army cavalrymen reached him, he was still laughing... while he lay on his back looking at the stars.

Father Goram sat on a bench in the chapel... the same place where his goddess, Althaya, and Aurora, the goddess of the rangers of Aster, appeared and first told him of the last empath. Since that evening so long ago, Father Goram had maintained the plants brought in at the time for Aurora's benefit. A small brook had been added which enhanced the chapel as a place of peace and solitude. In the peace of the chapel, people could find a quiet place for the contemplation of one's soul, a place to buoy lost spirits, and a place to grieve. At the moment, Father Goram was in need of all three. Autumn sat by his side with her arm interlocked with his.

"The Queen's safe," Autumn said, "only because of the decisions you made."

Father Goram didn't respond. He continued to stare into the shallow brook and listen to the water as it meandered over the rocks which lined the bottom.

Occasionally a dried leaf would move with the current. "The cost," he finally whispered before looking at his wife. "And now the Army marches against us."

"That has always been a possibility with or without the Queen here," Autumn replied. "Dear, this has been building for years. Ever since Martin was murdered... which I'm sure Mordecai had arranged."

Father Goram shook his head. "I should've been smart enough to head it off long ago. The animus between Mordecai and me goes back to a time before Martin came over from the Alfheim." Father Goram looked over at his wife. "Remember Hector? By the gods I loved that wolf. I love them all. Anyway, he didn't like Mordecai from the very moment he laid eyes on him. Hector was a brilliant judge of character." Father Goram beat his fist against his knee. "Damn! If only I'd done something back then before Mordecai gained true power!"

Autumn shook her head. "Your logic is flawed, my love. The only way you could've stopped this would've been to remove Mordecai from the equation."

Father Goram looked at Autumn.

"Assassins?" she said.

Father Goram said nothing. He turned and looked at the brook.

"Horatio," Autumn gasped. "You're better than that!"

"You didn't have a problem when I asked Mother Aubria for the same thing yesterday," he replied.

Autumn shut her mouth. "Now is different... it's war, Horatio," she said even though she still didn't approve of her husband using assassins. "But to do it simply because it's a political expediency... that's never right."

Father Goram sighed. "It wouldn't have been a political expediency. It would've been crushing a cockroach under my boot... nothing different. This war might have been prevented if I had the foresight to do it earlier." He turned to look at his wife. "What's worse for the soul, dear?" he asked. "One death? Hundreds? Thousands? Already Mordecai has taken more than I have the strength to endure. Maggie's dead because of him!"

"Landross wouldn't see it that way."

Father Goram exploded out of the bench. "The hell with a knight's honor!" he shouted. As soon as he said the words, he regretted them. Autumn shouldn't be made to bear the brunt of his anger... that should be reserved for Mordecai.

Bending over and framing Autumn's face with his hands, Father Goram kissed her on the forehead. "I'm sorry, sweetheart."

Autumn got up from the bench and tightly hugged her husband. "All is well, my beloved. I miss her too."

Four black-cloaked, hooded figures leaned over a communications crystal sitting on a small table. A simple candle provided the only light source in the otherwise dark room.

"We have our contract from Mother Aubria, master," one of the robed figures, a female, said into the crystal. "You risk our disclosure by calling us back together again."

"I understand, but this communication is necessary," a voice from the crystal replied. *"I want the entire guild on a new contract."*

The four figures exchanged glances. "And our current contract with Mother Aubria?"

"To be carried out as agreed," the voice responded. *"But this takes precedence."*

"As you wish, master. We're yours to command."

"You have my thanks and appreciation." the disembodied voice said. *"Everyone will receive double shares. Now here's who I want you to destroy..."*

Sorcerer and virtuoso assassin Eric the Black slipped the communications crystal back into his belt pouch. "You and your toadies took something from me that was precious beyond even my own life, Mordecai," he said to himself. "My friend Magdalena's dead and now I'll have my revenge."

Mordecai stared at General Narmolanya, who was standing at attention by the entrance doorway of Mordecai's lavish dining room. Mordecai and

Nightshade had just sat down for a late dinner, and the interruption didn't sit well with the self-proclaimed king of InnisRos.

Mordecai removed his crown and rubbed his forehead as if that simple gesture would chase away the now ever-present headache. "What is it, General?" he asked.

The general saluted. "Highness, I've just received word that a contingent of our mounted knights and cavalry have engaged the rebels in the north."

Mordecai looked at his Army chief. "Where in the north, General?"

"In the fields before the foothills of the North Spire Mountain range," the general replied.

Mordecai motioned for the general to take a seat. A servant rushed to offer the general a glass of wine... which he accepted after he had received a nod from Mordecai. Both Mordecai and Nightshade were drinking water and waved the servant off after he had served General Narmolanya.

"How did we fare?" Mordecai asked.

"Not well, Highness," the general said. "Mounted elements of the First Army Corps engaged what was reported to be Colonel Balthoron's battalion and a few of Father Goram's rangers." General Narmolanya took a sip of wine.

"Causalities, General?" Nightshade spoke for the first time.

"Seven hundred dead out of a total force of eight hundred." the General took another sip of wine.

"One battalion of regulars and a few rangers did all that damage?" Nightshade remarked incredulously. "To mounted knights?!"

471

The General looked into his wine cup. "They were reinforced by Landross and his knights from the monastery at Calmacil Clearing."

"Never mind that, General," Mordecai said. "What of the traitor Balthoron's battalion?"

"Completely destroyed, Highness."

Mordecai sat back in his chair. A smug look came over his face. "That's not so bad, General. We can replace our dead. Goram can't."

Nightshade looked over at Mordecai with disgust. "You fool!" she said. "Why would Landross' knights be afield? For that matter why would Balthoron engage his infantry against such a large number of knights? It's suicide!"

Mordecai frowned. "You're right." he said as he looked at the general.

"Is there more, General?" Nightshade asked.

"Yes ma'am," the general replied before taking a big gulp of his wine. "Though I've yet to get confirmation, it would appear the Queen is alive and has reached the monastery."

"What!" Mordecai screamed as he rose, knocking his chair to the floor behind him.

General Narmolanya cringed and ducked his head.

Mordecai began to pace. "The Navy's off playing war games and refusing to follow my orders and the Army is INCOMPETENT!"

"Highness... "

"SHUT UP, GENERAL!" Mordecai screamed.

Nightshade smiled. "This is working out nicely," she thought. Then she turned her attention back to Mordecai. "Calm down and stop your pacing," she said. "What's done is done. We need to think this through."

Mordecai frowned at Nightshade, but righted his chair, sat down, and took deep breaths to calm himself.

Nightshade nodded. "Now, General," she said. "When will your troops arrive at Calmacil Clearing?"

"The cavalry and knights by dawn's light tomorrow, I should think," he said after pausing to consider. "The infantry a day later... perhaps dusk or shortly thereafter."

"Is one army corps enough to lay siege?" Nightshade asked.

General Narmolanya nodded. "Yes, my lady... though it might take another corps to actually root the rebels out of the monastery. But one corps will certainly keep them bottled up."

"Excellent! See Mordecai, it's not so... " but Nightshade was interrupted by an onset of gagging by General Narmolanya. His eyes popped out of their sockets and hung by tendons as he grabbed his throat and stood. He then coughed bloody phlegm over the table as he fell. When he hit the floor, he went into a seizure. In seconds it was over.

"What the hell just happened?" Mordecai asked, mortified at the dead body lying on his dining room floor.

"Isn't it obvious?" Nightshade said as she visually examined the dead Army chief. "He's been poisoned."

"In my palace? How?"

Nightshade rose. "I've seen this type of poison before," she said. "Only an assassin would use it."

She turned, but the servant was already gone.

THE STRUGGLE FOR INNOCENCE

CHAPTER NINETEEN

Elanesse

*The universe has no stake in the struggle
between benevolence and malevolence... order and
chaos... light and dark. It continues to thrive despite the
individual outcome of these battles of opposites,
repeated over and over again. The concept of
benevolence and malevolence, and the subsequent
mêlée between the two, is a mortal construct... as are
the moral truths that rule a mortal's heart and mind.*

--From a Treatise Concerning the State of the
Universal Continuum...Author Unknown
-Book of the Unveiled

The attack came in three waves, was well orchestrated,
and flawlessly executed. The Purge-controlled humans
had climbed down the ropes that hung from the sewer
level to the cavern exposed by the earlier collapse.
Through sheer force of numbers they overcame the
magical wards Kristen had crafted for just this exigency.
Though many lay dead or unconscious from the wards,
even more climbed over their prone compatriots to
continue the assault. With the Purge controlling their
minds, it was an assault they couldn't retreat from even
if they wanted.

Though the Purge's generalship was on full
display, Tangus, with Lester and Mariko, were well

versed in combat tactics as well... particularly defensive measures. Kristen had placed her magical wards far enough down the corridor to allow plenty of time to react to the attack. The wards only lasted a few minutes, but it was enough time for Kristen to call forth two magical pillars of flame... positioned on opposites sides of the corridor approximately fifty feet away. This in effect funneled the attackers closer together. As the Purge forces ran past the flaming pillars... Tangus, Safire, and Jennifer picked them off with bow and arrow. Lester and Mariko stood behind them and in front of Kristen and Emmy.

The corridor quickly filled with dead and wounded humans. The narrow confines of the corridor, the distance to the flaming pillars, and the fallen bodies which had to be negotiated by the attackers, played in favor of the companions. None of the humans got within thirty feet before taking an arrow.

"I've only got six arrows left," Jennifer said.

Tangus looked down the corridor. "We're all getting short. I don't think we can stand another assault like that," he said.

"Indeed, friend Tangus," Lester quipped. "Perhaps the next time Mariko and I can take part."

Kristen ignored the banter and was studying the magical ward that sealed off this end of the tunnel... the tunnel that led to the surface entrance to the Grand Palace. "We need to get through this," she said, looking at her husband. "Who knows how many humans the Purge has at its beck and call?"

Tangus looked at Safire who nodded, signaling she should watch for signs of another attack. He turned and moved back to stand next to his wife.

"It's sorcerer magic, honey," Kristen said. "And it's powerful... maybe beyond my ability to comprehend."

"Not too surprising since it was meant to stop anyone from getting down here," Tangus replied. He reached out and cautiously touched the glimmering field of magic. It sparkled at the point of contact and sent a low-powered volt up his arm. It was uncomfortable but not too severe. There was no give in the wall of magic whatsoever, however.

"I've seen this before," Tangus said. "It's a barrier of force." He took a couple of steps back and studied it. "Elrond has not only cast this type of magic before... but he's also dispelled it." Tangus shook his head. "But nothing this strong. You can tell by the glimmer. See how it shimmers from one hue to another? Elrond told me this means the magic is constantly changing... now what did he call it... constantly changing frequencies, whatever those are."

"It means the magic is constantly changing from one type to another," Kristen said. "One second it might be protective, and the next invocative or enchantment. To dispel it, you'd have to know the correct sequencing."

Tangus looked confused. "Whatever you say, dear. That's your area, not mine. Even so, I've been around... not as much as Elrond or dear Max... but enough to know this was created by a very powerful sorcerer."

"Which means I'll not be able to dispel it," Kristen said with a sigh.

Tangus went up behind Kristen and massaged her shoulders. "Sweetie, even Elrond probably couldn't bring this down. But you see magic differently than he does. At least try."

Tangus's breath suddenly exploded out as if he had been hit by a thrown anvil. He then felt a sharp pain in his lower back. He dropped to one knee while pulling both Kristen and Emmy with him. He'd been wounded enough times to know he'd been hit by an arrow. Looking back up, he saw that Jennifer, Safire, and Lester were also struggling with their own wounds. Mariko had both her katanas out and several pieces of arrows laid at her feet. The narrow corridor, their advantage of just a few moments before, was now their disadvantage.

Tangus heard the release of bowstrings from down the corridor before he saw the arrows streaking by the flaming pillars. "Down!" Safire screamed. Tangus dropped and covered Kristen and Emmy as best as he could. As he waited for the flight of arrows to arrive, he heard shouts. Another wave of humans was attacking.

Romulus ran west, through the Forest of the Fey and into the foothills of the Olympus Mountains. He didn't know why he had chosen this path... but something inside... an unresolved feeling... told him this was the direction he must go. Mount Repose was his destination.

He stopped at a stream for a drink and rest. Though Althaya had made him long-lived, he was a normal dire wolf in all other respects... except for his great size, endurance, and even greater intelligence. A rigorous run still tired him as much as it did any other dire wolf... just not as quickly.

After satiating his thirst, he waded upstream and caught a fish for his dinner. He had eaten several rabbits along the way and appreciated the opportunity for the change to his diet. After he finished eating, he decided to take a short nap. Mount Repose could be clearly seen as it dwarfed the other mountains around it... as if it were the king and the smaller mountains served as its court. As Romulus stared, he felt once again the strange connection with the mountain. Something kept drawing him towards it... something he needed but thought he'd never have. "A mate," he thought. "That's what I seek." Just before Romulus drifted off he wondered for the hundredth time how Emmy would know such a thing.

"I'm so bored!" Elrond shouted.

The horses grazing under the protection of the Tree of Golden Radiance looked up and scolded Elrond with their eyes. Smoke and Arbellason whinnied their disdain.

Elrond looked down. "Well, I am," he whispered. When he looked back up, however, he had a gleam in his eye. He walked over to a pile of saddles and grabbed his along with his saddle blanket. Picking everything up, he went over to his horse.

"Ready for a little trip?" he said with a smile. His horse nodded his head and stomped a foot on the ground.

Elrond threw the saddle over the saddle blanket and fastened the cinch.

"What are you doing?" Elanesse asked in Elrond's head.

"Think I'll take a stroll into... well... into you," Elrond replied, then shook his head. "The city you, that is. That was strange."

"Do you not remember what the empath said?"

Elrond stopped what he was doing and thought back to the conversation...

"Mr. Elrond, you can't go with us," Emmy had said.

Elrond, taken aback by that announcement, asked, *"What do you mean, I can't go. You're going to need my help to defeat the Purge. And it's the only way I can be sure Elanesse is no longer threatened."*

"It's because of Elanesse that you can't go," Emmy replied. *"The Purge isn't something that can be easily destroyed. The magic that brought the Purge to life drew in and used the evil purpose in its creator's hearts. When faced with the reality of its own destruction, the Purge will seek a new host. It'll try to escape its fate. The only possibility is Elanesse. Mister Elrond, she'll need you to be here to help battle the Purge. If you don't, then our sacrifice to neutralize its influence will be for naught."*

"And if Elanesse and I succeed?" he had asked.

"Then the Purge will not be able to escape justice," Emmy replied. *"Like the mighty oak that dies,*

collapses, and returns to the earth, the Purge will have its essence torn apart and returned to the heavens if it doesn't find a refuge. I WILL kill it, Mr. Elrond... as long as it has no place to run."

Elrond leaned against his horse, shook his head, and sighed. "Damn," he whispered before taking the saddle and saddle blanket off the horse and putting them back with the others. Plucking fruit from the Tree of Golden Radiance, he sat down on a hollow log, causing the family of squirrels living within to scamper away, and took a bite.

"I'm so bored," Elrond said to one of the squirrels who had bravely returned to admonish him.

Safire's warning saved them. Except for a few minor scratches caused by the arrows as they shattered off the magical barrier, no one was the worse for wear from the second barrage. Mariko, the only one uninjured, stood to meet the advancing horde. As the humans streamed past the pillars of flame, screeching horrendous battle cries, Tangus and Lester joined Mariko, their weapons drawn, to make a last stand. Safire and Jennifer dropped their bows and drew their own swords.

Kristen, watching the scene unfold before her, knew that this could be the end if she didn't do something. She reviewed her spells, discarding those that either took too long to cast or those that would be ineffective for the circumstances. Emmy suddenly grabbed Kristen's hand.

"Concentrate on the bond, mother," the child said.

Kristen looked at Emmy, who nodded, and did as she was asked. By now she completely trusted her little girl's judgment. Kristen closed her eyes, felt the bond, and gasped. An incredible quantity of energy was flowing through it from Emmy to her... more energy than she had ever felt before... and it overwhelmed her. From somewhere far, far away, Kristen heard Emmy speak to Mariko.

"Mariko, cross your katanas," Emmy called to the assassin.

Mariko did as she was asked.

A wave of bright, sparkling energy coalesced on Mariko's crossed katanas. As the moving energy reached a pinnacle, it jumped off Mariko's katanas and rolled down the corridor. It was similar to a gigantic bundle of tangled snakes, torrents of energy contorting and snapping at everything in its path. Each human the energy touched vanished.

Tangus watched as the charging Purge-controlled humans vanished... though he wasn't sure if that's what was happening. The rolling sphere of energy left nothing alive in its wake. He'd seen disintegration spells used before, but this was nothing like that. When someone or something disintegrated, a powdery substance was always left behind. Once Elrond explained that disintegration only changes the material composition of the person or object... for example the ash left after a burned piece of wood in a fire. This magic caused the touched humans to disappear. There were no screams of pain, no struggling, no reaction. One moment there... the next not.

As everyone watched, the energy bundle moved past Kristen's pillars of flame. As it did so, strands of energy reached out and intermingled with both pillars, absorbing them and adding their power to its own. Then it disappeared down the corridor and into the darkness. All sounds of the attacking humans coming from the dark corridor ceased.

Kristen collapsed to the floor. Emmy, who had been holding her hand, did her best to break the fall.

"I'm sorry, mother, but I had to borrow some of your power," Emmy said to the now prone Kristen. "I had to use you and Mariko as conduits for the magic."

With Tangus' help, Kristen raised herself up and leaned on her elbows. "I'll be okay... just a little dizzy," Kristen said.

"Are you sure, love," Tangus replied concerned for his wife's wellbeing.

"Yes, dear," Kristen said. "Emmy, I'm sorry you had to kill."

Emmy shook her head. "I didn't kill them, though it probably would've been better if I had."

"What do you mean, child," Tangus asked.

"Their minds were destroyed by the Purge," Emmy answered. "They were nothing but automatons... shells of people whose will and conscious thought had been consumed. They lived and breathed only because the Purge allowed it." Emmy sighed. "I sent them into the void."

Jennifer, who'd been listening to the conversation, looked confused, "The void? What's that?"

Kristen stood and turned to Jennifer. "It's a difficult concept," she said. "The void is a place of nothing. It exists, yet it doesn't. Some believe it's a magical construct... but most, including me, believe it's a place created by the old gods to hide their mistakes... or punish their wicked. There's a host of things a sorcerer can do to manipulate it. For example, magic can beach it for protection or bend it for travel. But if the magic is somehow lost or taken away while someone is in the void... well, that soul is forever lost. Doomed to aimlessly roam in the void's great expanse for eternity." Turning to Emmy, Kristen said, "But these humans didn't have their souls, did they."

Emmy shook her head. A great sadness came over her. Kristen wrapped the child in her arms.

"But I still don't understand," Jennifer persisted. "How'd Emmy do it?"

Tangus looked at his daughter. He thought he knew what was unique about Emmy... but he didn't think it was his place to comment. Besides, his conclusions, at least on the surface, seemed ludicrous. Emmy was just special that's all... not a...

"Sweetie..." he said to Jennifer before being interrupted by Emmy.

"Sister, I'm the last empath," Emmy said. "At least for now. Each day I move further into my birthright. And each day, I discover new abilities I never knew I had." Emmy shrugged. "This was just one of those times."

Jennifer looked around at the faces staring at her... Emmy, Tangus, Kristen, and Mariko. Emmy and Mariko's eyes were scrupulously veiled and revealed nothing. But Tangus and Kristen seemed as confused and suspicious as she, yet neither were willing to take their suspicions further.

Jennifer smiled. "Sorry, Emmy. I've seen so much over the last few months that this shouldn't have surprised me." Turning to face Tangus, she said, "I'll go stand guard with Lester and Safire while you work on getting us around the barrier."

Kristen grabbed Jennifer's hand. "Let's see about healing your injuries first," she said. "The same goes for all of you."

Romulus ran through one of a network of passes that crisscrossed the Olympus Mountains. He relished the run... the freedom... the wind in his face. For the first time since being altered by the goddess Althaya, he felt he could just be a dire wolf... free of responsibility... free of obligation... and free to do silly little things like chasing butterflies. He wasn't sure how long his new-found liberty might last... so he took pleasure in every step.

The particular pass he was now moving through would take him close to the base of Mount Repose. He wasn't sure where he'd go once he got there, but reasoned everything would work itself out. The dire wolves of his original pack believed destiny drove all creatures... though through the years Romulus had come to realize he had some say in his future. Father Goram once called this control over one's actions free will. Destiny had put him on the path... but the freedom to chose one fork in the path over another was his to make. Not even destiny could change that. Father Goram always took the time to explain such matters. Unlike dire wolves, whose communication within the pack is simplistic and to the point, Father Goram's explanation of the affairs of his pack usually ended up as a complicated affair. The theory of free will and how it could change destiny caused Romulus' eyes to glaze over. While Father Goram droned on, his thoughts turned to big, fat, juicy haunches of venison. He was, after all, still a dire wolf.

Romulus stopped... he had caught a whiff of something that smelled of rotting corpses. He inspected the scent with his nose --- direction, distance, identification --- and decided he needed to get closer to the stench before he could decide its origin. He walked for several minutes before spotting an intersection in the path ahead. As Romulus cautiously approached, he ascertained other smells... different smells. The various scents where coming from a trail going further up into the mountains. It looked as if the trail went up to Mount Repose itself.

The magical barrier that separated the lower tunnels from the sewers... and the surface above... radiated strong magic. Kristen, as the only one familiar with the intricate knowledge needed to cast spells and cantrips, knew only she could solve the riddle of its construction and sequencing. Soon she had completely immersed herself in the challenge.

"Honey?" Tangus asked.

Kristen cleared her head and looked around. Several faces stared at her. "How long?" she asked.

"About an hour," Tangus replied. "We were getting worried."

Kristen stood and reached out to touch the barrier and seemed to lose herself in it again. "It's magnificent," she breathed. "Layer upon layer of protective and defensive magic. Each layer woven around and through each other, adding support to its neighbor... each component making the other parts around it stronger... more powerful. Think of homespun cloth, or better yet, the links in chain mail armor... except the open spaces in each small ring keeps changing." Kristen looked at Tangus. "It's efficient, brutally strong, and beautiful."

Tangus nodded. "Can we get through it?"

Kristen looked once again at the barrier. "No," she said. "This was made to last for an eternity."

There was a pause before Mariko asked, "Can we dig around it?"

Kristen shook her head. "The spell's creators made allowances for that. It's too pervasive."

"Can you... ?" Tangus asked.

"Dispel it?" Kristen replied. Then she laughed. "It's much too powerful for me. Even a sorcerer as powerful as Elrond, with all his magical trinkets, couldn't defeat it. Neither could my father, I suspect. Maybe a god..."

Tangus stole a glance at Emmy, but she didn't react. "Then we go back to the cavern and climb those ropes hanging from the sewer level... if they're still there," he said.

The smell of death was permeated the cavern where the ceiling had collapsed. Bodies buried in the rubble, and on top of it, were slowly decomposing. The natural chill that comes from being so far underground only delayed the process. Nothing can stop the unrelenting course of nature... ashes to ashes, dust to dust. One body wore a ragtag uniform with a lieutenant insignia on the epaulets of his shirt. Mariko noticed a folded piece of linen sticking out of a shirt pocket of the lieutenant. She grabbed it and stuffed it in her belt pouch without giving it a second thought.

To the relief of everyone, the ropes were still hanging from the sewer level. Mariko immediately selected a rope, pulled on it to test the strength, and effortlessly scrambled up it. Once she was on the sewer level above, she disappeared. After a few moments several muffled "clangs" could be heard from above as Mariko hammered steel spikes into the rock to further secure the rope. Poking her head over the breach above, she waved them up.

Tangus turned to Lester. "I want you to climb up first. I don't foresee a problem with Safire or Jennifer... but I'd like to tie them off with another rope held by you." Tangus looked at the two. "Just a precaution."

As Lester checked his grip, Tangus touched him on the shoulder. "You'll need to pull Kristen and Emmy up. Neither are experienced enough to do this on their own."

"Tangus, dear," Kristen objected. "We've rock-climbed together on InnisRos. I can do this."

Tangus shook his head. "This is a straight ascent. Yes, we've climbed... and rappelled down the side of a mountain. But you never trained for a dead-weight climb." Tangus then nodded at Lester who began his climb.

As Kristen watched Lester moved up the rope, she said, "You're probably right, Tangus. I don't think I could handle that."

Once Safire and Jennifer were up, Tangus took the rope and made a loop for Emmy to sit in. After he tied a safety rope around her waist, Lester hauled her up, and both ropes dropped back down.

"See you up-top," Tangus said to Kristen as he pulled on the safety rope to signal Kristen was ready.

Kristen looked at Tangus. "Promise?" she asked.

Tangus nodded and gave her a quick kiss on the forehead. "Promise."

Neither noticed the shadow behind one of the many stalagmites that grew out of the cavern floor.

The Purge felt the death of those it controlled below the city. The magic used to destroy its adherents was of empath origins... that much it knew... but it was far and away superior to anything the Purge had ever experienced. Now the only allies it controlled were the wild animals from the surrounding forests... the worgs. The saber cats and mountain wolves the Purge had once dominated rejected its control after a few days.

"Kill! Kill! Kill!"

The voices in the Purge's head were again repeating their mantra.

"Kill! Kill! Kill!"

"Shut up!" the Purge screamed.
But of course they didn't.
"Please shut up," the Purge implored with little hope of being listened to. "I can't kill the empath. She's too strong."

"Kill! Kill! Kill!"

The Purge had an evil madness that, while being almost completely insane, still maintained its calculating brilliance... and that brilliance had just hatched another plan. "No, I can't kill the empath... alone. But with help... yes... with help I can still attain my dream. The city... she's alive. What's her name? Elanesse? Yes... Elanesse. I can kill the empath if I can control Elanesse."

Romulus walked the trail warily. He had been climbing steadily for several hours and was now on the lower base of Mount Repose, which towered before him like another world. The higher he went, the colder it became. The trees and mountain grass that bordered the trail earlier had turned to snow... the landscape scarce except for the occasional mountain pine. As he exhaled, he could see his breath. The stench he followed, however, never diminished.

Romulus rounded a turn in the trail and came upon a "killing field". The trail before him had opened up after the turn and was about the size of a small clearing in a forest. The clearing was rimmed by the steep walls of the mountain. It was the perfect place for an ambush... the victims wouldn't know they were in trouble before it was too late. Here the victims were a pack of wolves. They had been pummeled to death by boulders.

Romulus approached one of the still forms and sniffed it. The scent, though familiar as a brother to his kind, was unknown. They were larger than the normal wolf he was accustomed to, but not as large as a worg or dire wolf. Each of the bodies was pure white... like the snow all around. Unlike the wolves he had ever known, however, the coloring of these wolves didn't vary. The sharp contrast of the red blood against the white fur served as a stark reminder of the danger all of nature's children faced... prey against predator. But what mountain predator makes prey of the wolf?

Romulus retreated so he'd be out of the clearing and sat to mull over how this might affect his search. Five crushed bodies lay in the bloodied snow, and there were indications that others had been dragged away up the trail at the other end of the clearing. Romulus heard stories told to Kristen by Father Goram about intelligent carnivores who lived above the tree line on mountains. The elf pack leader called them yeti. Like the dire wolf, they traveled and hunted in packs. And like the dire wolf, they had a den. Romulus considered continuing forward without investigating further, however, the thought of his wolf brethren being eaten by the yeti creatures didn't sit well with him. But what chance did he have against a whole pack of those creatures? A plan began to formulate in his mind.

Three yeti's were returning to the site of their ambush earlier in the day. Their full bellies made them slow... their reactions cumbersome. They didn't care... they were in their territory and had nothing to fear. All they wanted to do was return to their warm den and go to sleep. But first they had to bring back the rest of the wolf bodies. There was enough meat to keep the pack fed for another week, and opportunities like this didn't come often. They didn't notice the huge dire wolf upon them until it was too late.

As Tangus tied the safety rope around his waist before beginning his climb, he sensed something behind him. His first thought, as he cut the rope and turned to meet the menace, was that one or more of the Purge's followers had survived... but he quickly ruled that out. If it was a mindless follower, it wouldn't have waited until he was alone before attacking. instead, whatever was here cowered in the shadow of a stalagmite. It was hiding... not attacking.

"Tangus, what's wrong," Kristen called.

Tangus didn't want to spook whatever was in the cavern with him. He looked up at Kristen and waved... then he put a finger to his lips to quiet her. He turned and stared into the shadow. Nothing. Tangus drew his sword and moved cautiously toward the stalagmite.

Two small eyes peeked out of the shadow and quickly retreated. Tangus knew almost immediately those eyes were that of an animal. He took a deep breath, concentrated, and called forth his ranger's senses... a talent that allowed him to detect the emotional stability of an animal... and was bombarded with several emotions. Tangus felt confusion, fear, sadness, loss... and great pain. The animal was young, and the depth of these emotions caused Tangus' heart to lurch. "I need to save this baby," he thought as he slid his sword back into its scabbard.

Tangus knew any sudden move could force the animal to bolt. He slowly approached the stalagmite and peeked around it. What he saw explained a lot. The animal was a baby saber cat... about the size of a full-grown house cat. Tangus estimated it couldn't have

493

been more than a couple of days old. Its fur was snowy white with deep purple stripes.

"A Royal Mountain Saber Cat," Tangus said in wonderment as he got down on his knees to get on the cat's level. "You're supposed to be a legend. How'd you get here, little guy?"

The saber kitten backed up against a large boulder that looked as if had fallen from above. When the kitten moved, Tangus saw something was very wrong. He crawled closer. His elven sight and ranger senses penetrated the shadows, and it became clear what had happened. The boulder had fallen on one of the humans sent here by the Purge, hopelessly crushing him. His legs and one arm were sticking out from beneath the boulder. The arm still clutched a large satchel... and the lower part of the saber kitten's body appeared to be stuck in it.

"A poacher," Tangus muttered. "The Purge may have made this human a raving lunatic, but it would appear he still understood the value of a rare pelt."

Tangus recalled his knowledge of animal husbandry. Royal Mountain Saber Cats were thought to be animals of legend and lore... despite continued sightings in the remote mountain regions around Mount Repose and in the northern Mahtan Mountains. One such claim of the Royal's existence came from a dwarf hermit and was written about in the *'Tome of the Fantastic'*, a whimsical collection of essays describing all the strange and mythological creatures that roamed Aster. The tome was long on entertainment but short on the truth... at least as far as Tangus was concerned.

Tangus looked at the saber kitten. "I guess you give the tome some credence. It says you're a one-in-a-million offspring of two normal saber cats. It also says you'll only be male, bigger than normal, and unable to produce any of your own kittens." Tangus shook his head. "If the tome is to be believed, it says your mother and father left you to die because you're so different. That makes you a very rare fellow indeed."

The kitten swiped a paw at Tangus when he reached to stroke its head. But there wasn't much strength in the attempt and the kitten lost its balance and toppled over. Tangus petted the kitten, trying to give it as much reassurance as he could while using his extraordinary empathy for animals to calm it. The kitten fought Tangus' efforts to restrain it, but was too weak.

"A strong mind, eh little one?" Tangus whispered. "Let's see what's wrong."

"Tangus?" Kristen called.

"I'm okay," Tangus replied, though he never let his attention waver from the kitten. He tried to extract the kitten from the satchel... but the kitten snarled in pain. Tangus inspected the satchel more closely and saw that part of it was under the boulder. He took a knife and carefully sliced open the top half of the satchel to expose the back legs of the kitten. One leg was pinned under the boulder... clearly crushed.

"Oh no," he said as he looked at the kitten.

Upon closer inspection, Tangus could tell the leg had been nearly severed just above the middle joint. The only thing keeping the kitten from freedom was a thick piece of furred flesh. It appeared the bleeding had been controlled somewhat by the weight of the boulder which acted as a clamp on the major blood vessels.

Tangus frowned. "The minute I finish severing the leg, you'll bleed to death," he said. "But I can't just leave you here to die," Tangus said as he scratched the kitten behind the ears. "I'll get you out, little fellow. You just wait and see."

Tangus took out a jar of healing salve from a belt pouch and gently smeared it around the leg as best as he could. "That should help with the pain," he said before he stood and walked back over to the dangling rope.

"Kristen!" he called. He could make out several heads looking down on him from the hole one hundred feet above.

"What's going on, dear?"

"I've found an injured animal down here," Tangus responded. "It was being carried by one of the humans who fell to their death when the floor collapsed. It's hurt and alone."

Kristen looked at Jennifer who shook her head and said, "Father won't abandon that animal."

Kristen nodded. "I know. That's one of the many reasons I love him." She looked at Lester. "I'll need your help to go back down."

Emmy put a hand on Kristen's arm and shook her head. "Father must do this on his own."

"Why, honey?" Kristen asked.

"Because he needs this," Emmy replied. "It'll help to heal the hole left in his heart when Bitts died."

"Kristen?" Tangus called again.

Kristen nodded at Emmy. "What do you need?" she called to her husband.

"Do you have a potion or salve that helps to control bleeding?"

Kristen shook her head. "No. I do that using healing magic."

"Okay," Tangus said as his mind raced through possible scenarios. "I have to remove the leg to free the animal from a large boulder," he said. "I'll put him in a bag and tie it to the rope. When I tug, pull him up as fast as you can and then close the wound."

"Understood," Kristen replied. "Before you start..." Kristen said before she saw that Tangus had already left.

When Tangus returned to the kitten, it was unconscious and its breaths were fast and shallow. "It's gone into shock," Tangus said to himself. He cut a length of cloth and wrapped it around the upper part of the kitten's crushed leg. Then he tied the two ends around a wooden tobacco pipe he found on one of the bodies and twisted until he judged the blood flow had either slowed or stopped. After tying the tourniquet off so it wouldn't slip, he drew one of his swords and sliced through the flesh of the leg in one quick, powerful stroke. Tangus pulled the kitten from behind the stalagmite and checked the leg. The blood flow had stopped, but the kitten was now shivering uncontrollably.

"Stay with me, little guy," Tangus said as he wrapped the kitten in one of his empty sacks. He rushed over and tied the sack to the end of the rope and tugged. Instantly the kitten began his ascent to the level above.

As the kitten was hoisted up, Tangus returned to the stalagmite and double checked the satchel. In a side pocket of the satchel he found an old collar... much too big for the kitten... at least for now... and a small skin of milk. Tangus stood. "I'll be damned," he whispered. "He didn't want the kitten's pelt... he wanted the kitten as a pet."

Tangus walked over to the dangling ropes deep in thought. The enemy was the Purge. The humans and worgs it used to attack were its victims... not just mindless drones. Though Bitts viciously attacked him and had to be killed, was he to blame or any less loved? Of course not. And now this. One of the controlled humans somehow fought off the Purge just enough to rescue an abandoned saber kitten.

Tangus shook his head as he grabbed one of the ropes. "Evil is no match for even the simplest of kindly acts... compassion for the helpless."

Without further hesitation, or a safety rope, Tangus climbed up to join his family. He didn't remember the climb... but he remembered his newfound perspective.

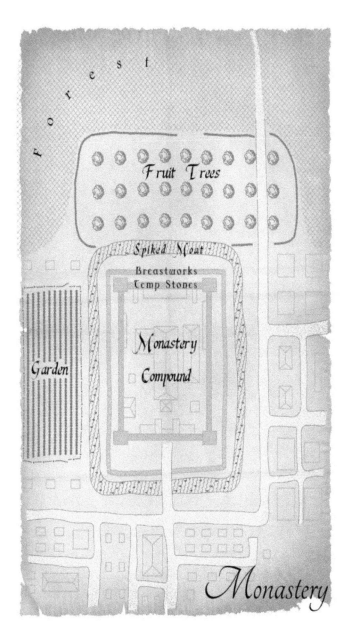

THE STRUGGLE FOR INNOCENCE

CHAPTER TWENTY

InnisRos

No fortification, regardless of size or strength, can survive a determined siege indefinitely. Only a foolish commander will retire behind four walls without plans to extricate his people from such a disastrous military position. I'm not a foolish commander.

-From the Letters of Father Horatio Goram to His Daughter, Kristen

"We're lost, aren't we, Daeron?" Nefertari said as she fed Miracle from the water skin. It had been several hours since they entered the forest. Night had fallen long ago and the dark trees began to run together... one looking just like the other.

Colonel Tirion stopped his horse and turned in the saddle to confront the priestess. "Lady, I'm not a ranger," he said testily. "The woods are as black as pitch and I've only visited Calmacil Clearing a few times." Colonel Tirion looked back out into the darkness. "Frankly, I expected to be met by Father Goram's rangers by now. Or maybe his wolves."

Maedhros Nénmacil descended through the trees to hover several feet above them. "They know we're here," he said as quietly as he could... though the vibration of his deep bass voice still caused a few leaves to fall off several tree branches. "We're being watched by several warriors and... I believe you called them wolves, Colonel. They have four legs and a tail. Amazing creatures... similar to the farmer's dog where I waited all those years... but very much larger. And they have..."

"Thank you, my friend," Nefertari interjected before the creation stone could ramble on further. "Why didn't you say something earlier?"

"My apologies, StarSinger," Maedhros Nénmacil replied sheepishly. "I thought you knew."

Nefertari shook her head. "No apologies necessary," she said. "I should've, but I let Miracle distract me. Daeron, it appears all we have to do is call out and we'll have our escort."

Colonel nodded. "Yes... but will it be in chains?" he asked.

"That's yet to be determined," a voice called out from the darkness as several rangers and wolves surrounded the four. "However, the Queen suggests we avoid conflict... particularly with that... that... that flying monstrosity. So, if it'll behave, we'll be just fine."

"I assure you, good ranger, we have the same desire," Nefertari said. "How fares my sister?"

"She is well, madam."

"And my Marines?" Colonel Tirion asked.

The figure studied the Marine colonel before continuing. "I'm sorry, Colonel. Only two arrived with the Queen. The others... well, I suspect they're dead."

Colonel Tirion dismounted his horse and nodded. "I should've known as much," he said as he rubbed his hand through his hair. "My sergeant and his men never passed on an opportunity to fight the good fight."

"Indeed!" the ranger said. "The two men who arrived with the Queen seemed quite despondent they were still alive."

Colonel Tirion held out his hand. "Colonel Daeron Tirion, First Marine Reconnaissance."

The ranger took the Colonel's hand. "Ranger Beren Goodfellow, Colonel. Now, if you'll please follow me, the Queen is most eager to reunite with her sister... and I believe Father Goram has a host of questions for all of you."

Before he turned to lead the way back to Calmacil Clearing, Beren Goodfellow eyed Maedhros Nénmacil suspiciously. "Excuse me, priestess..."

"StarSinger," Maedhros Nénmacil corrected abruptly. A few more leaves fluttered to the ground and several wolves growled.

Beren Goodfellow's eyes widened. "Um... well, yes... StarSinger," he stuttered. "Is... "

"Ranger Beren Goodfellow, meet Maedhros Nénmacil," Nefertari interrupted. "He's a very good friend of mine, and he won't harm you or anyone else."

"Unless of course you or anyone else attempts to harm the priestess," Colonel Tirion interjected.

"Or the child," the creation stone said.

Colonel Tirion nodded. "Or the child. Beren, I've already had this conversation with our flying companion. We should be safe enough as long as we stay on his good side."

"You mean the priestess' good side." Beren Goodfellow corrected.

Nefertari chuckled. "Of course, Ranger Beren Goodfellow. What other side is there?"

Maedhros Nénmacil booming laugh rattled all the rangers and wolves.

It was a quiet journey the rest of the way to Calmacil Clearing... except for an occasional deep giggle.

Fifty-seven anchors crashed into the waters of the Bay of Eltoria as the main battle fleet of InnisRos dropped anchor. Another seventeen warships from the northern fleet was on course to arrive in a few hours. Admiral Tári Shilannia leaned against a rail on the quarterdeck of Her Majesty's Ship the *Felicidade*, and drank coffee as she watched the sunrise. Marine Commander-General Aubrey Feynral stepped beside her with his own steaming mug. For a few minutes neither spoke. After the beauty of the sunrise gave way to the normalcy of a cloudless, sunny day, Admiral Shilannia broke the silence.

"Well, Aubrey?"

"Colonel Tirion reports that the Queen has arrived at Father Goram's monastery," General Feynral replied. "But there was a skirmish between the Army and Goram's forces, along with that Army battalion stationed at Calmacil Clearing... the one that remained in the Queen's service. I believe a Colonel Balthoron was its commander."

Admiral Shilannia sighed. "Definitely no turning back now. What happened?"

"This is only a preliminary report, but it appears the Army had several cavalry units north of the Aranel and Maranwe river junction," General Feynral said. "Father Goram had most of his rangers as well as Balthoron's battalion in the field to cover the Queen's retreat to Calmacil Clearing." General Feynral took a sip of coffee. "Goram's people were outnumbered and didn't survive... but from what Colonel Tirion told me, neither did the Army cavalry."

Admiral Shilannia nodded. "I never thought I'd see the day when civil war came to InnisRos." She turned to the general. "Aubrey, I knew Mordecai was no good. I should have taken him out when I had the chance."

"No blame on you, Tári," General Feynral replied. "None of us ever thought he'd go this far."

The *Felicidade's* Master-at-arms joined the two and saluted. "Admiral, the prisoner demands to speak with you."

"Demands, Lieutenant?" Admiral Shilannia said as she raised an eyebrow... then laughed. "Of course he does."

"I'd completely forgotten about him," General Feynral remarked.

"What do you think, Aubrey?" the admiral asked.

"I'd just throw him overboard. Let him swim for shore."

Admiral Shilannia shook her head. "No, Aubrey. As enticing as that sounds, we in the Navy do things with a bit less gusto than the Marines." The admiral turned to the lieutenant. "Give him a week's worth of standard issue rations and have him rowed to shore and left there. It's time I get that stink off my ship."

After the lieutenant left, the admiral threw what remained of her coffee over the side. "Let's get to work, Aubrey," she said. "Are your Marines ready?"

General Feynral nodded.

"Good." The admiral took one last look at the coastline which was about a mile away. "Let's review your plans one last time."

Jasmine Dubois, captain of the armed deep ocean merchant vessel *Freedom Wind*, sat impatiently in the outer office of their employer, Lane Cavanaugh Dular. Her First Officer, Thomas Krist, was by her side. He was leaning back in his chair and had his eyes closed. She nudged him.

"By the kraken, wake up!" Captain Dubois said.

Mr. Krist didn't open his eyes or change position. "I'm awake, Jasmine."

"How can you be so calm?" she asked.

"Because there's no reason to be concerned."

"The damage to the *Freedom Wind* cost over twenty-five thousand gold pieces to fix!" Captain Dubois replied.

"Work on vessels like the *Freedom Wind* doesn't come cheap. You know that." Mr. Krist opened his eyes and looked at his captain. "We've always said the *Wind* was under-sailed. Now the mizzenmast is twice as strong and carries more sail... as does the strengthened fore and main masts. And don't forget the other changes they engineered into the ship. I'm told by the shipwrights those improvements will add another seven to ten knots to her speed and will increase her stability." Mr. Krist looked away. "I'd be happier with a few more ballistae, but there wasn't room for them."

Captain Dubois nodded. "The *Freedom Wind's* better than ever, to be sure. But will I still be her captain?"

Mr. Krist took her hand. "Come down from your pity party, Jasmine."

That earned him an angry flash of her eyes.

"Good! That's the Jasmine Dubois we need... the Jasmine I need," Mr. Krist said with a smile. "We've gone over this several times. You can't control where or when a dragon will attack. Don't forget it was your tactics that prevented the *Freedom Wind* from going to the bottom of the ocean."

"Our passengers helped," Captain Dubois said.

"As did the crew," Mr. Krist added. "So quit worrying. You're the best ship's captain on Aster."

"What if they want to promote me to some type of executive position?!" Captain Dubois suddenly asked with panic in her voice.

Mr. Krist rolled his eyes, but before he could respond, a young woman walked out of the next room. "Mr. Dular will see you now."

Lane Dular's office was accommodating, though sparse... not the type of office one might expect from one of the wealthiest men on the mainland. Along one wall was a glass-covered display case that contained a large, wooden model of the largest ship either Captain Dubois or Mr. Krist had ever seen.

Lane Dular was a middle-aged human who didn't carry the responsibility of his family's merchant empire well. He was a diminutive man with prematurely gray hair and a hunched back. He looked tired with dark bags under his eyes and worry-lines crisscrossing his weathered face. But the light behind his eyes told a different story... intelligent, observant, experienced, and cunning.

"A pleasure to see you both again, Captain Dubois, Mr. Krist," he said as he stood and shook each hand. "I've got a little work to finish up, so make yourself at home. Go over and study the model." Neither wasted time as they moved over to the model to inspect it.

Lane Dular chuckled good-naturedly. "We start building the full-sized version by the end of the year," he said before turning his attention back to his paperwork.

"Four masts!" Mr. Krist whispered. The admiration in his voice was clear.

Captain Dubois nodded. "I've heard rumors about this ship," she said. "But I didn't know it was real... or that they were so close to building her."

"Impressive, isn't she," Lane Dular said as he came up from behind them a few minutes later.

Both Captain Dubois and Mr. Krist turned.

"That's a lot of cargo, sir," Mr. Krist said. "I'd wager she'll haul twice as much as the *Freedom Wind*."

"Oh, she'll not be used for cargo," Lane Dular said as he placed his hands on the glass display case... gently... almost like a caress. As he looked down at the ship model, Captain Dubois saw a familiar look come over his face. She recognized it because it was the same look most captains reserved for their ships... the same look she gave the *Freedom Wind.*

"Then?" Mr. Krist queried.

Lane Dular turned to them. "Exploration. We're going west past InnisRos." He looked back at the ship model. "We're going to see what's out there."

Mr. Krist marveled at the ambitiousness of the plan. "No one's ever returned from those waters," he said.

"No one's ever had a ship like this," Lane Dular said.

"What's her name, sir?" Captain Dubois asked.

Lane Dular paused before answering. His voice broke slightly. "She'll be named the *Adelaide Gail* after my daughter."

"I'm sure your..." Mr. Crist said before being nudged in the ribs by Captain Dubois.

Lane Dular didn't seem to hear. "Come, let's discuss why you're here," he said as he moved to a conference area and dropped into a large, over-stuffed leather chair.

"Why'd you elbow me?" Mr. Crist whispered.

Captain Dubois glanced at Lane Dular to make sure he was out of earshot. "Best to leave it alone. His daughter died recently in a riding accident. Broke her neck falling from a horse."

Mr. Krist nodded as he and Captain took their seats in a matching over-stuffed leather sofa.

"So, Captain, are you happy with the overhaul of the *Freedom Wind*?" Lane Dular asked.

"Indeed I am, sir," Captain Dubois responded. "Very happy. Her speed's almost doubled... and using her as a weapons platform, should that ever become necessary again, has been enhanced by the changes to her stability."

Lane Dular nodded. "I'm told she's ready to go."

"No sea trials, sir?" Mr. Krist asked.

"We don't have time, I'm afraid. You'll need to make any adjustments while on the way."

Captain Dubois looked at her employer, the concerns about her status as *Freedom Wind's* captain forgotten. "What's happened?" she asked.

"Civil war, Captain. Civil war on InnisRos... or so I've been informed by Father Goram," Lane Dular said as he opened a hand to reveal a communications crystal. "The Queen's accused of murder... but she escaped to Father Goram's monastery. Mordecai Lannian, the First Counselor, now fancies himself the king. He has their Army on the march and intends to take the Queen back to Taranthi for trial. Father Goram told me he won't let that happen."

"I wonder if Kristen or Tangus know?" Captain Dubois mused.

Lane Dular shook his head. "No, they don't. Father Goram knows you have a personal relationship with his daughter. At least he assumes so based on conversations he's had with her about you."

"He's right," Captain Dubois replied. "I consider her a good friend and told her if she needed help to contact me. She gave me a communication crystal linked to hers." Captain Dubois looked at Lane Dular. "Off the books."

Lane Dular raised an eyebrow.

"I don't charge friends for my assistance," Captain Dubois said with a defiant tone in her voice.

"Nor should you," Lane Dular responded. "But if it ever comes to that, I'd appreciate a heads up. The *Freedom Wind* is my family's ship and you're under contract. I can't let you go sailing where ever you want without at least a cargo. You want me to be able to pay your salary, don't you?"

An awkward silence followed before Lane Dular sighed.

"Oh hell, Captain... you know we value you far too much to ever let something like that interfere with your employment. Please... just make sure you tell me the next time."

Captain Dubois nodded.

"Superb. Moving on. You sail on the morning tide along with four of our faster schooners. That gives you the rest of today and tonight to do whatever you have to do to make ready for the voyage."

"What's our cargo, sir," Mr. Krist asked.

"There is none," Lane Dular said as he shook his head. "You'll be evacuating Queen Lessien and Father Goram's people from InnisRos."

After Mordecai had finished breakfast, he sat down to glance through the previous day's action reports... but his mind wasn't able to focus. The death of General Narmolanya to an apparent assassin attack the evening before had shaken him deeply. The papers before him blurred... and the headache caused by the crown he wore grew in severity. Finally, his irritation rose to the point where he couldn't take it anymore. He scattered the reports off his desk with a sweep of his arm, then stood, took off the crown, and threw it against a wall.

"Damn!" he shouted.

"What now?" Nightshade asked. She was sitting comfortably on a sofa and enjoying a glass of wine.

"I never thought Goram would go this far," he said. "Or maybe it wasn't even him. But if not, then who? Who got close enough to poison Narmolanya?!"

"Calm down and think about this rationally," Nightshade advised.

"What if I'm next?!"

"Then you'd already be dead," Nightshade replied. "The General's assassination was a warning." Though Nightshade wasn't at all sure about that. She'd been taken by surprise as much as Mordecai. Her attempts to find the assassins, or answers, during the night had failed... though several thugs paid a steep price for their ignorance.

There was a sharp rap on the door.

"Enter!" Mordecai shouted.

An Army colonel, escorted by several guards, marched into the room and saluted Mordecai. The colonel then bowed politely towards Nightshade who inclined her head.

"Yes, Colonel, let's have your report," Mordecai said impatiently.

"Ah... Your Highness... "

Nightshade perked up. "Something's happened," she thought. "Something I know nothing of."

"Speak up, Colonel!" Mordecai shouted.

"It appears every general in the city has been poisoned."

"What!" Nightshade said as she stood. Mordecai, however, slumped into his chair.

"Reports have been coming in from all over Taranthi for several hours now," the colonel said.

"And you thought to withhold this information until now?!" Nightshade barked.

The colonel cringed. "I didn't want to disturb you or his Highness until I had verified those reports."

Mordecai leaned forward in his chair. "Who's the ranking officer?" he asked. Nightshade could tell by the change in Mordecai's voice he had regained his resolve. "Good," she thought. "Stay confident. That'll make your fall even more enjoyable, you petty, little tyrant."

"I am, Your Highness," the colonel replied.

"You're my new Chief-of-Staff, General. Congratulations."

The colonel's eyes widened. "Begging your pardon, Highness, but I have a wife and five children. I respectively decline."

Mordecai wasted no time. "Sergeant of the Guard!" he said.

One of the guards took a couple steps forward and saluted. "Your Highness!"

"Take the Colonel outside and execute him!"

"But Your Highness," the sergeant stuttered as the colonel yelled, "No!"

Mordecai got up, walked over, and picked his crown up off the floor. Placing it back on his head, he faced the sergeant. "Do it... or join him."

As the struggling colonel was lead out of the room, Mordecai bellowed at the retreating backs. "And find me a colonel who wants to be a damn general!"

As the door shut behind the guards and struggling colonel, Mordecai turned to Nightshade. "They're as incompetent as my council."

Nightshade nodded, but inside she thought, "You're wrong about the generals, idiot. Whoever sent the assassins to kill the Army's high command in Taranthi struck a serious blow... but it also did my father a favor. Taking this island will be easy." Nightshade poured a fresh glass of wine for Mordecai and handed it to him, patting the sofa next to her. "Sit down, take a moment, and tell me how you're going to respond."

Mordecai accepted the wine gratefully and sat next to Nightshade. "I know Goram's behind this."

"Probably," Nightshade agreed, stoking the fire in Mordecai's belly. "What are you going to do about it?"

"I'll move the entire Army to Calmacil Clearing," Mordecai said. His voice dripped with hate. "I'll obliterate that monastery and everyone in it." Mordecai smiled. "Except for Goram. I'll keep him... and when I have his daughter and the empath, I'll make them watch as he's slowly skinned alive."

Nightshade smiled.

Father Goram, Autumn, Lessien, and Nefertari were on the western battlement watching the sunset in silence. Finley and Razor bracketed the Queen while Ajax sat at Father Goram's side. They had spent the entire day getting acquainted and going over plans for the upcoming siege. Everyone was tired, but each felt a need to witness one of nature's greatest sights... the end of the day and the coming of the night. The rays from the sun reflected off the clouds in the sky to radiate a kaleidoscope of orange, red, and purple hues. The late spring air was crisp and clean... but no smoke from fireplaces came from the buildings just outside the massive walls of the monastery. Father Goram had evacuated all civilians from Calmacil Clearing. Though a few resisted, Father Goram refused to be persuaded otherwise. He didn't want the blood of innocents on his hands. They could come back and rebuild when it was safe.

Below the massive stone walls of the western battlement, roughly two hundred yards from the monastery, a large, partially buried boulder lay on the ground, snoring softly. Maedhros Nénmacil suggested he remain in the town outside the monastery and be a boulder. He had argued that noone could play a boulder better than he... and that his surprise attack within the enemy's midst might actually save lives if timed properly. "People react most curiously when they see me smile for the first time," Maedhros Nénmacil said. "Their eyes get quite large and sometimes a dark spot appears on their trousers before they run away." Father Goram couldn't defeat that logic... and he was wise enough to understand it would be foolish to try even if he could.

"I've only been here a few days, but there's a lot of beauty in this world," Nefertari remarked in the stillness of the oncoming night. "But I've also witnessed ugliness."

"Don't judge our world quite yet, sister," Lessien said. "You've not seen us at our best."

"It's my world now as well." Nefertari replied.

Autumn looked over at the priestess. "Yes, dear, it is. And we're proud to have the long-lost sister of our Queen with us." Autumn then smiled as she looked down at the creation stone. "And of course we also welcome your friend Maedhros Nénmacil."

From below, the four elves and three dire wolves heard the rumble of Maedhros Nénmacil's laughter. Autumn looked surprise... then she too laughed... the sound of which made Father Goram's heart lighter. That feeling of content changed as the darkness skulked steadily forward, however.

"Look," Lessien said as she pointed to the southwest. The sky was lit with the light of a thousand of fires.

"The Army camps in the foothills," Father Goram said. "I expect the leading elements will be here tomorrow afternoon... and the main body by this time tomorrow night."

"Do you think they'll attack?" Autumn asked.

Father Goram shook his head. "Probably not tomorrow," he said, "unless Mordecai has other intentions. But if they do, the spiked moat should give them a little pause. We'll also buy time if they build siege engines."

"My source at the palace communicated Mordecai's anger at the loss of his Army generals,"

Lessien remarked. "He attributes that to you, Father. I think he'll attack as soon as his forces are marshaled." During the long day of briefings, Father Goram had mentioned his agreement with Mother Aubria to use assassins to destroy Mordecai's command structure. Landross had an apoplectic fit when he heard his side had used assassins... but calmed quickly. His military mind saw the logic and the advantage... even if his honor demanded a reaction.

"Again, I wish we knew for sure who this source was," Father Goram said. "We have no way to gage the truthfulness of the intelligence being passed along."

"I'd tell you if I could," Lessien replied. "But I don't know exactly. You know how much crystals can distort voices. I'm almost certain, however, it was Amberley. After all, she's the one who gave me the crystal."

"I still don't understand why she's so interested in helping you?" Autumn asked. "She's Mordecai's assistant... his lover. It makes no sense."

"Precisely," Father Goram said. "If it's her, she could be feeding you false information. But how would any of the information she's given you hurt us if it was false?"

"There's something Amberley said just before we parted." Lessien frowned as she tried to pull Amberley's words from the recesses of her mind. "She said, 'InnisRos is no longer yours. Leave as soon as possible for the mainland. But leave knowing that, though he doesn't yet understand, InnisRos won't be Mordecai's for much longer either.'"

No one said anything as they tried to decipher Amberley's meaning.

"Father," Lessien said. "What if my escape was necessary for something else altogether? What if *dear* Amberley," sarcasm dripped from Lessien's voice, "has her own plans for InnisRos? Now that I think upon it, perhaps that wasn't really Amberley at all. When last we spoke before I left the palace, her voice seemed... inhuman." Lessien turned to Father Goram. "Do you think Mordecai's consorting with demons?"

"It wouldn't surprise me," Father Goram replied. "And it sounds as if things are about to go very badly for the First Councilor."

Finley and Razor both growled... not because they sensed danger, but because their new master was angry.

"If true, my people are about to be subjugated to demons!" Lessien said. "I can't let that happen." Lessien shook her head. "I won't let that happen! There's no argument you can make that will now convince me to leave!"

Before Father Goram could respond, several riders broke from the surrounding forest and rode to the edge of the moat. Magical light stones, which surrounded the monastery, allowed those in the monastery to see the livery of the riders... which, unsurprisingly, was that of Army cavalry. With their horses dancing, each looked into the moat. The dark hid the spikes twenty feet below. "For your sake, I hope this isn't all you've got," one of the riders shouted.

"Speak your piece," Father Goram called down.

"You have until the morning after tomorrow to surrender your monastery in the name of King

Mordecai. If you haven't done so by then, three Army corps will take it by force."

"I'm your lawful Queen," Lessien said. "I demand you cease your illegal actions and follow me to arrest First Councilor Mordecai Lannian!"

The riders suddenly looked uncomfortable. One of the riders kicked his horse a few feet forward. "I would if I but could, Lessien Arntuile. But until you've been cleared of the murder charge, that's not possible. Goram, you have until dawn, day after tomorrow, to surrender. If you refuse to do so, you and your allies will be considered traitors and will be dealt with accordingly."

The riders retired and rode back into the forest.

"Three corps!" Father Goram whistled. "We're in trouble."

General Feynral knocked on Admiral Shilannia's cabin door. "Come," he heard a muffled voice in response to his request to enter. The general looked at the two Marine guards standing at attention next to the door.

"She retired only about an hour ago, General," one of them said. "She offered us a nightcap..."

"Excuse me?!" the general said as he looked at his Marines with disapproval.

"Of course we didn't accept, sir," the other Marine replied after giving the Marine who had spoken a look of disgust. "It's a ritual we go through whenever she's ready to retire for the evening."

General Feynral stared.

The Marine sighed. "The Admiral knows any good Marine can hold their liquor," he explained. "And a Marine with a drink is a happy Marine. At least that's what she always says."

General Feynral remained quiet... but his withering look never wavered.

"We never accept, General. Like I said, it's only a ritual."

General Feynral bent over and retrieved two small glasses which had been conveniently blocked from view by a leg. A small trickle of whiskey was still in the bottom of one. "Never accept, eh," he said as he handed a glass over to each Marine. "Next time just be honest about it," the general said as he opened the door.

Admiral Shilannia's long, silky hair was disheveled and her bunk unmade. She sat in her great chair, legs curled under her, and was drinking a mug of coffee. Unlike her hair and bunk, however, the rest of her spacious and luxurious cabin was in pristine condition... everything in its place. Even the stacks of paperwork on her desk had been neatly arranged.

"I assume you have news, Aubrey?"

General Feynral nodded and sat down in a chair next to the Admiral. "I do, Tári. I've heard from Colonel Tirion," he said.

Admiral Shilannia stared into her mug and waited as General Feynral poured his own mug of coffee.

"Mordecai's sending three Army corps... almost the entire Army... against the Queen and Father Goram. One Army corps is already there."

Admiral Shilannia shook her head. "Too much even for THAT monastery to defend against for long," she said. "I'm sure Father Goram and Sir Landross realize their precarious position. Does your colonel have any idea if Father Goram has any exit strategy?"

"I don't know... he's not privy to their preparations, although he did say the Queen's sister, the priestess Nefertari, is in their confidence. She may have more information about their plans later." General Feynral smiled. "I think the Colonel's a bit smitten with this Nefertari, Tári."

"Why do you say that, Aubrey?" the admiral asked.

"She has him and his two remaining Marines watching over a newborn rescued from the village of Ashakadi," the General replied. "He'd never allow himself to be trapped like that if he wasn't. And if I know my Marines, one child will probably keep all three of them busy," he added.

Admiral Shilannia looked at her Marine Commander-General... and both laughed.

There was a tentative knock on the door.

"Enter," Admiral Shilannia called out.

General Feynral's chief adjutant walked in, saluted both officers and laid a communications crystal on a table between the two.

"Admiral, General... the Queen wishes to speak to the both of you."

It was a hard night in Taranthi for Mordecai's council member collaborators. One by one each died a silent death. Some were poisoned, some had their throats slit, while others were strangled with a garrote. By night's end, the only true ally of Mordecai's left alive was Nightshade. The assassins, their contract concluded, disappeared into the city underbelly with the rest of the thieves, cutthroats, and those seeking anonymity.

This latest setback came close to breaking Mordecai's psyche. As his mind dove deeper and deeper into madness, Nightshade used her demon ability to manipulate his emotions. She worked to make sure he'd withstand this attack to his sanity... that he'd survive the depths of his personal hell of paranoia. Though her plans were already set into motion, she still needed Mordecai... at least for now. Eventually she'd grant Mordecai his journey into insanity... but only after he understood just how much she had betrayed him. Then, and only then, would she end him forever.

"We can't hold out against the whole army, Horatio," Landross said. "It's just too much."

Father Goram nodded. "Agreed, Landross. But we don't have a choice. I have transport ships coming from the mainland to evacuate everyone, but they won't be here for at least a month."

Lessien shook her head. "I've already told you I won't leave."

Father Goram looked at his queen. "It's only an option, Lessien. Let's not shut it down just yet."

"How about the Navy?" Cordelia asked.

"No," Queen Lessien said firmly. "They support me, but I've asked them to stay neutral. It's bad enough we must endure civil war... but the Navy is InnisRos' only protection from outside invaders. Besides, except for the Marines, there's not much more they can do short of emptying their ships of sailors to fight alongside us. I won't let that happen. Island nations MUST maintain strong navies."

"Your Highness, will at least the Marines help us?" Father Goram asked.

Lessien shook her head. "No, Father Goram, they won't. I've ordered them to stay neutral as well."

"So we're on our own," Eric the Black said. "Well, I've got a few surprises for them."

"They have sorcerers as well, Eric," Cameron pointed out. "It's possible they have more surprises in store for us then you do for them. After all, they are battle-hardened."

Eric the Black smiled. "Army sorcerers have little imagination," he said. He turned serious and directed his attention to the queen. "Your Highness?"

"Yes."

"Do I have your permission to conduct my magic unrestrained?" Eric the Black asked.

"That sounds ominous," Lessien replied.

Eric the Black nodded. "A lot of soldiers will die, Highness."

The war room grew very still as they waited the queen's response.

Lessien sighed. "My father taught me one of the most difficult things I'd face as a sovereign would be the setting aside of compassion during times of civil disobedience or war. He said the heart must not be allowed to interfere with reason... even though that will be a very difficult thing to prevent. In times of war, a ruler must be brutal and show no mercy. Any perceived weakness will only prolong the fight. And that adds to the number of casualties. There's no time for feelings until the enemy has been 'brought to the peace table', so to speak... or brought to their knees." Lessien paused for a moment. Her resistance to the hardness required for a war time ruler melted away. "There's only two ways I can stop this war... surrender, which I'll not do, or win."

"There's a third option, Your Highness," Father Goram said. "We could lose it."

Lessien shook her head. "No, my friend. That isn't an option. At least not as long as I draw breath." Lessien's eyes narrowed. "Eric... all of you. Do what needs to be done."

In Lessien's monastery room, her sword... the sword given to her by King Martin, her father... flared into brightness, burning into ashes the simple leather replacement scabbard which held it. The sword first took on a blood-red hue, followed by white, which turned to blue after a few seconds. A long slumbering consciousness that had been asleep since the day of Martin's exile from the Alfheim awoke. Broken so long ago by the dead king of the Alfheim, Argonne Quarion, the lone remaining shard of Martin's original sword, the same shard that had punctured his face and had been worked into the sword hilt, re-attuned itself to one of the Arntuile bloodline... Lessien.

"I am *Ah-HritVakha*!" it announced to the universe.

In the bottom of the crater that was Ashakadi, the body-burdened dirt shifted and moved. From a crack in the displaced earth a brilliant shaft of light reached to the heavens, then receded. A glowing scabbard rose slowly from the bottom of the crater, turned northeast, and flew away unnoticed. Its master, *Ah-HritVakha*, called to it.

A look suddenly came over Lessien's face none in the war room could recall ever having seen before. "Lessien, no!" Nefertari whispered. She knew the blank look. It was the same look her father had displayed when he was told she couldn't travel to Aster with him. It was anger, defiance, resolve, and loathing directed towards the subject of Martin's displeasure. They were the emotions caused by Martin's sword, *Ah-HritVakha*, in response to his initial anger. But Martin's mastery over the will of his sword was legendary, and he had quickly quenched its hunger for blood. Lessien didn't have that same mastery... at least Nefertari didn't think so.

"You must control the sword!" Nefertari pleaded.

But it was already too late. The Queen's face became hard and devoid of emotion. Her eyes sparkled like two crystal orbs... determination and clarity of purpose exposed in her gaze. There was also a feral gleam to them that caused everyone to stare. Both Finley and Razor growled in response to the emotion that had overcome their mistress.

"I will have my kingdom back," Lessien said as she stood. "This I promise before the gods of my father." Without another word she left the room with her two dire wolves trotting behind. Ajax rose and blocked his two pack members. But after a short wolf dialog between the three, Ajax nodded and back out of their way.

Nefertari got up. "Please excuse me," she said as she began to follow her sister out the door.

"What the hell just happened?" Cameron asked.

Nefertari paused, then turned to face the people in the room... the strangers who risked everything to help her sister. "Lessien is their liege," she thought. "They deserve answers." Nefertari returned to her chair and sat down.

"Very well," she said. "You know the story of my father's banishment from the Alfheim?"

Father Goram nodded. "Yes. Martin made sure everyone knew. He didn't want to be made king under false pretense. And he wanted everyone to know he'd never have a reason to abandon InnisRos "

"Then you know about his sword?" Nefertari asked.

Landross smiled. "The sword now carried by our Queen," he said. "A wonderful sword. King Martin commissioned its creation by the best blacksmith on Aster... Master Damien. This was shortly after he arrived from the Alfheim. Master Damien used..."

"Excuse me, Sir Knight," Nefertari interrupted. "Not that sword. I speak of the sword my father carried in the Alfheim... *Ah-HritVakha*, the Guardian Sword. It's a magical sword with awareness, though I wouldn't go so far as to say it was truly sentient... at least not how we think of such things. The sword, and in a more limited capacity the scabbard, magically connects with the one true guardian... one with pure Arntuile blood. It's a sword rarely seen... and it's extremely powerful. If not controlled by the chosen wielder, however, it can cause problems." Nefertari took a breath. "The look each of you saw on Lessien's face came from the sword. It's bloodthirsty."

"Martin mentioned that sword," Father Goram said. "When King Quarion rendered it useless and broke it, a shard from the blade buried itself into Martin's cheekbone." Father Goram paused. "Now things are beginning to make sense."

"Go on," Nefertari coaxed.

"Martin told me he had the shard, still bloodied, put into the hilt of his new sword... the sword Lessien now carries." Father Goram shook his head. "But I saw no sign it was anything more than just a magical heirloom."

Nefertari nodded. "That explains it. It must be that the magic of *Ah-HritVakha* was only rendered inert by King Quarion. As long as my father had at least a portion of it... the shard... the magic wasn't lost and the sword's purpose didn't die. Lessien must have just awoke it. I recognized its magic from the time my father carried it. What caused it to come out of its dormancy, I can't say... perhaps her dire circumstances... or her anger at what Mordecai has wrought. Regardless, it was bound to happen sooner or later. Now she needs to gain mastery over it. I can help her with that." Nefertari got back up and left the room without another word.

No one said anything for a few minutes until Landross broke the silence.

"It sounds like the perfect sword for a Queen."

Cameron scoffed. "Oh sure... the perfect sword," he said. "As long as the Queen can control its murderous tendencies."

"Times like this call for bloodthirstiness, don't you think, Cameron?" Eric the Black scolded. "It's civil war... people die. The more that die on the other side, the better!"

Cameron rose suddenly. His heavy chair crashed to the ground as he leaned onto the table facing Eric the Black, his fists clenched. "How can anyone take such a cavalier approach to death and destruction?!" he screamed.

Eric the Black stood as well and pointed a finger at Cameron. "You're either all in or you should pack up and leave. Do you think Landross' knights will hold back a killing thrust simply for... for... the sake of charity! For your vision of right and wrong? For some type of ... correctness?"

"All right you two, that's enough," Father Goram said over the din of the argument. But neither of the two were listening.

"I..." Cameron said before Eric the Black cut him short.

"There can be no indecision in this, Cameron!" Eric the Black shouted. "Fight, die, or run away. Which are you going to choose?"

Father Goram slammed an open palm on the table. "I said that's enough!" he shouted. Ajax, lying on the floor under the table at Father Goram's feet, growled.

Both stopped their quarrel and looked over at the priest.

Father Goram stared at both for a few seconds more, making sure his anger registered on them. "Please take a seat," he said.

Both did as ordered.

Father Goram sighed. "You're both right," he said. "We must kill as many as necessary to keep the Queen from being executed. That, gentlemen, is our priority." Father Goram paused and looked at Eric the Black. "But Eric, though war is brutal, we must not let it steal our compassion. I know how magic power can take a soul into very dark recesses... and those recesses expose themselves on the battlefield. Don't let that happen to you."

Eric the Black nodded. He was powerful, but young with 'rough edges'. He wanted Father Goram's tutelage... and respect. He'd been on his own far too long. In the short time he'd known Father Goram, the priest had become the father he never had.

Cameron reached out his open hand. Eric the Black looked at it with suspicion, but then he smiled and shook it to end the feud.

Father Goram nodded. "Now, moving on... "

Nefertari knocked on the door to Lessien's suite. "Lessien, it's me. May I come in?"

There was no answer, but when Nefertari turned the door latch, she discovered it wasn't locked. Slowly opening the door, her first sight was that of two massive dire wolf heads staring at her. Behind them, Lessien was sitting in a chair and holding up her sword... *Ah-HritVakha*. Blue arc's of magical energy jumped from the tip of the sword to the ceiling above... scorching the stone. Its mesmerizing gleam had captured Lessien's full attention... she seemed lost in its beauty.

Nefertari approached cautiously. Findley and Razor backed away as she did. They both sensed their mistress was in distress... and Nefertari could do more to help then they could. Standing in front of her sister, Nefertari knelt and placed her hands on Lessien's. Nefertari could feel the power of the sword. But she wasn't surprised. She'd felt that same power in the hands of her father before King Quarion banished him to Aster.

"Let's put the sword down, dear," Nefertari said as she unraveled her sister's fingers from around the hilt. Lessien didn't object as Nefertari took the sword, now no more dangerous than an ordinary sword, and carefully laid it on the floor.

"What are you seeing?" Nefertari asked as she cupped Lessien's face in her hands.

"Colors... beautiful colors," Lessien replied woodenly. "And power."

Lessien focused on her sister's face. "It's like I could rule the world. So much power."

Nefertari nodded. "Power you must control or it will eat away at your soul."

Lessien frowned.

"Its power is intoxicating, yes?" Nefertari questioned. "But it doesn't make you immortal. You MUST bend it to your will... just like father did."

"My father!" Lessien snapped back.

Nefertari shook her head. "No dear. In all respects except one he was truly my father as well."

Lessien's eyes welled up with tears. "I'm so sorry," she said. "Of course you're right. How could I be so hurtful?"

Nefertari smiled. "No harm done. Now, about the sword. Its name is..."

"*Ah-HritVakha,*" Lessien said without hesitation.

Nefertari nodded. "Yes. It's... shall we say... the little brother of *Ah-RahnVakha,* the royal sword of the Alfheim, and is traditionally awarded to the Commander-General of the elven armies and guardian of the rulers of the Alfheim."

"Are you familiar with *Ah-RahnVakha?*" Lessien asked.

Nefertari looked off into space before she answered Lessien's question. "Very familiar. *Ah-RahnVakha* was going to be my sword."

"Of course," Lessien sheepishly replied. "I wasn't thinking. I still don't understand..."

Nefertari held up a hand. "That's a discussion for another day."

Lessien nodded.

Nefertari picked up *Ah-HritVakha* and handed the sword to Lessien."Are you ready to begin?"

The following evening, the main body of the First Army Corps arrived on the outskirts of Calmacil Clearing. Its Army commanders immediately moved to surround the monastery and build war machines... catapults, ballista, and siege towers. The defenders within the monastery cringed as they listened to the sound of saw and ax destroying their beloved forest trees.

Sappers, who had been digging throughout the day, tunneled beneath the spiked moat that encircled the monastery. During the night, a slight rumble came from below... and the ground trembled. Though Landross wasn't sure if the Army would try to burrow underneath, he felt it prudent to arrange with Eric the Black to place a magic barrier below the earth... magic that was powerful enough to, once triggered, collapse the tunnel.

Most of the sappers died. The sorcerers assigned to the First Army Corps felt the release of magic and decided a response was not only justified, but required. Consequently, the war for the monastery began a few hours earlier than expected.

THE STRUGGLE FOR INNOCENCE

CHAPTER TWENTY-ONE

Elanesse

It can be argued the notion of 'good' or 'evil' doesn't exist in nature. But rather, it's kill or be killed. The worg is relentless in its pursuit of prey... and vicious in its attack. Conversely, the worg nurtures and cares for its young. Consider the hunter through the eyes of a deer. The hunter is also relentless in pursuit of prey... and vicious... at least to the deer who has fallen victim. Is the hunter evil? Some believe 'good' and 'evil' are simply creations of the self-aware mind... or the consensus of a society.

-The Book of the Unveiled

The female northern wolf, Sakkara, curled around her remaining pup in the crude, wooden cage that held her captive. All her pack, including her pups except the one she now protected, were dead... victims of a deadly ambush perpetrated by white, two-legged monsters. The cave, the stinking, dirty den of the two-legged monsters, was cold. The fire they had built... when they weren't fighting for the meat of her dead brethren... was small and did little to warm her cage.

As she watched the brutality of the monsters play itself out as they fought for their supper, she fell into the drowsy twilight of sleep. Unexpectedly, in the darkness of the entrance, she caught fleeting glance of a lupine form. Was she dreaming? Did her exhausted body and disheartened mind play a cruel trick on her? No! There it was again... coming closer. The movement was not a trick or hallucination! It was real! The form was much larger than any brethren wolf she was accustomed to seeing. She looked up, alert, and watched as the shade slinked through the shadows inside the cave towards her cage. She realized she couldn't smell the newcomer. Her joy... her elation... melted away as she considered the possibility it might be another predator trying to steal away a meal from the great white monsters. And if it was trying to help, what chance did they have of escaping?

Sakkara lost sight of the visitor until it was right behind her enclosure... out of sight of the meat-drunken white savages. It was another wolf... a male. He wasn't a lowland worg, but something different. The wolf was massive, easily twice the size of northern male wolves. He had rolled in mud, which was why she couldn't smell him. The mud also made it impossible to distinguish the coloring of his fur... but Sakkara suspected it was black.

As Sakkara watched, the wolf bit through the primitive plant fiber rope that held the cage together. She didn't move to help... but instead studied her rescuer, for she knew at once there was something more to him than just his massive size. There was a timelessness in his eyes... and intelligence. "At last," Sakkara thought, "my equal."

The male noticed Sakkara had been studying him and stopped. "Don't be afraid. My name is Romulus and I'm here to rescue you."

"I'm not afraid, Romulus. I'm Sakkara and I appreciate your help. But what you're doing is foolish. We'll never leave this cave alive. There are too many... even for a wolf as large as yourself. And this isn't the whole pack. Run while you can!"

Romulus looked at the snow white female. She wasn't as large or hardy as a female dire wolf... but she was beautiful... and, it appeared, very intelligent. "This is who Emmy said I should seek as a mate," Romulus thought with conviction. "I know it."

"The others of the pack no longer pose a threat to us... or anyone else," Romulus said out loud. "I've seen to that. As for these, I will kill them as well. Fear not, little one."

Sakkara bristled with anger. "Don't call me little one!" she growled back softly. "There are more ways to measure one's true worth then the size of one's paws! Or head!"

Romulus chuckled as he bit down on one bar of the cage and removed the side he had freed of rope. "Quickly, we must go."

Sakkara uncurled her body to reveal her pup. "Meet Kavik," she said.

Romulus didn't hesitate as he included the pup into his planned escape. "Can you run?" he asked Sakkara.

"Like the wind."

Romulus nodded. "I'll draw them to the back of the cave while you take Kavik and leave through the opening. Don't stop running until you're sure you're not being followed."

"What about you, Romulus?" Sakkara replied. "I'll never see you again." The concern in her eyes touched Romulus immensely.

"I'll find you, have no fear," he replied. "And I'll avenge your pack," he added.

Sakkara growled fiercely. "I should do that!"

"Yes," Romulus replied. "But you must take care of Kavik. Now prepare yourself."

Sakkara grabbed Kavik by the loose skin behind his head and nodded.

Romulus stealthily moved to the back of the cave while Sakkara prepared to run. Sakkara lost sight of him as he blended into the shadows. She then heard Romulus growl loudly. The yeti looked in his direction and charged. All except for one juvenile who was standing by the cave entrance. As Sakkara easily slipped past, hamstringing the yeti youth with a quick swipe of her paw, she could hear the battle begin behind her.

Elrond was dozing. It was early morning and a light rain was falling. The Tree of Golden Radiance, whose thick canopy extended several hundred feet, kept him dry. The comforting rhythm of the raindrops acted like a sedative. It hypnotized him into a light sleep which combated his boredom... and the worry he had for his friends.

Elrond's voyage into slumber was disturbed by the babblings of the squirrels who homed themselves in a hollowed log. He had once thought about supplementing his diet with a squirrel roasted over a fire... but discarded that notion almost as soon as he had it.

"Those critters are kind of cute," he had said aloud at the time. "Damn. Now I'm sounding like a ranger."

A strange chill suddenly overtook him. Elrond sat up and looked around. Everything appeared to be fine. Convinced it was only the remnants of a fleeting dream, he began to lay back down when something curious caught his eye. A leaf... a black leaf hanging against a background of gold.

"That wasn't there before," he thought to himself as he got to his feet and walked over to inspect it. As he looked closer, he became more concerned. It wasn't a dead leaf as he feared, but much worse. It was alive, and its base appeared to have tentacles that wrapped around the branch to which it was anchored.

"Elanesse?"

Elanesse didn't answer, however.

Elrond moved to the massive trunk and placed his hands on the rich, dark brown bark. He was instantly overcome with pain. He felt Elanesse undergoing an assault of incredible strength. It was powerful, it was evil, it was absolute, it was the Purge. Elrond knew Elanesse couldn't withstand the all-embracing might of the Purge without help.

"Elrond, you must stop contact with me," Elanesse said with difficulty. *"You... cannot... survive... this."*

"Neither can you!" Elrond said. But he removed his hands anyway. "How do I help," he asked the squirrel curiously looking at him.

By the time Tangus had reached the level above, Kristen and Emmy were leaning over the saber kitten and doing what they could to heal it. Tangus saw blue light come from between the two and knew his new charge was in the best of hands. "The kitten needs a name," Tangus said to no one in particular. "Think I'll call him Loki."

Tangus looked at the rest of his friends, but didn't see the assassin. "Where's Mariko?" he asked.

"She decided to scout ahead," Safire replied. "Hell, she's an assassin. I figure she can probably do that type of thing in her sleep."

"No doubt," Tangus said as he turned his attention back to his wife, daughter, and the kitten.

"You probably should've put that kitten out of its misery, friend Tangus," Lester remarked.

Tangus shook his head. "Not after watching him fight to stay alive." Tangus turned to the big knight. "Some things just feel right, Lester."

Lester nodded. "But three legs? That will make for a hard life."

"I've seen dogs get around fine with three legs," Jennifer opined. "Perhaps in the wild it might have been kinder to kill it. Better a quick death than a lingering starvation. But I know my father. It... Loki... will receive every chance to thrive."

Safire took Lester's hand. ""It's part of what we rangers do," she said.

Kristen and Emmy stood. Kristen held the saber kitten in her arms. She had wrapped it in a small blanket. Tangus looked at the sleeping saber kitten. Where before his fur was dull and dingy, now it radiated health and vigor. It glistened like an expensive piece of silk.

"His eyes have only recently opened," Kristen said. "I'd estimate he's only two or three days old."

Tangus nodded as he took the bundle and studied the slumbering saber kitten. "He'll be bigger than Bitts."

"But not as big as Romulus," Kristen said. There was a hint of pride in her voice.

"They'll be great friends," Emmy said with certainty. "Like brothers."

Lester and Safire welcomed Mariko as she trotted out of the darkness from her scouting foray. Everyone's attention immediately shifted to her.

"There's an open sewer grate about half a mile away," she said without preamble. "I saw no signs of humans... but plenty signs of wild animals. Worgs, I'd say."

Safire nodded. "That stands to reason. The Purge has been controlling worgs all along."

"I suspect the humans might be dead," Kristen said.

"Almost certainly, friend Kristen," Lester replied. "Most of them died below."

"Probably the Purge's last ditch effort to get at Emmy," Jennifer remarked.

"Unfortunately, I think we'll have a harder time dealing with the worgs. Mariko, could you get any feel for the number?" Tangus asked.

Mariko grimaced. "A whole forest full."

That silenced everyone as they stopped to consider the implication, and scope, of the statement. "That's a lot of worgs," someone whispered.

"Does anyone know where the Purge is?" Safire asked. "Emmy?"

The child shook her head. "I know the Purge can sense me... as I can it. But unlike the Purge who knows where I'm at, I don't know where it is... except somewhere close."

Mariko snapped the flat side of one of her katanas against her head. "My apologies, but I think I have something that might help." She pulled a piece of linen out of a belt pouch and gave it to Tangus. "A map of the city."

"How...?" Tangus said.

"I found it on one of the bodies below," Mariko replied. "It was the first time we went through the cavern. Other than quickly glancing at it, I put it out of my mind because of everything else going on."

Tangus handed Loki over to Emmy and opened the map without comment. "Where's the sewer entrance?" he asked Mariko.

"Right about here," Mariko responded as she pointed to a spot on the map. "Under the Great Obelisk. And if the map's correct, the Purge should be here," she said pointing to a spot on the map marked Pyramid of the Purge.

"That's pretty obvious," Lester remarked. "Maybe too obvious."

Tangus grunted. "Right now it's all we have."

"At least it's a starting point," Mariko observed. "My guess is the Purge will be well guarded. If we run into heavy resistance, we've probably stumbled upon the right place."

Tangus rolled up the map. He didn't offer it back to Mariko, however. Instead he slipped it into his tunic."Let's go."

The Great Obelisk was an impressive sight. It was surrounded by four ten foot high brick walls with twenty foot stone obelisks on each corner. The marble obelisk in the center rose one hundred feet above the ground.

"I know what this is," Kristen said as she rubbed her hands over the smooth, large obelisk in the center of the compound. "The middle obelisk is dedicated to the old elven goddess of the earth, Jörd. Each of the four corner obelisks represent the elements-earth, wind, fire and air.

Emmy, who was stroking the head of the sleeping saber kitten, said, "Jörd left this world long ago."

Everyone looked at Emmy, but she didn't elaborate. Instead she kept her head down and her attention riveted on her young charge bundled in her arms.

Tangus shrugged his shoulders. They had all grown used to Emmy's sudden bursts of wisdom and knowledge. "According to the map we need to go several hundred yards south to get to the pyramid."

"Maybe we should wait until night falls, friend Tangus," Lester offered.

Tangus shook his head. "No, that won't do. Worgs are nocturnal and hunt better at night." Tangus became silent as he thought about their situation. "I wish Romulus were here," he finally said wistfully.

"Romulus has his own fight," Emmy said. "But he'll join us as soon as he can."

"How do you know, Emmy?" Jennifer asked.

Emmy looked up from Loki and smiled. "Because I can sense him, dear sister."

Jennifer frowned.

"After all, he's one of my guardians," Emmy answered with a smile. "Just like all of you."

"Let's address the problem at hand, shall we," Tangus said. He wanted to shelve any discussion about Emmy's peculiarities for later.

Using foot and hand holds caused by erosion and time, Tangus climbed up the south wall to see if he could see the Pyramid of the Purge. Its massive size easily dwarfed the buildings that stood between it and the Great Obelisk.

Tangus jumped nimbly down from his handhold on the wall. "The pyramid's right where the map says it's supposed to be," he said."We have several buildings we can use for cover, but there's an open field between here and those buildings."

"Any sign of worgs?" Safire asked.

Tangus shook his head. "Which is a bit off. I would've thought they'd be concentrated around the pyramid if that's where the Purge is."

"Perhaps they're inside the pyramid," Jennifer observed.

Tangus nodded. "Well, it's certainly big enough."

"It goes down into the ground," Emmy remarked. "I saw it in a dream. There's an underground complex beneath the city... separate from the sewers or the deeper level below that."

"A dream?" Kristen asked.

Emmy nodded. "I have lots of dreams about Elanesse, mother," she said. "But I can't distinguish between those that show me what's real and those I must interpret."

"Well that's just wonderful," Safire said. "Another whole level to worry about."

Mariko shook her head. "No, that could be to our advantage."

Kristen nodded. "I see where you're going with this. If the Purge isn't in the pyramid perhaps we can search for it from beneath the city."

"Precisely."

"But won't the worgs be down there as well, friend Mariko?" Lester asked.

"Maybe," Tangus interjected. "But I'd rather face them one-on-one in a corridor than be surrounded out here." Tangus looked at Emmy. "Besides, I've seen what can be done with magic down a long corridor. But let's take it one step at a time. First we need to see what we find in the pyramid."

The small group moved into the open field outside the Great Obelisk. Tangus, holding Emmy, and Mariko took the lead. Lester stayed in the center with Kristen, who held Loki, while Safire and Jennifer, bows drawn and arrows notched, followed. The wind was blowing from the south. Tangus knew any worgs north of them would catch their scent... but there really wasn't anything he could do about it. The sprint across the field seemed to take forever.

They reached the first group of buildings and stopped to catch their breaths. Tangus put Emmy down and looked back at the Great Obelisk. He took a few moments to admire the architecture. The polished marble gleamed in the sunlight, and the pyramid top appeared to be made of, or covered with, crystal. As Tangus was looking at the top of the obelisk, movement below caught his eye. Worgs! A sea of worgs!

"We need to go... now!" Tangus shouted.

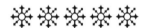

Romulus allowed two of the three seven feet tall male yeti's to flank him. He waited, growling, until they had worked themselves up into a frenzy. When they charged, waving their clubs, he sprinted between the two and attacked the third male who was protecting the females. As tall as the yeti's were, Romulus, when on his hind legs, was at least as tall... and much quicker. He was inside the yeti's reach before it had a chance to use its deadly club. Using his weight and momentum, Romulus knocked the yeti on its back and tore its throat out in one quick, practiced movement.

But that small delay proved costly as the other two males attacked. Romulus dodged one club, but not the other... and a glancing blow hit his upper thigh. Romulus heard bone crack, but ignored the pain as he whipped around and found a belly to sink his teeth into.

He shook his head a few times before he drew back, pulling intestines out of the screaming yeti... leaving it squirming and bleeding on the cave floor.

A second club hit Romulus on the back of the head, causing him to collapse to the ground, unconscious. The oblivion only lasted an instant and Romulus awoke just in time to move away from under another club attack. Romulus pivoted and jumped on the yeti. They both crashed down onto the hard cave floor, with Romulus on the yeti's chest and his teeth in the yeti's throat. But before he ripped the jugular and windpipe out, he glanced up at the females with his eyes. Each were visibly pregnant and didn't seem to have the will to endanger their unborn babies. The lone adolescent in the yeti pack was limping and holding its thigh. Sakkara must have wounded it on her way out... so it didn't look like it'd pose a danger.

Without at least one adult male, the females would have a very rough time of it... perhaps they wouldn't survive. The pain in both his head and thigh had become almost intolerable. Romulus wanted to leave... to find a safe place to sleep. He didn't need to kill again today.

Romulus carefully removed his clenched jaws from the throat of the yeti. He put his mouth in the yeti's face and growled... letting what gore and blood he hadn't spit out drip down into its frightened eyes. He looked up at the females and roared. They roared in return... but backed away into a corner. Romulus stared hard at them as he gathered his strength. He bound out of the cave and into the biting cold of the mountain air. He ran for about a mile back down the mountain before he found a large bushy tree. Romulus collapsed on the trail... his injured leg no longer able to support him. He crawled into the cover offered by the bushy tree before he drifted into a coma-induced sleep.

A few minutes later, Sakkara, who had been following Romulus since he left the den of the yeti, crawled next to Romulus, carefully placed Kavik down, and curled herself around both as best as she could.

Elrond felt helpless. Elanesse was dying and there didn't seem to be anything he could do about it. If the Purge took control of Elanesse, there wasn't any reason to think it couldn't kill Emmy. How do you fight a city that wants you dead?

"HOW DO I SAVE HER?!" Elrond screamed at the heavens. "TELL ME!"

But only silence answered his call. As he watched, several other gold leaves turned black. The Purge was spreading its influence faster now as Elanesse's defenses began to fail.

Elrond shook his head. "If you're going to die, so am I," he said to Elanesse as he reached out to touch the trunk once again.

"Wait!" a voice called from behind him. Elrond knew that voice as sure as he knew his own. "Max?" he said as he turned.

But Elrond didn't see Max... at least not right away. As he stared at the spot from which the disembodied voice came, he saw a form take shape.

"What trickery is this?" a startled Elrond asked as Max gained ghostly substance.

"No trickery, my dear friend," the apparition replied. *"We both knew the day would come when our luck would run out. Mine did below the city."*

Elrond dropped to his knees and let his tears flow freely. "Damn! I never said goodbye. We always considered that bad luck."

Max floated over and sat down beside him. *"Death's not so bad,"* he said. *"Oh, don't get me wrong. The whole dying aspect of it really pained me. Ha! Ha!"*

Elrond sat down as well and looked over at his lifelong friend. "Really, Max... even now?"

Max smiled. *"I'm at peace, Elrond. Death, our constant companion, no longer has its hold over me. I'm dead... but I've never felt more... alive."*

"No sane person would never believe I could have a conversation with the spirit of my dead friend," Elrond remarked.

Max laughed. *"We've never been normal!"*

There was a pause in the conversation. Although both had much to say to each other, neither thought it was really necessary. They'd been friends for so long neither felt the need to talk.

"Wish you could smoke," Elrond said as he pulled out a cigar, bit one end and spit it out, then lit the other with a simple fire spell.

"You need a good mug of ale to go with the cigar," Max said.

Elrond smiled. "So why are you here... to haunt me?"

Max chuckled. *"Every time you asked me to check for a trap, or pick a lock, I always thought to myself, 'If this kills me, I'll spook him to the end of eternity.' Ahhh... the good old days."* Max stopped smiling and grew serious. *"But that's not why I haven't moved on."*

Elrond looked at Max.

"You remember Angela?" Max asked. *"Of course you do... it hasn't been that long. She guarded Emmy for all those centuries. It was her purpose... her responsibility... before she could find the peace she deserved. Because of her love for Emmy, she would've sacrificed her whole eternity if necessary."* Max sighed. *"I, too, have such an obligation."*

Elrond waited.

"Remember when you met Elanesse for the first time? I'd never seen you like that before... not even with the Duke's sister, Bronwyn. From that moment I knew you'd never leave Elanesse. I knew that, for whatever reason, a connection between the both of you had sparked into being." Max smiled. *"I never thought you'd actually fall in love with someone... but knew that's what happened the moment you did."*

"It's all very strange, that's for sure," Elrond commented as he thought upon it. "But she..."

"She's become your purpose," Max finished for Elrond.

Elrond nodded. "I had no control over it. And I don't regret it, either."

"You couldn't regret it, my friend," Max said. *"It's your destiny."*

Elrond grunted. "Humph! Destiny... never really believed in it."

"What you believe doesn't matter, Elrond," Max replied.

Elrond looked at Max suspiciously. "You're an imposter, aren't you? The Max I know never went philosophical."

"Strange times, Elrond, strange times. Perhaps you'd like to hear about the time I was in the Dragon Teeth Mountains?"

"I was there, remember?" Elrond said. "I've heard you tell that story a hundred... oh... I understand."

"Precisely," Max said. *"Now listen closely. There's only one thing you can do to stop the Purge from controlling Elanesse."*

"I'm listening... because right now I feel useless." Elrond shook his head. "She's suffers so. Max, she's dying!"

"I know," Max acknowledged. *"But what you must do will be hard. You'll be changed both physically and mentally."* Max smiled. *"On the bright side you'll be almost immortal."*

Elrond looked at Max... then at the Tree of Golden Radiance. "I'd do anything for her, Max."

Max nodded. *"To prevent the Purge from destroying Elanesse, you must first cause her even more pain."*

Elrond hesitated... that was the last thing he wanted to do. But he understood the necessity. Far too many times he'd been forced to exorcise a limb filled with gangrene to save the body. "Tell me what I must do."

The Pyramid of the Purge was about one hundred feet in front of them on the other side of a small, grass and weed field. The worgs, however, were closing quickly. It was a race to see which of the two groups got to their destination first... and the worgs, with their greater speed, looked like they were going to win.

"I don't see a door," Safire shouted.

"I see it," Kristen said. "It's hidden in plain sight with magic. It may take a few moments to open it."

Tangus fell in beside Lester and handed Emmy over to him. "Get Kristen and Emmy inside. We'll hold them off as long as we can."

"I should stay," Lester protested.

Mariko took Emmy out of Lester's arms. "I'll protect them. You just stay in one piece until we can get you inside."

Tangus nodded. Who better than the assassin to guard his wife and daughter. Mariko's skill with her two katanas was unparalleled... even more so against a wall or in a doorway where she only had to defend in one direction.

"Jennifer, Safire... bows," Tangus said as he held up a few yards in front of the pyramid and used his own bow to lock in on a target. "Lester, watch our backs."

Tangus, Jennifer, and Safire stood in a line to meet the worg onslaught. Lester was a few feet behind, his great sword out and ready to kill any worg unlucky enough to get within his reach. The worgs began to die several hundred feet from where the four stood. The only weakness in Tangus' planning was the worgs outnumbered the arrows in their quivers. Behind them, Kristen was having difficulty defeating the magic of the entrance.

Robert E. Balsley, Jr

"Romulus, wake up!"

"Romulus, my special wolf, wake up!"

Romulus opened his eyes. He no longer felt the pain from his injuries. Instead, he felt refreshed and whole again. But Romulus was intelligent enough to know that he hadn't awakened in the real world of birds, trees, streams, forests... or the world of his friends and those he loved.

"Am I dreaming?" Romulus asked.

"In a manner of speaking," a female voice answered.

Romulus sat up and looked around. All he saw was white light... subdued and brilliant at the same time... comforting, loving, and reassuring. "I remember your voice from my puppyhood," he said, voicing the insight that had suddenly come to him. "I remember your touch as well. You're Althaya."

"Yes, Romulus, I am," Althaya replied, though she didn't reveal her form to him. "We are in your dreaming mind... but this isn't a dream. And I'm only the catalyst for what is to happen next." Althaya's voice faded away to be replaced by one more familiar... and welcomed.

"What trouble have you gotten yourself into, Romulus?" the voice asked.

"Emmy? But how?"

Emmy laughed. It sounded like the soft chime of bells. "Your mind is hearing what you want it to."

"To what purpose?" Romulus asked.

"Because you must survive," Emmy's voice said. "You're on the verge of giving up and you can't do that. Too many of your loved ones are relying upon your protection. Deep down inside of your soul you know that... but perhaps you need a reminder. That's why I'm here."

Romulus sighed. "I'm tired... so tired. I've lived a very long time for a dire wolf."

"And you'll live much longer, should you wish," Emmy replied. "But it's up to you. If you don't fight now, though, not only will you be giving up your present, but also your future."

Romulus considered Emmy's words. They were wise.

"Besides," Emmy said. "You now have a mate, if you wish. She won't leave your side unless you drive her away. She's intelligent, loyal, fearless, and very protective over those she loves. Much like you."

"I remember Mary McKenna as she died of old age," Romulus replied. "It was very sad. I howled to the heavens that day. I hope she has found peace in the afterlife."

"She has," Emmy said. "My dear Romulus, death is part of life and its inevitable conclusion. But, if you so choose, Sakkara and Kavik can be granted the same touch you received when you were but a puppy."

Romulus looked back to his memories of the cave and the caged white female wolf he encountered in it... the same wolf he'd been seeking. She'll make a good companion.

"Very well," Romulus said. "You've given me far more than I'll ever deserve. Thank you!"

"You're a very special wolf, Romulus," Emmy said. Though Romulus couldn't see her face, he could tell she was smiling. "And I love you."

Romulus awoke to see a tiny, furry face staring into his. He had a headache and his thigh was sore... but it felt as if he was on the mend.

"Mama hunts," Kavik said. "She'll be back soon with meat. How do you feel?"

Romulus smiled. "Much better, little one," he replied. "Much better."

Max, his duty discharged, was free to leave the mortal plane of existence and travel to whatever eternity he had earned. Elrond hoped it was a good one... and was encouraged that Max held no fear and eager to move on. Though Elrond was sad that his best friend, his brother, would never again enjoy a cigar with him... he didn't grieve. Max had died a warrior's death. Elrond hoped he would be so lucky.

Elrond turned his attention to Elanesse and what he must do to save her. What Max told him seemed unbelievable... but Elrond had seen stranger things in his lifetime. He walked over to the horses and untied their leads. He didn't fear they would stray... and they were safe enough under Elanesse... but he wanted to give them a chance at freedom just in case his friends didn't make it back.

Elrond pulled his spell-book out of his backpack and opened it to a blank page. Taking quill and ink, he penned a letter to his comrades. He briefly explained the danger the Purge had put Elanesse in and the actions he must take to save her from certain destruction. Elrond used one of his magical scrolls as a bookmark and placed the spell-book on his backpack in plain sight.

Elrond picked up his sword and drew it from its scabbard. Throwing the scabbard to the side, he walked over to the branch... the same branch the Purge had used to begin its assault... the same branch touched by a spreading contagion. Raising the gleaming, magical blade before him, he stared at the runes etched along its length.

"You must exorcise Elanesse of the contagion," Max had said. *"Then you must help her resist any further attacks by the Purge."*

"I'm so sorry for this, Elanesse," Elrond said. "But I believe it's the only chance you have."

"You don't have to do this," Elanesse replied. *"Perhaps I can fight the Purge off on my own."*

Elrond shook his head. "No, I'm afraid you can't. And I won't let you die if I can prevent it."

"You'll no longer be... who you are."

"Who I am was always a bit overrated," Elrond said. "Do you have something you can bite on?"

"I don't understand."

"Never mind," Elrond said as he raised his sword. "Prepare yourself."

Elrond brought the sword down and severed the branch in one, smooth, quick motion. Elanesse scream of pain in Elrond's mind brought tears, but he didn't let that distract him from what must be done. Firmly grasping the hilt of his sword, he conjured a magical spell on his hands and then on the sword. The blade became white-hot while a blue, cooling glow surrounded his hands. Elrond flipped the sword slightly so the flat of the blade faced the spot where the branch had been severed and, without hesitation, placed the blade against the newly cut stub of the branch. Again Elanesse screamed in Elrond's head. This time, however, reverberations of Elanesse's pain could be felt throughout the city.

"Hold on," Elrond said as he threw the offending sword to the side.

Elrond picked up the contaminated branch. Since it was no longer connected to Elanesse, the Purge retreated and the black leaves once again turned golden. But that didn't mean the Purge was defeated. Quite the opposite. Elrond grasped the branch with both hands and drove it into the soft earth with all his strength.

As soon as the branch contacted the soil, it vibrated. Roots grew out of the end of the branch that had been driven into the ground. Elrond watched as his hands, clutched to the branch, melded into the wood... becoming the wood. Elrond felt no pain... but instead a sense of completion. He felt strange sensations at the bottom of his feet, but when he looked down, he saw his feet had disappeared, and that his legs had fused together, along with his torso, to form the trunk of the tree he was becoming. The branch reached out to him with wooden tendrils... which Elrond gladly accepted. The essence of the branch was transferred to him... much like the blood of a mother is given to a child in her womb. Elrond grew and grew... limbs darted out of the trunk and reached to the sky. Green-bronze leaves sprouted into a stunning canopy that rivaled the beautiful golden tree standing next to him.

Elrond couldn't see, at least in the way a person could see. Instead, all of his other senses had been magnified enormously. He felt vivacious. He felt as vigorous and strong as he'd ever been.

"You are a very handsome tree, Elrond," Elanesse said... no longer from one mind to another... but rather in the way of one tree to another.

"There is one more thing I must do to help you resist the Purge," Elrond said.

Elanesse gasped then stilled. *"So this is how we fight the Purge together,"* Elanesse said.

"Yes," Elrond replied. *"My strength added to yours. Nothing shall ever separate or bring us down."*

Beneath the ground, Elrond's roots dove deep and far. As they did so, they interwove with the roots of Elanesse. Two trees... one root system. Strength multiplied through devotion, sacrifice, and love.

"It's open," Mariko called as she pushed the door inwards. Kristen, her cleric magic different in both form and structure from that of a sorcerer, couldn't defeat the magic of the door. Mariko, however, was able to use her assassin ability to get around the magic. It was, as she later remarked, a "rather clumsy attempt" to safeguard the entrance into the pyramid... but no one knew if that was the truth or braggadocio.

Tangus, Jennifer, Safire, and Lester had been forced to retreat by the worgs until they were only a few steps away. Each suffered from numerous claw and bite marks. Each looked as if they were in danger of collapsing where they stood.

As they backed toward the entrance, Tangus wasn't sure they would make even the few feet that remained. There were so many worgs. The worgs suddenly stopped their assault. They tilted their heads in unison as they listened to a silent command. As one they darted away. The defenders stood and watched in amazement.

"I wonder what that was all about?" Tangus said. "They were so close to breaking us."

Mariko stuck her head out the door. "The Purge isn't here," she said.

Tangus turned to look at her. "I'm not surprised," he commented. "The worgs came from the opposite direction, and they certainly wouldn't have broken off their attack if we posed a threat."

Kristen and Emmy stepped out of the pyramid. Kristen still held Loki, who, though awake, had remained calm... as if he understood the seriousness of the situation. "It was here," Emmy said. "This place was in my dream. I saw the Purge being created here."

"Do you know where the entrance into the tunnels below might be?" Tangus asked.

"I'm not sure... but there's at least one doorway out of the main room," Emmy replied.

Tangus nodded. "Let's get inside, everyone."

Magical light illuminated the inside of the pyramid. immediately inside the door was a large balcony. The pyramid was a hollowed-out stone shell.

The capstone of the pyramid, two hundred feet above, appeared to be made of clear crystal which allowed both sunlight and moonlight to shine through. Similar to an iceberg, the size of the pyramid from the surface up didn't tell the entire story. It also extended deep into the ground. Ten levels ringed the part of the pyramid that burrowed into the ground. Ten square balconies went around each level, with metal spiral stairs connecting each. Interspaced along the walls of each level were magnificent wooden doors. Every door gleamed as it still released the original protection magic cast upon it. Far below, on the bottom floor, was a ten foot diameter circular depression in the stone floor.

"Emmy, has anything changed from your dream?" Kristen asked.

Emmy closed her eyes and went into a trance-like state as she mentally studied each facet of her dream. "I don't think..." she said after she opened her eyes. "Wait! I remember the well down below on the floor. The well that held the Purge. It had glowing, magical runes that surrounded it. Now it doesn't."

"That makes sense if the Purge is no longer here," Safire commented. "Unless..."

"Unless the runes where only necessary to create the Purge, love," Lester said as he finished Safire's thought.

Tangus checked the closed entrance door to make sure it was secure. "Let's get our wounds looked at and then take a break. I don't know about the rest of you, but I feel like the walking dead."

Kristen, Emmy, and Mariko applied salves and bandages, as well as healing magic when necessary, to each. But the restoration of the body, though essential, couldn't take away the mental weariness each felt. They needed to rest.

Far below on the ground floor, looking out of an open door, a pair of human eyes watched what was happening above. He had seen the outline of the intruders silhouetted in the doorway when it opened. He watched the blue glow of healing magic. "The enemy," he grunted softly. "I know what to do... and it will please the master."

The Purge retreated in upon itself. Its attempt to dominate Elanesse was a complete failure... another, stronger force had somehow came into being. It had power that seemed similar to that of Elanesse, yet different. With the two of them together, the Purge knew it'd never be strong enough to command the intelligent city. Conversely, without the help of Elanesse, the Purge could never destroy the last empath... for she had grown much too powerful. But it could do damage beforehand... such as kill the empath held prisoner within itself.

"No! No! No!" the voices in its head cried in unison. *"That will bring about your extinction."*

"Then so be it," the Purge responded harshly. "My destruction already appears to be assured. At least I won't have to listen to you any longer!"

"Lady Esmeralda?" a voice said inside of Emmy's mind. *"Are you there?"*

"Charity? Is that you?" Emmy replied silently as she came out of a light slumber.

"Yes, mistress," Charity replied. *"I wasn't sure if I could contact you."*

"It's the ring I gave you. Are you in distress?"

Emmy could hear Charity sigh. *"The Purge has decided it's time for my end,"* Charity replied.

"That will kill it," Emmy said. "As you were part of its creation, so to would you be part of its destruction should harm ever befall you. Surely it knows that."

"It's ready to die," Charity said. *"Only the ring you gave me has kept it at bay... the ring and the distraction being caused by the others who don't wish the Purge to die. My lady, they have driven the Purge mad."*

"We're close, Charity. Very close."

"Please be careful, mistress," Charity replied before she ended the conversation. *"The Purge is much more dangerous now since it has nothing to lose... and only one thing sustaining it. Hate."*

CHAPTER TWENTY-TWO

InnisRos

Civility, honor, nobility... lofty goals when living one's life. However, it's unfair to judge the distance one has traveled towards the attainment of those goals during times of war. The barbarity and savagery of combat, combined with the innate desire for self-preservation makes it necessary to fight any such conflict with a cold heart. There's no need for self-recrimination afterwards.

-From the Chronicles of Commanding-General Martin Arntuile, the Alfheim

War is hell!

-Universal Truth

Several magical spheres of fire hit the magical barrier Eric the Black had cast to encircle the monastery. The force of the explosions rocked the brick and mortar and drove Eric the Black to his knees. Nefertari, standing next to him on the battlements overlooking the town of Calmacil Clearing, reached over and steadied him. She had used her own power to supplement Eric the Black's... but the blast didn't affected her the same as it did him.

Colonel Tirion, on Nefertari's other side, gripped his sword. "Hard for the common soldier to beat magic," he said.

Eric the Black nodded and turned to Nefertari. "Maybe it's time to awaken that flying boulder of yours?"

"Maedhros Nénmacil's never sleeps," Nefertari replied. "But he's not invulnerable to magical attacks."

"Meaning?" Eric the Black said.

Colonel Tirion answered for Nefertari. "Meaning he needs to be smart. Once he makes his first attack, he no longer has the element of surprise. One Army corps employs a lot of sorcerers... but three corps?"

"Not even a creation stone can withstand that," Nefertari finished.

Eric the Black shook his head. "Even with your help, priestess, I can't hold the force field much longer."

"Then all they have to do is keep pounding away until there's nothing left to pound," Colonel Tirion said.

"Perhaps it won't come to that," Eric the Black replied. "Father Goram has... how did he put it... oh yes... another card to play. What that might be I don't know. My orders are to do what I'm doing for as long as I can."

"You don't seem like the kind who takes orders easily," Colonel Tirion remarked.

Eric the Black grunted. "What business is that of yours?"

"Don't be offended," Nefertari said. "Daeron's just making an observation. Career Marines can be... shall we say... rather direct."

Colonel Tirion looked at Nefertari and then Eric the Black... but he didn't back off. "Everyone here seems to fit together well... like they've been working with each other for years. But around you, except for the good father, folks are tentative... like they're not sure just yet how close of an ally you are to their cause." Colonel Tirion looked out at the assembled army there to destroy them. "From what I've heard, Mordecai excels in planting spies upon his adversaries."

Nefertari lay a hand on Colonel Tirion's arm while she looked at Eric the Black. "Steady, good sorcerer."

The black-clad sorcerer smiled. "At least you're bold enough to say what you mean," Eric the Black replied to the big Marine's questioning. "Your scrutiny of my standing here is quite acute, Colonel. With the exception of Father Goram and Landross, I'm not yet completely trusted. Landross has become my friend. As for Father Goram... well, I'm not sure anything truly frightens him. He has certain... shall we say... ways to get to the truth of things. He knows well enough where I stand. Everyone else, though... it's as if they fear I'll turn them into toads, or some such nonsense, if they as much as look at me wrong."

Colonel Tirion and Nefertari remained silent but kept their attention directed on the sorcerer. Both understood Eric the Black may want to confide in them... not because they were friends, but because they were strangers.

Eric the Black continued, "Sorcerers, as a rule, don't have many friends... instead preferring to stay in their towers studying magic. I must admit I did try that for a while in the city of Elwing FeFalas... but found I still needed to put supper on the table. Becoming a military sorcerer didn't really appeal to me... so I tried entertaining children with simple cantrips. I found that the parents were quite appreciative. I'd unknowingly became somewhat of a surrogate babysitter for them while they ran their errands. They paid me very handsomely... but all of that soon became boring. Not that I disliked the children, mind you. I actually grew quite fond of them. But I was falling behind in my studies."

"How did you end up in Calmacil Clearing?" Colonel Tirion asked.

"Not by design," Eric the Black replied. "Happenstance... or fate as Magdalena used to tell me before she... before she was butchered by those bastards out there on the other side of this wall."

Colonel Tirion knew right away he'd hit a sensitive nerve. He saw the sorcerer's change in stance... he had suddenly become stiff. The inflection in his voice turned angry... and a look of pure hatred had been directed outward and into the night. It was time to end his interrogation before Eric the Black began to see at him as the enemy. Though he didn't believe Eric the Black was a spy, he believed there was more to the story than what he and Nefertari were being told. Something that involved Magdalena.

"Are you not well?" Nefertari asked.

Eric the Black reigned in his emotions and looked at the priestess. Finally he bowed his head and a single tear dropped and landed on his boot. "There was a child... Magdalena... she was... "

Before Eric the Black had a chance to finish, they heard movement behind them. The sorcerer quickly composed himself and everyone turned as Queen Lessien climbed the steps up to their position on the battlements. Razor and Findley preceded her, bounding up the stairs lightly, while Landross followed behind. The queen's sword, *Ah-HritVakha*, glowed brightly at her side, encased in its jeweled scabbard that mysteriously appeared in the queen's room a few hours before. Its emergence seemingly from out of nowhere left more than a few scratching their heads in confusion.

"Your Majesty," Colonel Tirion said with a slight bow. Eric the Black only nodded... but the queen took no offense, though Landross frowned at his sorcerer friend.

"Sister," Nefertari said. "Beautiful night, isn't it."

"It'd be much more beautiful if I didn't have to maintain this force field," Eric the Black commented. It was his way of saying he still had work to do and extra visitors distracting him wasn't going to make it any easier.

"Your Majesty..." Landross sputtered.

Lessien held up her hand. "Please, everyone. Stop with the 'Your Majesty' and 'Your Highness'. We're far from being at my court. And Landross, quit apologizing for everything."

As Lessien looked out at the bivouacked army, *Ah-HritVakha* suddenly flared... but dimmed after a few seconds.

"You need to keep your sword from doing that every time it spots the enemy," Nefertari suggested. "It reads your emotions and reacts accordingly. You've just given away your position."

Lessien looked down contritely. "I'm trying, sister," she said. "But it's as you said... very difficult."

Nefertari cupped Lessien's chin in her hand and gently raised the Queen's head so she could look into her eyes. "Remember our lessons. You're the master of the sword and he recognizes you as such. But *Ah-HritVakha*, like his brother, needs you to guide him. You must keep your emotions in check... at least until you're ready to use him."

Lessien nodded.

Nefertari smoothed a few strands of Lessien's unruly hair. "He'll never fail you. But his enthusiasm to please you can make him hard to handle." Nefertari studied her sister. "When it's time to use *Ah-HritVakha*, you must be here... and not here," Nefertari said as she first placed a finger to Lessien's head, then a hand to Lessien's heart.

"Everybody down!" Eric the Black cried out.

A bolt of green energy hit the sorcerer's protective force field, taking only a couple of seconds to drill its way through. The energy beam hit the wall below where they were standing and an explosion caused the monastery to tremble. Everyone was knocked to the floor of the battlements with scrapes and bruises... but the guard hut below them obliterated. Warriors lay scattered on the ground. Those still alive screamed as the shock of what just happened wore off and they felt the pain of their mutilated bodies. Within seconds people were running to inspect the damage and help the wounded. Father Goram, followed by Autumn and a host of dire wolves led by Ajax, bounded out of the main building to aid the injured and give orders.

Nefertari jumped off the battlements and, using the element of air, softly floated down into the middle of the confusion. The deep blue glow of her healing magic mixed with the lighter blue of Father Goram's, Autumn's, and the other priests and priestess's as wounds were healed and lives saved. Though Nefertari's magic was in sharp contrast to the other healing magic on the world of Aster, it accomplished the same objectives.

"I thought your force field was supposed to stop things like this from happening?!" Landross shouted as he helped the queen back on her feet.

Eric the Black was also getting to his feet. "A different type of magic," he said as he shook his head to clear it. "A different frequency."

"What?" Landross asked.

"Go easy on your friend, I beg you, Landross," Lessien said. "He couldn't do anything about it. The magic that just hit us came from another world."

Landross looked confused. "Another world?"

"The Alfheim to be specific," Eric the Black said.

"But how?" Landross asked.

Lessien looked out over the assembled army. "They have a sorcerer from the Alfheim."

Eric the Black nodded. "Think of it this way, Landross," he said. "If magic were fire, the magic we use on Aster is a torch, while the same magic used on the Alfheim is an inferno."

Landross stared.

"My father explained this to me, Sir Knight," Lessien said. "What it means is that Eric the Black isn't powerful enough to stop an Alfheim sorcerer. No sorcerer trained on Aster can."

"Trained on the Alfheim?" Father Goram asked. Queen Lessien, Nefertari, Colonel Tirion, and the entire monastery command team, led by Father Goram, sat around a large table in the war room.

"Correct, Father," Lessien replied. "The source of magic on the Alfheim is much stronger than here."

Father Goram nodded. "I understand that," he said. "Our glass is only half full while the Alfheim's is completely full."

"Ours is more like a sixteenth full," Eric the Black said.

Father Goram frowned at the sorcerer.

"Well excuse me, but I actually FELT the magic they used to break through my force field," Eric the Black countered. "It felt like I was protecting us with a piece of vellum."

"My point being," Father Goram continued unabated, "I didn't think any Alfheim sorcerer's were over here. The Alfheim banned the travel of their sorcerers to Aster generations ago."

Lessien shrugged. "No ban is one hundred percent effective," she said. "And I doubt Mordecai even knows about this sorcerer... or the significance of Alfheim training. If he did, he'd keep him... or her... close at hand. A precious commodity."

"A rogue sorcerer then," Landross remarked.

Lessien nodded. "Probably."

"But how can the Alfheim sorcerer use that magic on our world?" Autumn asked.

Eric the Black sighed. "It's not so much the magic being used... but rather HOW it's being used. As the Queen mentioned, it's the training. With the magic so abundant and readily available, Alfheim sorcerers see magic in a different way. That is, they observe certain aspects of its existence no sorcerer on Aster could ever hope to perceive. Consequently they're able to manipulate its composition. But there is one thing we have in our favor."

"Which is?" Colonel Tirion asked.

"They don't have access to as much magic as they'd have over on the Alfheim," Eric the Black replied. "Meaning they'll need time to gather energy before they can send another spell against us."

"How long?"

Eric the Black shrugged his shoulders. "I have no idea."

The small, black bat flew out from the monastery and unnoticed over the buildings that comprised Calmacil Clearing. It was early morning... the sun had yet to rise in the east... and the sentries of the Army below were drowsy and inattentive as their watch neared its end. Breakfast and their cots awaited... so a single bat flying in the sky wouldn't cause a stir, even though bats mostly inhabited the mainland and were only rarely seen on InnisRos.

The bat circled the Army encampment, searching, until it found a two-story building that appeared to be well guarded. Dipping its wings, it dived out of the sky and made a sudden, fluttered stop on the chimney. It delayed for a few moments as it looked for smoke and felt for heat. Having deemed the chimney safe, the bat dropped down into the dark vent to the hearth on the bottom floor. It flew out into the room, up to the ceiling, and landed gently on a candle chandelier. It didn't hang from its claws like a normal bat, but instead clung inconspicuously on the ceiling support strut. Perched as it was, it could spy on the room with little fear of detection. The bat waited.

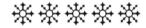

Moglor Calilimë sat in the middle of a small, barren room with his legs crossed, head bowed, upper arms against torso, and hands raised into the air at the elbows, palms facing inwards. He had been sitting in this position for hours as he chanted words learned in the Alfheim. Magic coalesced around him... filling his every pore with energy.

His eyes shimmered with power as he raised his head and smiled wickedly. Though he hadn't been evil when he surreptitiously crossed over to Aster, the strength he felt every time he gathered his will... strength that was his and his alone on this magic-deficient world... had warped his sense of responsibility to his vocation... and the innocent. He lived to dominate things... and people... with his magic.

"Just a little more energy," he thought. "Just a little more and I'll raze that monastery to the ground!"

The small bat cocked his head when it felt the strong magic radiate from above. He remained still for a few moments as he communicated his location. Then, in response to his master's command, he leaped off the chandelier, flew up the chimney, out into the early morning light, and returned to the monastery. The bat was happy during the short trip back... his master was very pleased. He jubilantly circled the monastery a couple of times before returning to his home in the bell tower... his happiness even further magnified by several unfortunate flying bugs. .

"We got him!" Eric the Black called out as he refocused his mind from the link he had with his bat familiar to the faces staring at him. "Ránëwén felt the magic he's gathering."

"Show me," Father Goram said as he looked at a map of Calmacil Clearing lying on the table in front of him. Eric the Black pointed to a large two-story building on the outskirts of the town.

Autumn shook her head. "You're kidding me... the hospital?" she exclaimed.

"We need to move fast, Father," Eric the Black said. "He'll have enough magic soon to do quite a bit of damage to my defenses."

"I'll take my knights..."

"My friend, you can't solve all the world's problems by charging your knights into the thick of things," Eric the Black said as he punched the armored knight on the shoulder. "This requires a more subtle approach."

Father Goram got up from the table. "Actually, Landross is right."

"You can't be serious," Eric the Black said, astonished that Father Gorem would even consider such a thing. "There's a whole army out there! He'd be cut down before he gets even half way!"

"We can make it, Horatio," Landross pleaded before he looked at Eric the Black. "Eric, have you ever seen what a full charge of several hundred knights on warhorses can do to infantry?"

"Infantry using buildings for cover?" Eric the Black snapped back. "All they need to do is pick you off with arrow-fire... and that's before the devastation the Army sorcerers will rain down upon your thick skulls with their magic."

"What choice do we have, Eric?" Landross asked. "What deep, dark magic can you cast to stop the foreign sorcerer? Anything?"

Eric the Black remained quiet. Landross was correct, he didn't have strong enough magic to get the job done. The building wasn't within line of sight... and one doesn't just cast spells blindly hoping to achieve a specific goal. It's too risky. Besides, he feared sending any magic against the Alfheim sorcerer. It would most likely be added to all the other magical energy being collected.

"Enough for now, gentlemen," Father Goram said. "I know what might work. Autumn, if you'll come with me up to the roof?"

"What...?" Landross asked before being cut off by Father Goram.

"A not-too-subtle answer to our dilemma," Father Goram said.

"Whatever it is, Father, make it quick," Eric the Black said. "Or all that's left of this monastery will be a slag heap."

Atop the roof of the monastery, looking menacing down to the ground below, were twelve delicately-carved crystal dragons... five to each side and one each in the front and back. Each of these dragons were twice the size of a messenger dragon and weighed approximately two thousand pounds. Inside each, invisible from the ground but easily seen through the crystal close up, were beating hearts.... no circulatory system... just the heart. The eyes of the dragons glistened with magic.

"So these are the 'watchers on the roof' you're always going on about," Autumn said. They were standing on a long balcony that ran the length of the roof. Steel rails had been built into the slate shingles along the edges for safety. It'd be a fatal fall to the ground.

"Crystal golems, my dear," Father Goram replied. "A gift from a long dead human sorceress. She was... my friend."

Father Goram walked over to the nearest one and ran his hands over the smooth crystal. The touch of Father Goram awakened the dragon golem. Its heart started to beat faster until blood flowed throughout its body. It turned its head to Father Goram and leaned in against his chest, coaxing the priest to pet it. As he did so, the clear crystal makeup of the body changed to deep purple.

"Nefertari has her creation stone," Father Goram said. "But I have my twelve dragons."

Father Goram then reached out his hand to Autumn. "Come, sweetheart."

Autumn cautiously approached and let Father Goram take her hand. The dragon watched her suspiciously, but other than that didn't seem to consider her a threat.

"The blood of the sorcerer, as well as my own, flows through the dragon," Father Goram explained. "Our mingled blood not only keeps it alive, but also allows it to recognize me. It will carry out my will. It will do whatever I ask of it."

Autumn was mesmerized. "Even its own destruction?"

Father Goram nodded. "I'd never ask that of them unless the circumstances were extremely dire. They're much too valuable to me." He took her unresisting hand and let Autumn pet it.

"It feels warm!" she exclaimed.

"He's awake," Father Goram replied, "and ready to do my bidding."

Autumn looked at her husband. "What do you have in mind?"

"First, I want you to control these dragons as I do," Father Goram said. "But it requires your blood."

Autumn trusted her husband completely and held out her arm to him without hesitation. Father Goram removed a knife from a sheath on his belt and pressed the razor-sharp edge against the skin of her upper arm. Without wavering, he cut deep. Autumn gasped and Father Goram had to catch her as she almost fainted from the pain. The color drained from her face and she breathed deeply, struggling for air. Then she retched.

"That's normal, Autumn," Father Goram assured her as he gently brushed back her sweat-matted hair with his hands. "It's almost over."

Autumn, secure in the strong arms of her beloved, didn't respond except to nod her head.

Father Goram lowered her to the roof. The dragon golem turned to face the two. Its movement was fluid and graceful as it covered the cut on Autumn's arm with its maw and drank the blood. When it had finished, it raised its head into the air and bellowed. The other eleven dragons suddenly joined their comrade with bellows of their own. The cut on Autumn's arm had disappeared without a trace.

Autumn sat up and shook her head. Except for sweat-drenched clothes, she looked and felt normal. Helped by her husband, she stood and placed her hand on the side of the dragon golem's face. "I'm Autumn," she said in her mind.

"I'm Golanth," the dragon replied. One by one, each of the other dragon golems also named themselves to Autumn.

"Now they'll respond to your authority," Father Goram said. "I'm sorry for not warning you about the pain you had to endure," he added contritely.

Autumn shook her head. "You were right not to. So, what do you have planned for our friends here?"

"It's pretty simple, actually... "

Several Army guards standing watch noticed something launch itself straight up into the sky from the roof of the main monastery building. But they were too far away and the strange object moved too fast for a closer look. Within a few seconds it had traveled out of sight. Each of the guards who had observed this spectacle decided it wasn't cause for alarm... that it'd be enough to put it in the end of watch report when their shift had concluded. They didn't realize their mistake until they heard a loud "boom" and saw the same object speeding straight down towards a building behind them.

Golanth flew to a height of two miles before he stopped his ascent. He hovered for a few seconds as he used his extraordinary eyesight to find his target... a two-story building that lay just outside the forest on the west end of Calmacil Clearing. Golanth sensed the strong magic that radiated from the building. It was getting stronger just as his master had told him.

The golem dragon began his descent, using his wings to adjust his position slightly until he was directly over the building. He flapped his wings to build up speed. At approximately one thousand feet over the building, he knew it was physically impossible for him to travel any faster. He folded his wings into his body to make himself as streamlined as possible.

Golanth traveled through the roof, second and first floors, and into the basement. Just before he crashed into the hard-packed earth, he wondered what death felt like for a golem. "I should have asked the master," he thought.

The energy of two thousand pounds of magical crystal traveling faster than the speed of sound, combined with the magical energy brought forth by the Alfheim sorcerer Moglor Calilimë, resulted in an explosion never before experienced in InnisRos's long history. A brilliant white light flashed in the sky, and the ground trembled with the force of the blast. A grim-looking mushroom cloud rose several thousand feet above the impact point. Everything within three hundred feet was instantly vaporized... while the concussive force reached out another thousand feet. It knocked over buildings and snapped trees in half. Only Eric the Black's force field prevented major damage to the monastery complex.

The wizards and the complete First Army Corps command structure ceased to exist. The remaining warriors suffered from shock and fell into complete disarray. The screams of the wounded and the dying could be heard through the falling dust and debris even before the rumble of the explosion had stopped. Soldiers walked out of the dust-cloud, slowly coming into view like a ghost slowly materializing into the physical world. But they acted like zombies... their movements stiff and unsteady. Most walked only a few feet before falling face first onto the rubble-strewn ground.

Father Goram gripped the steel rails of the roof's balcony and looked out upon the devastation he had created. "By the goddess, what have I done," he wailed with tears running down his face.

Autumn rubbed her husband's back in support... but tears were also forming in her eyes. "Please, my love. Don't... "

"You've done exactly what was needed," a voice said from behind. Queen Lessien, followed by her dire wolves, Landross, Nefertari, and Colonel Tirion, were standing at the doorway leading out onto the roof.

Father Goram nodded... but his queen's acceptance of his actions didn't ease his conscience.

Lessien turned and looked at Landross. "Now's the time to go out with your knights," she said. "I doubt you'll face much resistance."

"Yes, Your Majesty," Landross said as he saluted his queen.

As Landross was leaving, Lessien called to him. "Take as many clerics and healers as you can find. Save as many as possible."

"I'll go as well," Nefertari said as she pivoted and followed Landross.

"Colonel," Lessien said.

"Your Majesty?"

"I suspect you'll be the ranking officer down there. Defer to Sir Landross, but try to instill military order among the survivors."

"They may not take kindly to a Marine, My Queen."

Lessien nodded. "I understand," she replied. "But they'll be more inclined to take orders from you then from a monastery knight with a sword pointed at their throats. See what you can do."

Colonel Tirion saluted and turned to leave.

"Oh, and Colonel," Lessien said as she grabbed his shoulder. "See that no harm comes to my sister."

Colonel Tirion barked a short laugh.

Lessien looked at him sharply. "Were my orders amusing?"

Colonel Tirion looked at Lessien. "Huh? Oh... no, Your Majesty, of course not," he replied, but continued to smile. "It's just that Maedhros Nénmacil is down there. Nothing will get past him to threaten your sister."

Lessien nodded and smiled as Colonel Tirion left.

"I need to go down there as well, Lessien," Father Goram said as he turned to leave with Autumn on his arm.

Lessien shook her head. "No... we need to talk."

Father Goram paused. "I made a promise to someone," he insisted. "It's important I keep it. We'll talk later."

"You can keep your promise... just not now." Lessien shot back. From the tone in her voice there was little doubt she had just given Father Goram an imperial command. "I have something I wish to discuss with you that can't wait."

Both Father Goram and Autumn stared at Lessien. "You have no right to speak to my husband in that manner," Autumn said. "Not after all he's done for you!"

Father Goram squeezed Autumn's hand. "Darling, please. She's our Queen."

Lessien sighed. "You're right, Autumn," she said. "I owe your husband... and many others... my life. But we don't fight this war for me. We fight to deny Mordecai because we all know he'll ultimately destroy InnisRos if he's not stopped. We are ALL subservient to that goal... to that singular purpose." Lessien looked at Father Goram. "Isn't that correct, Father?"

Father Goram nodded.

Lessien took a deep breath. She didn't like what she had to say next. "Look out there, Horatio. Look what you've wrought."

"I'm very much aware, Lessien," he responded.

"Hundreds of my warriors lie dead and broken."

"They would capture you and give you back to Mordecai!" Autumn replied angrily. "Besides, you yourself said it needed to be done."

"You're correct, Autumn, on both counts," Lessien replied. "But Mordecai's the traitor... not my soldiers! They're just following orders!"

Father Goram kept quiet.

"Then what would you have us do?" Autumn asked.

Lessien became angry. Father Goram saw it in her eyes and thought it might be the influence of her sword.

"What would I have you do?!" Lessien shouted. "I'd have you TELL ME FIRST! Maybe there was an alternative to the death and destruction we've just witnessed! Maybe we could have figured out a way to kill only the Alfheim sorcerer! Yours is not the only opinion that matters!"

Complete silence followed the queen's emotional outburst.

Lessien's tone softened. "My kingdom is coming apart, don't you see that?"

"Of course we do, Lessien," Father Goram replied. "But that's not your fault. The blame lies with Mordecai. You're the rightful liege and should be re-installed onto the throne. No one here questions that... and we're willing to die to rectify this injustice. But only you can decide the cost you're willing to pay." Father Goram took a breath. "But there's more to it than that. You've only been here for a few hours... hours that have been extremely busy. There hasn't been enough time for what I need to tell you."

"Such as?" Lessien asked.

"We believe there's a deeper reason for Mordecai's treason," Autumn said. "And we think we know what that reason is."

"I'm listening," Lessien said.

Father Goram looked out over the remnants of Calmacil Clearing. "I'll be brief. Mordecai's found a way in which he can control all the magic of the Svartalfheim. If he succeeds, he can use the dark elf armies to invade Aster... and we believe eventually the Alfheim itself. We think his end game is to declare himself 'emperor' over three realms. For obvious reasons he doesn't feel his position as First Councilor afforded him the same opportunities to achieve his goals as being the King. So he had you removed on a trumped up murder charge."

Lessien said nothing... but she had a firm grip on the hilt of *Ah-HritVakha*. The sword flared in response to her anger... or was it fear?

"We have a day, possibly two, before the other two armies arrive," Father Goram said. "Plenty of time to have a more in-depth discussion concerning what we believe Mordecai's doing and what we've already done to stop him."

Lessien stared at the priest. "I'll hold you to that pledge."

Father Goram nodded. "Give me two hours."

"Very well," Lessien said. "Go fulfill your promise."

As Father Goram and Autumn turned to leave, Lessien held up her hand, stopping them. "Please believe I appreciate everything you've done for me."

Father Goram nodded. "We simply do our duty to our Queen... and Martin's daughter."

Father Goram and Autumn walked through the remains of Calmacil Clearing. Here and there pockets of disarmed soldiers were guarded by Landross's knights. Autumn left her husband's side to help the other clerics and healers in one of several triage areas that had been established for the wounded. The dead... those who hadn't been outright disintegrated... were placed on piles of wood and burned after their identification tags had been collected. By Queen Lessien's orders, monastery scribes began the tedious process of comparing the corps' payroll listings against the identification tags of the living and the dead to determine who disappeared without a trace in the blast. At some point Lessien felt she needed to notify the families.

The nearer Father Goram walked to the point of impact, the more desolate the area became. He'd never before seen an explosion of this magnitude. Ahead of him, Nefertari and Colonel Tirion were standing at the edge of the crater caused by the explosion. Maedhros Nénmacil was hovering nearby. Father Goram acknowledged the three as he came up and stood beside them.

"Your intervention, Father?" Nefertari asked. She could still feel the strong aura of Alfheim magic.

Father Goram didn't appear to hear Nefertari's question as he searched the crater bottom.

"Father Goram?"

"Huh... oh, sorry Nefertari. Yes, I suppose 'intervention' would be the correct term for it." Father Goram replied. "I only wanted to prevent the sorcerer from sending Alfheim-strength magic at us again. I miscalculated the strength of my response."

Colonel Tirion snorted. "I'd say your response was dead on. You not only stopped the magical attack... but you also negated the threat from this Army corps, giving us at least another day, perhaps two, to prepare for the other two corps coming." Colonel Tirion looked to the west. "One or two days of planning without interference from this corps will go a long way."

Father Goram sighed. "Since the Queen won't leave the island, all I want for now is a stalemate until we can figure out how to go on the offensive. A stalemate without further bloodshed."

Colonel Tirion shook his head. "I don't know how we can possibly go on the offensive from behind those stone walls of yours... especially when we'll be bottled up by two Army corps." Colonel Tirion considered. "But Mordecai, from everything I've heard of him, won't have the patience for that. Besides, he doesn't have to wait for us to surrender or starve as long as he can bring magic against us. We're limited in that department."

"Don't readily discount clerical magic, Daeron," Nefertari remarked. "You've seen what I can do. Then there's my friend Maedhros Nénmacil."

Colonel Tirion laughed. "I could never forget you or your flying boulder!"

Nefertari clasped hands with Colonel Tirion and smiled. She glanced at the priest and saw he was once again distracted by the bottom of the crater. "What troubles you so, Father?" she asked.

"I'm looking for something. I guess I'll have to go down to find it."

"Perhaps I can find it for you," Nefertari said. "If you'll permit me, of course."

Father Goram looked at Nefertari and frowned. "How?"

"Tell me what you seek and I'll show you," Nefertari answered.

"Do it, Father!" Colonel Tirion encouraged. "She does things like no priestess I've ever seen."

"Well?" Nefertari asked.

Father Goram nodded. "Very well. I'm looking for a huge crystal... hard as a diamond and just as beautiful. I sent it... him... to his death." Father Goram sighed. "It's important he have a place of honor in my home." Father Goram looked away and back into the crater. "That was all he asked."

Maedhros Nénmacil spoke for the first time. "He was your friend," he rumbled.

Father Goram nodded. "Yes."

"Let's see what we can do," Nefertari said. She closed her eyes and chanted.

"Aster earth formed long ago.
Search your depths both high and low.
A crystal, a gemstone, you must seek.
Through dirt and stone and mossy peat.

Open the dark, the black, your natural stealth.
Return this crystal from your inner self."

The earth at the bottom of the crater moved. A dome appeared and pushed upward. As loose earth dropped off the top of the dome, sunlight struck the clear crystal of the dragon golem and reflected out of the crater, its brilliance a beacon of multi-colored light.

Father Goram didn't hesitate. He slid down the side of the crater and walked over to the large mound of misshaped crystal. He felt along the side... it was cold.

Nefertari and Colonel Tirion came up beside the priest.

"This caused the explosion?" Nefertari asked.

Father Goram nodded. "One of my dragon golems. Unrecognizable because of the damage caused by the impact. This is Golanth. Of all my dragon golems, he was the one I liked the most... the one I trusted above all the others."

"He's rather large, Father," Colonel Tirion said.

"I have the magic necessary to get him back home," Father Goram remarked.

Maedhros Nénmacil gently bumped the slab of crystal and Father Goram felt a slight 'thump' underneath his hand and turned to the creation stone with a questioning look.

"I have, shall we say, empathy for stone and crystal," Maedhros Nénmacil replied with a smile. "And loyal friends should be given every opportunity, don't you think?"

Father Goram felt heat begin to radiate from the crystal. He put his ear against Golanth's side and listened. He couldn't believe what he was hearing... a heartbeat... getting stronger and stronger. Father Goram backed up and with his arms motioned for Nefertari and Colonel Tirion to do the same. As they watched, the lump of crystal reshaped itself into that of a dragon. Its color turned from clear to purple.

Golanth turned his head and looked at Father Goram. "I NEVER want to do that again!" he said as he flapped his wings.

Admiral Tári Shilannia felt an explosion in her cabin and, fearing something had happened to one of her ships anchored in the bay, rushed up to the deck. Joined by Marine Commander-General Aubrey Feynral, she surveyed the fleet... but saw no obvious signs of trouble. General Feynral tugged at her sleeve.

"Admiral, over there."

Admiral Shilannia looked towards the direction the General was pointing and saw a large mushroom cloud rising through the trees inland.

"That looks to be near the monastery," she said.

"Indeed it does."

Admiral Shilannia considered. "Aubrey, put a force together and get it checked out. I want eyes on the monastery as soon as possible."

General Feynral nodded and looked over to his adjutant, who saluted and ran below. "It's being done even as we speak, Tári."

Nightshade sat behind Mordecai's desk in his underground torture chamber. The *Ak-Séregon Stone* was sitting on the ground next to it. Mordecai was upstairs, still asleep even though it was mid-morning. Nightshade understood... it had been a long night for him. So many of his allies murdered. Maybe all of them. Nightshade smiled. "I wonder who managed that," she thought. She shrugged her shoulders and said out loud, "Oh well... it's not important."

She stood from behind the desk and moved to the center of the dark room. Nightshade took a deep breath. The room smelled of death. "Invigorating!" she said before sitting in front of the summoning circle. She chanted, and in a few moments a swirling mist appeared. Within the mist, the horrible countenance of her father emerged.

Aikanáro looked down at his daughter. "It's good to see you, Nightshade."

"Thank you, father," Nightshade replied. "Everything you planned has come to pass. I have the *Ak-Séregon Stone* and the armies of InnisRos will soon be concentrated in the northeast."

"The Navy?" Aikanáro asked.

Nightshade smiled. "Some things don't require manipulation. Most of the island's naval units are there as well, apparently of their own volition. It would seem they chose not to take part in the Queen's capture and might even have aided in her subsequent escape."

Aikanáro nodded. "I have the dark elves ready to invade," he said. "But it must be soon. They're most eager to start the campaign against the Alfheim."

"You must keep them under control, father," Nightshade remarked. "We need to wait until all of InnisRos's military are concentrated in one area before we invade. The island will be ours, but it must be done quickly before their allies from the mainland have a chance to respond. The fewer humans we have to kill, the greater our chance of success. We need their armies on the mainland as our allies or your dark elf army has no chance against Queen Kyleigh Angelus-Custos and her Elves of Light. "

Aikanáro guffawed. "The dark elves will move only when I say they will move."

Nightshade nodded. "Another day, two at the most, as this world measures time," she said. "I'll set the *Ak-Séregon Stone* and open the gate. Until then, father." She made a slight movement of her hand to banish the misty doorway. As it disappeared into the dark, she could hear her father laughing.

THE STRUGGLE FOR INNOCENCE

CHAPTER TWENTY-THREE

Elanesse

Prophets and oracles envision scenarios depicting the end of the world. Naysayers scoff at these preposterous sermons and see these divination's as either madness or the work of charlatans. Never once do they understand that their death is the ultimate proof of the prophets' veracity.

-Book of the Unveiled

By the time Romulus, with Sakkara and Kavik, emerged from the bramble, he had regained his strength and his wounds had were completely healed... a gift from Emmy. His heart, though still heavy with a sense of responsibility for his loved ones, was also filled with a sense of completion, for he had found a mate and a son to share his life.

"Where do we go, Romulus," Sakkara asked. "My pack is no more thanks to the white monsters."

"You're both part of my pack now," Romulus replied. "But they're in danger so we must travel quickly."

Sakkara grabbed Kavik by the scruff of his neck and waited. Romulus smiled in the way of the dire wolf and then throated a great howl of happiness and determination. As they started back down Mount Repose, Romulus never noticed the avalanche his howl had inadvertently started behind him.

The stone floor of the pyramid was dark, cold, and empty... except for the large, bare pool in the center. Massive marble columns, equally spaced around the circular room, stood solemn watch as they used their strength to support the balcony above. Underneath the balcony were closed doors... but unlike the doors on the upper levels, these doors didn't radiate protection magic.

With one exception, the doors led to empty rooms. The remaining door opened into a dark passageway.

Tangus, on a hunch, knelt to study the first few feet into the corridor.

"Someone's been here," he observed. "And not a worg. These are booted prints in the dust."

Safire knelt beside him. "Looks recent."

"I wish Romulus were here," Tangus remarked as he stood. "We have to assume someone knows we're down here."

"I'll lead," Mariko volunteered.

Tangus grunted consent.

Kristen cast a cantrip spell and a magical ball of light, the size of a small apple, appeared in front of Mariko. It was bright enough to light the entire corridor for approximately twenty feet, yet soft enough not to interfere with sensitive elven eyesight.

"Touch it, Mariko," Kristen said. "Once you do that, it'll obey your mental commands."

"Will it dim by command as well?" Mariko asked.

"If that's what you wish," Kristen replied.

Mariko touched the floating light and then sent it fifty feet forward down the corridor. She carefully inspected the floor, walls, and ceiling as it made the journey.

"Can I keep it?" Mariko inquired.

Kristen laughed. "It's yours."

Tangus had moved to stand by his wife and inspect Loki. The saber cat purred at his touch. "He seems to have recovered well. His eyes are clear and his color is back. He looks healthy."

"Mother and I have been able to heal all his physical wounds, father," Emmy said. "But Royal Mountain Saber Cats are keenly intelligent. He's aware of you and recognizes you as his family. But he's still mentally traumatized by his injuries. That'll take more time to overcome."

"Time I hope we have, dear one," Tangus said as he cupped Emmy's chin and kissed her forehead. He then leaned over and kissed Kristen.

"We'll be fine, honey," Kristen reassured him. "The Purge will soon be destroyed... after which we can start making Elanesse our home."

Tangus shrugged. "The Purge is only one of our problems. What's occurring on InnisRos is also worrisome."

"Father will handle it, you'll see," Kristen said with confidence... mostly for Emmy's sake. Deep down she wasn't so sure.

The path forward was filled with a myriad of twists and turns. Like a labyrinth, the corridor system they found themselves in was designed to trap the uninvited. With no idea where the Purge might be nesting, it'd be impossible to determine direction... and impossible to know which corridor was correct and which a dead end... except for the booted prints in the dust. Tangus didn't know if the prints would lead to the Purge, but without a better option, he decided the risk was worth it. Without Azriel and his instinctive dwarven ability to move unerringly underground, Tangus realized they'd probably be lost in short order if they followed any other course.

Tangus worked beside Mariko as they followed the booted prints. Each time they came to a fork, the booted prints went into a corridor with no indication of a pause. This reaffirmed his decision to use the prints as a guide. "If nothing else," Tangus thought, "at least this person knows where he's going."

Predictably they came to an intersection with an air shaft overhead. The air shaft in and of itself wasn't unusual. The architect of these corridors knew fresh air needed to be piped in from above and allowed for this in the design. But this was the first air shaft over an intersection. The circulation of air from the shaft kept the dust from settling on the stone floor. As a consequence, there were no prints to follow... and seven corridors branched off in different directions.

"I guess we search each corridor to see if we can pick up the prints again," Tangus said. "Lester, please stay with Kristen and Emmy. Safire, with me... Jennifer, go with Mariko. When the dust once again covers the floor in each corridor, check for booted prints. You shouldn't have to go too far in... maybe twenty, twenty-five feet. But don't wander too far... I don't want you to get lost."

"Don't worry about us," Mariko replied reassuringly. "We'll be fine. C'mon, Jennifer, let's get a move on it."

"Mark the corridors you've searched with chalk," Tangus called out to the retreating backs of his daughter and Mariko. In response, Jennifer didn't even stop or turn. She held up a piece of chalk for him to see as she continued walking.

It took fifteen minutes to check all the passageways.

As Jennifer and Mariko walked out of the last corridor, Tangus looked at them. "Anything?" he asked.

Jennifer shook her head.

Tangus was puzzled. He and Safire had found nothing either.

"That doesn't make sense, Tangus," Kristen remarked. "He had to go somewhere. He couldn't just vanish, could he?"

"Yes, maybe he could." Tangus frowned. "We've made too many assumptions and followed blindly. In retrospect, we don't really know what we're dealing with."

"We didn't have too many options at the time, friend Tangus," Lester observed.

"I suggest we stop for a few minutes to look at this more closely," Mariko commented. "You're correct, Tangus... we've been rushing forward with our eyes closed, so to speak, and instead relying on our instincts. Not all quandaries can be dealt with through instinct alone. While it's true we've had no choice, there must come a point wherein we pause and explore all our options."

"Father's trained me to the point I don't have to think about things... just react," Jennifer said. "If I'm shooting an arrow, I unconsciously judge wind speed, distance, intersection point if the target is moving, point of horizon, plus any other intangibles. The action of firing an arrow becomes instinctive BECAUSE of the training. The point is I don't have to waste time thinking about it."

Mariko nodded. "That's true for each of us... and it's kept us alive thus far. But some situations pose problems that can't be handled by instinct alone. You can't train for the unknown. Some problems need to be reasoned. Predicaments that, if we rely entirely upon our instincts to solve, may result in a poor outcome because we've not have considered all the options. As an assassin I've set up ambushes based upon how I know the quarry will act instinctively."

"And if they don't react instinctively?" This came from Safire.

"I don't give them that chance," Mariko replied. "Using reasoned thought and planning, I force them to respond in a manner that guarantees the outcome I desire. I force them to react instinctively because I can anticipate that." Mariko paused. "The point being each problem offers its own set of unique parameters. Instinct serves its purpose, but shouldn't be the end-all."

Everyone went silent. Her point had been well taken. They knew how effective Mariko was in her previous occupation.

"Sometimes, Jennifer," Mariko continued, "instincts can be used against you."

Jennifer shook her head. "I've honed my instincts through training. In battle, it's usually the only thing that saves our lives."

Mariko looked at Jennifer. "What you say is true. But, unless the battle is unexpectedly thrust upon you, it's YOUR decision when to go into that battle... or how you'll influence the enemy to your advantage. Your father's very good at this. But in my opinion we've been allowing ourselves to be manipulated."

"We're doing what we have to do to save Emmy from the Purge," Jennifer protested. "What other choice do we have?"

Mariko nodded. "Probably none. But that doesn't mean our responses can't be measured."

While Jennifer and Mariko were having their discussion, Kristen put Loki down in case he had business to attend. He didn't hesitate to try walking on three legs... and after several failed attempts seemed to get the feel of it and started to move with little problems.

"He's adjusting well," Lester observed.

Emmy smiled. "He doesn't have many memories of walking on four legs," she said. "So it's much easier for him."

Everyone's attention turned to more important matters... where to go from here.

"There must be a secret door somewhere," Safire said. "If not in here then perhaps in one of the corridors leading out."

Tangus nodded. "That's one possibility. Can anyone think of another?"

"Probably not the ceiling unless he could fly," Lester commented.

"We know nothing about who we're following, so let's not rule anything out," Tangus replied as he and everyone else looked up. The height of the ceiling opened up from fifteen feet in the corridors to twenty-five feet in the intersection.

"If he went up there I don't see how," Lester observed. "Looks to be solid stone."

"I'll look for any magical enchantments while the rest of you search for a secret door," Kristen said before she closed her eyes to cast the spell.

Everyone else, except for Emmy, began the meticulous search of the intersection for secret doors or passageways.

"Father," Emmy said.

"Not now, sweetie."

Emmy shrugged her shoulders and walked over to Loki. She had noticed him stop his exploration of the intersection and now he was staring at a spot almost dead center.

"What's up, little fellow," Emmy said as she knelt next to the saber kitten.

Then she felt it... almost imperceptible and virtually impossible to detect unless right over and on it.

"Good boy," she said as she picked up Loki and set him in her lap. "Father, Loki may have found what you're looking for."

Everyone stopped their search immediately and looked at Emmy who was sitting in the middle of the room. Kristen, her magical detection spell activated, glanced around, but sensed no unusual magical aura.

Tangus knelt next to Emmy. "What is it, honey?" he asked.

In response, Emmy took her father's hand and placed it slightly above the place Loki had found.

"I'll be damned," Tangus exclaimed. "Air... coming UP from the floor."

"A staircase?" Kristen speculated.

Tangus nodded. "Maybe. Everyone, down on your hands and knees. Let's see if we can map this out."

"You mean by feeling the floor for air?" Jennifer said.

Tangus looked at his daughter and nodded. "Lester, keep a watch. Everyone else, use your chalk to mark it." Within a few minutes they had a fifteen foot diameter circle outlined on the floor.

"I wish Max were here," Lester said, his voice solemn. "Obviously this has some sort of opening mechanism... and he'd most certainly find it with little problem."

Safire reached out and touched Lester on the arm, silently offering strength to her future husband. She knew Lester was still grieving the loss of his friend.

It took an hour, but they finally located a secret compartment in the wall next to the corridor they originally exited. The compartment door wasn't locked and opened easily. Inside was a lever.

"I don't know if there's a trap or not," Tangus whispered to no one in particular. "Or if the lever itself is trapped. But I doubt I'd be able to decipher it even if it is."

Cautious as always, Tangus moved everybody out of the room and into the nearest corridor. He pulled the lever and waited for the world to either explode or collapse, depending upon the type of trap that might be connected to the action.

Nothing happened.

In the dark recesses of the Purge's mind, a battle for survival was playing itself out between the empath Charity and the Purge. It was a battle no different from the one that was occurring in Elanesse... a life and death struggle between the light and the dark, reason and madness, innocence and corruption. Only the ring given to Charity by Emmy had thus far averted the Purge's advance toward its own self-destruction... the murder of the empath used in its creation.

Charity had retreated as far as she could, relying on the ring to stop the mental attacks directed at her by the Purge. She had no more places to hide... what small citadels of good that had remained with the Purge since its inception had been overrun by its madness and hate. The Purge bashed at her defenses relentlessly.

Charity didn't think she would survive.

"Stop! Stop! Stop!"

"Damn the voices!" the Purge screamed. "Damn the voices!"

"Stop! Stop! Stop!"

"Go away!" the Purge cried in anguish. But the voices didn't go away. Nor would they stop. They understood what killing the empath meant... their complete and utter destruction.

"How to escape? How to find the peace I knew during three millennia of sleep?" The Purge put nonexistent hands over nonexistent ears. "HOW TO DIE?!" it roared.

"Stop! Stop! Stop!"

The worg, along with many of its brethren, circled the base of the Tower of the Innocent in west Elanesse. It was guarding... watching... waiting... for any interloper to approach. It hadn't joined the brief migration into the southern part of the city, but noticed that many of those who did never returned. As the worg made another of what had been many journeys around the tower, it suddenly wondered why it was doing such a thing.

As one, the worgs in Elanesse abandoned the city and returned to their forest homes.

Romulus, Sakkara, and Kevik ran out of the Olympus Mountains' eastern foothills and entered the Forest of the Fey. Romulus, in his customary lead position, stopped. Worgs! The forest was filled with worgs!

Worgs are primitive off-shoots of the dire wolf lineage... and massive Romulus was the king of the dire wolves. Under normal circumstances, the worg wouldn't challenge the dire wolf... even if they had the advantage in numbers. But Romulus knew these worgs were being manipulated by the Purge... and would attack in a berserker rage. Chances were slim Romulus could fight his way out of the trap he found himself.

To his surprise, however, they weren't attacked. Sakkara, Kavik, and Romulus were ignored as the worgs wandered past. The only hint the worgs knew Romulus and his family were even there was when one would nod in Romulus' direction as it filtered through the forest.

"I don't understand," Sakkara said. She had put Kavik down.

Romulus sighed. "They were mind-controlled and viciously attacked my pack," Romulus replied. There was concern in his voice. "Now they just look confused. Remember what I told you of the Purge?"

"Yes."

Romulus continued to watch the worgs passing by. "These worgs return to their homes because the Purge is dead... or because the Purge has destroyed my pack and are no longer needed."

After a few moments, Tangus felt vibrations and heard the activation of machinery underneath the floor. A low grating sound, synchronized with the hidden apparatus below, forced everyone's attention to the center of the room. As they watched, the circle on the floor slowly moved back into the floor until it exposed a dark hole. The top of a stone spiral staircase going down began just a few inches below the floor. A closer look revealed the familiar booted prints in the dust.

"These look fresh," Tangus remarked as he got up from the floor. "No doubt our quarry. I guess we go down." He had a gleam in his eye as he brushed himself off. "When this is all over, I can't wait to map the tunnels beneath this city."

"I'm sure Azriel will be more than happy to help," Mariko said.

"Azriel-Ahlasim," Emmy corrected.

"My pardon."

"How far down, friend Tangus?" Lester asked.

"I can't tell," Tangus replied. "Too dark. Mariko, send your light sphere down to see what we're up against."

Tangus, Kristen, and Mariko looked into the opening. Tangus judged the stairway went down a one hundred feet before it reached bottom. The light sphere revealed a small chamber with only one exit. There was also a mummified figure at the base of the stairs.

"That's a bit disconcerting," Mariko remarked.

"Looks like whoever that is fell going down the stairs," Kristen said. "It's hard to tell from this far away, but from the positioning of the body, I'd say a broken neck at least... and probably a few other bones as well." Kristen leaned further into the opening. "His head looks caved in, though I can't say whether that injury was from the fall or being hit on the head before he fell."

"Well, it's obvious that's not who we're following," Tangus commented. "Whether from the fall or being hit on the head, that body tells us we need to be careful going down the stairs. It won't do us any good if one of us ends up with a broken neck ourselves. It's not essential we catch our quarry... just that we can follow him."

"Though it'd be a real shame if the person we're following isn't heading for the Purge," Kristen observed.

"We must hurry," Emmy interposed. She stood off to the side a few feet and was absentmindedly petting Loki.

Everyone looked at the young empath. "The Purge is trying to kill itself," Emmy said in response to their questioning glances.

"But that's a good thing, isn't it?!" Jennifer asked.

Emmy shook her head. "Not for Charity," she replied.

"Charity?"

Emmy paused. She hadn't really talked much about Charity and the part she had played in the creation of the Purge... or the fact she'd had conversations with the young empath. Her concern for Charity forced a slip of the tongue. "Charity's an empath. The Purge made her a prisoner and will surely kill her before it dies."

"I thought you were the last empath?" Jennifer persisted.

Tangus and Kristen, who both knew about Charity from conversations with Emmy, looked at each other. Kristen nodded.

"Jennifer," Tangus said, "do you trust me?"

"Of course I do! Why would you ask such a question?"

"Father... let me," Emmy said as she handed Loki over to Kristen and looked at Jennifer. "Sister, though I'm only a child in your eyes, I'm over three thousand years old. Things... things happened during my suspension in stasis. I gained knowledge... precognitive visions... comprehension of facts and the workings of the mortal body that can only be learned through training. Training I've never had... at least in any type of traditional way. I don't as yet understand how or why I came to be this way. But it can't be denied that I AM this way. I know not what the future holds or exactly what I'll become. But a doorway to my destiny will be opened once the Purge is at last defeated. Preventing the Purge from harming Charity further is necessary if that's going to happen. She's important."

"More important than you?" Jennifer asked.

Emmy thought about the question for a moment before answering. "Yes... or perhaps it'd be more precise to say only through her can I become what I must."

607

Jennifer nodded, then frowned. "I don't understand. But something about what you've explained has a ring of truth to it." Jennifer considered for a few moments before deciding to accept Emmy rationale. After all, wasn't Emmy her sister? "Very well."

Everyone else had also been listening to the conversation in rapt attention. Mariko was just as much in the dark as the others about what had just been disclosed about Emmy and her relationship with the other empath... but she accepted everything she had heard without question or reservation. Only she understood how deep her devotion to Emmy went. Lester and Safire also didn't seem to be bothered. They had both seen far too many things during their lifetimes, particularly in the last few weeks, to allow one more impossibility to throw them off balance.

The navigation down the stairs, though somewhat tricky, wasn't the problem everyone had expected. Though they descended with great care, there was a handrail around the central pillar to steady their descent. Once at the bottom it became clear to Kristen that the mummified body had succumbed to a blow to the head... probably from a club if the impact outline on the smashed skull was any indication. As expected, the booted prints in the dust clearly led into the only corridor going out the room.

Without warning, the dark corridor brightened in a flash of light... and a scream of excruciating pain followed moments later.

Elrond felt wonderful! Powerful... vibrant... immortal!

"You almost are," Elanesse remarked. Elrond's amazement at what he had become filled her heart with joy and laughter. Gold leaves shimmered in her delight.

"This must be how the oak feels," Elrond remarked. His green-bronze leaves shimmered as well.

"You're much more than the oak, Elrond," Elanesse said. "I'm a city... a home for all who wish peace and security within my walls. You're the mighty forest... my protector. How this came to be I cannot say. But it feels right. No longer will I fear the Purge, for together we have proven it cannot defeat us."

"You're correct, my beloved," Elrond replied. "But the Purge can still defeat our friends."

"Then we should help them, should we not?"

Elrond nodded... at least he felt as if he did. There was still much he had to learn about being the 'Elendrel-Telperiën' in the tongue of the ancient elves, or 'Tree of the Eternal Sentinel'. "How do I do that?" he asked. "I mean, how do I leave this form."

"You never leave what you are," Elanesse replied. "No... it's a matter of expanding who you are. You extend your consciousness out from your center. Every tree, every bush, every blade of grass within the forest is yours to command if you know how. Let me show you."

Romulus led Sakkara and Kavik through the Forest of the Fey. The migration of worgs they had seen earlier disappeared almost as quickly as it had materialized. They were still in the area... and they were still the same vicious and cunning predators as before. But now they had returned to their place in the natural hierarchy of the forest.

"How far is it to your friends?" Sakkara asked.

Romulus stopped and looked around. "Hard to tell, but no more than a few hours if we manage a steady pace."

"My stomach is growling, Romulus," Sakkara said. "And though Kavik doesn't complain, he's hungry as well."

"Do you wish me to hunt?" Romulus asked.

Sakkara stuck her nose into the air and then shook her head. "The worgs have driven all the game into hiding. We'll be fine for a few more hours."

Romulus suddenly had a thought. "Have you ever eaten fruit?" he asked.

"What self-respecting wolf would eat anything other than the rich meat from a fresh kill," Sakkara said as she wrinkled her nose.

Romulus showed his teeth in a wolf smile. "I once felt as you. But the fruit from the Tree of Golden Radiance is almost better than fresh meat. It's delicious... and... succulent. That's what my friend Max once said."

"What's 'succulent' mean?" Kavik wondered aloud as he tilted his head.

Romulus frowned. "I... I don't know." Romulus barked out a laugh. "You'll probably need a bath afterwards, little one, because the fruit is real juicy. You'll get it all over your fur."

Sakkara mouthed the loose skin on the back of Kavik's neck and picked him up. She was ready to travel. Romulus nodded and turned to lead her forward. As he did so, he stopped. All the branches and bushes had bent to the side, presenting a clear path through the forest.

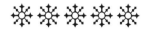

Elrond smiled. "Bring your family home, Romulus," he whispered. "We're waiting for you."

Tangus and Mariko were again in the lead as they moved slowly down the corridor. The light sphere Mariko controlled hovered twenty feet ahead of them. It had exposed an abrupt turn in the corridor to the right.

Tangus held an arm up to stop Mariko before he approached the turn. He put his back to the wall, closed his eyes and took several deep breaths before looking around the corner.

"By the goddess," he whispered as he stared at the form lying on the floor, just within the glow of the light sphere about thirty feet away. The lump moaned. Tangus stepped away from the corner and leaned against the wall.

"What?" Mariko whispered.

"Look for yourself, Mariko," Tangus replied. "I've... I've seen death many times. But this... this eclipses them all."

Mariko looked and then disappeared around the corner. "Tangus, come here!" she called.

Tangus looked back at the rest of his loved ones and friends. "Stay here for now," he said before joining Mariko.

It would've been impossible to identify the form lying on the floor as human... except for the head sitting in the approximate center of the mass of flesh. As Tangus looked closer, he made out internal organs - lungs, intestines, heart. As he looked closer, he saw the heart was still beating. This filled him with disgust, then dread that something like this could be done to a human being. Tangus studied the head and realized the open eyes were still shining with the last remaining gleam of life. Those eyes saw Tangus staring and blinked... a silent plea for mercy. But before Tangus could recover from the shock of seeing what lay before him, the last vestige of life left those suffering eyes.

Tangus glanced over at Mariko. "You don't seem too bothered by this. I mean, he's literally been turned inside out! How can you not be?"

Mariko had bent and was studying the cooling corpse. "I've seen this before," she said. Standing, she stepped over the carcass. "No footprints beyond this point. I'd have to assume this is who we've been following."

"Mariko!" Tangus bellowed... then looked around, embarrassed. Quietly, he said, "Please make your point. What did this?"

Mariko looked at Tangus as she pulled a blanket out of her traveling pack to cover the mangled body. "My people call it 'Qénsharma', or 'Soulreaver'." Mariko put her traveling pack back over her shoulders and picked up her two katanas. "Though I'm sure it goes by other names. It precedes the attack with a mind numbing flash of light. A single Soulreaver can decimate populations of entire villages."

"How'd it get here?" Tangus asked. "No. A better question... what's it look like?"

"Amorphous," Mariko replied. "No real shape or form. In the dark it can appear as a puddle on the ground... or a stain on a wall. The victim rarely knows it's there until it launches its light attack which blinds and stuns. Then it enters through any access point on the body... a wound, nose, ears, eyes," Mariko paused, "and other places. Once inside, it eats away at the skin and muscle until only the internal body organs are left. Anyone making a quick examination of the remains would think it's been turned inside out. But upon closer inspection of the carcass, you'd find there's no skin... except for the head... and no muscle tissue."

"Why not the head?"

"No one seems to know," Mariko replied to Tangus' question. "Though there's speculation it can't get through the skull or face bones to eat away the skin. Trial and error seems to bear out that line of inquiry."

"Speculation? Line of inquiry? Trial and error?" Tangus asked incredulously. "You mean this thing... this abomination... has been studied?"

"Of course," Mariko replied. "It's the perfect assassin's tool... like laying a trap. Remarkably efficient... and the head's left intact, as we've seen, leaving no doubt who the victim is. The assassin can't get paid if the client doesn't know for sure the job's done. And if you stop to consider, the Assassin's Guild is actually doing a public service by keeping these things out of circulation. We've been using Soulreavers for centuries."

Tangus stared at Mariko with his mouth open... then shook his head.

"As for the other part of your question, underground is the Soulreaver's natural habitat," Mariko continued. "Though rare, it's not impossible for it to be here. But really, I've never heard of one being this close to the surface. Usually, they're much deeper. Unless... "

"Unless?"

Mariko looked down the corridor. "Someone brought it here... or it came up on its own. And if one came up... "

"Then so could others," Tangus said, finishing her thought. "Though one seems bad enough."

"We don't have to be concerned about this one," Mariko remarked. "Once they've eaten they crawl away and go into hibernation for several weeks."

"Any easy way to spot them?" Tangus asked.

"Not really, except to avoid puddles or stains on walls and ceilings," Mariko responded. "I know what to look for, though. I've hunted Soulreavers before."

Tangus nodded and then sighed. "Guess I need to tell the others."

"I'll stay here and wait."

Tangus shook his head. "No Mariko, you'll not. I'll not allow you to be alone. Besides being a valued member of our family, you're the only one who can get us past the Soulreavers... if there's more down here, that is."

Mariko nodded. "Makes sense."

Kristen breathed a sigh of relief when she saw Tangus and Mariko turn the corner and head back towards them. But as they walked closer she saw the concerned look on her husband's face. She knew the news wouldn't be good.

Charity screamed in pain. The protective power of the ring was being drained at an increasingly faster rate by the Purge... and the ring no longer blocked all the attacks against her. Once its power was gone, she knew there was no hope.

"Mistress!" she called out in desperation. *"I'm lost!"*

There was no answering reply... only silence. Charity contorted as another wave of agony sent by the Purge radiated over her. The ring was now inert. Charity's head dropped in sorrow and tears came to her eyes.

"I'm sorry," she sobbed.

The corridor had no more intersections and ended in a stone door built seamlessly into a wall. Several hours had passed... the going had been deliberate as Mariko carefully examined each foot of floor, wall, and ceiling for any signs of a Soulreaver. Several false alarms slowed the march forward even further. When at last they reached the door, everyone turned to Emmy. If anyone could sense the Purge, it'll be her.

Emmy handed Loki over to Kristen. "I only have this one chance to save her, mother," she said. "This is why I'm here."

Kristen looked quizzically at her adopted daughter, but Emmy had already closed her eyes and withdrew her mind inward as she concentrated on what she must do.

"Emmy?" she asked. She hadn't expected an answer, however. Then she felt the bond disappear. Kristen had been so secure in its presence for so long it stunned her.

"What's going on?" Tangus asked, his concern deflected from the door to his wife and daughter.

Kristen looked at Tangus. "Emmy's removed our bond," she replied.

Tangus understood what was happening immediately. There could be only one reason she'd do that... to protect Charity from the Purge. "We're here!" he roared. "Open the door!"

Charity waited for the death that was rapidly approaching. In a way she felt relief... she had been caught in this nightmare for so long. Three millennia of guilt-ridden thoughts and self recriminations. Three millennia of enduring the hole left in her soul from the loss of all she held so close. Three millennia of struggling to turn evil to love so no more lives would be destroyed. The exhaustion Charity felt came from a deeper place than any physical discomfort. But the expected end never came. She felt warmth and comfort come from a dazzling white light that suddenly bathed her and lifted her spirits. She recognized the light. It was the same connection she had with her own mother. It was the bond between empath and protector.

"Is that you, mistress?" she asked. There wasn't an answer... but Charity didn't need one. She knew who it was.

Charity felt the Purge quake, and the other voices scream in pain. The force of the bond, and the love that the bond represented, not only shielded her, but was also striking a killing blow against the Purge. She felt the Purge retract its tendrils from throughout the city of Elanesse... but it was too late as each tendril separated from the host and shriveled up, much like a worm drying in the light of the day, withering until each disappeared. Charity then felt herself being pushed through filth and muck, moving faster and faster, until she was ejected into the air, landing hard on the floor. Charity took her first breath in over three millennia... then coughed out the slime that had infiltrated her lungs. As she lay on the floor, she saw five clerics... the same five clerics who were used in the creation of the Purge.

They were already standing. It looked as if they were preparing spells. The last thing Charity saw before she lost consciousness was a little girl running towards her.

"Mistress," she whispered.

Emmy bolted past a stunned Tangus and ran into the room. Mariko, though not quick enough to stop the empath, relied upon the lightning-quick reflexes she had developed as an assassin to stay close behind. She saw Emmy stop and kneel next to a gypsy-clad young girl of about twelve. Emmy gathered the girl on her lap and rocked back and forth while speaking softly into her ear.

Mariko's attention quickly diverted to the five clerics. The way they were moving their arms... and the words they were chanting... told her magical spells were about to be cast. She suddenly smelled brimstone... and the temperature in the room rose. She maneuvered herself between Emmy and Charity just as the flame of plasma fire engulfed her. Mariko screamed in agony as the pain overwhelmed her. When the darkness at last prevailed, its embrace was cool and welcomed.

Tangus watched as Mariko fell to the floor writhing, engulfed by the fire that had come from the clerics. She had given her life to save Emmy and the girl Emmy cradled in her lap. That must be Charity. As he rushed to attack, two of the clerics fell to arrows from Safire and Jennifer. Off to his right Tangus could hear the sound of armor. He looked over and saw Lester running next to him.

Screaming a battle cry, he raised his scimitars to avenge Mariko as he continued his quick advance. Two more arrows whizzed past him, but this time they hit something in mid-flight that caused them to shatter. "A wall of force!" Tangus screamed in his mind just before he crashed into it. The force of the impact knocked him back a few steps. Though he kept his footing, he stood quiet for a few moments while he regained his senses. His nose bled profusely from the collision... hideously broken... and he suffered from bruises and abrasions all over his body. A large rune-covered sword suddenly appeared out of thin air and swung at Tangus who only barely managed to jump out of the way of the first swing. The sword followed him and struck relentlessly. All Tangus could do was shield himself from the blows with his scimitars as he was forced back.

Lester had also crashed into the invisible barrier... but, unlike Tangus, couldn't keep his footing. The sound of his armor as it collided with the barricade rang through the room. Lester stumbled back a couple of paces before he dropped to the floor, unconscious. A large, two-handed war-hammer appeared in the air and beat the comatose knight savagely. Lester's heavy knight's armor protected him... but would do so for only for a few attacks. It was turning into a mangled metal coffin.

Kristen ran to Emmy and Charity. Placing Loki on the floor, she checked the two children for injuries. Finding none, she crawled over to Mariko. Astonishingly, the assassin was still alive... though she wouldn't be for long. The plasma fire had caused horrible burns to Mariko's entire body. The rasping, strangling sound Mariko made as she struggled for breath broke the priestess' heart. Kristen said a quick prayer to Althaya and began to heal her friend. She knew the massive burns made survival impossible even if she used her strongest healing spells. But perhaps she could make Mariko as comfortable as possible before she passed on to the next world.

Safire and Jennifer, finding that their arrows no longer effective, dropped their bows and pulled their swords as they charged into the room. Both understood the best chance for survival rested with Tangus and Lester getting back into the melee. Safire rushed to help Lester while Jennifer did the same for her father. As they intercepted the flying war-hammer and sword, they saw the two dead clerics rise. Their struggle with the magical weapons, however, forced them to redirect their attention away from that development and to the defense of their lives.

Kristen's primary concern was protecting her daughter. After pulling Mariko closer, Kristen closed her eyes. She called upon her goddess to grant her the power to bring forth magic. A blue glowing cage sprang into existence which surrounded Emmy, Charity, Mariko, Loki, and her. The *Bladebarrier Sanctuary* spell, a wall of magical force surrounded by an impenetrable barricade of hundreds of spinning knives, encircled them. It was only a temporary measure of protection... but Kristen had learned long ago that even the most dire situations can turn in an instant.

Jennifer had provided just enough distraction to allow Tangus to climb to his feet. Together the two forced the flying sword back. The sword countered a pivot by Jennifer and sliced under her guard to open a shallow wound across her belly. Tangus used the opportunity to advance... deflecting the sword as it tried to lunge. When it lunged a second time, Tangus was ready. He stepped across the attacking sword and brought both his scimitars down across the blade, snapping it in two. As the pieces of the enchanted sword dropped to the ground, Tangus looked at the clerics. He realized he was inside the perimeter of their magical barrier... which meant it was no longer there. One priest had his hand up and was finishing a chant. Tangus turned and knocked Jennifer to the floor just as a line of plasma fire exploded over the place they stood only moments before. Both of their backs were seared as the fire passed overhead.

The flying war-hammer was causing all kinds of difficulties for Safire. She swiftly discovered blocking a strike from the magical weapon resulted in her arm going numb. The first time Safire did this she only barely kept her grasp on her sword. It didn't take long before Safire realized she was outclassed and couldn't defeat the war-hammer on her own. It appeared to have better leverage and looked to be as heavy as she was. One misstep... one unblocked hit from the war-hammer... would leave her senseless if it didn't kill her outright. With a deftness even Tangus could admire, she danced with the war-hammer - feinting, sidestepping, ducking - every attack to buy time... time that would allow Lester to come out of his stupor. She didn't see the two undead zombies moving towards her until it was too late. They bore her down under their combined weight and began to rip through her light armor. The magical war-hammer once again began assaulting the metal shell that was protecting Lester.

Charity regained consciousness and stared into the eyes of Emmy, who still cradled Charity's head in her lap.

"Mistress!" Charity said as she rose into a sitting position.

"How do you feel?" Emmy asked as she captured a playful Loki and rubbed his belly.

"Unshackled," Charity replied with a smile. Then she looked around to see the battle that was occurring outside the *Bladebarrier Sanctuary*. "The Purge is dead, but it's evil lives on. Your family cannot defeat the clerics. They've had over three thousand years to hone their skills."

Emmy looked into Charity's deep brown eyes. "Good will prevail," she said. "As will our family."

"Our family," Charity repeated wistfully. Then she saw the disfigured, burned body of Mariko. "Oh, no!" she said as she scrambled over to the assassin.

Kristen looked at the girl. "Charity, I'm... "

"You're Kristen, my mistress' mother," Charity said as she examined Mariko. "I feel as though you're my mother as well."

"I AM your mother... at least I am from this moment on," Kristen replied. "You've been alone for so long. It's time you had a family who loves and treasures you."

Charity looked sad. "She still lives," she said, referring to Mariko.

Kristen nodded. "Only for a short time," Kristen replied. "I've made her comfortable, though. It won't be much longer."

Kristen looked away from Charity toward her husband with apprehension. She didn't like how the battle outside the *Bladebarrier Sanctuary* was progressing... and Charity's words regarding the evil clerics worried her even more. She never truly believed anything could defeat her husband, but now had serious doubts. "I need to help him," she thought.

While Kristen's attention was directed at the life and death struggle occurring outside her protective magic, Charity reached over and cupped Mariko's head in her hands. The blue glow of healing magic burst out of her and encompassed both her and Mariko.

"NO!" Kristen screamed as she reached to remove the girl's hands from Mariko's head. "She's too close to death for an empath to heal!"

But Emmy deflected Kristen's hands with unexpected strength. "Mother, she has to do this."

"Darling, it'll kill her! Does she know that?"

Emmy nodded. "Yes." Tears had formed in Emmy's eyes and ran down her cheeks.

"I don't understand," Kristen replied. "Why is she so willing to give up her life?"

Charity moaned and squirmed with the pain she was accepting from Mariko.

"Because she's an empath," Emmy replied as she took her mother's hands.

Kristen shook her head. "I don't understand."

Emmy looked at Charity. "For over three thousand years she's blamed herself for what happened to all the empaths of Elanesse. Though she understands no fault can be laid upon her, she accepts it nevertheless."

Mariko began to resume her normal appearance as the terrible burns transferred to Charity.

"She can have a normal life, Emmy," Kristen said. "She can be a little girl with a family who loves her."

"Charity knows she already has that," Emmy replied. "The moment the two of us saw each other in a dream all those days ago, she understood we were her family and we loved her. But this is something she must do for the peace of her soul."

"Emmy!" Kristen implored. She was crying herself. "You can stop this! She'll listen to you!"

Emmy bowed her head. "Perhaps... but I love her too much to take this away from her." Emmy sighed. "Her sacrifice will usher in a new age of the empath... and it's the only way to defeat the evil of the Purge."

"I thought the Purge was already dead?"

Emmy looked at the clerics who were feeling the effects of Charity's pain. Their assaults on her husband and her friends wavered as the agony of fire began to overtake them. "They're the real Purge. Charity was necessary because she allowed them to identify and know the empath... to know the essence of the empath. But during the creation of the Purge, she became strongly linked to them. Her good to their evil.

Her compassion to their indifference." Emmy paused. "The balance of the universe, mother. To the point that the clerics feel what she feels. To the point that now they can't live without her."

Kristen looked at Emmy in horror. "You mean you knew her death was necessary all along?"

"Not at first," Emmy replied. She wouldn't look at Kristen. "But eventually... yes. My part in all of this is to understand... to guide... to guarantee the transcendence of the empath race so no further harm shall befall them."

Charity moaned and collapsed. Mariko looked normal and appeared to be resting comfortably.

Emmy handed Loki over to a stunned Kristen and said, "It's time." She moved to Charity and cradled the young girl's head in her lap once again. An aura of blue light surrounded both children... though neither had been children for very long.

"Mistress," Charity whispered. Peace had come over her as Emmy blocked the pain. "Have I done well?"

Emmy bent over and kissed Charity on the forehead. "Better than any empath ever," she whispered into Charity's ear. When Emmy looked once again into Charity's eyes, they stared back blankly. Emmy closed them and hugged the girl tight, crying.

The five evil clerics screamed as one and turned to dust. An unfelt air vortex picked up the ashes and swallowed them. Suddenly, it was very still in the room.

Mariko awoke and looked around. "Where am I?" she asked.

Emmy, still hugging and rocking Charity, answered. "The Tower of the Innocent."

625

THE STRUGGLE FOR INNOCENCE

CHAPTER TWENTY-FOUR

InnisRos

The Planning and Operations general develops layered battle plans. That is to say, the battle plan is designed to include potential reactions by the adversary and developed contingencies for each, one after the other. But strict adherence to a pre-developed battle plan often leads to confusion on the battlefield if the enemy doesn't react as expected. Therein lies the importance of the Combat general. The Combat general develops battle plans in real time, compensating for the unpredictable nature of the opponent... because no enemy in any battle has ever always acted according to plan.

-From the Chronicles of Commanding-General Martin Arntuile, the Alfheim

Army General Tomas "The Screw" Singëril sat in one of many briefing rooms situated around the royal palace at Taranthi. The general was a stately, older elf and close to retirement... though he didn't know any other life. He kept his long, white hair braided in a fashion popular with many females. The general wasn't one to care about such things and endured playful comments from his friends for several reasons... he'd been doing it since before it became stylish and didn't want to change... and it hid several knives. The general never went unarmed... even in the presence of kings or queens. He was burly for an elf... probably as strong as any soldier in his Army... and maintained his strength by a strict regimen of daily exercise, diet, coffee in the morning and a glass of whiskey in the evening.

His right eye was missing, a victim of an old sword injury that started with the eye and ran down his cheek. Over the years several clerics had offered to remove the scar, but the general always politely refused. The missing eye, and the eye-patch covering it, was part of the rough and tumble persona he had developed for his soldiers.

Perhaps the one thing the general was most proud of was his nickname. His peers called him "The Screw" because his was the Army called upon whenever the enemy needed, in soldier vernacular, "the screws put to them." His warriors, however, called him that because they knew if they caught more than a passing glance of his good left eye, they were probably screwed. Still, every soldier considered it a badge of honor to be a regular member of the general's Army. He commanded an elite Army... three full corps of seventy five hundred soldiers each... that was used by InnisRos hierarchy for "special projects". At the moment, the enemy that needed "the screws put to them" was a large contingent of pirates trying to get a foothold in the Santea Archipelago to the north of InnisRos.

Sitting next to the general was his assistant, Lauran Ar-Feiniel. She was well past her youth, but still as beautiful as any elf on InnisRos. The general had kept in his personal employ for more years than he could count. He was as devoted to her as she was to him. Few knew she had been a very successful mercenary before her relationship with the general, and was his equal with a sword... and better with several other weapon types. Perhaps her greatest advantage was she had no qualms about breaking any honor system in a fight. If his life were in danger, there'd be no boundaries. She'd be as nasty as any assassin or shadow warrior.

General Singëril tapped his fingers impatiently on the table. They sailed around half the island to be here, and Mordecai didn't even have the good manners to be on time.

"Damn it, I've got a campaign to run," General Singëril said finally. Except for military planning and combat, patience had never been a strong suit for "The Screw".

Lauran laughed. It was rich, warm, and never ceased to raise his spirits and calm his intolerance. "Didn't you leave orders for your men to leave plenty of pirates for you?" she said.

"I did, didn't I." General Singëril smiled as he covered Lauran's hands on the table with his own. Since she didn't actually serve in the Army, fraternization wasn't an issue. Besides, the general put little stock in what other people thought... except for his soldiers.

The door to the briefing room opened and Nightshade, in her Amberley form, walked in and took a seat across from the two.

"Where's Mordecai?" General Singëril asked.

Nightshade put both elbows on the table, locked her hands together, and touched her lips with her two index fingers. Both the general and Lauran thought she was considering her answer... but in truth Nightshade was hesitating deliberately. She was the one in control.

"Mordecai is currently indisposed," Nightshade answered after several seconds. "I'm seeing you on his behalf."

General Singëril rose from his chair. "You're seeing... you're only his assistant!" he said angrily. "C'mon, Lauran, let's go back to our quarters and wait until Mordecai is no longer 'indisposed'."

"Take one step, General, and I'll have your head," Nightshade snapped. "Along with your pretty companion."

Nightshade and General Singëril stared at each other for several long seconds as Lauran tugged on the general's sleeve to pull him back down. Lauran had seen a flash of danger in Nightshade's eyes and had a feeling Mordecai's assistant could do as she said. General Singëril took his seat.

Nightshade nodded. "Wise, General. Very wise."

"Where's Mordecai?" General Singëril asked.

"Do you really care?" Nightshade responded. "We know where your loyalties lie, General. But Mordecai doesn't mind as long as you follow orders."

"Which are?" Lauran asked.

"So she does have a tongue!" Nightshade replied. "And here I thought she was nothing but your... whore." Nightshade smiled.

"She's baiting you, Tomas," Lauran said quickly.

But Lauran needn't have worried. General Singëril knew exactly what Nightshade was doing. "Very well, Amberley," he replied. His voice dripped with danger of his own... but he kept his composure. "But first you'll apologize to Lauran. That is, if you truly want my help."

Nightshade stared at the impudent general before nodding. "My apologies, miss," she cooed. "These are tough times and His Highness' conscience suffers greatly from the duty he must attend. Justice, General. Justice for dear Councilor Erin Mirie."

General Singëril cleared his throat. "What a load of crap," he thought. "What are Mordecai's orders," he said out loud.

"His Highness wants you to collect your Army and join the Second and Third Corps in the siege of the monastery at Calmacil Clearing," Nightshade replied. "Shall we say... oh, in a day or two?"

"A day or two? A day or two!" General Singëril bellowed. And just like that the situation began to escalate again. "Do you have any idea how many islands make up the archipelago? It'll take at least a week to disengage my army and arrange transportation."

"Oh, come now, General," Nightshade purred. "I know you have a communications crystal with you even as we speak. I also know your command and control is vastly superior to anything else the Army has to offer."

"But the navy... "

"Isn't cooperating. Yes, I know. But you have your own small fleet of barges and fishing vessels. Enough to serve your purposes." Nightshade smiled. "Any questions, General?"

Neither General Singëril nor Lauran Ar-Feiniel said anything.

"Very good," Nightshade said as she got up and pulled documents from a canvas folder she carried. "Here are your official orders," she said as she placed them on the table in front of the general. "Formalities being what they are and all. I'm sure you understand."

Nightshade left the briefing room as General Singëril and Lauran stared at the documents laying before them.

Nightshade accepted a crystal glass of wine from a waiting servant outside the briefing room. She laughed as the servant scurried away in fear. "In two days almost the entire armed forces of InnisRos will be north and concentrated around that monastery," she thought. "Even the navy is anchored up there. With the south practically undefended, father and his legions of dark elves will have no trouble with the populace. Then his dragons will tear the north apart."

Nightshade was still laughing when she entered Mordecai's apartment. He was sleeping... and the drugs she kept giving him would keep him that way until she was ready for him to witness her betrayal. "I will suck you dry, Mordecai," she said aloud to the empty foyer. "And you will feel the death of ten million cuts."

Marine Commander-General Aubrey Feynral led a force of three thousand Marines through the forest toward the monastery at Calmacil Clearing. His scouts reported monastery rangers shadowing his force... so he knew Father Goram was aware of his approach. Though he had taken all the steps he deemed necessary to protect his command against attack, he didn't try to be stealthy. He wanted the priest to understand he wasn't a threat.

A rider approached from the head of the column and stopped his horse in front of the general. He saluted. "Sir," he said, but delayed his report as he looked at the ground. His horse nickered and pawed at a loose stone.

General Feynral looked at the young elf. "Well, spit it out, lad," he commanded.

"The Queen's awaits your pleasure in a small clearing just ahead," the scout said.

"And?"

The scout swallowed hard. "She's not very happy, General."

General Feynral sighed. He was afraid this would happen. "Understood. You can return to your duties."

The scout paused.

"Is there something else?" General Feynral asked.

"Well sir, I'm not the best judge of how a Queen's supposed to look... but she looked almost... feral." The scout appeared to search for the right words to describe what he saw. "Like a warrior Queen, sir." The scout nodded vigorously. "Yes sir, like a warrior Queen. She looks ready for an awful lot of sh... "

"That'll be enough, soldier," the general interrupted. "You're dismissed."

The scout saluted and rode away.

"Weren't we ordered to stay neutral?" the general's adjutant said. It wasn't a question.

General Feynral didn't reply. "Have everyone stand down until I get back," he said as he rode forward... alone.

The adjutant was more than happy to stay behind. It sounded like 'the old man' was going to get a bit of a tongue lashing from the Queen. And only the gods knew what else. He certainly didn't want to be in the line of fire when it happened.

The queen did indeed look as described by the scout. She sat her horse as if she were the queen of the world... not someone accused of murder who's had her title stripped away. As her horse danced, the queen looked grimly at General Feynral when he entered the clearing. On both sides of the queen's horse sat two huge dire wolves. They both looked warily at the general... as if they were sizing him up for dinner. Hanging from the queen's belt was a brightly glowing sword. General Feynral recognized the mighty *Ah-HritVakha* from stories he'd heard told by Martin. Somehow the queen had brought it back to life.

Sitting on horses and slightly behind the queen were Father Goram and a couple members of his staff. General Feynral had a vague familiarity with Father Goram's people and recognized the cleric Autumn, who was also Father Goram's wife, and Cordelia, Father Goram's second-in-command. Of course the general couldn't overlook Ajax, Father Goram's own enormous dire wolf.

Last in the group waiting for the general was his own Colonel Tirion. When the two Marines made eye contact, the colonel shook his head slightly. General Feynral nodded in return, showing he understood the colonel's message... "Tread lightly with the Queen." Next to the colonel was an obvious priestess, though she was dressed in unfamiliar garb. It appeared Colonel Tirion and her were quite comfortable with each other. General Feynral dismounted and walked his horse the remaining ten yards to stand in front of Lessien. He bent a knee and lowered his head in acquiescence.

"Oh, stop being so formal, General," Lessien said as she dismounted her horse. Her party followed her lead. She bid him rise then, surprising all, suddenly hugged the large Marine brusquely.

Stepping back, Lessien frowned. "But it would seem that you, and by extension the navy, have chosen sides... but which one. Tell me, General, are you here with several thousand Marines to join me? Or do you think you can storm the monastery and do what the Army couldn't."

"My scout told me you reminded him of a warrior queen... like heroines from legends past," the general replied. "He wasn't far from being wrong."

Lessien nodded. "How can I be anything but? We're involved in civil war... the worst kind of war possible. My people die... both in defense of me and in seeking my removal." Lessien took a deep breath. "The only true enemy is Mordecai and his cohorts. Petty little people who strive only for power with no regard for the tragedy the nation must endure to satisfy these unlawful pursuits." Lessien pulled her sword from its scabbard and raised it in the air.

As General Feynral stared at the naked, gleaming blade, small spheres of lightening traveled from the hilt up to the tip, then back again. Barely perceptible cracks of thunder followed the spheres as they made their transit.

The general wasn't the only person mesmerized by *Ah-HritVakha*. Lessien also stared at the blade, lost in its message only she could hear.

"Lessien!" Nefertari said as she walked up to stand beside her sister. "Control the blade!"

Lessien shook off her communion with the sword and looked at the general. "This was my father's blade, did you know that?"

"Everyone knows that, Highness," General Feynral replied.

Lessien didn't seem to hear. "*Ah-HritVakha* has awakened something in me, General." Lessien said, suddenly focused. "I wasn't a true queen until I had learned the lessons of the sword. My father taught me wisdom, mercy, compassion, even-handedness. But the sword taught me how to be hard. I learn those lessons every day." Lessien sighed. "If I had learned them sooner, I might have recognized Mordecai for what he is and dealt with him much earlier," she lamented.

"Lessien?" Nefertari said after a few seconds of silence.

Lessien looked at her sister and smiled. "I'm fine," she said before directing her attention back to the general. "You never answered my question, General. Are you here to join me or oppose me?"

"My Marines, and Admiral Shilannia's Navy, support you, Highness."

Lessien nodded, but her voice took an ominous tone. "I had wished the Navy and Marines to remain neutral for a purpose, General. Our enemies are both here and out there." She looked to the east, towards the mainland, to emphasize her point. "Then there's those damned pirates in the archipelago. Who will keep the people of InnisRos safe while Mordecai and I settle our squabble if not the Navy and her Marines?"

"At least we don't have to worry about the pirates," Father Goram spoke for the first time. "General Singëril's handling them."

"Ah yes," the Queen said. "The one called 'The Screw'. Considering everything I've heard about General Singëril, it's my most ardent hope he doesn't show up outside the monastery gates instead."

"Doubtful, Highness," General Feynral stated. "At least not anytime soon. He's fighting on so many fronts it'll take days to disengage and move all his troops. Besides, I doubt Mordecai would be foolish enough to give such an order. The pirates are a direct threat to Tasartir on Listern Island. Without General Singëril, the city would fall in short order."

"Agreed," Father Goram said. "General, how many Marines do you have with you?"

"Three thousand, Father, and another two thousand still onboard the Navy's ships."

"Well, let's get food in their bellies," Autumn said.

Father Goram nodded. "There's much to discuss, General. And I've found planning always goes best over a hot meal."

The First Army Corps lost a little over one-quarter of its strength, approximately two thousand soldiers, in the magic-induced explosion caused by the dragon golem Golanth. The same explosion also killed all Corps sorcerers, most of the clerics, and the entire command structure. An additional five hundred soldiers were injured and being treated for their wounds. Though the remnants of the First Corps still represented a formidable force, the immediate aftermath of the explosion left them in disarray long enough for Landross' knights and infantry, though still well outnumbered, to sweep in and take control.

The queen asked the remaining soldiers of the First Corps to change allegiance from the pretend king, Mordecai, back to her. Surprisingly, most did. The approximate one thousand that didn't were given pardon upon their oath to defend the people of InnisRos and not take up arms against the monastery ever again. Though the Queen had misgivings and thought keeping the soldiers as prisoners for the duration was ill advised, Landross argued the common soldier understood honor perhaps more so than their commanders... and definitely more than their civilian leaders. Father Goram cringed at Landross' directness, but the queen didn't take offense. She just looked at him and nodded. Later she confided in Nefertari that she was heartened to hear Landross' high opinion of the ordinary soldier. She felt the same and that reaffirmation by Landross was encouraging. It also strengthened her resolve, for she understood the common soldier, who were almost exclusively drawn from the populace, and the people were one in the same. Both would suffer greatly under Mordecai's rule... and they deserved so much more.

Admiral Shilannia was ordered to resume normal naval activities. As much as the queen wanted the admiral and her ships to stay and support her against the two Army corps just hours away, her concern for the people was paramount. No island nation should ever go unguarded by its Navy.

General Feynral's three thousand Marines, along with the four thousand soldiers of the First Corps who chose to stay, stretched the monastery's resources beyond measure. The first consideration was housing. The monastery was never designed to accommodate that many people within its walls. Plans were drawn to bivouac General Feynral's Marines outside the walls and behind temporary stone breastworks. Eric the Black worked his magic to fuse the stone together for added strength. Once the fighting began, the civilians were to be herded into the tunnels and dungeons under the monastery for safety's sake... and to keep them out of the way.

Father Gorem's original intention to transport everyone off the island was now impossible. He hadn't contracted enough sailing ships from the mainland to take everyone, and the queen refused to use the navy to supplement the effort. After a lengthy and rather contentious discussion, the queen still insisted she'd not desert her people even if it was for her own safety... though she had no objections if others wished to leave. Father Goram and General Feynral relented before they raised the queen's ire even further. Both believed chances were somewhat high the number of monastery soldiers and civilians still alive by the time the transport ships arrived might make the point irrelevant.

Food and water was another serious consideration. Rangers and Ajax's dire wolf pack hunted fresh meat, barrels of water from a nearby stream were collected to supplement the water provided by the spring within monastery walls, and fruit, berries, and as many vegetables and tubers that could be found were harvested. But the additional food collected still wouldn't be enough to feed all the mouths in the monastery for more than a few weeks.

"So much for sitting out a protracted siege," Cordelia once remarked.

Landross laughed. "Hell, Cordelia, I've got enough soldiers and knights to take over the whole island!"

Cordelia smiled. But she knew Landross' empty boasting was only intended to make her feel better.

General Singëril had accomplished the impossible... which was one of his specialties. He left one of his corps behind in the archipelago to keep the pirates contained while he moved his remaining two corps south to the northern beaches of InnisRos. He approached the monastery from the northwest while the two regular Army corps marched from the southwest.

Four Army corps - thirty thousand warriors - were only hours away from their objective.

     The Second and Third Army Corps reached the southwest edge of the forest at dusk and made camp. General Singëril's two corps arrived at the northwest corner of the same forest a few hours later. In a coordinated effort, small units from both armies were dispatched into the forest with orders to reconnoiter. They were to avoid contact with monastery rangers or guards if at all possible. Except for General Singëril and his Corps commanders, who were planning the siege of the monastery, the main body of each Army settled in for the night. The following day portended to be long and bloody.

     When the full moon rose in the night sky, it was crimson. General Singëril , enjoying a nightcap of whiskey with Lauran Ar-Feiniel, cursed.

     Nightshade dragged a doped and semiconscious Mordecai off his horse and let him fall to the ground. They were deep in the forest on the western outskirts of Taranthi. Nightshade looked through the trees and into the night sky. The full moon seemed even larger than normal... and had taken on a sinister red hue. Several bats flew across the sky in front of the moon and wolves howled in the distance. Nightshade smiled. "Perfect," she said aloud.

She stepped over Mordecai and approached her horse. Opening a large pack, Nightshade withdrew the *Ak-Séregon* stone. She walked over to a spot where the light of the moon reached through the trees and touched the ground. Placing the stone in a shaft of moonlight, she backed away a few paces and sat down. Nightshade crossed her legs, raised her arms, and chanted in the demon tongue:

> *"Hail, Lord Vor Thalore!*
> *Prince of the Shadow Penumbra,*
> *Ruler of the Obsidian City.*
>
> *By the power of the crimson moon.*
> *To the spirits of dark I ask this boon.*
>
> *Open the door, open the gate.*
> *Let in your minions with venom and hate.*
>
> *Hail, Lord Vor Thalore!*
> *Prince of the Shadow Penumbra,*
> *Ruler of the Obsidian City.*
>
> *The end of good, the end of light.*
> *Corrupt this land, bring to it blight.*
>
> *Ak-Séregon stone, wise and true.*
> *Seek the Dark Elves, let them pass through.*
>
> *Hail, Lord Vor Thalore!*

Prince of the Shadow Penumbra,
Ruler of the Obsidian City."

A single pin-prick appeared in the air in front of Nightshade. Spinning and spinning, it was large enough to let an elf pass through within a few moments. But it didn't stop. It continued to grow at an enormous rate. Only darkness could be seen inside the now building-sized vortex... but Nightshade could hear the roars of creatures, mixed in with the screams of the Dark Elf invading army. They were very eager to cross over to Aster.

Nightshade stood with a smile on her face. She had a desire to whistle... something she had heard mortals do when they're happy... but she never learned how. She walked over to the prone Mordecai and looked at him. "Something's missing," she thought. Then she snapped her fingers... another thing she observed and picked up from mortals... and walked back over to her horse and rummaged through her saddlebag. She pulled out the jewel-encrusted, golden crown of InnisRos.

"Petty metal for an insignificant little tyrant," she said. "I wonder why this gave you a headache every time you put it on that weasel head of yours? Guilt? Wearing a crown never seemed to bother the Queen." Nightshade shrugged. "No matter."

Nightshade picked up Mordecai by the front of his favorite wolf fur coat. He groaned. "Good," she thought. "He's waking up." She rammed the crown down on his head hard enough to scrape skin and turned him to face the spinning vortex. As she stood behind him, she turned into her demon form and punctured

643

Mordecai's body with her talons. Not deep enough to kill... but enough so that he couldn't escape her grasp.

The vortex finished its expansion. Nightshade moved back, taking the talon-punctured Mordecai with her. He was still too much under the influence of the drug Nightshade had given him to feel pain or understand what was happening... but the stupor that guarded him from the knowledge of his short and terrifying future was rapidly fading way.

A massive figure emerged from the black of the swirling vortex. The head of a dragon - huge, horned, dark as pitch, with insidious and soulless eyes - appeared. The long, sinewy body soon filled the entire fifty foot high vortex and slinked into the world of Aster. Upon its back rode Nightshade's father, Aikanáro.

Mordecai shook the cobwebs out of his head as the last effects of the drug he was given wore off. The first thing he noticed was the pain he felt on both sides of his body. The pain was replaced by terror as he stared into the face of the fiercest dragon he'd ever seen. His first impulse was to run. But though he struggled, he only caused himself pain. Mordecai turned his head up and around to see what was preventing his escape.

"Nightshade?" he asked when he saw who was holding him. His eyes widened as it dawned upon him the only time Nightshade ever held a person as she was holding him was before she ate the soul. "What...?"

Nightshade's demon face looked into Mordecai's eye's. "I see you're beginning to comprehend the graveness of your situation."

"Release me this instant!" Mordecai screamed as he renewed his struggles, despite the pain it caused him. "I called you forth from the demon world! I'm your master!"

"Whatever gave you the idea you were powerful enough to hold me? I broke your hold weeks ago, Mordecai," Nightshade said. "I've not been your puppet... you've been mine. Now I have another surprise for you. Father!" she called.

Aikanáro dismounted the dragon and stood in front of Mordecai.

"You!" Mordecai shrieked. "But how... "

Mordecai suddenly became quiet and slumped, held up only by Nightshade's talons. She had injected him with paralyzing venom. His heart kept beating and his lungs kept working. His mind remained clear and alert, he could hear, see, and talk... but otherwise he couldn't move.

"Watch, Mordecai," Aikanáro said.

The dragon stepped aside to allow thousands of dark elves to march through the vortex in well-disciplined ranks. Above, hundreds of smaller two-legged dragons with barbed tails... wyverns... flew through and circled overhead, relieved to be away from their dark home world and in the clear, moonlit skies of Aster. An occasional full-sized dragon also fly through, barely fitting themselves through the vortex periphery.

"But what about the priestess and the empath?' Mordecai said. "Nightshade, we were going to rule the Svartalfheim and InnisRos together once the Queen was out of the way and we had those two. Even the whole of Aster and the Alfheim would've been within our sights."

Nightshade laughed.

"Did you think you could trust a demon, Mordecai?" Aikanáro asked. "Your idea was good, I'll grant you that, but not nearly ambitious enough. My daughter and I already have the Svartalfheim. We decided to take it in a different direction. The Alfheim. And we don't need the priestess or the empath to do it."

"You might have Aster, but the dark elves won't be enough to invade the Alfheim," Mordecai said. "You'll need human armies! I can make that happen. I'll be your loyal general. I'll be anything you want. Just don't eat my soul!"

Aikanáro considered, and Mordecai's eyes lit up with hope. "Perhaps you'd make a good general after all," Aikanáro said after a few moments. "You're smart... it didn't take long for you to recognize what I need for the next phase of my plan. You're devious and have a heart as depraved as any mortal I've ever known. And you're correct, I'll need an emissary."

"Yes!" Mordecai pleaded. "I'll deliver the human armies to you. You'll see!"

Aikanáro suddenly shaped-changed into an almost exact image of Mordecai. "Yes, I rather think you WILL deliver the human armies to me," he said. "It's not quite perfect, but good enough to fool most of the people. As for those it won't, they're either dead or soon will be." Aikanáro cocked his head. "Why Mordecai, I do believe you appear to be somewhat disconcerted." Aikanáro then roared with laughter... and continued to laugh as he saw the hope in Mordecai's eyes fade away and his chin drop to his chest. After a few minutes, Aikanáro, back in his demon form, raised Mordecai's head with a sharp talon. The gleam in

Mordecai's eyes had been extinguished. He nodded to his daughter as he turned away to direct his Army.

Nightshade neutralized the paralyzing venom that flowed through Mordecai's body and slowly ate him from the inside out... one nerve at a time. Mordecai's screams reverberated throughout the forest for a very long time that night... screams that could be heard in the capital city of Taranthi several miles away. Mordecai's black soul was the finest Nightshade had ever dined upon.

The corridor forced open between Aster and the Svartalfheim sent waves of magical energy into the depths of both worlds. On the Svartalfheim, these waves were welcomed and eagerly consumed by this magic poor world. On Aster, however, the waves dove deep within the earth and reverberated throughout. At an unfathomable depth beneath Elanesse the magical energy bombarded a honeycombed chamber as large as any city on the surface. Formless creatures stirred from their long slumber. The primordial guardians of Aster... the beings created by the gods to protect the newly born world until it could stand on its own... were once again needed. A small army of sylphs began their ascent to the surface.

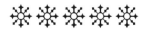

It was close to sunrise when the first contact between monastery rangers and a squad from General Singëril's Army occurred. Both sides maneuvered through the forest to gain the superior position for an attack. But the rangers knew the terrain far better than the Army. As a consequence, General Singëril's squad found themselves being led around in circles. But it didn't take long for the experienced squad leader to understand the deception taking place. He held his squad up while he reviewed the tactical situation in his head. He had the superior number of soldiers and could have made a stand... that is if the rangers wanted to challenge him. But as he saw it, he had several problems with that strategy. Most important, his orders were to stand down rather than make contact unless attacked. No one disobeyed an order from General Singëril. Secondly, he didn't know the lay of the land which put him at a distinct disadvantage. Additionally, he wasn't sure how many other ranger patrols might be close enough to reinforce those he followed. Underestimating the strength of the enemy, especially in their own territory, was tantamount to a death wish. Finally, he didn't relish fighting his own people.

One of his perimeter scouts ran up to him. "Sir, they've peeled off."

The sergeant-major looked at the young female. "Which direction?" he asked.

"To the south."

The sergeant-major shook his head. "That doesn't make any sense," he said to himself. "The monastery is east of here."

Then the sound of battle filtered through the forest trees. Each squad member heard the commotion at the same time and started to whisper amongst themselves. The sergeant-major motion for quiet with one hand.

"Maybe a klick away, sir," the nearest soldier said.

The sergeant-major nodded. "Agreed. Gear up, everyone. Let's see what's going on."

The closer they got, the more desperate the sound of the confrontation became. Screams echoed through the forest... screams intermixed with roars the likes of which the sergeant-major had never heard before.

The squad silently approached the struggle until they were close enough to see what was taking place. Several Army squads and monastery rangers were fighting against a common foe... two legged dragons. They were small for a dragon, but the sergeant-major could see they were still very formidable. They didn't use dragon's breath, but were much quicker than their larger cousins. At the tip of their tails were poison stingers, like that of a scorpion. The puncture wound from the stinger was large enough to kill... and the poison worked by causing huge rends to appear on the body, exposing the internal organs, which the creatures ate.

The sergeant-major and his squad barely hesitated before joining the fray. The force of Army soldiers and monastery rangers succeeded in driving the dragons away.

As clerics and medics treated the injured, leaders from both of the adversary groups came together to talk.

"I've never seen dragons the like of these before," the ranking ranger said. "Bigger than messenger dragons but smaller than a normal red or blue dragon."

"I know what they are," quipped another... a corporal. "But I've only seen illustrations in manuscripts. They're called wyverns."

The sergeant-major looked at one of the dead wyverns. "Where did they come from?" he asked.

The corporal shook his head. "Not from this world," he said. "According to the manuscript I read, they come from the land of the dark elves. They come from the Svartalfheim."

Everyone stared at the sergeant-major. "We have to let our commanders know," he said to the ranger leader.

The ranger leader turned as he pulled a communications crystal out of his shirt, but stopped and offered his hand to the sergeant-major. "Thank you," he said.

The sergeant-major smiled and took the offered hand without reservation. "You're not the enemy," he said before he shook his head. "We're just soldiers following orders... and we should never have been put in the position of adversaries in the first place. One thing's for sure, though. If wyverns from the Svartalfheim are here, so are the dark elves." The sergeant-major clenched his fists. "To hell with politics and power-grabs. Our duty is to the homeland regardless of what side our commanders are on. I think it's time the common soldier had a say in this mess we've gotten ourselves into. Luck go with you."

The ranger leader smiled and nodded before disappearing into the forest along with the rest of his people.

The sergeant-major took out his own communications crystal. "Let's head back to camp," he ordered as he activated the magic that would allow him to talk to General Singëril.

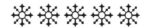

By dawn of the following day Taranthi had been completely surrounded by the dark elf Army. Two small Army outposts were overrun and obliterated before they could sound the alarm. With little hope of reinforcement since most of InnisRos' military were on the northern part of the island, the remaining Army forces surrounding the city retreated behind its massive fortifications before they could be cut off. But the great walls of Taranthi were little more than a minor inconvenience. Dark dragons appeared in the skies overhead and used their dragon breath weapons with great accuracy on selected targets... such as military barracks, catapults and ballistae, docks, and the ships in the harbor. Aikanáro and Nightshade didn't want to destroy the city or its populace... just bring them to heel. Taranthi would belong to Aikanáro... and her people his slaves.

Reports out of Taranthi became sketchy at best. It became clear to Eric the Black that magic was intercepting and draining all messages between communication crystals, resulting in an eventual blackout of the capital city. Messenger dragons were dispatched, but with no success. It would later be learned that wyverns frightened messenger dragons so much, they'd disregard their training and retreated as soon as they caught even the slightest hint of wyvern presence. But communications with the other major cities and military installations had not been affected. Within hours of the first reports of the wyverns, the naval base at Olberon, as well as the major cities of Elwing FeFalae and Tasartir on Listern Island, were warned. Runners with military escorts were sent to notify and collect as many civilians as possible from the surrounding country side, and plans were put into motion to form a civilian defense league. Veteran Army soldiers and Marines dusted off their weapons and reported for duty in droves. As many food animals - cows, sheep, goats, deer, pigs - as possible were rounded up and herded into several large caverns deep inside the North Spire Mountain Range... caverns discovered long ago and modified just this purpose.

By evening, while Aikanáro and Nightshade were consolidating their hold on Taranthi, the rest of the island had become nearly abandoned, except for the cities, bases, and other secret strongholds. The conquest of Aster began with InnisRos... but Aikanáro and Nightshade were about to learn it would be harder than they could ever have imagined.

Lessien waited on horseback in a small clearing with Father Goram, Autumn, General Feynral, Nefertari, and Maedhros Nénmacil. The creation stone floated behind the priestess and was there more for the effect his presence might cause rather than any true concern he'd be needed to protect his mistress. The Queen's two dire wolves, Findley and Razor, flanked Lessien in what was becoming their customary place at her side. Ajax sat between Father Goram and Autumn.

General Singëril and his assistant, Lauran Ar-Feiniel, with the commanders of the other two Army corps and their adjutants, faced the Queen on the opposite side of the clearing. If the general was surprised by Maedhros Nénmacil, he didn't show it. The rest of the officers, however, became very animated when they saw the creation stone. They didn't retreat, but there were whispers of the slaughter at Ashakadi.

"General...?" Lessien queried.

"Singëril, Highness. Tomas Singëril."

Lessien smiled. "Ah yes, the 'Screw'. I regret we've never met, thought I was getting regular reports about your success with the pirates in the archipelago. Impressive!"

General Singëril nodded. "Thank you."

The Queen's eyes narrowed. "I'm also impressed you made it south so quickly."

The General looked at the Lessien warily. "She's fishing for information," he thought before deciding now wasn't the time for deception. "A good general finds ways to do what's necessary. Over time I've put together a small navy of fishing vessels, small schooners, and captured pirate ships to move my army around the islands."

Lessien nodded. "And the pirates? If you're down here, who's up there keeping them bottled up? Listern Island would be a grand prize... and under our present circumstances, it might be a while before we could root them out if they take it. I'll not have my people suffer their brutality."

General Singëril went rigid. "You think I'd leave..." he said before Lauran cautioned him with a hand on his sleeve. After a deep breath, he said, "I've garrisoned Listern Island and left part of my army to keep the pirates attention on other things. They're contained for now, though I can't seem to deliver the knockout blow. There's far too many places in the archipelago to hide."

Lessien studied the general and his assistant, Lauran Ar-Feiniel. By her clothes Lessien could tell she wasn't part of the Army. She watched as they worked together, acting as perfect compliments to each other... like bookends. They'd been doing this for so long it seemed like they were communicating at some subconscious level... like Father Goram and Autumn. Lessien knew their relationship was by far more than professional. "Did you know thousands of years ago the northern half of InnisRos had a volcano on it?" she said. "It exploded and the archipelago, with its thousands of caves and secret niches, are what's left."

"Of course I do, Highness!" General Singëril snapped back with a tinge of impatience in his voice.

Lessien didn't let on that the slight bothered her... and she didn't hold it against the general. She'd heard gruffness was one of his distinctive characteristics. "Mordecai would've had a lesser soldier punished for that," she thought. "Regardless of rank."

Lessien jumped off her warhorse in a smooth, practiced move. The rest of her party followed suit. General Singëril nodded at his people as he dismounted.

"General," Lessien said, "I know why you've brought your Army here. But can we forego any discussion of my guilt or innocence for another time? There's an even greater threat to the people of InnisRos which requires our immediate... and cooperative... attention. Indeed, if our hunch is correct, the whole world of Aster may be in serious jeopardy."

"The wyverns," General Singëril said. "I'm told they're from the Svartalfheim."

Lessien nodded.

General Singëril continued. "Which begs the question... how did they get here?"

"You already know the answer to that," Lessien said.

General Singëril nodded. "I suspect I do. A corridor between Aster and the Svartalfheim has been opened."

"That's not easily done, General," Lessien stated. "Nor is it accidentally done. Someone had to use the *Ak-Séregon* stone."

General Singëril waited.

"Either Mordecai was directly responsible or played a hand in it... which makes him a traitor. Or perhaps it happened without his knowledge. That makes him either incompetent or dead." Lessien paused. "Either way, General, I don't think he's the one whose orders you should be following."

Lauran Ar-Feiniel spoke for the first time. "The Queen's right, Tomas. We should hear what she has to say before deciding which road to travel. But consider... we've both been questioning Mordecai's loyalty to her and InnisRos for some time now. We've also heard the rumors in Taranthi that the evidence for the Queen's arrest was either planted or contrived to lead the investigation to her. Not many people outside the palace believe it."

General Singëril looked at his love and nodded. "All right, Your Highness. I'm listening. But know that I don't take my orders lightly."

"I wouldn't have it any other way," Lessien responded. "With your permission, I'd like my sister to continue the narrative."

As Nefertari and Maedhros Nénmacil moved to stand by Lessien, General Singëril said, "Your sister?"

Lessien nodded. "I present StarSinger Nefertari Arntuile, High Priestess to the ancient Elder Goddess Sehanine StarEagle. With her is the creation stone named Maedhros Nénmacil."

One of General Singëril's commanders, a young colonel, said, "I've never heard of that goddess."

"Her followers left this world before recorded time," Maedhros Nénmacil rumbled in a grating voice. Everyone, including the general, lurched back in surprise, which caused Maedhros Nénmacil to laugh. "I'm pleased to meet you."

"Creation stones are rare in the universe, General," Nefertari said. "And almost as old. My friend here is one of but a dozen. And I can assure you, he's quite safe to be around if you don't threaten him... or me. Isn't that right, my friend."

"You are most correct, StarSinger," Maedhros Nénmacil replied with enthusiasm. But there was a grave seriousness in his eyes. "General, you'll find me as tame as a kitten... or as wild as a saber cat."

The general recovered quickly, but was worried and on guard nevertheless. What happened at Ashakadi, if true, spoke volumes to how dangerous this seemingly affable creature can be. He nodded at the creation stone before returning his attention to Nefertari. "StarSinger Nefertari, tell me how you know, and what you know, about the wyverns?"

"General, I was raised in the Alfheim," Nefertari said.

"Point in fact, General, she was raised to be the Alfheim's queen," Lessien added.

General Singëril looked at his queen incredulously.

Nefertari nodded. "That's a story for another time, General. The Alfheim's been invaded many times by the dark elves of the Svartalfheim, though never in my lifetime." Nefertari looked at General Singëril. "Believe me when I tell you I understand their tactics. Hundreds of wyverns are always sent ahead of the army to cause whatever mischief they can. They scare the populace and cause panic. They attack perimeter outposts to cut early warning. They kill anyone caring for livestock and take control of herd animals to feed the invading army. Obviously, since they fly, walls are ineffective. But General, the wyverns represent only the first phase of the Dark Elf invasion. They're the shock troops. Next, though not as many in number, full-sized spirit dragons follow. Don't let the name fool you... these dragons have plenty of substance. Their breath will melt flesh off of bone. With the dragons come the hydra... huge beasts with five heads, each spitting bolts of crackling energy. Nothing can withstand their assault. Only magic will bring them down." Nefertari paused and her voice became quiet as she spoke. "Finally the army arrives. Thousands upon thousands of dark elves hungry for conquest."

General Singëril considered Nefertari's words. He was a seasoned warrior, so he remained calm as Nefertari described an almost impossible force of conquest. But there were answers to every problem. One just had to know where... and how... to look "So what does the Alfheim do to stop them?"

Nefertari leaned against her staff as if she were tired. Maedhros Nénmacil started to move forward, but she waved him away. "My people..." Nefertari voice broke. "Sorry. For all the eagerness the Elves of Dark show each time they invade, the Elves of Light are just as motivated... more so... to defend the homeland. Even the civilians. We... they... never let the numbers diminish their resolve. But perhaps the greatest advantage the Elves of Light have is their ability to adjust tactics... and magic. Dark elves, though always having numerical superiority, have yet to develop a general to make sense of it all. In other words, they're somewhat out of their element when it comes to organized warfare. It's more like a disorganized mob."

"But they've apparently surrounded the capital," General Singëril remarked. "That seems like a sensible tactic to me."

"It does indeed, General," Lessien answered.

"That's why we think they finally have a general to lead them," Nefertari said. "And one other thing.

Whenever they attacked the Alfheim, they never had magic support. This was because they always foolishly used up their wizards to open a corridor between the two worlds. But in this instance they've had help. Somehow they got their hands on the *Ak-Séregon* stone. There can't be any other explanation. So they'll have their complete complement of wizards with them." Nefertari shook her head. "They not only have us out-manned... but also out-magicked."

Lessien looked at General Singëril. "If everything my sister has said is true, and I have no reason whatsoever to think otherwise, we can't stop the invasion. And with Taranthi already lost..." Lessien looked at Nefertari who nodded. "General, we need the human armies."

General Singëril shook his head. "The humans have no love for us. Besides, they're an ocean away. That will take time... time to sail over there, time to negotiate alliances, and time to get back. We'll be overrun long before the humans can make a difference. Assuming, of course, they decide to come at all."

Lessien put a hand on the general's sleeve. "Which is why I need you to fight the dark elf army for as long as you can. To give us the time we need. It's not just InnisRos we defend, but all of Aster as well. General Singëril, I'd like you to be my commander-in-chief."

Lauran Ar-Feiniel watched the exchange between Tomas, the Queen, and the Queen's sister. There was more the Queen wished to say to Tomas. "Your Highness?" Lauran prompted. "Was there something else?"

Lessien frowned at the older elf. She realized this one saw what the general apparently didn't. "Perceptive, madam," she said. "General Singëril, will you give me your sword?"

General Singëril blinked.

"Do it, Tomas," Lauran coaxed. Turning to the rest of the commanders and adjutants, she motioned for them to do the same. Each was hesitant, however, preferring to take their lead from the general.

General Singëril studied Lessien. Then it suddenly became very simple for him. He'd never follow a creature such as Mordecai. Not truly. Even if the Queen were guilty of murder, which General Singëril didn't believe, she was by far the best choice for InnisRos. He knelt, detached his scabbard and sword, and offered the sword hilt to Lessien. She removed the sword from the scabbard and placed the tip lightly on his chest, next to his heart. "Accepted," she said as she pulled the sword away and slammed it home back into its scabbard. Each commander standing behind the general knelt with sword and scabbard in hand and pulled their swords out just far enough so Lessien could see the blades. She nodded to them. Several swords slammed back into their scabbards as Lessien bid the general and his senior officers to rise.

"General Singëril, though reluctant at first, I've decided to take Father Goram's advice and leave the island. I must travel to the mainland to garner human allies," Lessien said. "Only I can make these alliances. In my place I leave my sister, Nefertari, to act as my regent. You'll follow her orders as you would mine."

The general nodded. "And if we should ever get our hands on Mordecai?"

Lessien thought upon it. Suddenly, words from her father came back to her:

"King Argonne Quarion of the Alfheim, having proof that his own brothers had betrayed him and plotted to have him murdered, personally executed both by taking their heads with his royal sword... Ah-RahnVakha. As sovereign, you must be prepared to administer any sentence of death to a royal or a traitor. Anything less would be an abdication of your duty ."

"Bring him to me, General." Lessien said grimly as she gripped the hilt of *Ah-HritVakha*. "Alive, if possible."

The hydra, a five-headed dragon, flew up the eastern coast of InnisRos. She was flanked by two spirit dragons. A third spirit dragon trailed behind. Though huge in their own right, the hydra's escorts were only half her size.

Below them two small sailing vessels made their way south towards the dark elf army which was laying siege to Taranthi. One of her attending travel mates glided down and destroyed them with its breath weapon... beams of invisible energy which melted flesh and charred wood without flame. The female hydra didn't even bother to look back or slow her pace. She had much larger prey to hunt and destroy.

Admiral Tári Shilannia came up from her stateroom to stand on the quarterdeck of her flagship, the *Felicidade*. She'd just had a long conversation with her Marine General Feynral via a communications crystal. As hard as it was to believe, it appeared InnisRos was being invaded by the dark elves from the Svartalfheim and all communication with Taranthi lost. It hadn't been determined if Mordecai was behind this treachery. But no matter... the Queen was now in complete command and Mordecai was the one being hunted. That is, if he was still alive.

Besides the invasion, other considerations weighed heavily upon her. She looked out over the bay and at the ships deployed there by her orders. There was talk of dragons accompanying the invading army. Ships didn't have many defenses against dragons... and plenty of reasons to fear them. She needed to get them to safe harbor, or she'd lose the Navy. But before she could do that she had to have the remaining two thousand Marines put ashore. Finally, she received a communication from the Queen. In it, the Queen outlined her desire to set sail for the mainland to ask the humans for help. The Queen would need a fast ship and escorts that could keep up. The thought of humans coming to the rescue of InnisRos made the admiral's teeth grind together in anger... but it was also very sobering. If the humans were needed, it could only mean InnisRos couldn't stand on its own.

Admiral Shilannia turned to her adjutant. "Commander, please send the following. I want the fast frigates Viper, A'aneas, and Chryseos prepared to accept the Queen and her retinue, such as it is. They're to set sail for the mainland as soon as the Queen is aboard."

"Very well, madam."

"Let's get the rest of our Marines moved to the shore. They're to reinforce the monastery at Calmacil Clearing." Admiral Shilannia looked at the commander. "They're on the troop carriers Saint Nezerine, Charon, and Erinyes?"

Her adjutant nodded. "The Charon and Erinyes are currently empty. Their Marine compliment are already at the monastery with General Feynral."

Tári Shilannia looked over the fleet. "Slow troop ships won't do us much good without troops to transport. Have the Saint Nezerine's captain run her aground. It'll make unloading faster. The captain and his crew are to go with the Marines to Calmacil Clearing."

"Yes, ma'am."

The Admiral paused to consider. "Leave the Charon and Erinyes anchored... they're not fast enough to stay with the fleet, but perhaps can serve as decoys. Have their crews transferred to other ships. "

"Aye."

"Provide a small force... let's say three frigates... to cover the disembarkation of the Marines," Admiral Shilannia said as she looked at the sun. "I wish you hadn't come up so early," she whispered. The sun's steady presence, normally a thing of comfort and great beauty, mocked her this morning. She sighed and

663

turned her attention back to her adjutant. "I want everyone else to weigh anchor and prepare to make a run out to sea. That'll be all."

The commander saluted and hurried away. Within a few seconds, signalmen were sending her orders to the fleet.

Admiral Shilannia left the quarterdeck and went down to the wheelhouse where the "Felicity's" captain stood behind the great rudder wheel, looking at charts lying on a wooden block table.

"Good morning, Admiral," the captain said as he nodded.

The admiral smiled and accepted a mug of coffee from an orderly standing nearby. "Anything interesting in those charts you're constantly studying?"

Felicity's captain smiled. "You can't..."

"Overstudy charts." Admiral Shilannia laughed. "I know... I was taught the same lesson." Admiral Shilannia paused before saying wistfully. "It seems so long ago."

"Admiral?"

Admiral Shilannia shook her head... clearing it of memories long since past. "Sorry. Captain, we need to scatter the fleet. I'm thinking some up in the archipelago... we already know about a few caves that will accommodate large sailing vessels."

The captain nodded.

"Get the slower fleet vessels up there. The rest will set sail for the Isile Silimaure... including the Felicity."

"The 'Magnificent Resolve', ma'am?" The captain looked confused. "We can't support the homeland from out there."

"I know, but we're sitting ducks for dragons in these shallows off the island," Admiral Shilannia replied. "We need open water to maneuver. InnisRos doesn't benefit if we're on the bottom of the sea."

"I understand, but..." The captain was interrupted by the lookout on the mainmast.

"Dragons astern on the port side!"

Both the admiral and the captain rushed up to the quarterdeck and used their field glasses to look in the direction the lookout was pointing. Four dragons, one with five heads, were just coming into view as they swung around and between the island and the base of The Arrow.

Admiral Shilannia collapsed her field glass. "We're too late," she whispered. She turned to the captain. "Signal all ships... 'Make sail and scatter. Godspeed.'"

The captain nodded and looked at the signalman who was already attaching flags to be hoisted. To his Officer of the Deck, he ordered, "Make sail and arm the ballistas! Set course to north by northeast!"

As the captain continued to give commands, Admiral Shilannia listened and mentally concurred with each. Satisfied all was in order, she looked back at the fast approaching dragons and shook her head. "We're too late."

THE STRUGGLE FOR INNOCENCE

EPILOGUE

Elanesse

The sojourn away from peace frequently takes place on well-traveled pathways.

-Book of the Unveiled

Kyleigh Angelus-Custos, Queen of the Alfheim, wandered the halls of her palace compound. It was late, well past the setting of the moon... but she couldn't sleep. Several hours earlier she had learned the *Ak-Séregon Stone* had been reactivated on Aster. That the power of the stone had gone missing for several days was troublesome enough. Now it was functioning once again... but the corridor it opened was not back to the Alfheim, as expected. Instead, it went to the Svartalfheim. "I just can't imagine Aster would make such a mistake," she thought, "or take the risk. This does not bode well... for Aster or the Alfheim."

      Kyleigh found herself in front of the apartment door of her first councilor, Robert Gareathe. It was common for her to seek his point of view whenever she had a vexing problem to solve. His guidance... and unbroken support... was the one thing she could always count upon. He was the one person above all others to whom she could express her true feelings... her misgivings... her fears. In some respects she loved him. But her love for her people... for the Alfheim... transcended all other considerations, including her own personal happiness. She rapped on his door lightly.

"Robert, are you awake?" she whispered. She didn't want to cause a disturbance so early in the morning. She heard movement from the other side and the door opened a few moments later. Robert invited her in with a wave of his hand.

"You couldn't sleep either, I see," Kyleigh said.

Robert Gareathe grunted. "Sleep! What's that?" he said as he pointed to a wheeled tray trolley. A silver coffee pot with several mugs sat on top. "I've just had it delivered not five minutes ago, so it should be plenty hot."

Robert, who had already poured his mug, sat down in a well worn padded chair. He didn't bother to serve her, knowing she'd only object and do it herself. When the two of them were alone together, they usually set aside all formality. The only reminder that Kyleigh was the queen was her sword, *Ah-RahnVakha*, which always rested in its scabbard on her side.

Kyleigh sat in another chair, similar to Robert's except not as worn, and blew on her coffee before she took a sip. "So, what do you think?" she asked Robert.

Robert snorted. "The fools opened a corridor to the Svartalfheim," he said derisively. "What other possible explanation could there be?"

Kyleigh shook her head. "Lessien wouldn't be so reckless. There has to be another reason."

"Okay," Robert said, "let's work off that assumption. But Kyleigh, only Lessien, or one or more of her most trusted advisors, can have the *Ak-Séregon Stone* triggered. If she had legitimate reasons to connect with the Svartalfheim, surely she'd have said gotten a message to you. She knows from Martin how dangerous the dark elves are. But the stone's been mysteriously quiet for several days until now, so there's no way to know. Perhaps she's gone rogue... or power mad."

"No, I don't think that's the case," Kyleigh said. "If she's anything like her father, she'd never jeopardize her people like that. Nor would she seek more power. I don't believe that's in her nature. Besides, InnisRos doesn't have the resources to challenge the Svartalfheim."

"Maybe she's made an alliance... or some other type of accommodation." Robert said. "People change, Kyleigh."

"Not Lessien."

"How do you know?" Robert countered. "You haven't seen her since she crossed over with her father. And then she was just a child."

"We've communicated through the corridor," Kyleigh countered. "On many occasions. You know that."

Robert nodded. "But Kyleigh, you've never looked into her eyes," he said. "Only through them can you read her soul."

"But I knew Martin!" the queen exclaimed. "I knew him very well."

Robert looked at Kyleigh.

"Oh stop," Kyleigh said. "It wasn't like that. He was too much in love with Denairis to betray her like that. And me? Well, let's just leave it. But we both had a shared interest... our love for our king and our homeland. Over the decades in Argonne's service, we became very close friends. It hurt deeply when Martin decided to leave the Alfheim for InnisRos."

Robert nodded. "Very well. If we give Lessien the benefit of the doubt, then who did? And why?"

Kyleigh shrugged. "Maybe the dark elves found a way to trigger the *Ak-Séregon Stone* from the Svertalheim."

"That doesn't explain why it went dark. And why would they go to Aster?" Robert asked. "We're their eternal enemy. I mean, if they can trigger the *Ak-Séregon* stone, they might be able to trigger the *Ak-Samarië Shard*."

"They've never needed the *Ak-Samarië Shard* to invade before," Kyleigh replied.

Robert took a sip of coffee before answering. "Which has always been their downfall," he said. "They use their sorcerers to open a corridor... but that has disastrous consequences. Without the added power of the *Ak-Samarië Shard*, the dark elf sorcerers are drained of their wizardry. With no sorcerers to support the invasions, the combined dark elf army, though vastly superior, doesn't stand a chance against us. That's why our sorcerers keep the shard so well protected."

Kyleigh stood and walked over to a glass-covered window. The sky was brightening and the magic of this world could be seen as multi-colored waves swimming through the atmosphere above. "This is why the dark elves covet this world so," she thought. "For the strong magic that inhabits its very essence. The earth, the sky, the trees, the water, every blade of grass... us." Kyleigh turned to Robert. "All right then... someone on Aster activated the *Ak-Séregon* stone. But I refuse to believe it was Lessien. Since she'd know if the stone were stolen and would have communicated that to me, it means she's either been removed from power or dead."

"That sounds like a reasonable conclusion," Robert replied as he got up and went over to stand next to Kyleigh.

"Recommendations?" Kyleigh said without looking at her First Councilor.

"Shut down the *Ak-Samarië Shard* and put the army on alert."

Kyleigh looked over at Robert. "You can't just shut down the shard."

"I know," Robert responded.

"You're advocating I have the shard destroyed?" Kyleigh said with surprise. "But that means..."

"It means cutting our link with Aster. Yes, that's what I'm suggesting." Robert looked at his queen. "If the dark elves invade us WITH their sorcerers, the outcome becomes much more problematic. Hell, Kyleigh, the link should never have been created in the first place. We should've left Aster alone. It's no place for an elf."

"But we did, Robert, and now they're paying the price. Don't we owe Aster some recompense?"

Robert shook his head. "Not at the expense of the Alfheim."

Kyleigh gave her half-finished mug of coffee to Robert, turned, and walked to the door of his apartment. As she grabbed the door knob, she stopped and looked over her shoulder. "Put the army on alert until further notice," she said. "I want a meeting with the military high command to go over options. Make it around noon... and the heavens help any general or admiral who's late. Convene the Council for three o'clock.

Finally, I want to see the master sorcerers of the Twelve Houses as well as all the high priests. Tell them they're cordially invited to dinner with their liege at six o'clock. Make sure they each understand I won't be very cordial if they don't show up."

Robert nodded. "Very well," he said. "And the shard?"

Kyleigh sighed. "I'll think upon it," she said before she opened the door and left.

Even though the dire threat the Purge represented had been eliminated, the return to the Tree of Golden Radiance was a somber affair. Lester was in the lead as he carried Charity's cloak-draped body. Though she was carefully shrouded below the city, Emmy insisted the dead child's face remain uncovered. Emmy said Charity deserved to bear witness to the peace her sacrifice had brought to the world. No one argued the sentiment. Charity looked to be at peace. All signs of the gut-wrenching pain the empath had endured before she died was no longer evident.

Emmy and Mariko walked on either side of Lester. Mariko couldn't contain her tears. The former assassin displayed emotions that wouldn't have been possible in her earlier life. On this journey, and with Emmy's guidance, she had undergone a startling metamorphosis. She was still one of the deadliest beings to walk Aster... but now her skills would now be used in the service of empaths... and Emmy

Tangus and Kristen were concerned about the impact Charity's loss would have on their little girl... but they needn't have worried. Emmy was handling it well. While she was saddened by the death of Charity, she told Kristen she was very proud of the empath and her willingness to sacrifice herself for another. Although Charity had seen it as a means to soothe her conscience... to expunge responsibility for her part in creating the Purge... it still took great courage. But it was her courage, and her dedication to the concept that good must prevail over evil regardless of the price, that told the real story. "She was so brave, mother!" Emmy had told Kristen. "But perhaps more importantly, in the end, she exposed the true soul of the empath for all the world to see."

The bond shared between Kristen and Emmy never returned. Kristen knew one day her daughter wouldn't need the bond to protect her against raw emotions such as hate, anger, or envy... but she wasn't prepared for the link to be broken so soon, or the emptiness it left. She and Tangus quietly discussed it on the way back to the Tree of Golden Radiance. Though Kristen was still unsettled, it was Tangus' pragmatic view of what had happened over the course of the last few weeks that convinced Kristen to let it be. It was obvious to Tangus that the young empath had experienced so much since her awakening she was forced to develop the fortitude necessary to function independently. Tangus had taken it even one step further. In Emmy he saw a strength of character that allowed her to not only survive, but to thrive. Over and over Emmy proved she had the ability to make decisions... difficult decisions such as allowing Charity to die for Mariko. "My love," Tangus had said. "She's transcended the bond. It doesn't mean she is not our daughter or she no longer needs our love. It only means she's reaching her full potential... wherever that leads. Another way to look at it... the last empath could also be the first empath. What better start to a new age?"

The Tree of Golden Radiance was not alone. Standing about fifty feet away was another huge tree, larger than its companion. Its green-bronze leaves waved in the light wind, and its massive branches grew around branches of the Tree of Golden Radiance... reinforcing and protecting the smaller tree... a lover's embrace. Of Elrond, there was no sign. The horses were safe, calmly grazing on the rich, green carpet of grass beneath the two trees and eating the occasional fruit that had dropped to the ground. They looked up from their meal as their masters approached, but other than snickering a welcome, continued to feast.

Romulus, with his new mate Sakkara and her son, Kavik, were also waiting for them when they arrived. Kavik and Loki, after a few indecisive moments, decided they would be great friends and at once began to play. Loki, still adjusting to the loss of one leg, was clumsy... but Kavik didn't seem to mind and would patiently wait while Loki picked himself up after a stumble. It soon became clear that the disability would not slow Loki down for long.

"Over here!" Lester called from a short distance away. While the others were either watching Loki and Kavik play or inspecting the new tree, he had lain the body of Charity next to a huge hollowed log.

Behind the log was a small campsite. A fire pit had been dug and lined with rocks and Elrond's sleeping blankets lay between it and the log. All his other equipment was there... backpack, cloak, weapons, and his magical items such as spellbook, staves, wands, potions, and scrolls. Lester gently put Charity down and held up several bags of gold and silver coins.

"Friend Tangus," Lester said. "Elrond would never leave behind magic or money. At least, not willingly."

Tangus, once his view of the campsite was no longer blocked by the log, shook his head. "No, Lester, he wouldn't. He'd die first."

"Elrond has changed much since we started our journey," Emmy said.

Lester nodded. "Yes, Miss Emmy, you're certainly correct about that. We've all been changed."

"Honey, do you know what's happened here?" Kristen asked.

Emmy looked at her mother, then at the new tree, and smiled. "He's found a higher purpose."

Everyone looked from Emmy to the tree.

"Are you saying..." Safire said before being interrupted.

"That's Elrond," Mariko said as she looked at the tree with the others.

"How do you know?" Safire asked.

Mariko shrugged. "It's just a feeling based upon the evidence. Besides, considering everything we've seen... we've endured... over the last few weeks, would it be so extraordinary?"

No one answered, but all were shaking their heads.

Emmy walked up to the tree and opened her arms as far around the trunk as she could, hugging it close. She then closed her eyes and placed her ear on the rough bark. "You have done well, my friend," she whispered.

Turning to face the stare of the others, Emmy smiled. "You're correct, my child," she said to Mariko. "This is Elrond, or perhaps I should say, 'Elendrel - Telperiën'... the 'Tree of the Eternal Sentinel'. He says he knows about Max. In fact, it was the spirit of Max that showed him the way... a way made necessary to fend off a direct attack against Elanesse made by the Purge. He congratulates you on your victory and wishes you peace and joy within his forest."

"His forest?" Tangus said.

In response to his query, the branches of small trees and bushes outside the joint canopy of Elrond and Elanesse moved into irregular shapes without the help of the wind. Tangus watched in astonishment as the branches spelled out the words, 'Yes! Mine and Elanesse's. Don't try to take it away!'

After a few brief, startled moments, both Tangus and Lester laughed. "One more thing Elrond claims is his," Lester said, doubled over and laughing harder than ever.

"And... and... the one thing he swore he wouldn't ever have," Tangus replied. He was laughing so hard tears rolled down his cheeks. "A wife."

Both warriors were now on their knees.

Lester, in between guffaws, said, "He... he... he vowed he'd never ..."

"... settle down and plant roots in one place!" Tangus snorted.

The sylphs Azriel-Ahlasim and Elbedreth-Ahlasim were in the tunnels below the Crystal Gardens. The magic of the crystals had healed each... but both were reluctant to leave and go back to their home in the corridors and caverns below the city of Elanesse. Instead, they used the time to explore each other's thoughts, feelings, and experiences. At one point Azriel-Ahlasim asked about the change that had made him a sylph. Elbedreth-Ahlasim told him only that it was meant to be... but when pressed, she admitted she didn't know. She then gently scolded him for seeking answers to questions about something that made them both complete. "And if you should find your answers?" she asked. "Let it lie, my love. Not all revelations are yours for the taking. Not all revelations are necessary to live the life given you." Nevertheless, Azriel-Ahlasim was determined to one day figure it out.

As each day passed, Azriel-Ahlasim became more and more comfortable with his new state of being. So much so that after a few days he no longer thought about the days when he was simply Azriel the dwarf... though he'd never forget the people he loved in that earlier life.

Though the way Azriel-Ahlasim thought... the way he viewed life... and death... had changed significantly, his resolve to guard and protect innocents remained strong. The young empath, Emmy, had forced him to realize his true calling, regardless of his incarnation. Azriel-Ahlasim decided the caverns and tunnels below Elanesse would be his to guard. No enemy will be allowed to come for his friends from that direction. To that end he and Elbedreth-Ahlasim constantly honed their fighting skills. Azriel-Ahlasim trained with his great magical battleaxe and steel quarterstaff, while Elbedreth-Ahlasim used her multitude of razor-sharp blades. When they practiced, they learned to work together. Battle to them became a ballet of sorts... their movements smooth and intimate. When they fought, they became one being... one being to match the lovers they had become.

Azriel-Ahlasim and his love were in the midst of a conversation regarding the significance of the moon's influence over elf and human behavior. Elbedreth-Ahlasim was fascinated about every aspect of surface life and couldn't get enough of the comments and observations Azriel-Ahlasim made when he was a dwarf. She did, however, have reservations regarding his claim that dwarves would one day be the dominant race... that is if they ever came out of their mines. Suddenly, something happened to stop short the conversation.

"Lassie! What was that?" Azriel-Ahlasim asked.

Elbedreth-Ahlasim paused before answering. She had also felt the disturbance.

"Great magic," she said. "The kind that happens only rarely. This cannot be good."

"A doorway between worlds?" Azriel-Ahlasim asked. "That'll sometimes occur between InnisRos and the Alfheim... though it's my understanding not as often as before. It's very powerful magic. Relic magic. Relics can only be made by the gods."

Elbedreth-Ahlasim nodded. "I've felt that magic before and this is similar, except much more powerful. Any doorway opened by this much magic would have to be huge."

"Perhaps large enough to let through an army?"

"Yes," Elbedreth-Ahlasim said. "But there's something different about the feel of this magic."

"In what way, lassie?" Azriel-Ahlasim asked.

Elbedreth-Ahlasim looked at her companion. "A doorway has been opened to another world... a place much more sinister than the other place you mentioned."

"The Alfheim?"

"Yes," Elbedreth-Ahlasim replied. "I feel a great threat coming from the magic."

Azriel-Ahlasim nodded. "I don't understand... but I feel it as well."

"You're responding to your nature as a sylph." Elbedreth-Ahlasim looked anxious.

Azriel-Ahlasim reached out to comfort Elbedreth-Ahlasim. "What's wrong?"

"This will awaken my people. It will free them."

"Lassie, I thought we were the only..."

Elbedreth-Ahlasim stared at the stone floor. "There are a number of things I've not told you, Azriel-Ahlasim, because I never believed something like this would ever happen. It's a long story... a story that goes back to the very creation of this world. I'll explain it to you along the way."

"We're going somewhere?" Azriel-Ahlasim asked.

"Far below," Elbedreth-Ahlasim answered. "To intercept my people."

"And if we don't?"Azriel-Ahlasim queried.

Elbedreth-Ahlasim sighed. "My people are the oldest beings to have ever lived on Aster. Created by the elder gods, they had one purpose and one purpose only... guard the world against any and all who would come to take it. The elder gods don't view time as we do... so Aster remained empty for eons. Long enough for my people to get comfortable with a world of their own. They guarded, and prospered, until the elder gods got around to populating Aster with humans, dwarves, giants, centaurs, and all the other races. The elves came later... but not by the hand of the elder gods. The sylph, no longer necessary on the view of the elder gods, were pushed out, betrayed, and imprisoned. Imprisoned for a very long time. They'll be furious."

Azriel-Ahlasim looked at Elbedreth-Ahlasim. "Angry at who?"

"Everyone. My people consider all the races of Aster to be their enemy... contagions that must be eliminated so they can once again have the world for themselves." Elbedreth-Ahlasim replied. "They'll not distinguish between good and evil." Elbedreth-Ahlasim stared at an unusually silent Azriel-Ahlasim. "We must convince them otherwise."

Azriel-Ahlasim looked at his mate. For the briefest of moments his face took on the appearance of the dwarf he used to be. "Aye, lassie. I couldn't have said it better."

Lord Ternborg, King of the Draugen Pesta and father of the Imperial Princess, Daphnia, waited atop a small hill with a company of riders from the First Phalanx, his daunting personal bodyguard. The horses he and his men sat upon were giants of their kind... thirty-five hands tall at the shoulder. They were jet black, snorted flames, and their hooves, as they danced around, created sparks whenever they hit the stones beneath their feet. In the valley behind the waiting contingent of warriors was an enormous army... enormous, but still only half the Draugen Pesta's total strength. The encampment stretched throughout the valley and overflowed up both sides of the hills surrounding it. The acrid smoke of its campfires filled the air.

There was little to distinguish Lord Ternborg from his men except for the light blue cloak he wore... which stood out in a remarkable contrast against the burgundy-trimmed black cloaks of his guard. His armor was no more functional or decorated. Nor was it any less battle-damaged. At twelve feet, the riders were giants. Lord Ternborg, however, was smaller by a foot. The Draugen Pesta celebrated battle... but theirs was also a very sophisticated society. They understood size and strength didn't always make for the best leaders. Their king or queen had to be smart, cunning, and above all else have the best interests of the kingdom at heart. Any abuse of power always resulted in removal... by efficient, yet brutal, means. Lord Ternborg had ruled with his people's approval and consent for over a century.

For the first time in its history, the king of Draugen Pesta was going to lead his armies against another land without having been attacked first. Lord Ternborg wasn't comfortable with the deal he had to make. But his precious daughter had been whisked away... kidnapped by an evil he couldn't comprehend... an evil he'd crush if he ever got the chance. He and his people would move the heavens and the earth to get her back. But for now, he must be patient.

The loss of the princess would by itself justify his actions. But there was also the promise of land. Lord Ternborg was a pragmatist. His people needed more room. Moving east against Draugen Pesta's hereditary enemy, the Hyrokkin, would've been much too dangerous. The best Draugen Pesta could ever hope to achieve against this kingdom was a stalemate... and sometimes an unsteady truce. Lord Ternborg realized going west to expand Draugen Pesta was his only choice.

A small, brilliant white light appeared in front of the waiting warriors and expanded into a swirling eddy of energy and magic. Through this doorway between space and time stepped the black form of Nightshade. She had discarded her mortal Amberley form now that the invasion of InnisRos had begun. She no longer cared about the charade she had been forced to play. Moving past the mounted warriors, she looked at the army waiting in the valley. Turning, she went back to stand in front of Lord Ternborg.

"Impressive!" she said. "Especially since you've only had two days to prepare."

"I'm so glad you approve," Lord Ternborg said through tight lips.

"Sarcasm, Ternborg?"

Lord Ternborg said nothing as he stared at the demon.

Nightshade shook her head. "No matter. As long as you do your part you'll get your daughter back... and the land you so desire to expand your empire."

"You needn't worry about my warriors, Nightshade," Lord Ternborg said with thinly veiled contempt. "We'll do our part."

Nightshade was getting bored with Lord Ternborg's attitude. "If this is so hard for you, perhaps someone else would be better suited to serve your people."

"That's always their choice," Lord Ternborg replied. "But it's a choice only they will make, Nightshade. You may understand the politics of InnisRos, but you're far from knowing what motivates the people of Draugen Pesta. Your invasion of the elven island would be tenuous at best if I were to throw the weight of my army behind them. And if it wasn't for my daughter, I might've done just that. If our legends are correct, the dark elves are scum and have no place on Aster."

"Don't threaten me, Ternborg!" Nightshade railed... but she knew he was right and opted to change the subject. "Are your Doom Warriors ready?"

At the mention of Doom Warriors, all the horses snorted fire from their nostrils and danced around again.

"Horses don't like the Doom Warriors," Lord Ternborg said. "Neither do my people."

Nightshade grunted with impatience and snapped her fingers. The horses quieted... though their irritation was still plain to see. "That's not what I asked, Ternborg," Nightshade said.

Lord Ternborg shook his head. "Not yet, Nightshade, but soon. As you know, they're not easily controlled."

Nightshade smiled. "That's why they're so valuable," she said.

"They're an abomination," Lord Ternborg replied.

"Even so," Nightshade said. "You're to move southwest and meet with the armies of both Madeira and HeBron."

"I thought those two city states hated each other?"

Nightshade nodded. "But they now have a shared interest."

Lord Ternborg raised an eyebrow.

"That's none of your concern," Nightshade replied to Lord Ternborg's unspoken question. "But they'll follow you. Like you, they've been... shall we say... motivated? Once you've combined your armies, sweep down and take control of everything east of the Olympus Mountains."

"Resistance?"

"Havendale has a large standing army and powerful sorcerers." Nightshade grimaced. "It's a sorcerer's stronghold. I recommend you send the soldiers of Madeira and HeBron against the city first. They're more expendable. Other than that, there's only a few smaller cities and towns protected by the Riders of Elderdale... a loose-knit organization of mounted volunteers guarding that part of the country. Questions?"

Lord Ternborg nodded. "The city of Elanesse in the Forest of the Fey and The Hammer in Knights Lament pass?"

"Bypass Elanesse," Nightshade replied. "The Hammer doesn't really need to be taken."

Lord Ternborg stared at Nightshade as thoughts ran through his mind.

"You have other concerns?" Nightshade asked.

"How does this benefit you?" he asked.

Nightshade shrugged. She respected Lord Ternborg's mental acuity and his devotion to his people. Unlike Mordecai, or her father, who only thought about themselves and the power they could take and control, Lord Ternborg was sincerely concerned about his daughter and his people. Over the course of her long association with the mortals of Aster, she found she actually preferred the company of the righteous. But that didn't mean she was going to make it easy for him.

Lord Ternborg persisted. "As soon as we cross the Greater Boreskyre Mountains and into the land of the humans, their armies will combine to stop us. Whether we can keep the land east of the Olympus Mountains, even with HeBron and Madeira as allies, is problematic."

Nightshade remained silent as she waited for Lord Ternborg to draw his own conclusions.

Lord Ternborg paused for a few moments as he thought about Nightshade's strategic use of his army. "You want to make sure the humans don't reinforce InnisRos... at least not before your dark elves secure the island."

Nightshade said nothing, but she confirmed his reasoning with a slight nod. "Eventually we'll need the humans for a much larger task, so try not to kill too many of them. Just keep them busy for a few weeks."

"Doom Warriors won't hold back," Lord Ternborg said. "They're incapable of making that distinction."

Nightshade nodded. "So keep them reigned in, Ternborg."

Lord Ternborg stared.

"Oh for goodness sakes, Ternborg, think!" Nightshade scolded. "The Doom Warriors will scare the hell out of the humans. What better way to scale down causalities."

"What about my daughter?"

Nightshade made a few movements with her hands and a small window appeared in the air in front of the Draugen Pesta king. Through it Lord Ternborg could see his young daughter in a luxurious room and playing with an amazingly huge white and gray wolf. Lord Ternborg drew back with fear and looked wildly at Nightshade. His warriors, who had also seen the princess and the beast, drew their swords and pointed them at the demon.

Nightshade laughed. "Don't worry, Ternborg, it's not Fenrisúlfr... only one of his sons. His coloring wasn't to Fenrisúlfr liking, so he was given to me as a gift." Nightshade looked through the window herself. "It appears they've become excellent friends."

And it did look that way. Daphnia was laughing and crawling all over the beast who was patiently enduring the child's play... not unlike any other tamed, loving household pet. When Daphnia put her arms around the huge neck of the wolf, it licked her, which made the child laugh that much harder. It didn't look to

Lord Ternborg that his daughter was in any danger whatsoever.

"How do I know you're not tricking me with some sort of elaborate ruse?" Lord Ternborg asked.

"Speak to her."

Lord Ternborg looked at Nightshade and nodded. "Honey, can you hear me?"

"Daddy!" Daphnia replied as she disengaged herself from hugging the wolf and looked around. *"I don't see you."*

"I can see you, sweetie. Who's your friend?"

The child climbed onto the back of the wolf. *"I call him Adimar,"* she said. *"The nice lady said he's mine. Say hi to daddy, Adimar."*

The wolf howled. "That'll take some getting used to," Lord Ternborg thought. "Wait, did she say it was hers?" he said aloud.

"Indeed she did, Ternborg," Nightshade said. "He may not be Fenrisúlfr... but he's damn sure going to get as big as the Father of Wolves." Nightshade laughed again. She was enjoying herself. "Do your part and you'll get your daughter back... with the added bonus of a giant wolf as her companion."

Lord Ternborg watched as the wolf... Adimar... rolled over on his back so Daphnia could scratch his belly. "I wonder if he's housebroken," Lord Ternborg thought before shaking his head. "Honey, can you hear me still," he called to his daughter.

Daphnia was laughing. *"Yes, father."*

"You stay there and play with Adimar. I'll come to get you soon."

"Okay, father." the child responded before the window blinked out of existence.

687

"Satisfied?" Nightshade asked.

Lord Ternborg shook his head. "Not really," he said as he stared into the empty space that moments before contained the vision of his daughter. "I won't be satisfied as long as my daughter's being held captive. Nightshade, there's no reason to keep her prisoner. You have my word I'll do what you require."

Nightshade turned serious. "Come now, Ternborg. I'm not stupid. Your daughter will be safe. On that you have MY word."

Lord Ternborg snorted. "I'm to believe the word of a demon? You can't be..."

"I'm very serious," Nightshade interrupted. "Now get your Doom Warriors ready to cross the Greater Boreskyre Mountains. You have a land to invade." Nightshade cast a magical spell which opened a doorway in the air. Without another word she stepped into it and disappeared.

It had been a long day. Elliott was in the foothills of the Greater Boreskyre Mountains... on the western slope... and half-way home. But it would be dangerous to continue down the foothills in the dark. Around him his family's herd of mountain goats were busy munching grass while Elliott's two dogs, Boomer and Pokey, stood guard not far away. He had built a large fire to ward away the chill of the night and keep nocturnal predators at bay. As daylight retreated over the horizon Elliott, warm in his sleeping blankets, watched the fire while it tempted him into a well-earned sleep.

Elliott suddenly startled awake. It was deep into the night and the fire was almost out. As he sat up to add wood, he noticed how unusually quiet it was. He looked around, still wiping the sleep from his eyes, and discovered the goats and his dogs were nowhere to be seen. Further down the foothills he made out the bleating of the sheep and the howling of his dogs.

"Oh great," Elliott said as he threw off his blankets. He was getting up when he felt warm breath on the back of his neck. Elliott froze. An eerie chill ran down his spine as he slowly turned to look behind him.

Five huge horses stared down at him. Hints of flame came out of their nostrils as they exhaled. As large as the horses were, the giants who sat upon their backs appeared even larger.

"Black Death," Elliott whispered before he got up and ran down the mountain. Boomer and Pokey weren't too far ahead, and Elliott soon managed to catch up with them. He, along with his dogs, urgently herded the mountain goats ahead of them as they ran for their lives.

"Do you want me to retrieve the young man, Major?" one of the mounted warriors asked.

The leader considered the request then shook his head. "No, Sergeant, that won't be necessary. They won't believe him. Those people think of us as legends. They hide their heads in the sand and pretend we don't exist."

"Yes, sir."

"Instead, send a runner to the King," the major said. "Tell Lord Ternborg we've encountered no resistance." The major chuckled. "Make that only minor resistance."

As the major listened to the horse of the messenger gallop away, he looked down at the moonlit land below him. There were only a few lights shining in the countryside though the city lights of Madeira lit up the sky several miles away. "They're all asleep," he said.

The major turned to his sergeant. "Time to give those folks down there a wake-up call."

Jasmine Dubois and her First Officer, Thomas Krist, stood on the quarterdeck of the *Freedom Wind* as the ship made her way through gale-laced water. Both of the officers and the crew on the deck of the massive ship were tied off and hooked to retractable stanchions fastened into the deck to guard against being washed overboard.

The storm had come upon the small fleet of five ships, the *Freedom Wind* and four smaller schooners, unexpectedly... preceded by a spectacular lightning storm which lit the night sky with horizontal bolts of energy. Each wave crest was the equivalent of climbing a mountain while the troughs were virtual free-falls. More than one of the experienced crew lost their supper as the *Freedom Wind* struggled to stay afloat. Three of the smaller schooners used their speed to escape... choosing to return to their home port rather than continue the voyage on such dangerous waters. The fourth, however, was broken up by the fifty foot waves and quickly sank. The entire crew went down with the ship.

The much larger *Freedom Wind* didn't have the speed or maneuverability to change course. Captain Dubois realized the only chance she had of saving her ship was to turn into the tempest and hope the extra stability recently added would be enough to allow the *Freedom Wind* to survive in one piece. She knew her ability to captain a ship would be severely challenged over the course of the next few hours.

His voice barely perceptible over the sound of crashing waves and the rumble of thunder, the fore-mast lookout yelled, "Waterspout dead ahead!"

Captain Dubois and Mr. Krist raised their spyglasses to the front of the ship. "He's got good eyes," Captain Dubois commented to Mr. Krist. "I can barely see it."

Leaning over the rail in front of her, she shouted orders to the officer in charge of the men manning the ships' wheel. "Three degrees to port, Mr. Carlowe, if you please."

"Aye, Captain. Making my course three degrees to port."

Captain Dubois looked over at Mr. Krist. "The waterspout's moving perpendicular to us," she explained. "Our new course should get us safely past while keeping us into the wind."

Mr. Krist nodded. "Aye," he said while studying the waterspout. "Jasmine, it has an unnatural look to it. I have this strange feeling it doesn't belong here... and that its searching for something. Like its lost. Let's hope it stays on its present course. I don't want to be caught in that."

Mr. Krist remained calm and steady as he stood next to his captain... his feet seemingly planted into the very deck of the ship. Captain Dubois relied upon that strength during times such as this. Without taking her spyglass off the waterspout, she said, "I have the same feeling, Thomas. Every nerve in my body is warning me to get away as fast as possible."

"This course will take us dangerously close to the Dragon's Maul," Mr. Krist observed.

Captain Dubois looked worriedly at her first officer. "I know."

The Dragon's Maul is an area in the Ocean of the Heavens that covered approximately one thousand square miles. It was known for its frequent whirlpools... the size of which varied greatly. They'd been seen as small as one hundred yards and as big as five nautical miles in diameter. Whirlpools had been observed to occur in batches with several spinning simultaneously. Like everything else about the whirlpool, the length of time they existed was unpredictable. Some had lasted as long as several days while others only a few minutes. Traveling through the Dragon's Maul had been described as walking across a bridge of rotten boards. Or, according to the ancient poet Uripidis, who penned its name, the whirlpools compared to sailing into the mouth of a dragon... you didn't know which tooth was going to crush you and you probably weren't going to get out. No one had ever determined the cause of this phenomenon... except to say it seemed to be natural and not magical.

For the next hour the *Freedom Wind* battled the waves and cyclone-strength winds. The rain, pushed by the wind, flew into the faces of the crew... stinging like angry bees protecting their queen. Though the ship made little headway, she didn't break up... which was a testament to the skill of her captain and crew... not that the crew thought they had anything to do with it. To a person they felt the only reason the *Freedom Wind* didn't sink was because her captain willed it to stay afloat.

The wind, and the waves driven by the wind, abruptly changed direction from the southwest to the northeast at an alarming rate. This one hundred and eighty degree turn was unprecedented in the sailing annuals of Aster... and Captain Dubois, Mr. Krist, and every man and woman in the crew knew it. Before the sails could be set to adjust for the new wind direction, the *Freedom Wind* was traveling with the waves at breakneck speed. Each time they dipped down the side of a wave, picking up tremendous velocity as they headed for the trough, it felt as if the ship would surely be driven under the water and straight to the bottom of the ocean.

Again Captain Dubois and Mr. Krist gave the orders that saved the ship. And again the marvelous crew responded like the family they had become under the captain's tutelage. Not only was the *Freedom Wind* still sailing, but not a single crewmember had been lost... though the ship was still in dangerous waters.

"Whirlpool four points starboard!" one of the main-mast lookouts yelled.

Both Captain Dubois and Mr. Krist turned and focused their spyglasses in the called-out direction. In the few seconds it took for them to find the whirlpool, the ship was already moving past it.

"We're in the Dragon's Maul," Mr. Krist shouted.

"Probably," Captain Dubois shouted back. "But I've never seen weather like this."

Mr. Krist shook his head. "Me neither."

"So how can we be sure?"

Before Mr. Krist could answer, another lookout shouted, "Whirlpool dead ahead!"

"I guess now we're certain," Captain Dubois said as she grabbed the railing in front of her. She knew there wasn't any way the ship could avoid it. She only hoped it was small enough to allow them to skip over.

"Hang on," Mr. Krist yelled.

But the *Freedom Wind* didn't drop into the whirlpool. In the blink of an eye, the ship and her crew found themselves enshrouded in a dense fog. The water was calm, and the wind had stopped blowing. The fog was dry... more like smoke than a regular fog, which was always wet. For a moment, the entire crew did nothing except look around, trying to make sense of what had just happened. No one felt relief from avoiding the whirlpool... for each suspected they were in a place much more threatening. As quickly as the fog had come, it disappeared.

"Jasmine, the sky!" Mr. Krist said as he pointed upwards. "Those aren't our stars!"

As Captain Dubois looked up, the unknown sky began to fog again. She hurriedly pulled a sextant out of a tool crib attached to the railing and tried to get a fix on their location, hoping she could find a familiar constellation. But Mr. Krist was right... she recognized none of them. She sighed as her observations became obscured by the unknown miasma that closed around them once again.

"What the hell is going on?" Captain Dubois wondered aloud. She wasn't ready to admit the obvious... they were no longer on Aster.

For the second time in as many minutes, the fog disappeared to reveal bright sunlight. Captain Dubois let out the breath she didn't know she was holding. It looked to be Aster's sun.

"Rocks dead ahead!"

Mr. Krist was already looking forward with his spyglass. "Helm, make your course two degrees to port!" he ordered.

"Aye, sir. Making my course two degrees to port!"

"You know what that is, Jasmine?" Mr. Krist said as he pointed to the island-sized barriers sliding by each side of the *Freedom Wind*.

Captain Dubois nodded. "Yes, Thomas. The Isile Silimaure. InnisRos is just beyond the horizon."

Mr. Krist put his hand over Captain Dubois' as she gripped the rail. "We've been through an unknown storm... no, an impossible storm. We found ourselves surrounded by a strange fog which moved us from Aster to a world unknown... and back again. Now we find we've just crossed three-quarters of the ocean in only a few hours. How?"

Captain Dubois shook her head. She didn't have an answer.

Kyleigh Angelus-Custos, Queen of the Alfheim, along with her First Councilor, Robert Gareathe, had sequestered themselves with the Alfheim's military leaders while they discussed strategy to counter the dark elf invasion of Aster. Against Robert Gareathe's advice, Kyleigh decided not to destroy the *Ak-Samarië Shard*... so the corridor between the two worlds could still be opened when they were ready to support their brothers and sisters on InnisRos. A tentative knock on the council room door brought the conversation to a halt.

Kyleigh looked at the door with irritation. "Robert, please remind the guards I don't wish us to be disturbed."

Robert Gareathe nodded and stood to do Kyleigh's bidding.

Everyone around the conference table engaged in small talk as they awaited the first councilor. When he reappeared a few minutes later, he ushered in an impossibly old elf dressed in a grease-stained robe. His long, white hair wasn't in much better shape... except it looked as if he had wetted his hands and ran them through it in an attempt to tame his frazzled appearance. In his left hand he held a staff. Glowing runes circled the ancient wood that moved from the bottom up to the clear crystal hour-glass shaped figure on the top end. Inside the hour-glass crown were what looked to be miniature tomes, scrolls, manuals, and books floating in liquid.

Robert left the old elf standing next to the door as he walked over to Kyleigh and whispered in her ear. "You need to give this gentleman a private audience."

"I don't recognize him," Kyleigh whispered back. "Is he from one of the Twelve Houses?"

Robert shook his head. "He works for you."

This drew Kyleigh back. "Works for me?! But..." Kyleigh stopped and turned to her generals. "I'm sorry, but I need to attend to this. We'll continue this discussion at another time. My First Councilor will let you know when. Dismissed."

The generals rose, bowed, and filed out of the room. Robert brought the old sorcerer over and indicated he should take a chair.

"You're Master Zacharias, aren't you?" Kyleigh asked.

"Yes, Your Highness," Zacharias replied.

"I've seen your name mentioned as I glossed over expense accounts," Kyleigh said. "Much to my chagrin, we've never met. I apologize."

Zacharias shook his head. "There's nothing to apologize for, Your Highness. I rarely come out of my quarters. I live in the levels beneath the south tower. King Argonne graciously provided a laboratory, food and drink, a monthly stipend, and access to all the written knowledge of the Alfheim so I can conduct my research."

"Which is what, exactly?" Robert asked.

Zacharias frowned. "I've never tried to explain what I do to anyone before. King Argonne was only interested in results... though, since I never really gave him any, perhaps it'd be better to say he just put up with an old, eccentric sorcerer to keep him off the streets. The King was hard when he had to be. But he had a generous heart."

"Zacharias," Kyleigh chided gently. "What do you do?"

"Oh... sorry. My work involves... how should I put it... the theoretical effect of a relic's magic on the universal continuum." Zacharias was beaming by the time he had finished. "No one ever asks me what I do. It's exciting."

Kyleigh and Robert looked at each other. "Go on," Kyleigh said.

"My instruments recently picked up something most puzzling. I'd have said something earlier, but I wanted to check the results before I came to speak with you."

"I'm glad you decided to speak to me, Zacharias," Kyleigh said. "What did your instruments detect?"

"A disturbance in the magic that makes up the *Ak-Samarië Shard* relic," Zacharias replied. "Actually, to be more specific, the *Ak-Séregon Stone* has been used to create another dimensional corridor without the magical aid of the *Ak-Samarië Shard*."

"You know about that?" Robert asked.

"Yes, yes... of course," Zacharias replied. "But what's most troubling is where the *Ak-Séregon Stone* magic has been directed. It's been used to open a corridor from Aster to the Svartalfheim."

"We know that, good sorcerer," Kyleigh said. "The dark elves are invading Aster, and that world is ill-prepared to defend against such an invasion. That's what I was doing before you arrived. Discussing and planning for the rescue of Aster with my generals."

Zacharias became agitated. "But don't you see, the danger to Aster is much greater than that!" Zacharias exclaimed.

"Explain."

"You see, we all use magic... but very few of us UNDERSTAND magic. As you know, the *Ak-Samarië Shard*, with the *Ak-Séregon Stone*, opens a corridor between our world and Aster. But this can be done safely only if the two are working in concert with each other."

"But the dark elves do it with magic alone."

Zacharias nodded. "And their sorcerers die as a result. That's why their invading armies have no magic support when they've reached the Alfheim. It's a simple matter of cause and effect. Besides, their world is much closer to ours then it is to Aster. Think of it as our next-door neighbor. Not nearly as much magic is needed for travel between the two realms."

Both Kyleigh and Robert looked confused.

"Let me explain it this way," Zacharias said. Kyleigh and Robert could tell he was flustered because they didn't comprehend. "Like the Svartalfheim, the Alfheim and the world of Aster do not exist in the same planes of existence. Nor does time necessarily flow similarly for both. The *Ak-Samarië Shard* and the *Ak-Séregon Stone* work collectively to bring the two together. For example, my right fist is the Alfheim." Zacharias took his fist and stuck it up into the air above him. "And Aster..."

"Please, Zacharias, we don't really need to know how the shard and stone work," Kyleigh said.

The Queen's mild rebuff caused Zacharias to wince and duck his head. He laid his hands on his lap and looked down. "Yes, Your Highness," he responded.

Robert watched the exchange and felt sorry for the old sorcerer. "Zacharias, it's just that we're laymen and couldn't possibly understand the intricacies of your trade."

Kyleigh was quick to understand her crassness and Robert's attempt to salvage the conversation. "My First Councilor's correct, Zacharias," she said gently. "You're the expert and we'll never have your understanding of such things. I only need you to identify the problem and find me the answer... if there's one to be found."

Zacharias brightened up and nodded. "I can do that! In fact, I already have... at least I think I have. But I don't think you'll like the answer."

"Please continue."

"Please keep in mind, Your Highness, this is only a working theory... but as I previously stated, I've verified the readings and my conclusions are solid based upon the data," Zacharias said. He had fallen into a lecture mood. "This isn't about the *Ak-Samarië Shard*. That's a full relic created by the gods with the capacity to operate independent of any other magical source. The *Ak-Séregon Stone* is a different matter altogether."

"Why's that?" Robert asked.

"The stone was created by mortal sorcerers to augment the magic of the shard," Zacharias replied. "Nothing occurs in our reality without consequence. As I mentioned earlier, cause and effect. Using the shard and the stone together as one is a way of getting around this universal truth. They allow us to travel between the two worlds safely and without upsetting the balance."

Kyleigh and Robert were both beginning to understand the problem. "So... by using the stone without the shard there will be, as you said, consequences," Kyleigh remarked.

"Correct," Zacharias replied. "I believe, because the shard has forged a pathway to Aster so many times, it no longer needs the stone. It's a familiar route. That plus the fact that it's a relic. But forcing the stone to open a corridor from Aster to the Svartalfheim without the shard to assist it will... well, unfortunately it's going to have planetary effects on Aster."

"What kind of effects?" Robert asked.

Zacharias sighed. "That's the one thing the data can't tell me."

"Your best guess."

"Strange weather patterns, I suppose."

"And the end result for Aster?" Kyleigh asked. "What's your best guess on that."

Zacharias' eyes widened. "Oh, I don't have to guess," he said. "Aster will eventually phase out of its current position in time and space. Who knows where or when the world will reappear. But wherever or whenever that is, Aster will be nothing but a lifeless hunk of rock after the transition."

Kyleigh and Robert stared at the old sorcerer for several seconds. Finally Kyleigh said, "That's a problem." She turned to Robert. "It's a good thing I decided not to destroy the shard. We need to get as many of Aster's people over here as we can."

"Your Highness," Zacharias said. "Perhaps you SHOULD destroy the shard."

"And condemn Aster?" Kyleigh objected. Her tone sounded like a reprimand. "How could you even suggest such a thing?"

Zacharias looked at his hands.

Kyleigh sighed. "It's alright. Tell us why you think the shard should be destroyed."

Zacharias looked up and met the queen's eyes. "Blowback, Your Highness. The link between the shard and the stone is strong... and it's been in place for millennia." Zacharias pulled out two buttons and a piece of string from his robe and placed them on the table, tying each button to an end of the string before doing so. "The buttons represent the Alfheim and Aster. The string is the corridor between the two." Zacharias moved one of the buttons around the table. The other, attached to the other end of the string, followed. "This link remains in effect even if the corridor is not active. Where Aster goes, so will the Alfheim."

Silence dropped down on Kyleigh and Robert like a net. They didn't move... they didn't speak... they didn't breathe as the implications of Zacharias' conclusions came to roost in their minds. Finally Kyleigh asked the question she suspected she already knew the answer to. "How do we stop this?"

Zacharias leaned back in his chair and furrowed his brow. "As I see it, there are two options. You can do as I recommended and cut the link between the two worlds by destroying the shard."

Kyleigh shook her head. The abandonment of Aster might be necessary... but only as a last resort.

"Or you can go to Aster and find the *Ak-Séregon Stone*. If it's realigned with the shard before it's too late, I think everything will go back to normal."

"How long do we have?" Robert asked.

Zacharias shook his head. "I don't know. And there's one other thing."

Kyleigh nodded as her shoulders slumped. "Of course there is," she said. "What would that be, good sorcerer."

"There's only one person who knows the correct magic needed to bring the shard and the stone back together."

"And that is?" Robert asked.

"Me."

Robert shook his head. "You'd never survive the transition from here to Aster without the shard and stone working together! You're too..."

"Too old and infirm?" Zacharias finished for Robert.

Robert nodded.

"Surely there's another way to re-attune the shard and the stone without you going to Aster?" Kyleigh asked.

Zacharias remained silent... thinking.

"Well?" Kyleigh repeated.

"The only other way is to bring the shard and stone together," Zacharias replied. "A simple touch between the two is all that's needed. At least I believe this to be true."

Robert shook his head. "So all we have to do is find the *Ak-Séregon Stone*, steal it away from the dark elves, bring it back across, and hope you're right. Tall order."

"Oh no, you can't do that!" Zacharias replied. "You can't bring the *Ak-Séregon Stone* to the Alfheim. The resulting explosion once it was in the corridor would have dire consequences for both worlds... and the passageway between the two forever lost. It'd hardly do Aster any good with the stone here and no way to get it back."

Kyleigh sighed. "Do you have any other suggestions?"

Zacharias shook his head. "I'm sorry Your Highness. But if you'll..." He paused and his eyes lost focus for a few seconds.

"You were saying, Zacharias?" Robert said.

"Huh... oh, frightfully sorry, sir, Your Highness," Zacharias replied. "I was going to ask permission to return to my quarters to look for more alternatives."

Kyleigh nodded and both her and Robert watched him get up and shuffle away.

"Did you see that, Kyleigh?" Robert asked after Zacharias had left the room.

"Indeed, I did," the Queen responded. "He thought of something... something he didn't want to share. Robert, have him watched."

Zacharias walked the hallways of the palace with purpose. He knew where he was going... the reliquary of the *Ak-Samarië Shard*... and he knew what he needed to do. Because of Zacharias' penchant for privacy, only the late King Argonne knew he claimed to be the foremost authority on the shard and stone... though the King never gave the sorcerer any true credence. Nevertheless, Zacharias was granted unfettered access to the shard... something he'd never actually used since the King's death.

The guards nodded and stood aside as Zacharias walked up to the double doors of the reliquary. He paused and took a deep breath. One guard, misreading his delay as reluctance or confusion, opened one of the doors for him. Zacharias looked at the guard, smiled, and nodded before stepping into the reliquary. The door silently closed behind him.

The size of the room was that of a closet rather than a legitimate room. It measured five feet by five feet and was empty except for the *Ak-Samarië Shard*, which floated in the center behind an invisible, magical barrier thought to be impenetrable. The shard itself looked like nothing more than a huge, magnificent green emerald. It shimmered with power. Roughly the size of a large chest, it was shaped like a teardrop with the tip pointed towards the floor. The many-faceted shard had been perfectly cut and Zacharias, as he'd done each time he visited, took a few moments to admire its exquisiteness. In his mind's eye nothing compared favorably to the shard's beauty. Nothing except life.

Zacharias closed his eyes. "Please forgive me, but two worlds depend on this," he whispered. Tears ran down his cheek. "Seek Queen Kyleigh Angelus-Custos. She'll know what to do."

He set the tip of his staff on the floor and concentrated. His personal spell book appeared before him in the air and opened to a page near the end. Zacharias, reading from the book, mumbled words known only to sorcerers while he made symbols in the air with his free hand. When he had finished his incantation, brilliant energy leaped from his closed fist and surrounded the magical barrier surrounding the shard. The energy coalesced to a pinprick, fought the barrier for several seconds before pushing through, and struck the shard. The room exploded with an unworldly release of energy.

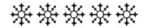

As soon as Zacharias' magic penetrated the barrier surrounding the *Ak-Samarië Shard*, magical alarms sounded. The explosion that followed the alarms shook the palace. Guards, sorcerers, and everyone of importance in the palace dropped what they were doing and sprinted towards the shard reliquary. The massive double doors to the reliquary had been knocked from their hinges and the guards lay on the floor, unconscious.

By the time Kyleigh and Robert reached the reliquary, a crowd of people had gathered and were milling around the door. Kyleigh heard one of the guards shout "Make way for the Queen!" and everyone parted to make a lane and bowed... everyone except Master Xanthus, Court Sorcerer and leader of one of the Twelve Houses. He blocked the way into the room. As Kyleigh approached with Robert, Master Xanthus bowed deeply.

"Your Highness," he said.

"The shard?" Kyleigh asked.

Master Xanthus shook his head. "Damaged. To what extent I'm still trying to ascertain."

"Walk me through it," Kyleigh said as she stepped around the sorcerer and looked into the room. Lying before the shard was a charred body. A sorcerer's staff and spell book laid next to it. The shard itself appeared to be unharmed... no, that wasn't quite true.

Master Xanthus stood beside Kyleigh. "That's what's left of Master Zacharias. He apparently decided to destroy the shard," he said. "He breached the force field and, using a spell I've never seen before, attacked it. We'll have the force field back up soon... after we've determined the extent of Zacharias' success."

Kyleigh nodded to Master Xanthus before kneeling next to the body. "Thank you," she said to Zacharias' remains before reaching over to grab his staff and spell book. Standing, she handed both to Master Xanthus before she approached the shard. Its appearance hadn't changed... except for the small piece of it laying on the floor. About the size of an arrow head, it was a complete replication of the larger shard. When she picked it up, she could feel the power radiating from it.

"Zacharias wasn't trying to destroy the shard," Kyleigh said. "He was providing an answer to a particularly vexing problem."

"The dark elf invasion of Aster," Master Xanthus said.

"Correct, good sorcerer," Robert said, speaking for the first time.

Kyleigh looked at Master Xanthus. "That spell book you hold in your hands represented Zacharias' life work. I suspect no one knew more about the *Ak-*

707

Samarië Shard except the gods that created it. Take whomever you need and go to his quarters. Study the spell book and everything else you find. I want it all documented. Every single bit of it. Be prepared to brief me when you're finished." Kyleigh placed her hand on Master Xanthus' sleeve. "We don't have much time."

"Yes, Your Highness," the sorcerer replied. "As soon as we..."

Kyleigh interrupted him. "The shard is fine. And a new force field isn't necessary. She can protect herself."

Master Xanthus shook his head. "Excuse me?" he said. Not much surprised the sorcerer... but this did.

"Come now. Surely you understand the nature of relics," Kyleigh said. "The gods that create them grant intelligence... but they only communicate when they see fit."

"Well yes, I understand that. But..." Master Xanthus frowned. "You think the shard was communicating with Zacharias?"

Kyleigh nodded. "I know so," she answered. "She's talking to me now. And she understands it's not just Aster that's in danger."

Master Xanthus looked at Kyleigh quizzically.

"I began to hear her shortly after the explosion," Kyleigh said. "Zacharias... let's see... how should I articulate this? He put in a good word for me." Kyleigh smiled. "Yes, that's what he did. I'll handle things here. Now, go find for me everything Zacharias' research had to say on the shard."

Master Xanthus nodded, bowed, and left.

Kyleigh signaled to several of the palace staff waiting in the hallway. "Please have Zacharias' body taken and prepared for a state funeral. I'll go over the specifics with Chief Seneschal Duncan later. Be certain to treat the body with respect."

After the servants had removed Zacharias, and the guards had dispersed the crowd, Kyleigh turned to Robert, who was staring at the shard. "Beautiful, isn't she," Kyleigh said.

"I've never seen the shard before," Robert replied. He still hadn't taken his eyes off the relic. "I wasn't sure what to expect. Yes... yes, exquisite. Stunning, in fact."

"Robert?" Kyleigh prodded when he continued to stare. "Focus."

"Sorry, Kyleigh," he replied. "Do you really think that piece of shard will realign the stone?"

Kyleigh held the small teardrop piece of shard up against light. It shimmered and sparkled with power. In all respects except size, it WAS the *Ak-Samarië Shard*. "Yes," she answered. "And I'll be the one to do it."

THE STRUGGLE FOR INNOCENCE

AUTHOR'S NOTE

In the world of Dungeons and Dragons... a world I frequent... as well as the majority of fantasy books I've read over the years, magic users (sorcerers and clerics) generally release their magic by a series of words (incantations). This is normally accompanied by hand manipulations, reading from a magical tome, or using a magical item such as a staff. Usually the words themselves are magical and used to focus the energy of the spell just before it's discharged. Since the words are, for the most part, unique to the discipline of either the sorcerer or cleric, I felt they needed to be set apart. To do this, I converted the words or phrases I developed to Latin. (Although I took two years of Latin in high-school, my present knowledge of the language is no more than that of someone who's never studied it.) I used translators I found on Google. If you're so inclined, you can use Google or any other search engine to go back to the English translation... though it's not critical to the story. Some mysteries, particularly those of respected sorcerers and clerics, should remain secret.

Lightning Source UK Ltd.
Milton Keynes UK
UKHW010639231120
373916UK00001B/55